BREAKING BAILEY'S RULES

BY
BRENDA JACKSON

Mills & Boon (UK) Limited's policy is to use papers that are natural, renewable and recyclable products and made from wood grown in sustainable forests. The logging and manufacturing processes conform to the legal environmental regulations of the country of origin

Printed and bound in Spain by
CPI, Barcelona

MILLS & BOON

Published in Great Britain 2015
by Mills & Boon, an imprint of Harlequin (UK) Limited,
Eton House, 18-24 Paradise Road, Richmond, Surrey, TW9 1SR

© 2015 Brenda Streater Jackson

ISBN: 978-0-263-25284-2

51-1115

Harlequin [...] paper [...] from [...] papers that are natural, renewable and recycl[...] [...] grown in sustainable forests. The loggin[...] [...] to the legal environmental regulation[...]

Printed an[...]
by CPI, Ba[...]

Why was she feeling such a strong attraction to Walker?

This wasn't usually how it worked with her and men. Most of the time she thought of them as a nuisance, not an attraction.

"You okay?"

The truck had slowed down for traffic again and she took a quick glance over at him, then wished she hadn't when she saw he was gazing at her with those gorgeous dark eyes. "Yes. Why would you think not?"

"You shivered just now."

He had to have been watching her mighty close to have known that. "Just felt a little chill."

"Then maybe I should turn up the heat."

Turn up the heat?

She was feeling hot enough already!

* * *

Breaking Bailey's Rules
is part of *New York Times* bestselling
author Brenda Jackson's Westmorelands
series—A family bound by loyalty...and love!

Brenda Jackson is a *New York Times* bestselling author of more than one hundred romance titles. Brenda lives in Jacksonville, Florida, and divides her time between family, writing and traveling.

Email Brenda at authorbrendajackson@gmail.com or visit her on her website at www.brendajackson.net.

To the man who will always and forever be
the love of my life, Gerald Jackson, Sr.

Pleasant words are a honeycomb.
Sweet to the soul and healing to the bones.
—Proverbs 16:24

Prologue

Hugh Coker closed his folder and looked up at the five pairs of eyes staring at him.

"So there you have it. I met with this private investigator, Rico Claiborne, and he's convinced that you are descendants of someone named Raphel Westmoreland. I read through his report and although his claims sound pretty far-fetched, I can't discount the photographs I've seen. Bart, every one of your sons could be a twin to one of those Westmorelands. The resemblance is that strong. I have the photographs here for you to look at."

"I don't want to see any photographs, Hugh," Bart Outlaw said gruffly, getting out of his chair. "Just because this family might look like us doesn't mean they are related to us. We are Outlaws, not Westmorelands. And I'm not buying that story about a train wreck over sixty years ago where some dying woman gave her baby to my grandmother. That's the craziest thing I've ever heard."

He turned to his four sons. "Outlaw Freight Lines is

a multimillion-dollar company and people will claim a connection to us just to get what we've worked so hard to achieve."

Garth Outlaw leaned back in his chair. "Forgive me if I missed something, Dad, but didn't Hugh say the Westmorelands are pretty darn wealthy in their own right? I think all of us have heard of Blue Ridge Land Management. They are a Fortune 500 company. I don't know about the rest of you, but Thorn Westmoreland can claim me as a cousin anytime."

Bart frowned. "So what if they run a successful company and one of them is a celebrity?" he said in a cutting tone. "We don't have to go looking for any new relatives."

Maverick, the youngest of Bart's sons, chuckled. "I believe they came looking for us, Dad."

Bart's frown deepened. "Doesn't matter." He glanced at Hugh. "Send a nice letter letting them know we aren't buying their story and don't want to be bothered again. That should take care of it." Expecting his orders to be obeyed, Bart walked out of the conference room, closing the door behind him.

Sloan Outlaw stared at the closed door. "Are we going to do what he says?"

"Do we ever?" his brother Cash asked, grinning while watching Hugh put the papers back in his briefcase.

"Leave that folder, Hugh," Garth said, rubbing the back of his neck. "I think the old man forgot he's no longer running things. He retired a few months ago, or did I imagine it?"

Sloan stood. "No, you didn't imagine it. He retired but only after the board threatened to oust him. What's he's doing here anyway? Who invited him?"

"No one. It's Wednesday. He takes Charm to lunch on Wednesdays" was Maverick's response.

Garth's brow bunched. "And where is Charm? Why didn't she attend this meeting?"

"Said she had something more important to do," Sloan said of their sister.

"What?"

"Go shopping."

Cash chuckled. "Doesn't surprise me. So what are we going to do Garth? The decision is yours, not the old man's."

Garth threw a couple of paperclips on the table. "I never mentioned it, but I was mistaken for one of those Westmorelands once."

Maverick leaned across the table. "You were? When?"

"Last year, while I was in Rome. A young woman, a very beautiful young woman, called out to me. She thought I was someone named Riley Westmoreland."

"I can see why she thought that," Hugh said. "Take a look at this." He opened the folder he'd placed on the conference room table earlier and flipped through until he came to one photograph in particular. He pulled it out and placed it in the center of the table. "This is Riley Westmoreland."

"Damn," chorused around the table, before a shocked silence ensued.

"Take a look at the others. Pretty strong genes. Like I told Bart, all of you have a twin somewhere in that family," Hugh said. "It's—"

"Weird," Cash said, shaking his head.

"Pretty damn uncanny," Sloan added. "Makes the Westmorelands' claims believable."

"So what if we are related to these Westmorelands? What's the big deal?" Maverick asked.

"None that I can see," Sloan said.

"Then, why does the old man have a problem with it?"

"Dad's just distrustful by nature," Cash answered Maverick, as he continued to stare at the photographs.

"He fathered five sons and a daughter from six different women. If you ask me, he was too damn trusting."

"Maybe he learned his lesson, considering that some of our mothers—not calling any names—turned out to be gold diggers," Sloan said, chuckling.

Hugh shook his head. It always amazed him how well Bart's offspring got along, considering they all had different mothers. Bart had managed to get full custody of each of them before their second birthdays and he'd raised them together.

Except for Charm. She hadn't shown up until the age of fifteen. Her mother was the one woman Bart hadn't married, but the only one he had truly loved.

"As your lawyer, what do you want me to do?" Hugh asked. "Send that letter like Bart suggested?"

Garth met Hugh's gaze. "No. I believe in using more diplomacy than that. I think what has Dad so suspicious is the timing, especially with Jess running for senator," he said of their brother. "And you all know how much Dad wants that to happen. His dream has been for one of us to enter politics. What if this is some sort of scheme to ruin that?"

Garth stood and stretched out the kinks from his body. "Just to be on the safe side, I'll send Walker to check out these Westmorelands. We can trust him, and he's a good judge of character."

"But will he go?" Sloan asked. "Other than visiting us here in Fairbanks, I doubt if Walker's been off his ranch in close to ten years."

Garth drew in a deep breath and said, "He'll go if I ask him."

One

Two weeks later

"Why are they sending their representative instead of meeting with us themselves?"

Dillon Westmoreland glanced across the room at his cousin Bailey. He'd figured she would be the one with questions. He had called a family meeting of his six brothers and eight cousins to apprise them of the phone call he'd received yesterday. The only person missing from this meeting was his youngest brother, Bane, who was on a special assignment somewhere with the navy SEALs. "I presume the reason they are sending someone outside their family is to play it safe, Bailey. In a way, I understand them doing so. They have no proof that what we're claiming is the truth."

"But why would we claim them as relatives if they aren't?" Bailey persisted. "When our cousin James contacted you a few years ago about our relationship with them, I don't recall you questioning him."

Dillon chuckled. "Only because James didn't give me a chance to question anything. He showed up one day at our Blue Ridge office with his sons and nephews in tow and said that we were kin. I couldn't deny a thing when looking into Dare's face, which looked just like mine."

"Um, maybe we should have tried that approach." Bailey tapped a finger to her chin. "Just showed up and surprised them."

"Rico didn't think that was a good idea. From his research, it seems the Outlaws are a pretty close-knit family who don't invite outsiders into their fold," Megan Westmoreland Claiborne said. Rico, her husband, was the private investigator hired by the Westmorelands to find members of their extended family.

"And I agreed with Rico," Dillon said. "Claiming kinship is something some people don't do easily. We're dealing with relatives whose last name is Outlaw. They had no inkling of a Westmoreland connection until Rico dropped the bomb on them. If the shoe was on the other foot and someone showed up claiming they were related to me, I would be cautious, as well."

"Well, I don't like it," Bailey said, meeting the gazes of her siblings and cousins.

"We've picked up on that, Bay," Ramsey Westmoreland, her eldest brother said, pulling her ear. He then switched his gaze to Dillon. "So when is their representative coming?"

"His name is Walker Rafferty and he's arriving tomorrow. I thought that would be perfect since everyone is home for Aidan and Jillian's wedding this weekend. The Atlanta Westmorelands will be here as well, so he'll get to meet them, too."

"What does he intend to find out about us?" Bailey wanted to know.

"That you, Bane, Adrian and Aidan are no longer hellions," Stern Westmoreland said, grinning.

"Go to—" Bailey stopped and glanced at everyone staring at her. "Go wash your face, Stern."

"Stop trying to provoke her, Stern," Dillon said, shaking his head. "Rafferty probably wants to get to know us so he can report back to them that we're an okay group of people. Don't take things personally. Like I said, it's just a precaution on their part." He paused as if an idea had come to him. "And, Bailey?"

"Yes?"

"Since you're the most apprehensive about Mr. Rafferty's visit, I want you to pick him up from the airport."

"Me?"

"Yes, you. And I expect you to make a good impression. Remember, you'll be representing the entire family."

"Bailey representing the entire family? The thought of that doesn't bother you, Dil?" Canyon Westmoreland said, laughing. "We don't want to scare him off. Hell, she might go ballistic on him if he rubs her the wrong way."

"Cut it out, Canyon. Bailey knows how to handle herself and she will make a good impression," Dillon said, ignoring his family's skeptical looks. "She'll do fine."

"Thanks for the vote of confidence, Dillon."

"You got it, Bailey."

Bailey knows how to handle herself and she will make a good impression.

Dillon's words rang through Bailey's head as she rushed into the airport fifteen minutes late. And she couldn't blame her delay on traffic.

That morning she had been called into her boss's office to be told she'd been promoted to features editor. That called for a celebration and she'd rushed back to her desk to call her best friend, Josette Carter. Of course Josette had insisted they meet for lunch. And now Bailey was late doing the one thing Dillon had trusted her to do.

But she refused to accept that she was off to a bad start...even if she was. If Mr. Rafferty's plane was late it would not hurt her feelings one iota. In fact today she would consider it a blessing.

She headed toward baggage claim and paused to look at an overhead monitor. Mr. Rafferty's plane had been on time. Just her luck.

Upon reaching the luggage carousel for his plane, she glanced around. She had no idea what the man looked like. She had tried looking him up online last night and couldn't find him. Josette had suggested Bailey make a sign with his name, but Bailey had rolled her eyes at the idea. Now, considering how crowded the airport was, she acknowledged that might have been a good idea.

Bailey checked out the people retrieving their luggage. She figured the man was probably in his late forties or early fifties. The potbellied, fiftysomething-year-old man who kept glancing at his watch with an anxious expression must be her guy. She was moving in his direction when a deep husky rumble stopped her in her tracks.

"I believe you're looking for me, Miss Westmoreland."

Bailey turned and her gaze connected with a man who filled her vision. He was tall, but that wasn't the reason her brain cells had suddenly turned to mush; she was used to tall men. Her brothers and cousins were tall. It was the man's features. Too handsome for words. She quickly surmised it had to be his eyes that had made her speechless. They were so dark they appeared a midnight blue. Just staring into them made her pulse quicken to a degree that ignited shivers in her stomach.

And then there was his skin tone—a smooth mahogany. He had a firm jaw and a pair of luscious-looking lips. His hair was cut low and gave him a rugged, sexy look.

Gathering her wits, she said, "And you are?"

He held his hand out to her. "Walker Rafferty."

She accepted his handshake. It was firm, filled with authority. Those things she expected. What she didn't expect was the feeling of warmth combined with a jolt of energy that surged through her body. She quickly released his hand.

"Welcome to Denver, Mr. Rafferty."

"Thanks. Walker will do."

She tried to keep her pulse from being affected by the throaty sound of his voice. "All right, Walker. And I'm—"

"Bailey Westmoreland. I know. I recognized you from Facebook."

"Really? I looked you up but didn't find a page for you."

"You wouldn't. I'm probably one of the few who don't indulge."

She couldn't help wondering what else he didn't—or did—indulge in, but decided to keep her curiosity to herself. "If you have all your bags, we can go. I'm parked right outside the terminal."

"Just lead the way."

She did and he moved into step beside her. He was certainly not what she'd expected. And her attraction to him wasn't expected, either. She usually preferred men who were clean shaven, but there was something about Walker Rafferty's neatly trimmed beard that appealed to her.

"So you're friends with the Outlaws?" she asked as they continued walking.

"Yes. Garth Outlaw and I have been best friends for as long as I can remember. I'm told by my parents our friendship goes back to the time we were both in diapers."

"Really? And how long ago was that?"

"Close to thirty-five years ago."

She nodded. That meant he was eight years older than she was. Or seven, since she had a birthday coming up in a few months.

"You look just like your picture."

She glanced at him. "What picture?"

"The one on Facebook."

She changed it often enough to keep it current. "It's supposed to work that way," she said, leading him through the exit doors. And because she couldn't hold back her thoughts she said, "So you're here to spy on us."

He stopped walking, causing her to stop, as well. "No. I'm here to get to know you."

"Same thing."

He shook his head. "No, I don't think it is."

She frowned. "Either way, you plan to report back to the Outlaws about us? Isn't that right?"

"Yes, that's right."

Her frown deepened. "They certainly sound like a suspicious bunch."

"They are. But seeing you in person makes a believer out of me."

She lifted a brow. "Why?"

"You favor Charm, Garth's sister."

Bailey nodded. "How old is Charm?"

"Twenty-three."

"Then, you're mistaken. I'm three years older so that means she favors me." Bailey then resumed walking.

Walker Rafferty kept a tight grip on the handle of his luggage while following Bailey Westmoreland to the parking lot. She was a very attractive woman. He'd known Bailey was a beauty because of her picture. But he hadn't expected that beauty to affect him with such mind-boggling intensity. It had been a while—years—since he'd been so aware of a woman. And her scent didn't help. It had such an alluring effect.

"So do you live in Fairbanks?"

He looked at her as they continued walking. Her cocoa-colored face was perfect—all of her features, including a full pair of lips, were holding his attention. The long brown hair that hung around her shoulders made her eyes appear a dark chocolate. "No, I live on Kodiak Island. It's an hour away from Fairbanks by air."

She bunched her forehead. "Kodiak Island? Never heard of the place."

He smiled. "Most people haven't, although it's the second largest island in the United States. Anchorage and Fairbanks immediately come to mind when one thinks of Alaska. But Kodiak Island is way prettier than the two of them put together. Only thing is, we have more bears living there than people."

He could tell by her expression that she thought he was teasing. "Trust me, I'm serious," he added.

She nodded, but he had a feeling she didn't believe him. "How do people get off the island?"

"The majority of them use the ferry, but air is most convenient for me. I have a small plane."

She lifted a brow. "You do?"

"Yes." There was no need to tell her that he'd learned to fly in the marines. Or that Garth had learned right along with him. What he'd told her earlier was true. He and Garth Outlaw had been friends since their diaper days and had not only gone to school together but had also attended the University of Alaska before doing a stint in the marines. The one thing Garth hadn't done with Walker was remain with him in California after they left the military. And Garth had tried his hardest to talk Walker out of staying. Too bad he hadn't listened.

He'd been back in Alaska close to ten years now and he

swore he would never leave again. Only Garth could get him off the island this close to November, his son's birthday month. Had his son lived he would be celebrating his eleventh birthday. Thinking of Connor sent a sharp pain through Walker, one he always endured this time of year.

He kept walking beside Bailey, tossing looks her way. Not only did she have striking features but she had a nice body, as well. She looked pretty damn good in her jeans, boots and short suede jacket.

Deciding to remove his focus from her, he switched it to the weather. Compared to Alaska this time of year, Denver was nice. Too damn nice. He hoped the week here didn't spoil him.

"Does it snow here often?" he asked, to keep the conversation going. It had gotten quiet. Too quiet. And he was afraid his mind would dwell on just how pretty she was.

"Yes, usually a lot this time of year but our worst days are in February. That's when practically everything shuts down. But I bet it doesn't snow here as much as in Alaska."

He chuckled. "You'd bet right. We have long, extremely cold days. You get used to being snowed in more so than not. If you're smart, you'll prepare for it because an abundance of snow is something you can count on."

"So what do you do on Kodiak Island?" she asked.

They had reached her truck. The vehicle suited her. Although she was definitely feminine, she didn't come across as the prissy type. He had a feeling Bailey Westmoreland could handle just about anything, including this powerful-looking full-size pickup. He was of the mind that there was something innately sensuous about a woman who drove a truck. Especially a woman who was strikingly sexy when she got out of it.

Knowing she was waiting for an answer to his question, he said, "I own a livestock ranch there. Hemlock Row."

"A cattle ranch?"

"No, I raise bison. They can hold their own against a bear."

"I've eaten buffalo a few times. It's good."

"Any bison from Hemlock Row is the best," he said, and didn't care if it sounded as if he was bragging. He had every right to. His family had been in the cattle business for years, but killer bears had almost made them lose everything they had. After his parents' deaths he'd refused to sell and allow Hemlock Row to become a hunting lodge or a commercial fishing farm.

"Well, you'll just have to send me some to try."

"Maybe you'll get to visit the area one day."

"Doubt it. I seldom leave Denver," she said, releasing the lock on the truck door for him.

"Why?"

"Everything I need is right here. I've visited relatives in North Carolina, Montana and Atlanta on occasion, and I've traveled to the Middle East to visit my cousin Delaney once."

"She's the one who's married to a sheikh, right?" he asked, opening the truck door.

"Jamal *was* a sheikh. Now he's king of Tehran. Evidently you've done research on the Westmorelands, so why the need to visit us?"

He held her gaze over the top of the truck. "You have a problem with me being here, Bailey?"

"Would it matter if I did?"

"Probably not, but I still want to know how you feel about it."

He watched her nibble her bottom lip as if considering what he'd said. He couldn't help studying the shape of her mouth and thinking she definitely had a luscious pair of lips.

"I guess it bothers me that the Outlaws think we'd claim

them as relatives if they weren't," she said, her words breaking into his thoughts.

"You have to understand their position. To them, the story of some woman giving up her child before dying after a train wreck sounds pretty far out there."

"As far-out as it might sound, that's what happened. Besides, all it would take is a DNA test to prove whether or not we're related. That should be easy enough."

"Personally, I don't think that's the issue. I've seen photographs of your brothers and cousins and so have the Outlaws. The resemblance can't be denied. The Westmorelands and the Outlaws favor too much for you not to be kin."

"Then, what is the issue and why are you here? If the Outlaws want to acknowledge we're related but prefer not to have anything to do with us, that's fine."

Walker liked her knack for speaking what she thought. "Not all of them feel that way, Bailey. Only Bart."

"Who's Bart?" she asked, breaking eye contact with him to get into the truck.

"Bart's their father," he answered, getting into the truck, as well. "Bart's father would have been the baby that was supposedly given to his grandmother, Amelia Outlaw."

"And Amelia never told any of them the truth about what happened?" Bailey asked, snapping her seat belt around her waist. A waist he couldn't help notice was pretty small. He could probably wrap his arms around it twice.

He snapped his seat belt on, thinking the truck smelled like her. "Evidently she didn't tell anyone."

"I wonder why?"

"She wouldn't be the first person to keep an adoption a secret, if that's what actually happened. From what Rico Claiborne said, Clarice knew she was dying and gave her baby to Amelia, who had lost her husband in that same wreck. She probably wanted to put all that behind her and start fresh with her adopted son."

After she maneuvered out of the parking lot, he decided to change the subject. "So what do you do?"

She glanced over at him. "Don't you know?"

"It wasn't on Facebook."

She chuckled. "I don't put everything online. And to answer your question, I work for my sister-in-law's magazine, *Simply Irresistible*. Ever heard of it?"

"Can't say that I have. What kind of magazine is it?"

"One for today's up-and-coming woman. We have articles on health, beauty, fashion and, of course, men."

He held her gaze when the truck came to a stop. "Why 'of course' on men?"

"Because men are so interesting."

"Are we?"

"Not really. But since some women think so, we have numerous articles about your gender."

He figured she wanted him to ask what some of those articles were, but he didn't intend to get caught in that trap. Instead, he asked, "What do you do at the magazine?"

"As of today I'm a features editor. I got promoted."

"Congratulations."

"Thanks." An easy smile touched her lips, lips that were nice to look at and would probably taste just as nice.

"I find that odd," he said, deciding to stay focused on their conversation and not her lips.

The vehicle slowed due to traffic and she looked at him. "What do you find odd?"

"That your family owns a billion-dollar company yet you don't work there."

Bailey broke eye contact with Walker. Was he in probing mode? Were her answers going to be scrutinized and reported back to the Outlaws?

Walker's questions confirmed what she'd told Dillon. Those Outlaws were too paranoid for her taste. As far as she was concerned, kin or no kin, they had crossed the line by sending Walker Rafferty here.

But for now she would do as Dillon had asked and tolerate the man's presence…and his questions. "There's really nothing odd about it. There's no law that says I have to work at my family's corporation. Besides, I have rules."

"Rules?"

"Yes," she said, bringing the truck to a stop for a school bus. She looked over at him. "I'm the youngest in the family and while growing up, my brothers and cousins felt it was their God-given right to stick their noses in my business. A little too much to suit me. They only got worse the older I got. I put up with it at home and couldn't imagine being around them at the office, too."

"So you're not working at your family's company because you need space?"

"That's not the only reason," she informed him before he got any ideas about her and her family not getting along. "I'm not working at Blue Ridge Land Management because I chose a career that had nothing to do with real estate. Although I have my MBA, I also have a degree in journalism, so I work at *Simply Irresistible*."

She was getting a little annoyed that she felt the need to explain anything to him. "I'm sure you have a lot of questions about my family and I'm certain Dillon will be happy to answer them. We have nothing to hide."

"You're assuming that I think you do."

"I'm not assuming anything, Walker."

He didn't say anything while she resumed driving. Out of the corner of her eye, she saw he'd settled comfortably in the seat and was gazing out the window. "First time in Denver?" she asked.

"Yes. Nice-looking city."

"I think so." She wished he didn't smell so good. The scent of his aftershave was way too nice.

"Earlier you mentioned rules, Bailey."

"What about them?" She figured most people had some sort of rules they lived by. However, she would be the first to admit that others were probably not as strict about abiding by theirs as she was about abiding by hers. "I've discovered it's best to have rules about what I will do and not do. One of my rules is not to answer a lot of questions, no matter who's asking. I put that rule in place because of my brother Zane. He's always been too nosy when it came to me and he has the tendency to take being overprotective to another level."

"Sounds like a typical big brother."

"There's nothing typical about Zane, trust me. He just likes being a pain. Because of him, I had to adopt that rule."

"Name another rule."

"Never get serious about anyone who doesn't love Westmoreland Country as much as I do."

"Westmoreland Country?"

"It's the name the locals gave the area where my family lives. It's beautiful and I don't plan to leave. Ever."

"So in other words, the man you marry has to want to live there, too. In Westmoreland Country?"

"Yes, if such a man exists, which I doubt." Deciding to move the conversation off herself and back onto the Outlaws, she asked, "So how many Outlaws are there?"

"Their father is Bart and he was an only child. He has five sons—Garth, Jess, Cash, Sloan and Maverick—and one daughter, Charm."

"I understand they own a freight company."

"They do."

"All of them work there?"

"Yes. Bart wouldn't have it any other way. He retired last year and Garth is running things now."

"Well, you're in luck with my brother Aidan getting married this weekend. You'll see more Westmorelands than you probably counted on."

"I'm looking forward to it."

Bailey was tempted to look at him but she kept her eyes on the road. She had to add *sexy* to his list of attributes, no matter how much she preferred not to. Josette would be the first to say it was only fair to give a deserving man his just rewards. However, Bailey hated that she found him so attractive. But what woman wouldn't? Manly, handsome and sexy was a hot combination that could play havoc on any woman's brain.

"So were you born in Alaska or are you a transplant?" she asked him out of curiosity.

"I was born in Alaska on the same property I own. My grandfather arrived in Fairbanks as a military man in the late 1940s. When his time in the military ended he stayed and purchased over a hundred thousand acres for his bride, a woman who could trace her family back to Alaska when it was owned by Russia. What about your family?"

A smile touched Bailey's lips. "I know for certain I can't trace my grandmother's family back to when Alaska was owned by Russia, if that's what you're asking."

It wasn't and she knew it, but couldn't resist teasing him. It evidently amused him if the deep chuckle that rumbled from his throat was anything to go by. The sound made her nipples tingle and a shiver race through her stomach. If the sound of his chuckle could do this to her, what would his touch do?

She shook her head, forcing such thoughts from her mind. She had just met the man. Why was she feeling such a strong attraction to him? This wasn't usually how it worked with her and men. Most of the time she thought of them as a nuisance, not an attraction.

"You okay?"

The truck had slowed down for traffic again and she took a quick look over at him. She wished she hadn't when she met those gorgeous dark eyes. "Yes, why would you think I'm not?"

"You shivered just now."

He had to have been watching her mighty close to have known that. "Just a little chill."

"Then, maybe I should turn up the heat."

Turn up the heat? She immediately jumped to conclusions until he reached out toward her console and turned the knob. *Oh, he meant that heat.* Within seconds, a blast of warmth flowed through the truck's vents.

"Better?"

"Yes. Thanks," she said, barely able to think. She needed to get a grip. Deciding to go back to their conversation by answering his earlier question, she said, "As far as my family goes, we're still trying to find out everything we can about my great-grandfather Raphel. We didn't even know he had a twin brother until the Atlanta Westmorelands showed up to claim us. Then Dillon began digging into Raphel's past, which led him to Wyoming. Over the years we've put most of the puzzle pieces together, which is how we found out about the Outlaws."

Bailey was glad when she finally saw the huge marker ahead. She brought the truck to a stop and looked over at him. "Welcome to Westmoreland Country, Walker Rafferty."

Two

An hour later Walker stood at the windows in the guest bedroom he'd been given in Dillon Westmoreland's home. As far as Walker could see, there was land, land and more land. Then there were the mountains, a very large valley and a huge lake that ran through most of the property. From what he'd seen so far, Westmoreland Country was beautiful. Almost as beautiful as his spread in Kodiak. Almost, but not quite. As far as he was concerned, there was no place as breathtaking as Hemlock Row, his family home.

He'd heard the love and pride in Bailey's voice when she talked about her home. He fully understood because he felt the same way about his home. Thirteen years ago a woman had come between him and his love for Hemlock Row, but never again. Now he worked twice as hard every day on his ranch to make up for the years he'd lost. Years when he should have been there, working alongside his father instead of thinking he could fit into a world he had no business in.

But then no matter how much he wished it, he couldn't change the past. Wishing he'd never met Kalyn wouldn't do because if he hadn't met her, there never would have been Connor. And regardless of everything, especially all the lies and deceit, his son had been the one person who'd made Walker's life complete.

Bringing his thoughts back to the present, Walker moved away from the window to unpack. Earlier, he'd met Dillon and Ramsey, along with their wives, siblings and cousins. From his own research, Walker knew the Denver Westmorelands' story. It was heartbreaking yet heartwarming. They had experienced sorrows and successes. Both Dillon's and Ramsey's parents had been killed in a plane crash close to twenty years ago, leaving Dillon, who was the eldest, and Ramsey, the second eldest, to care for their thirteen siblings and cousins.

Dillon's parents had had seven sons—Dillon, Micah, Jason, Riley, Canyon, Stern and Brisbane. Ramsey's parents had had eight children, of which there were five sons— Ramsey, Zane, Derringer and the twins, Aidan and Adrian—and three daughters—Megan, Gemma and Bailey. The satisfying ending to the story was that Dillon and Ramsey had somehow managed to keep all their siblings and cousins together and raise them to be respectable and law-abiding adults. Of course, that didn't mean there hadn't been any hiccups along the way. Walker's research had unveiled several. It seemed the twins—Adrian and Aidan—along with Bailey and Bane, the youngest of the bunch, had been a handful while growing up. But they'd all made something of themselves.

There were definitely a lot of Westmorelands here in Denver, with more on the way to attend a wedding this weekend. The ones he'd met so far were friendly enough. The ease with which they'd welcomed him into their group was pretty amazing, considering they were well aware of the reason he was here. The only one who seemed bothered by his visit was Bailey.

Bailey.

Okay, he could admit he'd been attracted to her from the first. He'd seen her when she'd entered the baggage claim area, walking fast, that mass of curly brown hair slinging around her shoulders with every step she took. She'd had a determined look on her face, which had made her appear adorable. And the way the overhead lights hit her features had only highlighted what a gorgeous young woman she was.

He rubbed his hand down his face. The key word was *young*. But in this case, age didn't matter because Kalyn had taught him a lesson he would never forget when it came to women, of any age. So why had he suddenly begun feeling restless and edgy? And why was he remembering how long it had been since he'd been with a woman?

Trying to dismiss that question from his mind, Walker refocused on the reason he was here...as a favor to Garth. He would find out what his best friend needed to know and return to Kodiak. Already he'd concluded that the Westmorelands were more friendly and outgoing than their Alaskan cousins. The Outlaws tended to be on the reserved side, although Walker would be the first to say they had loosened up since Bart retired.

Walker knew Garth better than anyone else did, and although Garth wasn't as suspicious as Bart, Garth had an empire to protect. An empire that Garth's grandfather had worked hard to build and that the Outlaws had come close to losing last year because Bart had made a bad business decision.

Still, Walker had known the Outlaws long enough to know they didn't take anything at face value, which was why he was here. And so far the one thing he knew for certain was that the Westmorelands and the Outlaws were related. The physical resemblance was too astounding for them not to be. Whether or not the Westmorelands had an ulterior motive to claiming the Outlaws as relatives was yet to be seen.

Personally, he doubted it, especially after talking to Megan Westmoreland Claiborne. He'd heard the deep emotion in her voice when she'd told him of her family's quest to find as many family members as they could once they'd known Raphel Westmoreland hadn't been an only child as they'd assumed. She was certain there were even more Westmoreland relatives out there, other than the Outlaws, since they had recently discovered that Raphel and Reginald had an older brother by a different mother.

In Walker's estimation, the search initiated by the Westmorelands to find relatives had been a sincere and heartfelt effort to locate family. It had nothing to do with elbowing in on the Outlaws' wealth or sabotaging Jess's chances of becoming an Alaskan senator, as Bart assumed.

Walker moved away from the window the exact moment his cell phone rang. He frowned when he saw the caller was none other than Bart Outlaw. Why would the old man be calling him?

"Yes, Bart?"

"So what have you found out, son?"

Walker almost laughed out loud. *Son?* He shook his head. The only time Bart was extranice was when someone had something he wanted. And Walker knew Bart wanted information. Unfortunately, Bart wouldn't like what Walker had to say, since Bart hated being wrong.

"Found out about what, Bart?" Walker asked, deciding to be elusive. He definitely wouldn't tell Bart anything before talking to Garth.

He heard the grumble in Bart's voice when he said, "You know what, Walker. I'm well aware of the reason

Garth sent you to Denver. I hope you've found out something to discredit them."

Walker lifted a brow. "Discredit them?"

"Yes. The last thing the Outlaws need are people popping up claiming to be relatives and accusing us of being who we aren't."

"By that you mean saying you're Westmorelands instead of Outlaws?"

"Yes. We *are* Outlaws. My grandfather was Noah Outlaw. It's his blood that's running through my veins and no other man's. I want you to remember that, Walker, and I want you to do whatever you have to do to make sure I'm right."

Walker shook his head at the absurdity of what Bart was saying. "How am I to do that, Bart?"

"Find a way and keep this between us. There's no reason to mention anything to Garth." Then he hung up.

Frowning, Walker held the cell phone in his hand for a minute. That was just like Bart. He gave an order and expected it to be followed. No questions asked. Shaking his head, Walker placed a call to Garth, who picked up on the second ring.

"Yes, Walker? How are things going?"

"Your father just called. We might have a problem."

"I heard Walker Rafferty is a looker."

Bailey lifted the coffee cup to her lips as Josette slid into the seat across from her. Sharing breakfast was something they did at least two to three times a week, their schedules permitting. Josette was a freelance auditor whose major client was the hospital where Bailey's sister Megan worked as a doctor of anesthesiology.

"I take it you saw Megan this morning," Bailey said, wishing she could refute what Josette had heard. Unfortunately, she couldn't because it was true. Walker was a looker. Sinfully so.

"Yes, I had an early appointment at the hospital this morning and ran into your sister. She was excited that the Outlaws had reached out to your family."

Bailey rolled her eyes. "Sending someone instead of coming yourself is not what I consider reaching out. One of the Outlaws should have come themselves. Sending someone else is so tacky."

"Yes, but they could have ignored the situation altogether. Some people get touchy when others claim them as family. You never know the reason behind it."

Since Bailey and Josette were pretty much regulars at McKays, the waitress slid a cup of coffee in front of Josette, who smiled up at the woman. "Thanks, Amanda." After taking a sip, Josette turned her attention back to Bailey. "So tell me about him."

"Not much to tell. He looks okay. Seems nice enough."

"That's all you know about him, that he looks okay and seems nice enough?"

"Is there something else I should know?"

"Yes. Is he single? Married? Divorced? Have any children? What does he do for a living? Does he still live with his mother?"

Bailey smiled. "I didn't ask his marital status but can only assume he's single because he wasn't wearing a ring. As far as what he does for a living, he's a rancher. I do know that much. He raises bison."

"I take it he wasn't too talkative."

Bailey took another sip of coffee as she thought of the time she'd spent with Walker yesterday. "He was okay. We had a polite conversation."

"Polite?" Josette asked with a chuckle. "You?"

Bailey grinned. She could see why Josette found that amusing. Bailey wasn't known for being polite. "I prom-

ised Dillon I'd be on my best behavior even if it killed me."
She glanced at her watch. "I've got to run. I'm meeting
with the reporter taking my old job at nine."

"Okay, see you later."

After Bailey walked out of the restaurant, she couldn't
help but think about Josette's questions. There was a lot
Bailey didn't know about Walker.

She'd remedy that when she saw him later.

Walker was standing in front of Dillon's barn when
Bailey's truck pulled up. Moments later he watched as
she got out of the vehicle. Although he tried to ignore it,
he felt a deep flutter in the pit of his stomach at seeing her
again. Today, like yesterday, he was very much aware of
how sensuous she looked. Being attracted to her shouldn't
be anything he couldn't handle. So why was he having a
hard time doing so?

Why had he awakened that morning looking for her at
the breakfast table, assuming she lived with Dillon and
his wife, since she didn't have her own place? Later, he'd
found out from her brother Ramsey that Bailey floated,
living with whichever of her brothers, sisters or cousins
best fit her current situation. But now that most of her relatives had married, she stayed in her sister Gemma's house
since Gemma and her husband, Callum, had their primary
home in Australia.

He continued to watch her, somewhat surprised by his
own actions. He wasn't usually the type to waste his time
ogling a woman. But with Bailey it couldn't be helped.
There was something about her that demanded a man's attention regardless of whether he wanted to give it or not.
Her brothers and cousins would probably skin him alive if
they knew just where his thoughts were going right now.

The cold weather didn't seem to bother her as she moved
away from the truck without putting on her coat. Dressed

in a long-sleeved shirt, a long pencil skirt that complimented her curves and a pair of black leather boots, she
looked ready to walk the runway.

Squinting in the sun, he watched as she walked around
the truck, checking out each tire. She flipped her hair away
from her shoulders, and he imagined running his fingers
through every strand before urging her body closer to his.
There was no doubt in his mind he would love to sample
the feel of their bodies pressed together. Then he would
go for her mouth and—

"Walker? What are you doing here?"

Glad she had interrupted his thoughts, he replied, "I'm
an invited guest, remember?"

She frowned as she approached him. "Invited? Not the
way I remember it. But what I'm asking is why are you out
here at the barn by yourself? In the cold? Where is everyone? And why didn't you say something when I got out of
the truck to let me know you were over here?"

He leaned back against the barn's door. "Evening, Bailey. You sure do ask a lot of questions."

She glared at him. "Do I?"

"Yes, especially for someone who just told me yesterday
that one of her rules is not answering a lot of questions,
no matter who's asking. What if I told you that I happen
to have that same rule?"

She lifted an angry chin. Was it his imagination or was
she even prettier when she was mad? "I have a right to ask
you anything I want," she said.

He shook his head. "I beg to differ. However, out of
courtesy and since nothing you've asked has crossed any
lines, I'll answer. The reason I'm outside by the barn is because I just returned from riding with Ramsey and Zane.
They both left for home and I wasn't ready to go in just
yet."

"Zane and Ramsey actually left you out here alone?"

"Yes, you sound surprised that they would. It seems there are some members of your family who trust me. I guess your brothers figure their horses and sheep are safe with me," he said, holding her gaze.

"I didn't insinuate—"

"Excuse me, but I didn't finish answering *all* your questions," he interrupted her, and had to keep from grinning when she shut her mouth tightly. That same mouth he'd envisioned kissing earlier. "The reason I didn't say anything when you got out of the truck just now was because you seemed preoccupied with checking out your tires. Is there a problem?"

"One needs air. But when I looked up from my tires you were staring at me. Why?"

She had to know he was attracted to her. What man in his right mind wouldn't be? She was beautiful, desirable— alluring. And he didn't think the attraction was one-sided. A man knew when a woman was interested.

But he didn't want her interest, nor did he want to be interested in her. He refused to tell her that the reason he hadn't said anything was because he'd been too mesmerized to do so.

"I was thinking again about how much you and Charm favor one another. You'll see for yourself when you meet her."

"*If* I meet her."

"Don't sound so doubtful. I'm sure the two of you will eventually meet."

"Don't sound so sure of that, Walker."

He liked the sound of his name from her lips. Refusing to go tit for tat with her, he changed the subject. "So how was your day at work, Bailey?"

Stubbornly, Bailey told herself he really didn't give a damn how her day went. So why was he asking? Why did she find him as annoying as he was handsome? And why, when she'd looked up to see him staring at her, had she felt something she'd never felt before?

There was something so startling about his eyes that her reaction had been physical. For a second, she'd imagined the stroke of his fingers in her hair, the whisper of his heated breath across her lips, the feel of his body pressed hard against hers.

Why was her imagination running wild? She barely knew this man. Her family barely knew him. Yet they had welcomed him to Westmoreland Country without thinking things through. At least, that was her opinion. Was her family so desperate to find more relatives that they had let their guard down? She recalled days when a stranger on their land meant an alarm went out to everyone. Back then, they'd never known when someone from social services would show up for one of their surprise visits.

Knowing Walker was waiting for her to answer, she finally said, "It went well. It was my first day as a features editor and I think I handled things okay. You might even say I did an outstanding job today."

He chuckled. "No lack of confidence on your part, I see."

"None whatsoever." It was dusk and being outside with him, standing by the barn in the shadows, seemed way too intimate for her peace of mind. But there was something she needed to know, something that had been on her mind ever since Josette had brought it up that morning.

Not being one to beat around the bush when it came to things she really wanted to know, she asked, "Are you married, Walker?"

Walker stared at her, trying to fight the feel of air being sucked from his lungs. Where the hell had that question come from? Regardless, the answer should have been easy enough to give, especially since he hadn't been truly married even when he'd thought he had been. How could there be a real marriage when one of the parties took betrayal to a whole new level?

Silence reigned. Bailey had to be wondering why he hadn't answered. He shook off the unpleasant memories. "No. I'm not married." And then he decided to add, "Nor do I have a girlfriend. Any reason you want to know?"

She shrugged those beautiful shoulders that should be wearing a coat. "No. Just curious. You aren't wearing a wedding ring."

"No, I'm not."

"But that doesn't mean anything these days."

"You're right. Wearing a wedding ring doesn't mean anything."

He could tell by her frown that she hadn't expected him to agree with her. "So you're one of those types."

"And what type is that?"

"A man who has no respect for marriage or what it stands for."

Walker couldn't force back the wave of anger that suddenly overtook him. If only she knew how wrong she was. "You don't know me. And since you don't, I suggest you keep your damn assumptions to yourself."

Then, with clenched teeth, he walked off.

Three

The next morning Bailey sat behind the huge desk in her new office and sipped a cup of her favorite coffee. Yesterday had been her move-in day and she had pretty much stayed out of the way while the maintenance crew had shifted all the electronic equipment from her old office into this one. Now everything was in order, including her new desk, on top of which sat a beautiful plant from Ramsey and Chloe.

She couldn't help thinking, *You've come a long way, baby.* And only she and her family truly knew just how far she'd come.

She'd had some rebellious years and she would be the first to admit a little revolutionary spirit still lived within her. She was better at containing it these days. But she still liked rousing her family every once in a while.

Growing up as the youngest Westmoreland had had its perks as well as its downfalls. Over the past few years, most of her family members had shifted their attention away from her and focused on their spouses and children. She adored the women and men her cousins, brothers and sisters had married. And when she was around her family she felt loved.

She thought of her cousin Riley's new baby, who had been born last year. And there were still more babies on the way. A whole new generation of Denver Westmorelands. That realization had hit her like a ton of bricks when she'd held Ramsey and Chloe's daughter in her arms. Her first niece, Susan, named after Bailey's mother.

Bailey had looked down at Susan and prayed that her niece never suffered the pain of losing both parents like Bailey had. The agony and grief were something no one should have to go through. Bailey hadn't handled the pain well. None of the Westmorelands had, but it had affected her, the twins—Adrian and Aidan—and Bane the worst because they'd been so young.

Bailey cringed when she thought of some of the things she'd done, all the filthy words that had come out of her mouth. She appreciated her family, especially Dillon and Ramsey, for not giving up on her. Dillon had even taken on the State of Colorado when social services had wanted to take her, Bane and the twins away and put them in foster care.

He had hired an attorney to fight to keep them even with all the trouble the four of them were causing around town. Because somehow he'd understood. Somehow he'd known their despicable behavior was driven by the pain of losing their parents and that deep down they weren't bad kids.

"Little hell-raisers" was what the good people of Denver used to call them. She knew it was a reputation the four of them were now trying to live down, although it wasn't always easy. Take last night, for instance.

Walker Rafferty had almost pushed her into reacting

like her old self. She hated men who messed around after marriage. As far as she was concerned, the ones who messed around before marriage weren't any better but at least they didn't have a wedding ring on their finger.

Pushing away from her desk, she moved to the window. Downtown Denver was beautiful, especially today, seeing it from her new office. The buildings were tall, massive. As far as she was concerned, no other city had more magnificent skyscrapers. But even the breathtaking view couldn't make her forget Walker's callous remark.

Just like Bailey would never forget the pain and torment Josette had suffered while being married to Myles. Against their parents' wishes the two had married right out of high school, thinking love would conquer all as long as they were together. Within a year, Josette found out Myles was involved with another woman. To add insult to injury, he'd blamed Josette for his deceit, saying that it was because she'd decided to take night classes to get a college degree that she'd come home one night to find him in their bed with another woman. A woman who happened to be living in the apartment across the hall.

That was why Bailey had been so mad about Walker's insinuations that wearing a wedding ring meant nothing to a man. She'd been so angry that she'd only hung around Dillon's place long enough to hug his sons, Denver and Dade, before leaving.

It was obvious that Walker was just as mad at her as she was with him, but she didn't have a clue as to why. Yes, maybe her reaction had been a bit too strong, but seriously, she didn't give a royal damn. She called things the way she saw them. If he hadn't meant what he said, he should not have said it.

The beeping of the phone on her desk got her attention and she quickly crossed the room to answer it. It was an interoffice call from Lucia. Ramsey's wife, Chloe, was the magazine's founder and CEO but it was Chloe's best friend Lucia who ran things as editor in chief. Lucia was married to Bailey's brother Derringer. Although it was nice having her sisters-in-law as first and second in command at the magazine, it also put a lot of pressure on Bailey to prove that whatever accolades and achievements she received were earned and well deserved and not the result of favoritism. Just because Chloe and Lucia were Westmorelands, that didn't mean Bailey deserved preferential treatment of any kind. And she wouldn't have it any other way.

"Yes, Lucia?"

"Hi, Bailey. Chloe stopped by and wants to see you."

Bailey raised an arched brow. What could have brought Chloe out of Westmoreland Country so early today? It wasn't even nine in the morning yet. After marrying Ramsey, Chloe had pretty much decided to be a sheep rancher's wife and rarely came into the office these days.

Bailey slid into her jacket. "Okay. I'll be right there."

Deciding to take the longest route back to Dillon's place, Walker rode the horse and enjoyed the beauty of the countryside. There was a lot about Westmoreland Country that reminded him of Kodiak Island, minus the extremely cold weather, of course. Although the weather here was cold, it was nothing compared to the harsh winters he endured. It was the middle of October and back home the amount of snowfall was quadruple what they had here.

But the differences in the weather weren't what was bothering him today. What bothered him today had everything to do with the dreams he'd had last night. Dreams of Bailey. And that talk they'd had by the barn.

Even now the memory of their conversation made him angry. She'd had no right to assume anything about him. No right at all. She didn't know him. Had no idea the hell he'd been through or the pain he'd suffered, and was still suffering, after almost ten years. Nor did she have any idea what he'd lost.

By the lake, he slowed the horse and took a deep breath. The mountain air was cleansing; he wished it could cleanse his soul, as well. After bringing the horse to a stop he dismounted and stared at the valley below. *Awesome* was the only word he could use to describe what he saw.

And even though he was mad as hell with Bailey, a part of him thought she was pretty awesome, as well. What other way was there to describe a woman who could rile his anger and still star in his erotic dreams? He had awakened several times during the night with an erection. It had been years since that had happened. Not since he'd returned to Kodiak from California.

He had basically thrown himself into working the ranch, first out of guilt for not being there when his father had needed him, and then as a therapeutic way to deal with the loss of Connor. There were some days he'd worked from sunup to sundown. And on those nights when his body had needed a woman it had been for pleasure and nothing else. Passionate but emotionless sex had become his way of life when it came to relationships, but even that had been years ago.

Walker no longer yearned for the type of marriage his parents and grandparents had shared. He was convinced those kinds of unions didn't exist anymore. If they did, they were the exception and not the norm. He would, however, admit to noticing the ease with which the Westmoreland men openly adored their wives, wearing their hearts on their sleeves as if they were a band of honor. So, okay, Walker would include the Westmorelands in the exceptions.

He remounted the horse to head back. Thoughts of Bailey hadn't ended with his dreams. Even with the light of day, she'd invaded his thoughts. That wasn't good.

He had told Dillon he would leave the Monday after this weekend's wedding, but now he figured it would be best if he returned to Kodiak right after the wedding. The farther, and the sooner, he got away from Bailey, the better.

He'd learned enough about the Westmorelands and would tell Garth what he thought, regardless of Bart's feelings on the matter. If Bart thought he could pressure Walker to do otherwise, then he was mistaken.

Walker had nothing to lose since he'd lost it all already.

Bailey walked into Lucia's office to find her sisters-in-law chatting and enjoying cups of coffee. Not for the first time Bailey thought her brothers Ramsey and Derringer had truly lucked out when they'd married these two. Besides being beautiful, both were classy women who could be admired for their accomplishments. Real role models. The two had met at a college in Florida and had remained best friends since. The idea that they'd married brothers was remarkable, especially since the brothers were as different as day and night. Ramsey was older and had always been the responsible type. Derringer had earned a reputation as a womanizer of the third degree. Personally, Bailey had figured he would never settle down and marry. Now not only was he happily married but he was also the father of a precious little boy named Ringo. He had stepped into the role of family man as if he'd been made for it.

Chloe glanced up, saw Bailey standing in the doorway, smiled and crossed the room to give her a hug. "Bay, how are you? You rushed in and out of Dillon's place last night. We barely spoke, let alone held a conversation. How's day two in your new position?"

Bailey returned her sister-in-law's smile. "Great. I'm

ready to roll my sleeves up and bring in those feature stories that will grow our readership."

Chloe beamed. "That's good to hear. I wanted to congratulate you on your promotion and let you know how proud I am of you."

"Thanks, Chloe." Bailey couldn't help but be touched by Chloe's words. She had begun working for the company as a part-timer in between her classes at the university. She had liked it so much that she'd changed her major to journalism and hadn't regretted doing so. It was Chloe, a proponent of higher education, who had encouraged her to also get her MBA.

"So what brings you out of Westmoreland Country so early?"

"I'm meeting Pam in a little while. She wants me to sit in on several interviews she's hosting today. She's hiring a director for her school."

Bailey nodded. Dillon's wife, Pam, was a former actress and had opened an acting school in her hometown of Gamble, Wyoming, a few years ago. The success of that school had led her to open a second one in Denver.

Taking her by the arm, Chloe said, "Come sit with us a minute. Share a cup of coffee and tell me how you like your office."

"I love it! Thanks to the both of you. The view is simply stunning."

"It is, isn't it?" Lucia said, smiling. "That used to be my office and I regretted giving it up. But I have to admit I have a fantastic view in here, as well."

"Yes, you certainly do," Bailey said, agreeing, glancing around the room that was double the size of her office. When her gaze landed on Lucia's computer screen, Bailey went still.

"Recognize him?" Lucia asked, adjusting the image of a face until it took up the full screen.

Bailey sucked in a deep breath as she felt the rapid thud of her pulse. Even if the clean-shaven face had thrown her for a quick second, the gorgeous eyes staring at her were a dead giveaway, not to mention that smile.

"It's Walker Rafferty," she said. He looked years younger, yet his features, sharp and sculpted, were just as handsome.

Chloe nodded, coming to stand beside her. "Yes, that's him. At the time these photos were taken most people knew him as Ty Reklaw, an up-and-coming heartthrob in Hollywood."

Shocked, Bailey looked back at the computer screen. Walker used to be an actor? No way. The man barely said anything and seemed to keep to himself, although she knew he'd formed a pretty solid friendship with her brothers and male cousins.

What had Chloe just said? He'd been an up-and-coming heartthrob in Hollywood? Bailey studied his image. Yes, she could definitely believe that. His grin was irresistibly devastating, to the point where she felt goose bumps form on her arms.

She glanced back at Chloe and Lucia. "He's an actor?"

"He used to be, around ten years ago and he had quite a following. But then Ty Reklaw left Hollywood and never looked back," Chloe said, sitting back down in her chair.

A frown bunched Bailey's forehead. "Reklaw? As in Reklaw, Texas?"

Lucia chuckled as she poured Bailey a cup of coffee. "I doubt it. Probably Reklaw as in the name Walker spelled backward. You know how movie stars are when they don't want to use their real names."

Bailey's gaze narrowed as an idea popped into her head. "Are you sure Walker Rafferty is his real name?"

"Yes. I asked Dillon."

Bailey's brow raised. "Dillon knew who he was?"

"Only after Pam told him. She remembered Walker

from the time she was in Hollywood but she doubted he remembered her since their paths never crossed."

Bailey nodded. Yes, she could imagine any woman remembering Walker. "So he used to be an actor with a promising future. Why did he leave?"

Lucia took a sip of her coffee. "Pam said everyone assumed it was because of the death of his wife and son. They were killed in a car accident."

"Oh, my God," Bailey said. "How awful."

"Yes, and according to Pam it was quite obvious whenever he and his wife were seen together that he loved and adored her. His son had celebrated his first birthday just days before the accident occurred," Lucia said. "The loss was probably too great and he never recovered from it."

"I can understand that." Having lost both her parents in a tragic death a part of her could feel his pain. She reflected on their conversation last night when she'd asked if he was married. He'd said no and hadn't told her he was a widower.

She then remembered the rest of their conversation, the one that had left them both angry. From his comment one might have thought the sanctity of marriage didn't mean anything to him. Or had she only assumed that was what he'd meant? She shuddered at the thought.

"Bailey? Are you okay?"

She looked up at the two women staring at her. "Not sure. I might have offended Walker big-time last night."

"Why? What happened?" Lucia asked with a look that said she wished she didn't have to ask.

Bailey shrugged. "I might have jumped to conclusions about him and his attitude about marriage and said something based on my assumptions. How was I to know he'd lost his wife? I guess he said what he did because the thought of marrying again is painful for him."

"Probably since, according to Pam, he was a dedicated husband and father, even with his rising fame."

Bailey drew in a deep breath, feeling completely awful. When would she learn to stop jumping to conclusions about everything? Dillon and Ramsey had definitely warned her enough about doing that. For some reason she was quick to automatically assume the worst about people.

"Is that why you rushed in and out of Dillon and Pam's place last night? Because you and Walker had words?" Chloe asked.

"Yes. At the time I was equally mad with him. You know how I feel about men who mess around. Before marriage or after marriage."

Chloe nodded. "Yes, Bailey. I think we all know. You gave your poor brothers and cousins hell about the number of girlfriends they had."

"Well, I'm just glad they came to their senses and settled down and married." Bailey began pacing and nervously nibbled her bottom lip. Moments later she stopped and looked at the two women. "I need to apologize to him."

"Yes, you do," both Lucia and Chloe agreed simultaneously.

Bailey took a sip of her coffee as a question came to mind. "If Walker was so hot in Hollywood, then why don't I remember him?"

Lucia smiled. "If I recall, ten years ago you were too busy hanging with Bane and getting into all kinds of trouble. So I'm not surprised you don't know who was hot and who was not. I admit that although I remember him, he looks different now. Still handsome but more mature and definitely a lot more rugged. The beard he wears now makes him nearly unrecognizable. I would not have recalled who he was if Pam hadn't mentioned it. Of course when she did I couldn't wait to look him up this morning."

"Was he in several movies?" Bailey asked. She intended to find any movies he'd appeared in as soon as she left work.

"No, just two. One was a Matthew Birmingham flick, where Walker played opposite actress Carmen Atkins, as her brother. That was his very first. He was hot and his acting was great," Chloe said, smiling. "According to Pam, although he didn't get an award nomination, there are those who thought he should have. But what he did get was a lot of attention from women and other directors in Hollywood. It didn't take him long to land another role in a movie directed by Clint Eastwood. A Western. He'd just finished filming when his wife and son were killed. I don't think he hung around for the premiere. He left for Alaska and never returned."

Bailey didn't say anything. She was thinking about how to get back in Walker's good graces. "I'll apologize when I see him tonight."

"Good luck," Chloe said, chuckling. "When I left this morning, Thorn and his brothers and cousins had arrived for the wedding and you know what that means."

Yes, she knew. There would be a card game tonight. Men only. And she had a feeling Walker would be invited. Then she had an idea. For the past ten years Walker had lived on his ranch on that remote island. He'd indicated last night that he wasn't married and didn't have a steady girlfriend, which meant he was a loner. That made him just the type of man she needed to interview for one of the magazine's spring issues. She could see him being the feature story. She'd wait and share her idea with Chloe and Lucia until she had all the details worked out.

Bailey then recalled that Walker would be returning to Alaska on Monday after the wedding. That didn't give her much time. She looked back down at Walker's photo.

Getting an exclusive interview with him would definitely mean big sales for the magazine.

She took another sip of her coffee. Now, if she could only get Walker to agree.

Four

Walker threw out a card before glancing at the closed door. How many times had he done that tonight? And why was he expecting Bailey to show up at a men-only card game? The main reason was because it was Bailey, and from what he'd heard from her brothers and cousins, Bailey did whatever Bailey wanted to do. But he'd heard more fondness than annoyance in their voices and figured they wouldn't want it any other way.

So here he was, at what had to be close to midnight, in what was known as Dillon's man cave, playing cards with a bunch of Westmorelands. He would admit that over the past three days he'd gotten to know the Denver Westmorelands pretty well, and today he'd met their cousins from Atlanta, which included those living in Montana.

Walker couldn't help but chuckle at Bart's accusation that the Westmorelands had targeted the Outlaws for monetary gain. Walker knew for a fact that wasn't true. Even if their land development company wasn't making them

millions, from the talk around the table, the horse train-
ing business a few of the cousins owned was also doing
extremely well.

"I hear you chuckling over there, Walker. Does that
mean you have a good hand?"

He glanced over at Zane and smiled. "If I did you'd be
the last person to know until it counted."

That got a laugh from the others. In a way, he was surprised at the ease he felt being around them, even those
Westmorelands he'd only met that day. When he'd returned
to Kodiak from his stint in Hollywood, he'd shut himself
off from everyone except the Outlaws and those members
of the community he'd considered family. As an only child,
he wasn't used to a huge family, but he was being educated
about how one operated, Westmoreland-style.

Thorn was telling everyone about the bike he'd just built
for a celebrity. Walker just continued to study his hand. He
could have added to the conversation, since he happened
to know the man personally. But he stayed silent. That was
a life he'd rather not remember.

Walker heard the knock on the door and all it took was
the tingle that moved up his arm to let him know it was
Bailey. The mere thought that he could want her with such
intensity should have frozen him cold, especially after
what she'd accused him of last night. Instead, the opposite
was happening. He had dreamed of her, allowed her to invade his mind all day, and now his body was responding
in a way it did whenever a man wanted a woman.

"Come in," Dillon yelled out. "And whoever you are,
you better be a male."

Bailey stuck her head in the door. "Sorry to disappoint
you, Dil. I decided to check and make sure all of you are
still alive and in one piece. I can just imagine how much
money has been lost about now," she said with a grin as
she stepped into the room.

Walker was the only one who bothered to look up at her. She was gorgeous. Her hair hung like soft waves across her shoulders and her outfit, a pair of jeans and a blue pullover sweater, emphasized her curves, making her look feminine and sexy as hell.

All he could do was stare at her, and then she met his eyes. Bam! The moment their gazes connected he felt something slam into him. He was sure it had the same effect on her. It was as if they were the only two people in the room, and he was glad her family was more interested in studying their cards than studying them.

One of the things he noticed was the absence of that spark of anger in her eyes. It had definitely been there last night. Instead, he saw something else, something that had heat drumming through every inch of his body. Had frissons of fire racing up his spine. Was he imagining it?

"Go away, Bay. You'll bring me bad luck," wailed her cousin Durango, who'd flown in from Montana. He held his gaze steady on the cards in his hand.

"You're probably losing big-time anyway," she said, chuckling, breaking eye contact with Walker to look at Durango. "Another reason I'm here is to rescue Walker." Her gaze returned to Walker. "He's probably tired of your company about now, but is too nice to say so. So I'm here to rescue him."

Walker saw twelve pairs of eyes shift from their cards to him, but instead of seeing even a speck of curiosity, he saw pity as if they were thinking, *We're glad it's you and not us*. Their gazes then returned to their cards.

"We're not stupid, Bay," Zane Westmoreland said, grinning and throwing a card out. "You think you can pump Walker for information about our plans for Aidan's bachelor party. But we've told Walker the rules. What we say in this room stays in this room."

"Whatever," she said, rolling her eyes. "Well, Walker, do you want to be rescued?"

He didn't have to think twice about it, although he was wondering about her motive. "Why not," he said, sliding back his chair. "But it's not because I haven't enjoyed the company," he said, standing and placing his cards down. "It's because I refuse to lose any more money to you guys. All of you are professional gamblers whether you admit it or not."

Dillon chuckled. "Ian is the only true gambler in the family. We're just wannabes. If he was here you wouldn't be walking out with your shirt on, trust me."

Walker smiled. "Can't wait to meet him." He moved across the room toward the door where Bailey stood. "I'll see you guys in the morning."

"Not too early, though," Zane cautioned, throwing out a card. "This game will probably be an all-nighter, so chances are we'll all sleep late."

Walker nodded. "I'll remember that."

"Any reason you felt the need to rescue me?"

Bailey glanced over at Walker as they headed toward the stairs. "I thought you might want to go riding."

"Horseback riding? This time of night? In this weather?"

She chuckled. "Not horseback riding. Truck riding. And yes, this time of night or, rather, this time of morning since it's after midnight. And it's a nice night. At least nicer than most. Besides, there's something I need to say to you."

He stopped walking and held her gaze. "Didn't get all your accusations off your chest last night?"

She knew she deserved that. "I was out of line and jumped to conclusions."

He crossed his arms over his chest. "Did you?"

"Yes, and if it's okay with you I'd like to talk to you

about it. But not here. So if you're up to riding, I know the perfect place where we can have a private conversation."

From his expression she could tell he was wondering what this private conversation would be about. However, instead of asking he merely nodded and said, "Okay, lead the way."

Bailey nodded, too, and then moved forward. Once they made it downstairs she grabbed her coat and waited while he got his. The house was quiet. Everyone with a lick of sense had gone to bed, which didn't say a lot for herself, Walker, her cousins and brothers. But she had been determined to hang around and talk to Walker.

When they stepped outside she saw the temperature had dropped. It was colder than she'd thought. She glanced over at him. "It won't take long for Kent to warm up."

"Kent?"

She nodded, shoving her hands into the pockets of her coat. "Yes. My truck."

He chuckled. "You gave your truck a name?"

"Yes. He and I go a long way back, so we're best buds. I take care of him and he takes care of me." She smiled. "Let me rephrase that. JoJo helps me take care of him."

"JoJo is Stern's wife, right? The mechanic?"

"Yes," Bailey said, reaching her truck. "The best in Denver. Probably the country. The wor—"

"Okay, I get the picture."

She threw her head back and laughed as she opened her truck door. She climbed inside, buckled up and waited until he did the same. "So where are we headed?" he asked.

She looked over at him. "Bailey's Bay."

Walker had heard about Bailey's Bay and had even covered parts of it yesterday while out horseback riding with Ramsey and Zane. He'd been told by Dillon that Westmoreland Country sat on over eighteen hundred acres.

Since Dillon was the eldest, he had inherited the main house along with the three hundred acres it sat on. Everyone else, upon reaching the age of twenty-five, received one hundred acres to call their own. Bailey had decided to name each person's homestead and had come up with names such as Ramsey's Web, Stern's Stronghold, Zane's Hideout, Derringer's Dungeon and Megan's Meadows. She had named hers Bailey's Bay.

"I understand you haven't built on your property yet," he said, looking out the window. Because of the darkness, there wasn't much to see.

"That's right. There's no need. I have too many cousins and siblings with guest rooms at their homes. And then there's Gemma's house that sits empty most of the time since she's living in Australia."

He didn't say anything but figured shifting from guest room to guest room and from house to house would get old. "You do plan to build one day though, right?"

"Yes, eventually. Right now Ramsey uses a lot of my land for sheep grazing, but that won't stop me when I'm ready. I know exactly where I intend to sit my home, and it's far away from the grazing land."

"I bet your place will be a beauty whenever you decide to build." He had seen all the other homes. Each one was breathtaking and said a lot about the owners' personalities. He wondered what design Bailey would choose. Single story that spread out with several wings? Or a two-story mansion erected like a magnificent piece of art? Either one would be a lot of house for one person. But then didn't the same hold true for the house he lived in? All that land and all that house.

"Yes. I plan to make it a masterpiece."

He didn't doubt that and could even visualize the home she would probably build for herself.

"Bailey's Bay was chosen for me and sits next to Zane's

and between Ramsey and Dillon's properties." She chuckled. "That was a deliberate move on my brothers' and cousins' parts since they figured Zane would stay in my business, and Dillon and Ramsey were the only two people I would listen to."

"Are they?"

"Pretty much, but sometimes I won't listen to anyone."

He couldn't help but smile. Bailey was definitely a rebel. That was probably some of her appeal. That, along with her sensuality. He doubted she knew just how sensual she was. It would be any man's downfall when she did realize it.

They didn't say anything for a while, until she brought the truck to a stop. "Here we are."

Thanks to the full moon and the stars overhead he could make out the lake. It stretched wide and endless and the waters were calm. From riding out here with Zane and Ramsey he knew the lake ran through most of the West-moreland land. "Gemma Lake, right?"

"Yes. Raphel named it after my great-grandmother. I never knew them, or my grandparents for that matter. They died before I was born. But I heard they were great people and they left a wonderful legacy for us to be proud of."

Walker thought about the legacy his own parents, grand-parents and great-grandparents had left and how he'd al-most turned his back on that legacy to go after what hadn't been his dream but had been Kalyn's dream. Never again would he allow any woman to have that much power over him.

So why was he here? He had been in a card game and Bailey had showed up, suggesting they leave, and he had. Why? Was he once again allowing a woman to make de-cisions for him?

Walker glanced over at her. She stared straight ahead and he wondered what she was thinking. He looked back at the lake. It was peaceful. He liked being here with Bailey, parked, sharing this moment with her.

He was well aware they were attracted to each other, although neither of them had acted on it. But the desire was there nonetheless. Whenever they were alone there was always some sort of sexual aura surrounding them. Like now.

Even when there were others around he was aware of her. Like that first night when everyone had shown up at Dillon's for dinner. Walker had kept looking across the table at her, liking the sexy sound of her laugh. He had to be honest with himself—he had deliberately waited for her last night, outside by the barn, knowing she would eventually drop by Dillon's house since Zane had mentioned she did it every day.

The effect she was having on him bothered him, which was why he'd changed his plans so he could leave Saturday evening after the wedding instead of on Monday. The last thing he needed was to get involved with Bailey Westmoreland. He would never marry again, and all he could ever offer her was an affair that led nowhere. That wouldn't be good for her and could affect the friendships he'd made with her family.

He glanced over at her. "You said you wanted to talk," he prompted. The sooner they finished the sooner they could leave. Being out here alone with her could lead to trouble.

She looked over at him. He could barely see her features in the moonlight but he didn't need a bright light to know she was beautiful. She had rolled down the window a little and the cold air coming in enhanced her scent. It was filling his nostrils with the most luscious aroma.

But her looks and her scent weren't the issue; nor should they be. He had to remember he deserved better than a woman who could be another Kalyn.

"About last night."

That got his attention. "What about it?"

"I owe you an apology."

"Do you?"

"Yes. I made accusations that I should not have."

Yes, she had, but he couldn't help wondering what had made her realize that fact. "What makes you so sure?"

She frowned. "Are you saying that I was right?"

"No, that's not what I'm saying. You need to do something about being quick to jump to conclusions."

She waited a second, tapping her fingers on the steering wheel before saying, "I know. My family warns me about it all the time."

He touched her shoulder for emphasis. "Then, maybe you should listen to them."

He suddenly realized touching her had been a mistake. With her layered clothing he was far from coming into contact with bare skin, but he could still feel sensuous heat swelling his fingertips.

"I try to listen."

The catch in her voice sent a ripple of desire through him. He shifted in his seat when a thrumming dose of heat ripped through his gut. "Maybe you should try harder, Bailey."

What made Walker so different from any other man? His touch on her shoulder affected her in a way no man's touch had ever affected her before. How did he have the ability to reach her inner being and remind her that she was a woman?

Personal relationships weren't her forte. Most of the guys in these parts were too afraid of her brothers and cousins to even think of crossing the line, so she'd only had one lover. For her it had been one and done, and executed more out of curiosity than anything else. She certainly hadn't been driven by the kind of sexual desire she was feeling with Walker.

There was a spike of heat that always rolled in her stomach whenever she was around him, not to mention the warmth that settled in the area between her legs. Even now, just being in the same vehicle with him was making her breasts tingle. Had his face inched a little closer to hers?

Suggesting they go for a late-night ride might not have been a good idea after all. "I'm not perfect," she finally said softly.

"No one is perfect," he responded huskily.

Bailey drew in a sharp breath when he rubbed a finger across her cheek. She fought back the slow moan that threatened to slip past her lips. His hand on her shoulder had caused internal havoc; his fingers on her face were stirring something to life inside her that she'd never felt before.

She needed to bring an end to this madness. The last thing she wanted was for him to misunderstand the reason she'd brought him here. "I didn't bring you out here for this, Walker," she said. "I don't want you getting the wrong idea."

"Okay, what's the right idea?" he asked, leaning in even closer. "Why did you bring me out here?"

Nervously, she licked her lips. He was still rubbing a finger across her cheek. "To apologize."

"Apology accepted." Then he lowered his head and took possession of her mouth.

Five

Walker deepened the kiss, even while trying to convince himself that he should not be kissing Bailey. No way should his tongue be tangling with hers or hers with his.

But she tasted so damn good. And he didn't want to stop. Truth be told, he'd been anxiously waiting for this minute. He would even admit he'd waited ever since that day at the airport when he'd first thought her lips were a luscious pair. A pair he wanted to taste. Now he was getting his chance.

Her tongue was driving him insane. Her taste was hot, simply addictive. She created a wildness within him, unleashing a sexual beast that wanted to consume every bone-melting inch of her. When had he kissed any woman so thoroughly, with such unapologetic rawness?

He tangled his fingers in her hair, holding her mouth captive as his mouth and tongue sucked, licked and teased every delicious inch of her mouth. This kiss was so incredibly pleasurable his testicles ached. If he didn't end things now, this kiss could very well penetrate his very soul.

He reluctantly broke off the kiss, but made sure his mouth didn't stray far. He could feel the sweet, moist heat of her breath on his lips and he liked it. He liked it so much that he gave in to temptation and used his tongue to trace a path along her lips. Moments later that same tongue tracked a line down her neck and collarbone before returning to her mouth.

She slowly opened her eyes and looked at him. He knew he shouldn't be thinking it, but at that moment he wished the truck had a backseat. All the things he would do to her filled his mind.

"That was some acceptance," she whispered hotly against his lips.

He leaned forward and nibbled around her chin. "Acceptance of what?"

"My apology. Maybe I should apologize more often."

He chuckled lightly, leaning back to meet her gaze. "Do you often do or say things that require an apology?"

"So I'm told. I'm known to put my foot in my mouth more often than not. But do you know what?"

"What?"

"I definitely like your tongue in my mouth a lot better, Walker."

Walker drew in a ragged breath. He was learning there was no telling what would come out of that luscious mouth of hers. "No problem. That can be arranged."

He leaned in and kissed her again; this time was more intense than the last. He figured he needed the memory of this kiss to take back to Kodiak for those long cold nights, when he would sit in front of the fireplace alone and nurse a bottle of beer.

She was shivering in his arms and he knew it had nothing to do with the temperature. She was returning his kiss in a way that ignited every cell in his body, and tasted just as incredibly sexy as she looked. Never had he sampled a woman whose flavor fired his blood to a degree where he actually felt heat rushing through his veins.

He could do a number on her mouth forever, and would have attempted to do so if he hadn't felt her fingers fumbling with the buttons on his shirt. He needed to end this now or else he would be a goner. There was only so much he could take when it came to Bailey.

Walker broke off the kiss, resting his forehead against hers. The needs filtering through him were as raw as raw could get. Primitive. It had been years since a woman had filled him with such need. He was like a starving man who was only hungry for her.

"I didn't bring you out here for this, Walker."

Her words had come out choppy but he understood them. "You said that already." He kept his forehead plastered to hers. There was something so alluring about having his mouth this close to hers. At any time he could use his tongue to swipe a taste of her.

"I'm saying it again. I only wanted to park and talk."

He chuckled against her lips. "That's all?"

Now it was her turn to chuckle. "You are so typically male. Ready to get laid, any time or any place."

"Um, not really. I have very discriminating taste. And speaking of taste," he said, leaning back slightly so he could look into her eyes, "I definitely like yours."

Bailey nervously licked her lips. What was a woman supposed to say to a line like that? In all honestly, there was nothing she could say, especially while gazing into the depths of Walker's dark eyes. He held her gaze hostage and there was nothing she could do about it. Mainly because there was nothing she wanted to do about it. His eyes had her mesmerized, drawing her under his spell.

The same thing had happened earlier when she'd watched his two movies back-to-back. What Chloe had said was true. His performances in both roles had been award-worthy material. Sitting there, watching him on her television screen, was like watching a totally different person. She could see how he'd become a heartthrob in a short period of time. His sexiness had been evident in his clothes, his voice and the roles he'd chosen. And those lovemaking scenes had blazed off the charts. They'd left her wishing she had been the woman in those scenes with him. And tonight, as unbelievable as it seemed, she had lived her own memorable scene with him.

She had to remember the reason she had brought him here. Apologizing for last night was only part of it. "There's something else I need to talk to you about, Walker."

He tipped his head back. "Is there?"

"Yes."

"Can I kiss you again first?" he asked, rubbing his thumb over her bottom lip.

Bailey knew she should say no. Another kiss from him was the last thing she needed. She feared it would detonate her brain. But her brain was halfway gone already, just from the sensuality she heard in his voice. His thumb gently stroking her lip stirred a need that primed her for something she couldn't define but wanted anyway.

He was staring at her, waiting for an answer. She could feel the effects of his spellbinding gaze all over her body. Suddenly she felt bold, empowered, filled with a burning need. Instead of answering him, she pushed in the center console, converting the truck from bucket seats to bench seats. Easing closer to him, she wrapped her arms around his neck and tilted her mouth up to his. "Yes, Walker. You can kiss me again."

And as if that was all he needed to hear, he swooped down and sucked her tongue into his mouth. Bailey couldn't help but moan. He was consuming her. She sensed a degree of hunger within him she hadn't recognized in the other kisses. It was as if he was laying claim to her mouth, branding it in a way no other man had or ever would, and all while his knuckles softly stroked her jaw.

She kissed him back with the same greediness. No matter what costar she'd watched him with earlier, he was with her now. This was real, no acting involved. The only director they were following was their own desire, which seemed to be overtaking them.

Walker's hand reached under her sweater to caress her stomach, and she moaned at the contact. The feel of his fingers on her bare flesh made her shiver, and when he continued to softly rub her skin she closed her eyes as awareness spiked fully into her blood.

The moment he released her mouth, she leaned closer and used her tongue to lick the corners of his lips. His hand inched upward, stroking her ribs, tracing the contours of her bones until he reached her breasts. She drew in a deep breath when his fingertips drew circles on the lace bra covering her nipples. The twin buds hardened and sent a signal to the juncture of her thighs. When he pushed her sweater out of the way, her body automatically arched toward him.

As if he knew what she wanted, what she needed, he undid the front clasp of her bra. As soon as her breasts sprang free, he lowered his mouth to them. Her nipples were hard and ready for him and he devoured them with a greediness that had her moaning deep in her throat.

When she felt the truck's leather touch her back, she realized he had lowered her onto her back. She ran her hands over his shirt and began undoing the buttons, needing to touch his bare skin like he was touching hers. Moments later, her fingers speared into the hair covering his chest.

She heard him growl her name seconds before he captured her wrists, holding her captive while his tongue swirled languorously over her stomach. Her skin sizzled everywhere his mouth touched. And when his mouth reached her navel, he laved it with his tongue. Her stomach muscles flexed beneath his mouth.

Walker was convinced Bailey's body was calling out to him. He was determined to answer the call. She tasted wonderful and when she rocked her body beneath his mouth he couldn't help but groan. His control was eroding. He'd thought all he wanted was a kiss to remember, but he discovered he wanted something more. He wanted her. All of her. He wanted to explode in the heat she was generating. But first, he wanted to fill her with the rapturous satisfaction she needed.

Raising his head, he met her gaze. The fire in her eyes almost burned him. "Lift up your hips, Bailey," he whispered.

When she did as he requested, he unsnapped her jeans and worked the denim down past her thighs. He then grazed his fingers against the scrap of lace covering her femininity. He inhaled deeply, drawing her luscious scent through his nostrils. His heart pounded hard in his chest and every cell in his body needed to please her. To give her a reason to remember him. Why that was important, he wasn't sure. All he knew was that it was.

His erection jerked greedily in anticipation of her feminine taste. When he lowered his head and eased his tongue inside her, he forced himself not to climax just from the delicious flavor of her. She pushed against his shoulders and then, seconds later, gripped him hard, holding his mouth right there as she moaned his name. He delved deep inside, stroking her, lapping up her taste with every inch of his tongue.

She lifted her hips to his mouth and he gripped her thighs tightly, devouring her in a way he'd dreamed of doing every night since he'd met her. Her scent and her taste filled him with emotions and sensations he hadn't felt in years.

He felt her body jerk beneath his mouth in an explosive orgasm. She screamed his name, but he kept his mouth crushed to her, sucking harder and hoping this was one intimate kiss she would never, ever forget.

Moments later, after he felt her body go still, except for the shuddering of her breath, he slowly withdrew his tongue—but not before brushing his lips over her womanly mound. Marking. Branding. Imprinting.

"Walker…"

"Yes, baby. I'm here." He eased over her body and kissed her.

Bailey's breath caught in her throat. When Walker finally released her mouth, she could only lie there enmeshed in a web of sensations that had left her weak but totally fulfilled. Never in her life had she experienced anything like what Walker had done. How he had made her feel. The pleasure had been so sharp she might never recover. He had taken her to rapturous heights she hadn't known existed between a man and a woman.

"I think we better go," Walker said softly as he rezipped her jeans, placing a kiss on her stomach. When she felt the tip of his tongue around her belly button, she whispered his name.

He took his time refastening her bra, cupping her breasts and licking her nipples before doing so. Then he pulled her sweater down before helping her into a sitting position. She was tempted to resist. She wanted to lie there while memories washed over her.

"Your breasts are beautiful, you know, Bailey."

She shook her head. No, she didn't know. No other man had ever complimented her breasts. But then, no other man would have had a reason to do so. She drew in a deep breath, rested her head against the seat and closed her eyes. Had she actually experienced an orgasm from a man going down on her? In a parked truck?

"The lake is beautiful tonight."

How could he talk about how beautiful the lake was after driving her into a sexual frenzy and blowing her mind? And just think, he hadn't even made love to her. What he'd given her was an appetizer. She could only imagine what the full course meal would be like.

She slowly opened her eyes and followed his gaze through the windshield to the lake. She knew he was giving her time to pull herself together, clear her head, finish straightening up her clothes. She took another deep breath. In her mind she could still feel his mouth on her breasts and between her thighs. It took her a while to respond to what he'd said. "Yes, it's beautiful. I love coming here. Day or night. Whenever I need to think."

"I can see this being a good thinking spot."

She decided not to add that he'd just proved it was a good making-out spot, as well. She glanced over at him and saw the buttons of his shirt were still undone, reminding her of when her tongue had licked his skin. Her blood seared at the memory.

"What we did tonight was wrong, Bailey. But I don't regret it."

She didn't regret it, either. The only thing she regretted was not taking things further. They were adults, not kids. Consenting adults. And if they had enjoyed it, then what was the problem? "And why was it wrong?"

"Because you deserve more than a meaningless affair and that's all I can offer you."

She didn't recall asking for more. "What makes you think I want any more than that, Walker? I'm not into serious relationships, either. They can get messy."

He lifted a brow. "How so?"

"Men have a tendency to get possessive, territorial. Act crazy sometimes. Trust me, I know. I grew up with twelve of them. That's why I have my rules."

"Bailey's Rules, right?"

"Yep. Those are the ones."

"So if you don't do affairs, what do you do? I assume you date."

"When it suits me." No need to tell him she'd never had a steady boyfriend. "I assume you date, too."

"Yes, when it suits me," he said, repeating her words.

"So we understand each other," she said, wondering if they really did.

"Yes, I guess you can say that," he said, buttoning his shirt. "And now is as good a time as any to mention that I've decided to return to Kodiak right after the wedding on Saturday instead of on Monday as planned."

Her jaw dropped in surprise. "You're leaving Saturday?"

"Yes."

"Why?"

He looked over at her. "There's no need to stay here any longer than that. What I have to tell the Outlaws won't change. Your family is good people, and it will be Garth and his brothers' loss if they listen to Bart and decide not to meet all of you."

She didn't say anything while she considered her plans for him to be interviewed by one of her writers. "I need you to stay until Monday...at least."

He glanced over at her with keen, probing eyes. "Why do you need me to stay until Monday?"

Something cautioned her to choose her words carefully. "Remember earlier, I told you there was something else I needed to discuss with you?"

He nodded. "Yes, I remember."

"Well, it was about a favor I need to ask."

"What kind of favor?"

She nervously nibbled at her bottom lip. "Today I found out that you used to be an actor. Ty Reklaw."

He didn't say anything for a minute. "So what of it? And what does that have to do with me staying until Monday?"

She heard a tinge of annoyance in his voice and had a feeling he didn't like being reminded of his past. "I understand you were at the peak of your acting career when you left Hollywood to return to Alaska. I was sorry to hear about you losing your family. Must have been a difficult time for you."

She paused and when he didn't say anything, she pressed on. "It's been almost ten years and you're still alone, living on your island. It just so happens that *Simply Irresistible* will be doing an article about men who are loners and I would love to make you our feature story."

He still didn't say anything. He merely stared at her. She swallowed deeply, hesitating only a second before asking, "So will you do it? Will you let me schedule an interview for you with one of my writers to be our feature story?"

It was then, there in the moonlight, that she saw the stiffening of his jaw and the rage smoldering in his gaze. "No. And you have a lot of damn nerve. Is that what this little truck ride was about, Bailey? How far did you intend to go to get me to say yes?"

Her gaze narrowed. "What are you asking? Are you insinuating I used my body to get my way?"

"Why not? I've been approached in the past by reporters who will do just about anything for a story."

"Well, I'm not one of them. The main reason I asked you here was to apologize for my behavior last night. Then I wanted to ask a favor of you."

"And why do you think I would want to be interviewed?

I left Hollywood for a reason and I've never looked back. Why would I want to relive those years?"

"You have it all wrong. The article we plan to publish will have nothing to do with your time in Hollywood. You're a loner and we want to find out why some men prefer that kind of life."

"Have you ever considered the fact that not everyone needs to constantly be around people? It's not as if I'm some damn recluse. I have friends. Real friends. Friends who know how to respect my privacy when I need them to. And they are the ones whose company I seek."

"Yes, however—"

"But you wouldn't understand that. You're dependent on your family for your livelihood, your happiness and your very reason for breathing. That's probably why you've made it one of your rules never to stray too far away from them."

His words fired her up. "And is there anything wrong with that?"

"Not if that's how you choose to live. Which is nobody's business. Just like how I choose to live is nobody's business, either. What makes you think I want to broadcast how I chose to live after losing two of the most important people in my life?"

He wasn't letting her get a word in. "If you just let me finish, I can explain wh—"

"There's nothing to explain. You just got this promotion to features editor and you need a story. Sorry, I refuse to accommodate you. Go find your story someplace else."

An hour or so later, Walker was back in his guest room and still finding it hard to accept the ease with which Bailey had asked that favor of him. Did she not realize the magnitude of the favor she'd asked or did she not care? Was she so into her family that she had no understanding or concept that some people preferred solitude? That not everyone wanted a crowd?

He could only shake his head, since he doubted he could get any angrier than he was at that minute. And he had just warned himself not to let her or any woman who'd shown the same persuasive powers Kalyn had possessed to get close to him. Yet he'd fallen under Bailey's spell after that first kiss. After the second, he'd been a goner.

Even now, memories of those kisses were embedded into the core of his soul. The mere idea of another woman getting that much under his skin stopped him cold with a helplessness he felt in every bone of his body.

He let out a slow, controlled breath. In less than a week he'd allowed Bailey to penetrate an area of his mind he'd thought dead forever. And earlier tonight when he'd reached across the seat and dragged her body against his, it hadn't mattered that they were both fully clothed. Just the idea of her being in his arms had brought out his primitive animal instincts. He'd wanted to mate with her. How he'd found the strength to deny what they'd both wanted was beyond his ability to comprehend, but he had. And for that he was grateful. There was no telling how far she would have gone to get her story. She might have had him eating out of her hands while he spilled his guts.

A part of him wanted to think she was just a woman, easy to forget. But he knew she wasn't just any woman. She wasn't the only person with rules, and somehow Bailey had breached all the rules he'd put in place. At the top of his list was not letting another woman get to him.

Whether it was her making him smile or her making him frown, or her filling him with the degree of anger like he was feeling now—she made him feel too much.

He heard the sound of doors opening and closing downstairs and figured the card game had run its course. Pretty much like he'd run his.

It would be to his advantage to remain true to what he knew. Bailey called it being a loner, but he saw it as surviving.

Bailey glanced at her watch as she got out of her truck once she'd reached Ramsey's Web. Most of her day had been filled with meetings, getting to know her new staff as they got to know her management style. It was important for them to know they were a team.

However, no matter how busy she'd stayed today, thoughts of Walker had filled her mind. He was furious with her, angrier than he'd been two nights ago. Was his anger justified? Had she crossed the line in asking him to do that piece for the magazine?

She was still upset about his insinuation that she would go as far as to use her body to get what she wanted. She didn't play those kinds of games, and for him to assume she did didn't sit well with her. So the way she saw it, they'd both been out of line. They'd both said things they probably regretted today. But she had to remember that Walker was a guest of her family, and the last thing she wanted to be was guilty of offending him. Dillon had placed a lot of confidence in her, and her family would never forgive her if she had offended Walker.

She needed to talk to someone about it before she saw Walker today, and the two people she could always go to for advice were Dillon and Ramsey. There was a chance she would run into Walker at Dillon's place, so she thought it best to seek out Ramsey and ask how she could fix things with Walker before the situation got too out of hand.

She found her eldest brother in his six-car garage with his head stuck under the hood of his Jeep. She loved Ramsey's Web and during her brother's before-Chloe days, she'd spent time here getting deliberately underfoot, knowing he wouldn't have it any other way. The two years when Ramsey had lived in Australia had been hard for her.

The sound of her footsteps must have alerted him to her presence. He lifted his head and smiled at her. "Bay? How are things going?"

"Fine. I would give you a hug but I don't want grease all over me. Why are you changing your oil instead of letting JoJo do it?"

Ramsey chuckled as he wiped his hands. "Because there are some things I'd rather do myself, especially to this baby here. She's been with me since the beginning."

Bailey nodded. She knew the Jeep had been Ramsey's first car and the last gift he'd gotten from their parents. It had been a birthday gift while he'd been in college. "You still keep it looking good."

"Always." He leaned back against the Jeep and studied her curiously. "So what's going on with you, Bailey Joleen Westmoreland?"

This was her eldest brother and he'd always had the ability to read her when others couldn't. "It's Walker."

He lifted a brow. "What about Walker?"

She glanced down at her pointed-toe boots a second before meeting Ramsey's gaze. "I think I might have offended him."

Ramsey crossed his arms over his chest, and she could tell from his expression that he didn't like the sound of that. "How?"

"It's a long story."

"Start from the beginning. I have time."

So she did, not rushing through most of the story and deliberately leaving out some parts. Such as how she'd found Walker utterly attractive from the first, how they'd both tried to ignore the sexual chemistry between them and how they'd made out in her truck last night.

"Well, there you have it, Ram. I apologized to him last

night about my wrong assumptions about his feelings on marriage, but I made him mad again when I asked him to do the interview."

Ramsey shook his head. "Let me get this straight. You found out he used to be a movie star who left Hollywood after the deaths of his wife and child, yet you wanted to interview him about being a loner since that time?"

Ramsey sounded as if he couldn't believe she'd done such a thing. "But that wasn't going to be the angle to the story," she argued. "*Simply Irresistible* isn't a tabloid. I'm not looking for details of his life in Hollywood. Women are curious about men who hang back from the crowd. Not everyone is interested in a life-of-the-party type of male. Women see loners as mysterious and want to know more about them. I thought Walker would be perfect since he's lived by himself for ten years on that ranch in Alaska. I figured he could shed some light on what it's like to be a loner."

"Think about what you were asking him to do, Bay. You were asking to invade his space, pry into his life and make public what he probably prefers to keep private. I bet if you had run your idea by Chloe or Lucia, they would have talked you out of it. Your plan was kind of insensitive, don't you think?"

With Ramsey presenting it that way she guessed it was. She honestly hadn't thought about it that way. She had seen an opportunity and jumped without thinking. "But I would have made the Hollywood part of his life off-limits. It was the loner aspect I wanted to concentrate on. I tried to explain that to him."

"And how were you planning to separate the two? Our pasts shape us into the people we are today. Look at you. Like him, you suffered a double loss. A quadruple one, to be exact. And look how you reacted. Would you want someone to show up and ask to interview you about that?

How can you define the Bailey you are today without remembering the old you, and what it took to make you grow from one into the other?"

His question had her thinking.

"And I think you missed the mark on something," he added.

She lifted a brow. "What?"

"Assuming being a loner means being antisocial. You can be a loner and still be close to others. Everybody needs some *me* time. Some people need it more so than others. Case in point, I was a loner before Chloe. Even when I had all of you here with me in Westmoreland Country, I kept to myself. At night, when I came here alone, I didn't need anyone invading my space."

She nodded, realizing something. "But I often invaded it, Ram."

"Yes, you did."

Bailey wondered, for the first time, if he had minded. As if reading her thoughts, he said, "No, Bay. Your impromptu visits never bothered me. All I want you to see is that not everyone needs a crowd. Some people can be their own company, and it's okay."

That was practically what Walker had said. In fact, he had gone even further by saying she was dependent on a crowd. Namely, her large family.

"Looks as if I need to apologize to Walker again. If I keep it up, he's going to think 'I'm sorry' is my middle name. Guess I'll go find him."

"That's going to be pretty difficult."

Her brow furrowed. "Why?"

"Because Walker isn't here. He's left."

"Left?"

"Yes, left. He's on his way back to Alaska. Zane took him to the airport around noon."

"B-but he had planned to stay for the wedding. He

hadn't met everyone since some of the cousins won't be coming in until tomorrow."

"Couldn't be helped. He claimed something came up on his ranch that he had to take care of."

What Ramsey didn't say, but what she figured he was thinking, was that Walker's departure had nothing to do with his ranch and everything to do with her. "Fine. He left. But I'm going to apologize to him anyway."

"Um, I probably wouldn't ask Dillon for Walker's phone number if I were you, especially not if you tell him the same story you just told me."

Bailey nibbled her bottom lip. How was she going to get out of the mess she'd gotten herself into?

Six

"So tell me again why you cut the trip short."

Walker glared across the kitchen at his best friend, who had made himself at home, sitting at Walker's table and greedily devouring a bowl of cereal.

"Why? I've told you once already. The Westmorelands are legit. I didn't have to prolong the visit. Like I said, no matter what Bart believes, I think you and your brothers should take them seriously. They're good people."

Walker turned to the sink with the pretense of rinsing out his coffee cup. What he'd told Garth about the Westmorelands being good people was true—up to a point. As far as he was concerned, the jury was still out on Bailey.

Bailey.

There was no way Walker could have hung around another day and breathed the same air that she did. He clenched his jaw at the thought that he had allowed her to get under his skin. She was just the type who could ge embedded in a man's soul if he was weak enough to let it happen.

On top of everything else, she was as gutsy as the day was long. She'd definitely had a lot of nerve asking him to do that interview. She was used to getting what she wanted, but he wasn't one of her brothers or cousins. He had no reason to give in to her every wish.

"You actually played cards with Thorn Westmoreland?" Garth asked with what sounded like awe.

"Yes," Walker said over his shoulder. "He told us about the bike he's building for some celebrity."

"Really? Did you mention that you used to be an actor and that you know a lot of those folks in Hollywood?"

"No."

"Why not?"

Walker turned around. "I was there to get to know them, not the other way around, Garth. They didn't need to know anything about me other than that I was a friend to the Outlaws who came in good faith to get to know them."

But that hadn't stopped them from finding out about his past anyway. He wasn't sure who all knew, since the only person who'd mentioned anything about his days in Hollywood was Bailey. If the others knew, they'd been considerate enough to respect his privacy. That had been too much to expect of Bailey. All she'd seen was an opportunity to sell magazines.

"I think I'll take your advice and suggest to the others that we pay those Westmorelands a visit. In fact, I'm looking forward to it."

"You won't be disappointed," Walker said, opening the dishwasher to place his cup inside. "How are you going to handle Bart? Do you have any idea why he's so dead set against any of you establishing relationships with your new cousins?"

"No, but it doesn't matter. He'll have to get over it."

Garth glanced at his watch. "I hate to run but I have a meeting back in Fairbanks in three hours. That will give Regan just enough time to fly me out of here and get me back to the office."

Regan Fairchild had been Garth's personal pilot for the past two years. She'd taken her father's place as the corporate pilot for the Outlaws after he retired. "I'll see you out."

When they passed through the living room, Garth glanced over at Walker. "When you want to tell me the real reason you left Denver early, let me know. Don't forget I can read you like a book, Walker."

Walker didn't want to hear that. "Don't waste your time. Go read someone else."

They had almost made it across the room when Walker's doorbell sounded. "That's probably Macon. He's supposed to stop by today and check out that tractor he wants to buy from me."

They had reached the door and, without checking to see who was on the other side, Walker opened it. Shocked, his mouth dropped open as his gaze raked over the woman standing there.

"Hello, Walker."

He recovered, although not as quickly as he would have liked. "Bailey! What the hell are you doing here?"

Instead of answering, her gaze shifted to the man standing by his side. "Hey, you look like Riley," she said, as her face broke into a smile.

It was a smile that Garth returned. "And you look like Charm."

She chuckled. "No, Charm looks like me. I understand I'm older."

"Excuse me for breaking up this little chitchat, but what are you doing here, Bailey?" Walker asked in an annoyed tone.

"Evidently she came here to see you, and on that note,

I am out of here. I need to make that meeting," Garth said, slipping out the door. He looked over his shoulder at Walker with an expression that clearly said, *You have a lot of explaining to do.*

To Bailey, Garth said, "Welcome to Hemlock Row. I'll let the family know you're here. Hopefully Walker will fly you into Fairbanks."

"Don't hold your breath for that to happen," Walker said. He doubted Garth heard as he quickly darted to his parked car. His best friend had a lot of damn nerve. How dare he welcome anyone to Walker's home?

Walker turned his attention back to Bailey, trying to ignore the flutter in his stomach at seeing just how beautiful she looked. Nor did he want to concentrate on her scent, which had filled his nostrils the moment he'd opened the door.

Walker crossed his arms over his chest. "I've asked you twice already and you've yet to answer," he said in a harsh tone. "What are you doing here?"

Bailey blew out a chilled breath, wrapped her arms around herself and tried not to shiver. "Could you invite me inside first? It's cold out here."

He hesitated, as if he were actually considering doing just the opposite, and then he stepped back. She hurriedly came inside and closed the door behind her. She had dressed in layers, double the amount she would have used in Denver, yet she still felt chilled to the bone.

"You might as well come and stand in front of the fireplace to warm up."

"Thanks," she said, surprised he'd made the offer. After sliding the carry-on bag from her shoulders, she peeled off her coat, then her jacket and gloves.

Instead of renting a car, she had opted for a cab service, even though the ride from the airstrip had cost her a pretty penny. But she hadn't cared. She'd been cold, exhausted and determined to get to Walker's place before nightfall.

The cabbie had been chatty, explaining that Walker seldom got visitors and trying to coax her into telling him why she was there. She'd let him talk, and when he'd figured out she wasn't providing any information, he'd finally lapsed into silence. But only for a little while. Then he'd pointed out a number of evergreen trees and told her they were mountain hemlocks, a tree common to Alaska. He'd told her about the snowstorm headed their way and said she'd made it to the island just in time or she would have been caught in it. Sounded to her as if she would get caught in it anyway since her return flight was forty-eight hours from now. The man had been born and raised on the island and had a lot of history to share.

When the cabbie had driven up to the marker for Hemlock Row, the beautiful two-story ranch house that sat on Walker's property made her breath catch. It was like looking at a gigantic postcard. It had massive windows, multiple stone chimneys and a wraparound porch. It sat on the Shelikof Strait, which served as a backdrop that was simply beautiful, even if it was out in the middle of nowhere and surrounded by snow. The only other house they'd passed had to be at least ten to fifteen miles away.

Walker's home was not as large as Dillon's, but like Dillon's, it had a rustic feel, as if it belonged just where it sat.

"Drink this," Walker said, handing her a mug filled with hot liquid. She hadn't realized he'd left her alone. She'd been busy looking around at the furniture, which seemed warm and welcoming.

"Thanks." She took a sip of what tasted like a mixture of coffee, hot chocolate and a drop of tea. It tasted delicious. As delicious as Walker looked standing directly in front of her, barefoot, with an open-collar sweater and jeans riding low on his hips. What man looked this mouthwatering so early in the day? Had it really been a week since she'd seen him last? A week when she'd thought about him every day, determined to make this trip to Kodiak Island, Alaska, to personally deliver the apology she needed to make.

"Okay, now that you've warmed up, how about telling me what you're doing here."

She lowered the cup and met his gaze. After telling Lucia and Chloe what she'd done and what she planned to do, they had warned her that Walker probably wouldn't be happy to see her. She could tell from the look on his face that they'd been right. "I came to see you. I owe you an apology for what I said. What I suggested doing with that piece for the magazine."

He frowned. "Why are you apologizing? Doing something so inconsiderate and uncaring seems to be so like you."

His words hurt but she couldn't get mad. That was unfortunately the way she'd presented herself since meeting him. "That goes to show how wrong you are about me and how wrong I was for giving you reason to think that way."

"Whatever. You shouldn't have bothered. I don't think there's anything you can do or say to change my opinion of you."

That angered her. "I never realized you were so judgmental."

"I'm as judgmental as you are."

She wondered if all this bitterness and anger were necessary. Possibly, but at the moment she was too exhausted to deal with it. What should have been a fifteen-hour flight had become a twenty-two-hour flight when the delay of one connection had caused her to miss another. On top of everything else, due to the flight chaos, her luggage was heaven knew where. The airline assured her it would be found and delivered to her within twenty-four hours. She hoped that was true because she planned to fly out again in two days.

"Look, Walker. My intentions were good, and regardless of what you think of me I did come here to personally apologize."

"Fine. You've apologized. Now you can leave.'

"Leave? I just got here! Where am I to go?"

He frowned. "How did you get here?"

"I caught a taxi from the airport."

A dark brow lowered beneath a bunched forehead. "Then, call them to come pick you up."

He couldn't be serious. "And go where? My return flight back to Denver isn't for forty-eight hours."

His frown deepened. "Then, I suggest you stay with your cousins in Fairbanks. You've met Garth. He will introduce you to the others."

Her spine stiffened. "Why can't I wait it out here?"

He glared at her. "Because you aren't welcome here, Bailey."

Walker flinched at the harshness of his own words. He regretted saying them the moment they left his lips. He could tell by the look on her face that they'd hurt her. He then remembered how kind her family had been to him, a virtual stranger, and he knew that no matter how he felt about her, she didn't deserve what he'd just said. But then what had given her the right to come here uninvited?

He watched as she placed the cup on the table and slid back into her jacket. Then she reached for her coat.

"What the hell do you think you're doing?" he asked, noticing how the loud sound of his voice seemed to blast off the walls.

She lifted her chin as she buttoned up her coat. "What does it look like I'm doing? Leaving. You've made it clear you don't want me here, and one thing I don't do is stay where I'm not wanted."

He wanted to chuckle at that. Hadn't her cousins and brothers told him, jokingly, how she used to impose herself on them? Sometimes she'd even done so purposely, to rattle any of their girlfriends she hadn't liked. "Forget what I said. I was mad."

When her coat was buttoned practically to her neck, she glared at him. "And you're still mad. I didn't come all the way here for verbal abuse, Walker. I came to apologize."

"Apology accepted." The memory of what had followed the last time he'd said those words slammed into his mind. He'd kissed her, feasting on her mouth like a hungry man who'd been denied food for years.

He could tell from the look in her eyes that she was remembering, as well. He figured that was the reason she broke eye contact with him to look at the flames blazing in the fireplace. Too late—the wood burning wasn't the only thing crackling in the room. He could feel that stirring of sensual magnetism that always seemed to surround them. It was radiating more heat than the fireplace.

"Now that I think about it, staying here probably isn't a good idea," she said, glancing back at him.

He released a deep breath and leaned back on his heels. She was right. It wasn't a good idea, but it was too late to think about that now. "A storm's headed this way so it doesn't matter if you don't think it's a good idea."

"It matters to me if you don't want me here," she snapped.

He rubbed his hand down his face. "Look, Bailey. I think we can tolerate each other for the next forty-eight hours. Besides, this place is so big I doubt if I'll even see you during that time." To be on the safe side, he would put her in one of the guest rooms on the south wing. That part of the house hadn't been occupied in over fifteen years.

"Where's your luggage?" he asked. The quicker he could get her settled in, the quicker he could ignore her presence.

"The airline lost it, although they say it has just been misplaced. They assured me they will deliver it here within twenty-four hours."

That probably wasn't going to happen, he thought, but figured there was no reason to tell her that. "Just in case they're delayed, I have a couple of T-shirts you can borrow to sleep in."

"Thanks."

"If you're hungry I can fix you something. I hadn't planned on preparing dinner till later, but there are some leftovers I can warm up."

"No, thanks. I'm not hungry. But I would appreciate if I could wash up and lie down for a bit. The flight from Anchorage was sort of choppy."

"Usually it is, unfortunately. I'll show you up to the room you'll be using. Just follow me."

Seven

The sound of a door slamming somewhere in the house jarred Bailey awake and had her scrambling to sit up in bed and try to remember where she was. It all came tumbling back to her. Kodiak Island, Alaska. Walker's ranch.

She settled back down in bed, remembering the decision she had made to come here. She could finally admit it had been a bad one. Hadn't Walker said she wasn't welcome? But she had been determined to come after deciding a phone-call apology wouldn't do. She needed to tell him in person that she was sorry.

And she would even admit that a part of her had wanted to see him face-to-face. Everyone in the family had been surprised he'd left early, and although no one questioned her about it, she knew they suspected she was to blame. And she had been. So no one had seemed surprised when she announced her plans to travel to Kodiak. However, Dillon had pulled her aside to ask if that was something she really wanted to do. She'd assured him that it was, and told him she owed Walker an apology and wanted to deliver it to him personally.

So here she was, in an area as untamed and rugged as the most remote areas of Westmoreland Country. But there were views she had passed in the cab that had been so beautiful they had almost taken her breath away. Part of her couldn't wait to see the rest of it.

Bailey heard the sound of a door slamming again and glanced over at the clock on the nightstand. Had she slept for four hours?

She suddenly sniffed the air. Something smelled good, downright delicious. Walker had been cooking. She hoped he hadn't gone to any trouble just for her. When her stomach growled she knew she needed to get out of bed and go downstairs.

She recalled Walker leading her up to this room and the two flights of stairs they'd taken to get here. The moment she'd followed him inside she'd felt something she hadn't felt in years. Comfort. Somehow this guest room was just as warm and welcoming as the living room had been.

It might have been the sturdy-looking furniture made of dark oak. Or the huge bed that had felt as good as it looked. She couldn't wait to sleep in it tonight. Really sleep in it. Beneath the covers and not on top like she'd done for her nap. Getting out of bed, she headed for the bathroom, glad she at least had her carry-on containing her makeup and toiletries.

A few minutes later, feeling refreshed and less exhausted, she left the guest room to head downstairs. She hoped Walker was in a better mood than he'd been in earlier.

Walker checked the timer on the stove before lifting the lid to stir the stew. He'd cooked more than the usual amount since he had a houseguest. Bailey had been asleep for at least four hours and even so, her presence was disrupting his normal routine. He would have driven around his land by now, checking on the herds and making sure everything was ready for the impending snowstorm. He'd talked to Willie, his ranch foreman, who had assured him everything had been taken care of.

That brought his thoughts back to Bailey, and he uttered an expletive under his breath. He'd figured out the real reason, the only one that made sense, as to why she was here, using an apology as an excuse. She probably thought she could make him change his mind about doing the interview, but she didn't know how wrong she was.

As far as he was concerned, she'd wasted her time coming here. Although he had to admit it had been one hell of a gutsy move. As gutsy as it was crazy. He'd warned her the first day they'd met that winters in Alaska were a lot worse than the coldest day in Denver. Evidently she hadn't believed him and now would find out the truth for herself. She had arrived nearly frozen.

But nearly frozen or not, that didn't stop the male in him from remembering how good she'd looked standing on his porch. Or how she'd looked standing by his fireplace after she'd removed layer after layer of clothing.

He had awakened this morning pretty much prepared for anything. He figured it was only a matter of time before Garth showed up. And a snowstorm blowing in was the norm. What he hadn't counted on was Bailey showing up out of Alaska's cold blue sky. When he'd left Denver, he had assumed their paths wouldn't cross again. There was no reason why they should. Even if the Outlaws kindled a relationship with the Westmorelands, that wouldn't necessarily mean anything to *him*, because he lived here on the island and seldom flew to Fairbanks.

"Sorry I overslept."

He turned around and then wished he hadn't. She was

still wearing the clothes she'd had on earlier, since she didn't have any others, but his gaze moved beyond that. From what he could tell, she wasn't wearing any makeup and she had changed her hairstyle. It no longer hung around her shoulders but was pulled back in a ponytail. The style made her features look younger, delicate and sexy enough to make his lower body throb.

"No problem," he said, turning his attention back to the stove.

He'd seen enough of her. Too much for his well-being. Having her standing in the middle of his kitchen, a place he'd never figured she would be, was sending crazy thoughts through his head. Like how good she looked in that particular spot. A spot where Kalyn had never stood. In fact, his wife had refused to come to Kodiak. She hadn't wanted to visit the place where he was born. Had referred to it as untamed wilderness that lacked civilization. She hadn't wanted to visit such a remote area, much less live there. She was a California girl through and through. She'd lived for the beaches, the orange groves and Hollywood. Anything else just didn't compute with her.

"What are you cooking? Smells good."

He inwardly smiled, although he didn't want to. Was that her way of letting him know she was hungry? "Bison stew. My grandmother's recipe," he said over his shoulder.

"No wonder it smells good, then."

Now, aren't you full of compliments, he thought sarcastically, knowing she was probably trying to be nice for a reason. But he wasn't buying it, because he knew her motives. "By the time you wash up I'll have dinner on the table."

"I've washed up and I can help. Thanks to Chloe I'm pretty good in the kitchen. Tell me what you need me to do."

"Why Chloe?"

"In addition to all her other talents, she is a wonderful

cook and often prepares breakfast for Ramsey and his men. Remind me to tell you one day how she and Ramsey met."

He came close to saying that he wouldn't be reminding her of anything, and he didn't need her to do anything, unless she could find her way back to the airport. But he reined in his temper and said, "You can set the table. Everything you need is in that drawer over there." He never ate at a set table but figured it would give her something to do so she wouldn't get underfoot. Not that trying to put distance between them really mattered. Her scent had already downplayed the aroma of the stew.

The ringing of his cell phone on the kitchen counter jarred him out of his thoughts. He moved from the stove to pick it up, recognizing his foreman's ringtone.

"Yes, Willie? What is it?"

"It's Marcus, boss," Willie said in a frantic tone. "A big brown's got him pinned in a shack and nothing we can do will scare him off. We've been firing shots, but we haven't managed a hit."

"Damn. I'm on my way."

Walker turned and quickly moved toward the closet where his parkas hung and his boots were stored. "Got to go," he said quickly. "That was Willie Hines, my foreman. A brown bear has one of my men holed up in a shack and I need to get there fast."

"May I go?"

He glanced over his shoulder to tell her no. Then he changed his mind. It probably had something to do with that pleading look on her face. "Yes, but stay out of the way. Grab your coat, hat and scarf. And be quick. My men are waiting."

She moved swiftly and by the time he'd put on his boots she was back. He grabbed one of the rifles off the rack. When she reached up and grabbed a rifle off the rack as well, he stared at her. "What do you think you're doing?"

"I'm not a bad shot. Maybe I can help."

He doubted she could and just hoped she stayed out of the way, but he didn't have time to argue. "Fine, let's go."

"I thought bears normally hibernated in the winter," Bailey said, hanging on in the Jeep. Walker was driving like a madman and the seat belt was barely holding her in place. On top of that, her thick wool coat was nothing against the bone-chilling wind and the icy slivers of snow that had begun to fall.

"It's not officially winter yet. Besides, this particular brown is probably the same one who's been causing problems for the past year. Nothing he does is normal. There's been a bounty on his head for a while now."

Bailey nodded. Although bears were known to reside in the Rockies, they were seldom seen. She'd known of only one incident of a bear in Westmoreland Country. Dillon had called the authorities, who had captured the bear and set him free elsewhere. She then remembered what Walker had told her the first day they'd met. There were more bears than people living on Kodiak Island.

The Jeep came to a sudden stop in front of three men she figured worked for Walker. He was out of the truck in a flash and before she could unbuckle her seat belt, he snapped out an order. "Stay put, Bailey."

She grudgingly did as she was told and watched him race toward the men. They pointed at the scene taking place a hundred or so feet ahead of them. The creature wasn't what she'd expected of a brown bear. He was a huge grizzly tearing away at a small, dilapidated shack, pawing through timber, lumber and planks trying to get to the man trapped inside. Unless someone did something, it wouldn't take long for the bear to succeed. And if anyone tried shooting the bear now, they would place the man inside the shack at risk.

She didn't have to hear what Walker and his men were saying to know they were devising a plan to pull the bear's attention away from the shack. And it didn't take long to figure out that Walker had volunteered to be the bait. Putting his own life at risk.

She watched, horrified, as Walker raced forward to get the bear's attention, coming to a stop at what seemed to be just a few feet from the animal. At first it seemed as if nothing could dissuade the bear. A few more loose timbers and he would get his prey. She could hear the man inside screaming in fright, begging for help before it was too late.

Walker then picked up a tree limb and hit the bear. That got the animal's attention. Bailey held her breath when the bear turned and went charging after Walker. The plan was for Walker to lure the bear away from the shack so his men could get a good shot. It seemed the ploy was working until Walker lost his balance and fell to the ground.

Bailey was out of the Jeep in a flash, her rifle in her hand. She stood beside the men and raised her gun to take a shot.

"There's no way you can hit that bear from here, lady," one of the men said.

She ignored his words, knowing Walker would be mauled to death unless she did something. She pulled the trigger mere seconds before the bear reached Walker. The huge animal fell and it seemed the earth shook under the weight.

"Did you see that?"

"She got that grizzly and her rifle doesn't even have a scope on it."

"How can she shoot like that? Where did she come from?"

Ignoring what the three men were saying, she raced over to Walker. "Are you okay?"

"I'm fine. I just banged my leg against that damn rock when I tripped."

Placing her rifle aside, she leaned down to check him

over and saw the red bloodstain on the leg of his jeans. He wasn't fine.

She turned to his men, who were looking at her strangely. "He's injured. I need two of you to lift him and take him to the Jeep. The other one, I need to check on the man in the shack. I think he passed out."

"I said I'm fine, Bailey, and I can walk," Walker insisted.

"Not on that leg." She turned to the men. "Lift him and take him to the truck," she ordered again.

"Don't anyone dare lift me. I said I can walk," Walker snapped at the two men who moved toward him.

"No, you can't walk," she snapped back at him. She then glared at his men, who stood staring, unsure whose orders to follow. "Do it!" she demanded, letting them know she expected her order to be followed regardless of what Walker said.

As if they figured any woman who could shoot that well was a woman whose order should be obeyed, they quickly moved to lift Walker. He spewed expletives, which they all ignored.

"I'll call Doc Witherspoon to come quick," one of the men said after they placed Walker in the Jeep. "And we'll be right behind you to help get him out once you reach the ranch house."

She quickly got in on the driver's side. "Thanks."

She glanced over at Walker, who was now unconscious, and fought to keep her panic at bay. Of all the things she figured she'd have to deal with upon reaching Alaska, killing a grizzly bear hadn't been one of them.

Eight

Walker came awake, then reclosed his eyes when pain shot up his leg. It took him a while before he reopened them. When he did, he noted that he was in his bed and flat on his back. It didn't take him long to recall why. The grizzly.

"Bailey?" he called out softly when he heard a sound from somewhere in the room.

"She's not here, Walker," a deep masculine voice said.

He didn't have to wonder who that voice belonged to. "Doc Witherspoon?"

"Who else? I only get to see you these days when you get banged up."

Walker shook his head, disagreeing. "I never get banged up."

"You did this time. Story has it that bear would have eaten you alive if that little lady hadn't saved you."

The doctor's words suddenly made Walker remember what he'd said earlier. "Bailey's not here? Where is she?"

"She left for the airport."

Airport? Bailey was returning to Denver already? "How long have I been out, Doc?" he asked. A lot of stuff seemed fuzzy in his mind.

"Off and on close to forty-eight hours. Mainly because I gave you enough pain pills to down an elephant. Bailey thought it was best. You needed your rest. On top of all that, you were an unruly patient."

Who cared what Bailey thought when she wasn't there? He then replayed in his mind every detail of that day with the bear. "How's Marcus?"

"I treated him for shock but he's fine now. And since he's a ladies' man, he's had plenty of women parading in and out of his place pretending to be nurses."

Walker nodded, trying to dismiss the miserable feelings flooding through when he thought about Bailey being gone. She'd told him she was returning to Denver within forty-eight hours, so what had he expected? Besides, hadn't he wanted her gone? Hadn't he told her she wasn't welcome? So why was he suddenly feeling so disheartened? Must be the medication messing with his mind.

"You have a nasty cut to the leg, Walker. Went real deep. You lost a lot of blood and I had to put in stitches. You've got several bruised ribs but nothing's broken. If you stay off that leg as much as possible and follow my orders, you'll be as good as new in another week or so. I'll be back to check on you again in a few days."

"Whatever." Walker knew Doc Witherspoon would ignore his surly attitude; after all, he was the same man who'd brought Walker into the world.

Walker closed his eyes. He wasn't sure how long he slept, but when he opened his eyes some time later, it was a feminine scent that awakened him. Being careful not to move his leg, he shifted his head and saw Bailey sitting in the chair by the bed reading a book. He blinked to make sure he wasn't dreaming. It wouldn't be the first time he'd dreamed of her since leaving Denver. But never had he dreamed of her sitting by the bed. In all his dreams she had been in the bed with him.

He blinked again and when she still sat there, he figured it was the real thing. "Doc said you left for the airport."

She glanced over at him and their gazes held. Ripples of awareness flooded through him. Why was her very presence in his room filling every inch of space within it? And why did he want her out of that chair and closer to the bed? Closer to him?

She broke eye contact to brush off a piece of lint from her shirt. "I did leave for the airport. Their twenty-four hours were up and I hadn't gotten my luggage."

"You went to the airport to get your luggage?"

"Yes."

He couldn't explain the relief that raced through him. At the moment he didn't want to explain it. He felt exhausted and was in too much pain to think clearly. "I thought you were on your way back to Denver."

"Sorry to disappoint you."

He drew in a deep breath. She'd misunderstood and was assuming things again. Instead of telling her how wrong she was, he asked, "Well, did you get your luggage?"

"Yes. They'd found it, but were taking their time bringing it here. I guess I wasn't at the top of their priority list."

He bet they wished they hadn't made that mistake. She'd probably given them hell.

"You want something to eat?" she asked him. "There's plenty of bison stew left."

Walker was glad because he was hungry and remembered he'd been cooking the stew when he'd gotten the call about Marcus. "Yes. Thanks."

"I'll be right back."

He watched Bailey get out of the chair and place the

book aside before heading for the door. He couldn't help but appreciate the shape of her backside in sweats. At least his attention to physical details hadn't lessened any. He brought his hand to his jaw and realized he needed to trim his beard.

When Bailey pulled the door shut behind her, Walker closed his eyes and again remembered in full detail everything that had happened down by the shack. The one thing that stuck out in his mind above everything else was the fact that Bailey Westmoreland had saved his life.

"Yes, Walker is fine just bruised and he had to get stiches in his leg," she said to Ramsey on the phone. "I hated killing that bear but it was him or Walker. He was big and a mean one."

"You did what you had to do, Bay. I'm sure Walker appreciated you being there."

"Maybe. Doesn't matter now, though. He's confined to bed and needs help. The doctor wants him to stay off his leg as much as possible. That means I need to tell Chloe and Lucia that I'll need a few more days off. Possibly another week."

"Well, you're in luck because Lucia is here, so I'll let you speak to both her and Chloe. You take care of yourself."

"Thanks, I will. I miss everyone."

"And we miss you. But it's nice to have you gone for a while," he teased.

"Whatever," she said, grinning, knowing he was joking. She was certain every member of her family missed her as much as she missed them.

A short while later she hung up. Chloe and Lucia had understood the situation and told her to take all the time she needed to care for Walker. She appreciated that.

Drawing in a deep breath, she glanced around the kitchen

Over the past three days she had become pretty familiar with it. She knew where all the cooking equipment was located and had found a recipe book that had once belonged to Walker's grandmother. There was a family photo album located in one of the cabinets. She'd smiled at the pictures of Walker's family, people she figured were his parents and grandparents. But nowhere in the album did she find any of his wedding pictures or photographs of his wife and child.

She looked out the window. It was snowing hard outside and had been for the past two days. She had met all the men who worked on Walker's ranch. They had dropped by and introduced themselves and told her they would take care of everything for their boss. News of her encounter with the bear had spread and a lot of the men stared at her in amazement. She found them to be a nice group of guys. A number of them had worked on the ranch when Walker's father was alive. She could tell from the way they'd inquired about Walker's well-being that they were very fond of him and deeply loyal.

She snorted at the thought of that. They evidently knew a different Walker from the one she'd gotten to know. Due to all the medication the doctor had given him, he slept most of the time, which was good. And he refused to let her assist him to the bathroom or in taking his baths. Doctor Witherspoon had warned him about getting the stitches wet and about staying off his leg as much as possible, so at least he was taking that advice. One of his men had dropped off crutches for him to use, and he was using them, as well.

Snow was coming down even worse now and everything was covered with a white blanket. The men had made sure there was plenty of wood for the fireplace and she had checked and found the freezer and pantry well stocked, so there was nothing for her to do but take things one day at a time while waiting for Walker to get better.

Garth had called for Walker and she'd told him what had happened. He'd left his number and told her to call if she needed anything or if Walker continued to give her trouble. Like she'd told Garth, Walker had pretty much slept for the past three days. When he was awake, other than delivering his meals and making sure he took his medication, she mostly left him alone.

But not today. His bedroom was dark and dreary and although the outside was barely any better, she intended to go into his room and open the curtains. And she intended for him to get out of bed and sit in a chair long enough for her to change the linens.

According to Garth, Walker had a housekeeper, an older woman by the name of Lola Albright, who came in each week, no matter how ugly the weather got outside. She had located Ms. Albright's phone number in the kitchen drawer and called to advise her that she need not come this week. Somehow, but not surprisingly, the woman had already heard what happened. After complimenting Bailey for her skill with a gun, she had thanked Bailey for calling and told her if she needed anything to let her know. Ms. Albright and her husband were Walker's closest neighbors and lived on a farm about ten miles away.

Grabbing the tray with the bowl of chicken noodle soup that she'd cooked earlier, Bailey moved up the stairs to Walker's bedroom. She opened the door and stopped, surprised to see him already out of bed and sitting in the chair.

The first thing she noticed was that he'd shaved. She couldn't stop her gaze from roaming over his face while thinking about just how sexy he looked. He was as gorgeous without facial hair as he was with it. He had changed clothes and was looking like his former self. A part of her was grateful he was sitting up, but then another part of her was annoyed that he hadn't asked for her assistance.

"Lunchtime," she said, moving into the room and putting the tray on a table beside his chair. She wanted to believe he said thanks, although it sounded more like a grunt. She moved across the room to open the curtains.

"What do you think you're doing?"

Without turning around, she continued opening the curtains. "I thought you might want to look outside."

"I want the curtains closed."

"Sorry, but now they're open." She turned back around and couldn't help but shiver when she met his stare. His *glare* was more like it, but his bad mood didn't bother her. After five brothers and a slew of male cousins she knew how to deal with a man who couldn't have his way.

"Glad you're up. I need to change the linens," she said, moving toward the bed.

"Lola's my housekeeper. She's coming tomorrow and can do it then."

"I talked to Lola this morning and told her there was no need for her to come out in this weather. I can handle things while I'm here."

He didn't say anything but she could tell by his scowl that he hadn't liked that move. And speaking of moves, she felt his eyes on her with every move she made while changing the sheets. She could actually feel his gaze raking across her. When she finished and turned to look at him, his mouth was set in a hard, tight line.

"You know, if you keep looking all mean and cranky, Walker, you might grow old looking that way."

His frown deepened. "No matter what you do, I won't be changing my mind about the interview. So you're wasting your time."

Drawing in a deep, angry breath, she moved across the room to stand in front of him. She leaned down a little to make sure her eyes were level with his. "You ungrateful bastard!"

That was followed by a few more obscenities she hadn't

said since the last time Dillon had washed out her mouth with soap years ago. But Walker's accusations had set her off. "Do you think that's why I'm here? That I only killed that bear, hung around, put up with your crappy attitude just because I want an interview? Well, I've got news for you. I don't want an interview from you. You're no longer a viable candidate. Women are interested in men who are loners but decent, not loners who are angry and couldn't recognize a kind deed if it bit them on the—"

She hadn't expected him to tug on a lock of her hair and capture her mouth. She hadn't expected him to kiss her with a hunger that sent desire raging through her, flooding her with memories of the night they'd parked in her truck at Bailey's Bay.

Convincing herself she was only letting him have his way with her mouth because she didn't want to move and hurt his leg, she found herself returning the kiss, moaning when his tongue began doing all kinds of delicious things to hers.

They were things she had dreamed about, and craved—but only with him. She could admit that at night, in the guest room, in that lonely bed, she had thought of him, although she hadn't wanted to do so. And since all she had were memories, she had recalled how he had licked a slow, wet trail from her mouth to her breasts and then lower.

Her thoughts were snatched back to the present when she felt Walker ease up her skirt and softly skim her inner thighs. His fingers slipped beneath the elastic of her panties before sliding inside her.

She shuddered and his finger moved deeper, pushing her over the edge. She wanted to pull back but couldn't. Instead, she followed his lead and intensified the kiss while his fingers did scandalous things.

Then he released her mouth to whisper against her wet lips, "Come for me again, Bailey."

As if his request was a sensual command her body had to obey, ragged heat rolled in her stomach as her pulse throbbed and her blood roared through her veins. Her body exploded, every nerve ending igniting with an intensity that terrified her. This time was more powerful than the last, and she had no willpower to stop the moan released from her lips. No willpower to stop spreading her thighs wider and arching her mouth closer to once again be taken.

That was when Walker placed his mouth over Bailey's again, kissing her with no restraint. He deepened the kiss, pushing his fingers even farther inside her. He loved the sounds she made when she climaxed; he loved knowing he was the one to make it happen. And he intended to make it happen all over again. Moments later, when she shuddered and groaned into his mouth, he knew he had succeeded.

She grabbed his shoulders, and he didn't flinch when she dug her fingers into his skin. Nor did he flinch when she placed pressure on his tongue. He merely retaliated by sucking harder on hers.

He had been hungry for her taste for days. Each time she had entered his bedroom, he had hated lying flat on his back, not being able to do the one thing he'd wanted to do—kiss her in a way that was as raw as he felt.

Most of the time he'd feigned sleep, but through heavy-lidded eyes he had watched her, studied her and longed for her. He'd known each and every time she had walked around his room, cursing under her breath about his foul mood, using profanity he'd never heard before. He had laid there as his ears burned, pretending to sleep as she called him every nasty name in the book for being so difficult and pigheaded.

He'd also known when she'd calmed down enough to sit quietly in the chair by his bed to read, or softly hum while flipping through one of his wildlife magazines. And he would never forget the day she had worn a sweater and a pair of leggings. She had stretched up to put something away on one of the top shelves in his room and caused his entire body to harden in desire watching her graceful movements. And the outlines of her curves covered by those leggings… His need for her had flowed through him like a potent drug, more intoxicating than the medication Doc Witherspoon had him taking. Knowing she was off-limits, because he had decided it had to be so, had only sharpened his less-than-desirable attitude.

But today had been different. He had awakened with his raging hormones totally out of control. He'd felt better and had wanted to clean himself up, move around and wait for her. He hadn't anticipated kissing her but he was glad he had.

There were multiple layers to Bailey Westmoreland, layers he wanted to unpeel one at a time. The anticipation was almost killing him.

Growling low in his throat, he slowly pulled his mouth away and pulled his fingers from inside her. Then, as she watched, he brought those same fingers to his lips and licked them in slow, greedy movements.

He held her gaze, tempted to take possession of her mouth again. Instead, he whispered, "Thank you for saving my life, Bailey."

He could tell his words of thanks had surprised her. Little did she know she would be in for a few more surprises before she left his ranch to return to Denver.

"And thank you for letting me savor you," he whispered. "To have such a filthy mouth, you have a very delicious taste."

And he meant it. He loved the taste of her on his fingers. Bailey was a woman any man would want to possess. The good. The bad. And the ugly. And for some reason that he didn't understand or could explain, he wanted that man to be him.

With that thought planted firmly in his mind, he leaned close, captured her mouth with his and kissed her once again.

Nine

"What have you gotten yourself into, Bailey?" she asked herself a few days later while standing outside on Walker's front porch.

This was the first time the weather had improved enough for her to be outside. As far as she could see, snow covered everything. It had seemed to her that it hadn't been snowflakes falling for the past several days but ice chips. The force of them had hit the roof, the windowpanes and blanketed the grounds.

Yesterday, Josette told her a bad snowstorm had hit Denver and threatened to close the airport. Bailey had endured Denver's snowstorms all her life, but what she'd experienced over the past few days here in Alaska was far worse. Even though parts of this place reminded her of Denver, looking out at the Strait from her bedroom window meant she saw huge glaciers instead of mountains. And one of the ponds on Walker's property had been a solid block of ice since she'd arrived.

Wrapping her hands around the mug of coffee she held in her hand, she took a sip. Would her question to herself ever be answered? Was there even an answer? All she knew was that she had to leave this place and return home before…

Before what?

Already Walker had turned her normally structured mind topsy-turvy. It had started the day he'd kissed her in his bedroom. Oh, he'd done more than kiss her. He had inserted his fingers inside her and made her come. Just like before. But this time he had tasted her on his fingers, letting her watch. And then he'd kissed her again, letting her taste herself on his lips.

At least when that kiss had ended she'd had the good sense to get out of the room. And she had stayed out until it was time to deliver his dinner. Luckily when she'd entered the room later that day, he had been asleep, so she had left the covered tray of food by his bed. Then Willie had dropped by that evening to visit with Walker and had returned the tray to the kitchen. That had meant she didn't have to go up to his room to get it.

She had checked on him before retiring for the night and he'd been sitting up again, in that same chair. After asking him if there was anything he needed before she went to bed, she had quickly left the room.

That had been three days ago and she'd avoided going into his room since then. She'd only been in to deliver his food. Each time she found him dressed and sitting in that same chair. It was obvious he was improving, so why hadn't she made plans to leave Kodiak Island?

She kept telling herself she wanted to wait until Dr. Witherspoon assured her that Walker could manage on his own. Hopefully, today would be that day. The doctor had arrived an hour ago and was up there with Walker now. It shouldn't be long before Bailey could work her way out of whatever she'd gotten herself into with Walker.

Knowing that if she stayed outside any longer she was liable to turn into a block of ice, she went back inside. She was closing the door behind her as Dr. Witherspoon came down the stairs.

"So how is our patient, Doctor?" she asked the tall, muscular man who reminded her of a lumberjack more than a doctor.

"Walker's fine. The stiches are out and he should be able to maneuver the stairs in a day or so. I'm encouraging him to do so in order to work the stiffness out of his legs."

Bailey nodded as she sat her coffee mug on a side table. "So he's ready to start handling things on his own now?"

"Pretty much, but I still don't want him to overdo it. As you know, Walker has a hard head. I'm glad you're here to make sure he doesn't overexert himself."

Bailey nibbled her bottom lip before saying, "But I can't stay here forever. I have a job back in Denver. Do you have any idea when it will be okay for me to leave?"

"If you have pressing business to attend to back home then you should go now. I'm sure Lola won't mind moving in for a few days until Walker's fully recovered."

Dr. Witherspoon was giving her an out, so why wasn't she taking it? Why was she making herself believe she was needed here?

"Just let me know when you plan to leave so I'll know what to do," the doctor added. "I'm sure you know Walker would prefer to be by himself after you leave, but that's not wise. Personally, I think he needs you."

The doctor didn't know just how wrong he was. Sure, Walker liked kissing her, but that didn't mean he needed her. "I doubt that very seriously. He'll probably be glad to have me gone."

"Um, I don't think so. I've known Walker all his life. I

delivered him into the world and looked forward to delivering his son, but his wife wouldn't hear of it. She wanted their son born in California. She wasn't too fond of this place."

Dr. Witherspoon paused, and a strange look appeared on his face, as if he'd said too much. "Anyway, if you decide to leave before the end of the week, let me know so I can notify Lola."

"I will."

Before reaching the door, the doctor turned. "Oh, yes, I almost forgot. Walker wants to see you."

Bailey lifted a brow. "He does?"

"Yes." The doctor then opened the door and left.

Bailey wondered why Walker would ask to see her. He'd seen her earlier when she'd taken him breakfast. She hadn't been able to decipher his mood, mainly because she hadn't hung around long enough. She'd placed the tray on the table and left. But she had seen that he'd opened the curtains and was sitting in what was evidently his favorite chair.

After taking a deep breath, she moved toward the stairs. She might as well go see what Walker wanted. All things considered, he might be summoning her to ask her to leave.

"Dr. Witherspoon said you wanted to see me."

Walker turned around at the sound of Bailey's voice. She stood in the doorway as if ready to sprint away at a moment's notice. Had his mood been as bad as Doc Witherspoon claimed? If so, she had put up with it when any other woman would not have. "Come in, Bailey, I won't bite."

He wouldn't bite, but he wouldn't mind tasting her mouth again.

She hesitated before entering, looking all around his bedroom before looking back at him. That gave him just enough time to check her out, to appreciate how she looked in her sweats, sweater and jacket. She wore her hair pinned back from her face, which showed off her beautiful bone structure. Although he hadn't stuck around to meet her sister Gemma, he had met Megan. There was a slight resemblance between the two but he thought Bailey had a look all her own. Both were beautiful women but there was a radiance about Bailey that gave him pause whenever he saw her.

"Okay, I'm in," she said, coming to stand in front of him. However, he noted she wasn't all in his face like last time. She was keeping what she figured was a safe distance.

"You're standing up," she observed.

"Is there a reason for me not to be?"

She shrugged. "No. But normally you're sitting down in that chair over there."

He followed her gaze to the chair. "Yes. That chair has special meaning for me."

"It does? Why?"

"It once belonged to my mother. I'm told she used to sit in it and rock me to sleep. I don't recall that, but I do remember coming in here at night and sitting right there on the floor while she sat in that chair and read me a story."

"I heard you tell Dillon you're an only child. Your parents didn't want any more children?"

"They wanted plenty, which is why they built such a huge house. But Mom had difficulties with my birth and Doc Witherspoon advised her not to try again."

"Oh."

A moment of silence settled between them before Bailey said, "You didn't say why you wanted to see me."

No, he hadn't. He stared at her, wishing he wasn't so fascinated with her mouth. "I need to apologize. I haven't been the nicest person the past several days." No need to tell her Doc Witherspoon hadn't spared any punches in telling Walker just what an ass he'd been.

"No, you haven't. You have been somewhat of a grouch, but I've dealt with worse. I have five brothers and a slew of male cousins. I've discovered men can be more difficult than sick babies when they are in pain."

"Regardless, that was no reason to take out my mood on you and I apologize."

She shrugged. "Apology acc—" As if remembering another time those words had set off a kiss between them, she quickly modified her words. "Thank you for apologizing." She turned to leave.

"Wait!"

Bailey turned back around. "Yes?"

"Lunch."

She raised a brow. "What about it?"

"I thought we could eat lunch together."

Bailey eyed Walker speculatively before asking, "Why would you want us to eat lunch together?"

He countered with a question of his own. "Any reason we can't? Although I appreciate you being here, helping out and everything, you're still a guest in my home. Besides, I'm doing better and Doc suggested I try the stairs. I figured we could sit and eat in the kitchen. Frankly, I'm tired of looking at these four walls."

She could see why he would be. "Okay, I'll serve you lunch in the kitchen."

"And you will join me?"

Bailey nibbled her lips. How could she explain that just breathing the same air as him was playing havoc on her nervous system?

Even now, just standing this close to him was messing with her mind. Making her remember things she shouldn't. Like what had happened the last time she'd stayed this long in this bedroom. And he wanted them to share lunch? What would they talk about? One thing was for certain— she would let him lead the conversation. She would not give him any reason to think she was interviewing him undercover. He'd already accused her of having under-handed motives.

When she'd walked into this room, she hadn't counted on him standing in the middle of it. She'd been fully aware of his presence the moment she'd opened the door. He was dressed in a pair of well-worn jeans and a flannel shirt that showed what an impressive body he had. If he'd lost any weight she couldn't tell. He still had a solid chest, broad shoulders and taut thighs. She'd been too taken with all that masculine power to do anything but stand and stare.

Without the beard his jaw looked stronger and his mouth—which should be outlawed—was way too sexy to be real.

Bailey couldn't stop herself from wondering why he wanted to share lunch with her. But then, she didn't want to spend time analyzing his reason. So she convinced her-self it was because she would be leaving soon, return-ing to Denver. Then there would be no reason for their paths to cross again. If things worked out between the Westmorelands and the Outlaws, she could see Walker hanging out with her brothers and cousins every now and then, but she doubted she would be invited to attend any of those gatherings.

Knowing he was waiting for an answer, she said, "Yes, I'll share lunch with you."

Ten

"So, Bailey, who taught you how to shoot?"

She bit into her sandwich and held up her finger to let him know it would be a minute before she could answer because she had food in her mouth. Walker didn't mind watching her anyway.

"The question you should probably ask is who *didn't* teach me to shoot. My brothers and cousins were quick to give me lessons, especially Bane. He's so good that he's a master sniper with the navy SEALs. Bane taught me how to hit a target. I don't want to sound as if I'm bragging, but I'm an excellent shot because of him."

"You're not bragging, just stating a fact. I'm living proof, and note I said *living* proof. There's no doubt in my mind that grizzly would have done me in if you hadn't taken it down."

"Well, I'm glad I was there."

He was glad she'd been there, too. At the sight of a huge grizzly any other woman would have gone into shock. But not Bailey. She had showed true grit by bringing down that bear. She'd made that shot from a distance he doubted even he could have made. His three men had admitted they could not have made it without running the risk of shooting him.

"My men are in awe of you," he added. "You impressed them."

She frowned. "I didn't do it to impress anyone, Walker. I did what I felt I had to do. I wasn't going after accolades."

That, he thought, was what made her different. Most of the women he knew would use anything to score brownie points. Hadn't making a good impression meant everything to Kalyn?

"I think you're the real hero, Walker. You risked your life getting that bear away from the shack before it got to Marcus."

He shrugged. "Like you said, I did what I felt I had to do. I wasn't going after accolades." He blinked over at her and smiled. He was rewarded when she smiled back.

Just what was he doing flirting with her? He was pretty rusty at it. There hadn't been a woman he'd really been attracted to since Kalyn. He'd had meaningless affairs solely for the purpose of quenching raging hormones, but he hadn't been interested in a woman beyond sex…until now.

He bit into his sandwich. "This is good. I hope I didn't get underfoot while you prepared lunch, but I couldn't stay in my bedroom a minute longer."

"Thanks, and no, you didn't get underfoot."

But he had made her nervous, he was sure of it. She'd been leaning over looking into the refrigerator when he'd walked into the kitchen. The sight of her sweats stretched over a curvy bottom had definitely increased his testosterone level. He had been happy just to stand there, leaning against the kitchen counter with an erection, and stare. After closing the refrigerator she'd nearly dropped the jars of mayo and mustard when she'd turned around to find him there. Of course she'd scolded him for coming down the stairs without her assistance, but he'd ignored all that. He wasn't used to a woman fussing over him.

She'd made him sit down at the table and had given him a magazine that had been delivered by the mailman earlier. Instead of flipping through the pages, he'd preferred watching her move around the kitchen. More than once she'd caught him staring and he'd quickly glanced back down at the magazine.

Walker would be the first to admit he'd picked up on a difference in the atmosphere of his home. It now held the scent of a woman. Although the guest room she was using was on the opposite side of the house, the moment he'd walked out of his bedroom, the scent of jasmine had flowed through his nostrils. At first he'd been taken off guard by it but then he decided he preferred it to the woodsy smell he was used to. It was then that he realized someone other than himself occupied the house for the first time since his parents' deaths. His privacy had been invaded, but, surprisingly, he didn't have a problem with it. Bailey had a way of growing on a person.

"Will you be returning to your room after you finish lunch?" she asked.

He glanced over at her. "No. There're a few things I need to do."

"Like what?"

He lifted a brow. Did she think whatever he did was any of her business?

As if she read his mind, she said, "I hope you're not planning to do anything that might cause a setback, Walker."

He heard the concern in her voice and clearly saw it in her eyes. It reminded him of what had been missing in his life for almost ten years. A woman who cared.

A woman he desired.

Although they had never made love, they had come close. It didn't take much to remember a pair of perfectly shaped breasts or the wetness of her femininity. Going down on a woman wasn't part of his regular lovemaking routine, but Bailey's scent had made him want to do it for her, and after that first time he'd found her flavor addictive.

So yes, he desired her. With a passion. Whenever he saw her, his mind filled with all the things he'd love to do to her. It had been a long time since he'd slept with a woman, but that wasn't the issue. He desired Bailey simply because she was a woman worthy of desiring. There had been this attraction between them from the start, and they both knew it. The attraction was still alive and kicking, and they both knew that, as well.

How long were they planning to play the "try to ignore it" game?

"No setbacks for me. I intend to follow Dr. Witherspoon's orders."

"Good."

Did Bailey realize she liked getting in the last word? "I need to go over my books, replenish my stock and order more branding equipment. I'll be fine."

She nodded before getting up from the table. She reached for his plate and he placed his hand on hers. He immediately felt a sizzle race up his spine and he fought to ignore it. "I can take care of my own plate. I appreciate you being here but I don't want you to feel as if you have to wait on me. I'm doing better."

What he didn't add was that he was doing well enough for her to go back home to Westmoreland Country. However, for reasons he wasn't ready to question, her leaving was not what he wanted.

"Fine," she said, moving away from the table.

He tried concentrating on his cup of coffee, but couldn't.

He watched her move around the room, putting stuff away. He enjoyed watching how her body looked in sweats. Whenever she moved, so did his sex as it tingled with need.

"Any reason you're staring?" she asked, turning to meet his gaze.

She looked younger today. Softer. It could be the way the daylight was coming in through the window. "You got eyes in the back of your head, Bailey?"

"No, but I could feel you staring."

In that case there was no need to lie. "Yes, I was staring. You look good in that outfit."

She looked down at herself. "In sweats? You've got to be kidding me. You must have taken an extra pill or two this morning."

He smiled as his gaze raked over her. "No, I didn't take an extra pill or two. Just stating the facts."

He sensed she didn't believe him. She brushed her fingers through her hair as if his comment had given her reason to wonder if she looked just the opposite. Possibly disheveled and unkempt. He found that interesting. How could she not know she looked good no matter what she wore? And she probably had no idea that her hot, lush scent filled the kitchen instead of the scent of what she'd prepared for lunch.

As if dismissing what he'd said, she turned back to the sink. "Are you going to sit there and stare or are you going to work in your office?" she asked over her shoulder a few moments later.

"I think I'll just sit here and stare for a while."

"It's not nice to stare."

"So I've heard."

She swung around and frowned at him. "Then, stare at something else, Walker."

A smile touched the corner of his lips. "There's noth-

ing else in this kitchen I would rather stare at than you."
And he meant it.

"Sounds as if you've got a case of cabin fever."

"Possibly, but I doubt it."

She placed the dish towel on the counter. "So what do
you think it is?"

He placed his coffee cup down, thinking that was easy
enough to answer. "Lust. I'm lusting after you, Bailey."

A drugging urgency slammed into Bailey's chest, making her nipples pucker and fire race through her veins.
Now, more than before, she felt the weight of Walker's
gaze. She didn't usually feel feminine in sweats, but he
had a way of making her feel sexy even when she didn't
have a right to feel that way.

And while he sat there, watching her every move, she
was fully aware of what was going through his mind. Because she was pretty certain it was the same thing going
through hers. This seductive heat was beginning to affect
her everywhere—in her breasts, deep in the juncture of
her thighs and in the middle of her stomach. The memories of those two kisses they'd previously shared only
intensified the hot, aching sensations overwhelming her
common sense.

She heard him slide the chair back and watched as he
slowly stood. "You can come here or I'm coming over
there," he said matter-of-factly in a deep voice.

She swallowed, knowing he was serious. As serious as
she was hot for him. But was she ready for this? A meaningless affair with Walker? Hadn't he told her that night
in the truck at Bailey's Bay that all he could offer was a
meaningless affair? At the time, she'd responded by saying that kind of relationship didn't bother her. Her future
was tied to Westmoreland Country and not to any man.
There wasn't that much love in the world.

But there was that much passion. That much desire. To a degree she'd never encountered before. She couldn't understand it, but there was no denying the way her body responded to him. It responded in a way it had never reacted to another man. A part of her believed this was no accident. What was taking place between them was meant to be. Not only was that thought a discovery, it was also an acceptance.

It was that acceptance that pushed her to say, "Meet me halfway."

He nodded and moved toward her. She moved toward him. Bailey drew in a deep breath with every step, keeping her gaze fixed on his face. That strong, square chin, those gorgeous dark eyes, his delicious mouth. He was such a striking figure of a man whose looks alone could make a woman shiver. Toss in her nightly naughty dreams and it made her bold enough to turn those dreams into reality.

When they met in the center of the kitchen, he wrapped his arms around her with a possessiveness that took her breath away.

"Be careful of your leg," she warned softly after managing to breathe again. She liked the feel of his body pressed hard against hers.

"My leg isn't what's aching," he said with a huskiness she heard. "Something else is."

She knew what that something else was. She could feel his erection pressed against the juncture of her thighs. Even while recovering from his injury, his strength amazed her. Although he annoyed her at times by not asking for help, his willpower and independence were admirable. And the thought that this was one particular area where this strong, sexy specimen of a man *did* need her sent her mind and body soaring.

He pulled back slightly to look down at her and she almost melted from the heat in his eyes. The feel of him cupping her bottom to keep their middles connected wasn't helping matters. "Our first time making love should be in a bed, Bailey. But I'm not sure I can make it that far. I need you now," he said in a voice filled with need.

"I'm okay with that, Walker. I need you now, too." She was being honest with him. When it came to sex, she felt honesty was the best policy. She detested the lies and games some couples played.

He pulled her back into his arms when he said, "There's something I need to warn you about."

Now she was the one to pull back slightly to look up at him. "What?"

"It's been a long time since I've been with a woman. A few years. About five."

The information, which he hadn't had to give her, tugged at something deep inside her. "It's been a long time since I've been with a man, as well. More than five years."

He smiled and she knew why. She'd been around the males in her family long enough to know they had no problems with double standards. They could sleep around but didn't want to know their women had done the same.

She wrapped her arms around his neck. "What about your leg? How do you plan for this to work? Got any ideas?"

"I've got plenty and I plan to try out every last one of them."

His words made her heart pound hard against her chest. "Bring it on, Walker Rafferty."

"Baby, I intend to do just that." And then he lowered his mouth down to hers.

Eleven

Sensation ripped through Walker the moment their mouths connected. He eased his tongue into her mouth and kissed her with a hunger that had her groaning. In response his erection pressed even harder against his zipper.

He captured her tongue with his and did the kinds of erotic things he'd dreamed of doing. He sucked as if the need to taste her was as essential to him as breathing. He deepened the kiss and tightened his arms around her. She tasted of heat and a wildness that he found delectable.

But then he found everything about her delectable—the way she fit in his arms, the way their bodies melded together like that was the way they were supposed to be.

Walker slowly eased away from her mouth and drew in a deep satisfying breath, missing the feel of her already. "Take off your clothes," he whispered against her lips.

She raised a brow. "In here?"

He smiled. "Yes. I want to make love to you here. We'll try out all the other rooms later."

She chuckled. "Horny, aren't we?"

He leaned in and licked her lips. "Like I said, it's been five years."

"In that case…"

Moving out of his arms, she took a few steps back and began removing her clothes. He watched her every move, getting more turned on with each stitch she discarded. When she had stripped down to nothing but her panties and bra, he finally released the breath he'd been holding.

He was weak in the knees from looking at her and he leaned against the breakfast bar for support. He needed it when she removed her bra and then slowly peeled her panties down her thighs. He couldn't help growling in pleasure.

It was only then he remembered something very important.

"Damn."

She lifted a concerned brow. "What's wrong?"

"Condoms. I don't have any down here. They're upstairs in my nightstand."

She shook her head. "No need, unless you're concerned about it for health reasons. I'm on the pill to regulate my periods."

He nodded. The thought of spilling inside her sent all kinds of luscious sensations through him. "No concerns. I'm okay with it, if you are."

"I'm okay with it."

He couldn't help but rake his gaze over her naked body. "You are beautiful, Bailey. From the top of your head to your pretty little feet, you are absolutely beautiful."

Bailey had never allowed any man's compliments to go to her head…until now. Walker sounded so serious and the look on his face was so sincere that her heart pounded in appreciation. She wasn't sure why his opinion of how she looked mattered, but it did. And she immediately thought of a way to thank him. Reclaiming the distance separating them, she leaned up on her toes and brushed her lips across his. Then she licked a line from one corner of his mouth to the other in a slow and provocative way.

She smiled in pleasure when she heard his quick intake of breath, glad to know she was getting to him as much as he was getting to her. "Now for your clothes, Walker, and I intend to help you." She intended to do more than that but he would find that out soon enough. He braced against the breakfast bar as she bent down to remove his shoes and socks.

Now for his shirt. She leaned forward and undid the buttons while occasionally leaning up to nip and lick his mouth. The more he moaned the bolder she got as she assisted him out of his shirt and then his T-shirt.

Wow, what a chest. She ran her fingers through the coarse hair covering it. She loved the feel of it beneath her hands. She trailed kisses from his lips, past his jawline to his chest and then used her teeth to nibble on his nipples before devouring them with her tongue and lips.

"Bailey." He breathed out her name in a forced whisper. "I need you."

She needed him, too, but first...

She reached down and unsnapped his jeans before easing down his zipper. Then she inserted her hand into the opening to cup him. She smiled at how thick he felt in her hand. "Um, I think we should get rid of your jeans and briefs, don't you?"

Instead of giving him a chance to answer, she kissed him again, using her tongue to further stir the passion between them. She heard him moan, which was followed by a deep growl when she sucked on his lower lip.

"Don't think I can handle this much longer," he said through clenched teeth.

"Oh, I think you can handle more than you think you can, Walker. Let's see."

She helped him remove his jeans and briefs and then stood back and raked her gaze over him before meeting his eyes. "You are so buff. So gorgeously handsome. So—"

Before she could finish he pulled her to him, capturing her lips in an openmouthed kiss as raw as it was possessive. And when she felt his hand between her legs, she broke off the kiss to ease out of his arms.

"Not so fast. I'm a guest in your home, so today I get to have my way," she whispered.

With that, her fingers gripped his hardness and gently squeezed, loving the feel of his bare flesh in her hands.

"Don't torture me, baby."

Torture? He hadn't endured any torture yet, she thought, as she continued to fondle his thick width, texture and length, loving every minute of it. He was huge, and she intended to sample every single inch.

In a move she knew he was not expecting, she dropped down on her knees and took him into the warmth of her mouth.

"Bailey!"

Walker grabbed her head but instead of pulling her mouth away, he wrapped his fingers in the locks of her hair. He lost all control while watching her head bob up and down. Every muscle in his body trembled and his insides shivered with the impact of her mouth on him. She was pushing him deliciously over the edge. He felt ready to explode.

It was then that he tugged on her hair, using enough force to pull her mouth from him. She looked up at him and smiled, licking her lips. "I need to get inside you now," he said in a guttural growl. He had reached his limit.

In a surprise move, he pulled her up and lifted her to sit on the kitchen table, spreading her legs wide in the process.

Thanks to her, his control was shot to hell. He trailed his fingers through the curls surrounding her feminine folds. She wasn't the only one who wanted a taste. He lowered his head to her wetness.

"Walker!"

He ignored her screaming his name as his tongue devoured her as she'd done to him. And when she wrapped her legs around his neck and bucked her hips against his mouth he knew he was giving her a taste of her own medicine.

When he'd pushed her far enough, he spread her legs farther, positioned his body between them and thrust until he was fully embedded within her. Then he held tight to her hips as he went deeper with every plunge.

Something inside him snapped, and his body moved with the speed of a jackhammer. When she wrapped her legs around his waist he threw his head back and filled his nostrils with her scent.

They came together, him holding tight to her hips. Why this felt so right, he wasn't sure. All he knew was that it did. He needed this. He needed her. And from the sounds of her moans, she needed him.

They were both getting what they needed.

Bailey came awake and shifted in Walker's arms, recalling how they'd made it out of the kitchen to the sofa in his living room. She eased up and tried to move off him when she remembered his leg.

His arms held tight around her like a band of steel. "Where do you think you're going?"

She looked down at him and remembered why he was down there and she was on top. Upon his encouragement, she had shown him that she wasn't only a good shot. She was a pretty damn good rider, as well.

She glanced at the clock. It was close to eight. They had slept almost through dinner. Okay, she would admit they hadn't slept the entire time. They had slept in between their many rounds of lovemaking.

"Your leg," she reminded him, holding his gaze.

He had a sexy, sluggish look in his eyes.

"My leg is fine."

"It's after eight and you didn't take your medicine at five."

A smile curved his lips. "I had another kind of medicine that I happen to like better."

She shook her head. "Tell that to your leg when it starts hurting later."

"Trust me, I will. Making love to you is better than any medicine Doc Witherspoon could have prescribed for me." And then he pulled her mouth down to his and kissed her in a slow, unhurried fashion that clouded her mind. She was grateful for the ringing of her cell phone until she recognized the ringtone.

She broke off the kiss and quickly scooted off Walker to grab her phone off the coffee table, being careful not to bump his leg. "Dillon! What's going on?"

"Hey, Bay. I was calling to check to see how Walker is doing."

She glanced over at Walker who was stretched out naked on the sofa. She licked her lips and then said to Dillon, "Walker is doing fine. Improving every day. The doctor is pleased with his progress."

"That's good to hear. And how are you doing? Is it cold enough there for you?"

"Yes, I'm doing good," she said, glancing down at her own naked body. It was a good thing Dillon had no idea just how good she was doing. "There was a bad snow-storm here."

"I heard about that. You took plenty of heavy clothing didn't you?"

"Yes, I'm good."

"You most certainly are," Walker whispered.

She gave Walker a scolding glance, hoping Dillon hadn't heard what Walker had said.

"Do you have any idea when you'll be coming back home?" Dillon asked.

She swallowed hard and switched her gaze from Walker to the window when she said, "No, I don't know when I'll be back. I don't want to leave Walker too soon. But when the doctor says Walker can handle things on his own, I'll be back."

"All right. Give Walker my regards and tell him the entire family is wishing him a speedy recovery."

"Okay. I'll tell him. Goodbye, Dillon."

"Goodbye, Bay."

She clicked off the phone and held it in her hand a second before placing it back on the table.

"What did Dillon want you to tell me?"

"That the family is wishing you a speedy recovery."

He nodded and pulled up into a sitting position. "That's nice of them."

She smiled and returned to the sofa to sit beside him. "I have a nice family."

"I'll have to agree with you there. You didn't say how the wedding went."

Her smile widened. "It was wonderful and Jill made a beautiful bride. I don't know who cried the most, Jill, Pam or their other two sisters." She paused and then added, "Ian, Reggie and Quade hated they didn't get the chance to meet you."

"And I hate I didn't get the chance to meet them."

She couldn't help but remember he'd left because of her. She looked at him. "Do you think you'll ever return to Denver to visit?"

Walker captured the back of her neck with his hand and brought her mouth closer to his. He nibbled around her lips before placing an openmouthed kiss on her neck. "Um, will you make it worth my while if I do?"

She closed her eyes, loving the way Walker ravished her with his mouth and tongue. Desire coiled in her stomach. "I can't make any promises, but I'll see what I can do."

He pulled back slightly and she opened her eyes and met his gaze. She saw a serious glint in the dark depths as he said, "Dillon asked when you were coming home."

He'd presented it as a statement and not a question. "Yes. I told him when you got better."

He nodded, holding fast to her gaze. "I'm better."

Bailey drew in a deep breath, wondering if he was telling her that because he was ready for her to leave. "Have I worn out my welcome?"

He gently gripped her wrist and brought it to his lips, placing a light kiss on her skin. "I don't think that's possible."

She decided not to remind him he was a loner. A man who preferred solitude to company. "In that case, I'll stay another week."

He flashed a sexy smile. "Or two?"

She tried not to blink in surprise that he was actually suggesting she hang around for two weeks instead of one. She glided her hand across the firmness of his jaw. "Yes. Or two."

As if he was satisfied with her answer, he leaned in and opened his mouth against hers.

Twelve

Walker left his bathroom and glanced across the room at his bed and the woman in it. This was the third night she'd spent with him and it was hard to remember a time when she hadn't. A part of him didn't want to remember it.

He rubbed a hand down his face. Bailey in his bed was something he shouldn't get used to. It was countdown time, and in a little less than two weeks she'd be gone and his life would return to normal.

Normal meant living for himself and nobody else. Garth often teased him about living a miserable life. Misery didn't need company. *He* didn't need company, but Bailey had made him realize that five years had been too long to go without a woman. He was enjoying her in his bed a little too damn much. And that unfortunately wasn't the crux of his problem. The real kicker was that he was enjoying her…even without the sex.

He hadn't gotten around to working until yesterday, and she had found what she claimed was the perfect spot in his office to sit and work on the laptop she had brought with her. That way she was still connected to her job in Denver.

They had worked in amicable silence, although he'd been fully aware of her the entire time. Her presence had made him realize what true loneliness was because he didn't want to think of a time when she wouldn't be there.

Forcing that thought to the back of his mind, he moved across the room to rekindle the flames in the fireplace. While jabbing at the wood with the poker, he glanced back over his shoulder when he heard Bailey shift around. She looked small in his huge bed. She looked good. As if she belonged.

He quickly turned back to the fire, forcing his thoughts off her and onto something else. Like Morris James's visit yesterday. The rancher had wanted to meet Bailey after hearing all about her. Word of how she'd downed that bear had spread quickly, far and wide. Morris wanted to present Bailey with the ten-thousand-dollar bounty she'd earned from killing the animal.

Bailey had refused to take it and instead told Morris she wanted to donate the money to charity, especially if there was one in town that dealt with kids. The surprised look on Morris's face had been priceless. What person in her right mind gives up ten thousand dollars? But both Walker and Morris had watched her sign the paperwork to do just that.

As he continued to jab the poker in the fire another Bailey moment came to mind. He recalled the day he'd stepped out onto his front porch for the first time in a week. While sipping a cup of coffee he'd watched in fascination as Bailey had built a snowman. And when she'd invited him to help her, he had. He hadn't done something like that since he was a kid and he had to admit he'd enjoyed it.

For a man who didn't like having his privacy invaded, not only had she invaded that privacy, but for the time being she was making privacy nonexistent. Like when he'd come downstairs for breakfast this morning to find all four of his men sitting at his table. Somehow she'd discovered it was Willie's birthday and she'd wanted to do something special. At first Walker had been a little annoyed that she'd done such a thing without confiding in him, but then he realized that was Bailey's way—to do as she pleased. He couldn't help but smile at that.

But then he frowned upon realizing it was also Bailey's way to be surrounded by people. Although he was used to loneliness, she was not. She had a big family and was used to having people around all the time. He figured the loneliness of Alaska would eventually drive her crazy. What if she decided to leave before the two weeks?

Why should he give a damn if she did?

He returned the poker to the stand, not wanting to think about that. He was expecting another visit from Doc Witherspoon tomorrow. Hopefully it would be his last for a while. He couldn't wait to take out his plane and fly over his land. And he didn't want to question why he wanted Bailey with him to share in the experience.

"Walker?"

He glanced across the room. Bailey was sitting up in his bed. Her hair was mussed up and she had a soft, sleepy and sexy look on her face. Although she held the covers up to her chest, she looked tempting. Maybe because he knew that beneath all those bedcovers she was naked. "Yes?"

"I'm cold."

"I just finished stoking the fire."

"Not good enough, Alaskan. I'm sure you can do better than that."

Oh, yes, he definitely could. He removed his robe and headed for the bed, feeling a deep ache in his groin. The moment he slid in bed and felt her thigh brush against his, the ache intensified. He pulled her into his arms, needing to hold her. He knew there would come a time when he wouldn't be able to do that. The thought had him drawing in a deep, ragged breath.

She pulled back and ran her gaze over his face. "You okay?"

"Yes."

"Your leg?"

"Is fine. Back to the way it used to be. Only lasting reminder is that little scar."

"Trust me, Walker, no woman will care about that scar when you've got this to back things up," she said, reaching her hand beneath the covers to cup him, then stroke him. Walker drew in another ragged breath. Bailey definitely knew how to get to the heart of the matter. And when he saw the way she licked her lips and how the darkness of her eyes shone with desire, his erection expanded in her hand.

She leaned close to his ear and whispered, "Okay, Walker, what's it going to be? You ride me or I ride you? Take your pick."

He couldn't stop the smile that curved his lips. It was hard—damn difficult, outright impossible—not to tap into all his sexual fantasies when she was around and being so damn accommodating. And she would be around for eleven more days. He intended to make the most of what he considered the best time of his life.

"Um," he said, pulling her back into his arms. "How about if we do both?"

Over the next several days Walker and Bailey settled into a gratifying and pleasurable routine. Now that Walker was back at 100 percent, he would get up every morning around five o'clock to work alongside his men. Then at nine, instead of hanging around and eating Willie's cooking like he normally did, he hightailed it back to the ranch house, where Bailey would have breakfast waiting on him. No matter how often he told her that she didn't have to go out of her way, she would wave her hand and brush off his words. After placing the most delectable-looking meal in front of him, she would go on and on about what a beautiful kitchen he had. It was one that would entice someone to cook whether they wanted to or not, she claimed.

He began to see his kitchen through her eyes and finally understood. In all the years he had lived here, he'd never thought of his kitchen, or any kitchen, as beautiful. It was a place to cook meals and eat. But she brought his attention to the space, its rustic look. But what she said she liked most was sitting at the table and looking out at the strait. On a clear day the waters looked breathtaking. Just as breathtaking as Gemma Lake, she'd told him. It was during those conversations that he knew she missed her home. Hadn't one of her rules been to never venture far from Westmoreland Country for too long?

Garth had dropped by twice to check on Walker, and because his best friend had been calling every day to see how he was doing, Garth wasn't surprised to find Bailey still there. Garth didn't seem surprised at how comfortable she'd made herself in Walker's home, either. And Walker had caught Garth staring at them with a silly-looking grin on his face more than once.

Garth had mentioned to Bailey that he'd gotten in touch with her family and had spoken to Dillon and Ramsey, and that he and his brothers would be flying to Denver in a few weeks. Bailey mentioned that she would be back home by then and that she and her family would anxiously await Garth's visit. Her comment only made Walker realize that he didn't have a lot of time left with her.

Lola was back on her regular housekeeping schedule and told him more than once how much she liked Bailey. He figured it was because Bailey was chattier with her than he'd ever been. And he figured since Lola had only one bed in the house to make up, the older woman had pretty much figured out that he and Bailey were sharing it. That had suited Lola since she'd hinted more than once that he needed a woman in his life and that being alone on the ranch wasn't good for him.

Walker took a sip of his coffee while looking out at the strait. He remembered the day Bailey had gone into town with him to pick up supplies. News of her and the bear had spread further than Walker had imagined it would, and she'd become something of a legend. And if that wasn't enough, Morris had spread the word about what she'd done with the bounty money. Her generous contribution had gone to Kodiak Way, the local orphanage. Walker hadn't visited the place in years, not since he'd gone there on a field trip with his high school. But he'd decided on that particular day to stop by with Bailey, so she could see where her money had gone.

It had amazed him how taken she'd been with all the children, but he really should not have been surprised. He recalled how much she adored her nieces, nephews and little cousins back in Denver and just how much they'd adored her. He and Bailey had spent longer at the orphanage than he had planned because Bailey couldn't miss the opportunity to take a group of kids outside to build a snowman.

He then recalled the day he'd taken her up in his single-engine plane, giving her a tour of his land. She had been in awe and had told him how beautiful his property was. When she'd asked him how he'd learned to fly, he'd opened up and told her of his and Garth's time together in the marines. She'd seemed fascinated by everything he told her and he'd gotten caught up in her interest.

It had been a beautiful day for flying. The sky had

been blue and the clouds a winter white. From the air he had pointed out his favorite areas—the lakes, small coves, hidden caves and mountaintops. And he'd heard himself promising to one day cover the land with her in his Jeep.

And then there had been the day when she'd pulled him into his office, shoved him down into the chair at his desk and proceeded to sit in his lap so she could show him what she'd downloaded on his desktop computer. Jillian and Aidan had returned from their three-week honeymoon to France, Italy and Spain, and had uploaded their wedding video. Bailey thought that since he'd missed the wedding, he could watch the video.

As far as weddings went, it had been a nice one. Bailey had pointed out several cousins he hadn't met and their wives and children. He agreed that Jillian had been a beautiful bride and he'd seen the love in Aidan's eyes when she'd walked down the aisle on Dillon's arm.

Watching the video made Walker recall his own wedding. Only thing, his wedding had been nothing more than a circus. His parents and Garth had tried to warn him with no luck. A few nights ago he'd dreamed about Kalyn and Connor. A dream that had turned into a nightmare, with Bailey waking him up.

The next day, even though he'd seen the probing curiosity in her eyes, she hadn't asked him about it and he hadn't felt the need to tell her.

Walker took another sip of his coffee and glanced down at his watch. Bailey should be coming down for breakfast any minute. He had finished his chores with the men earlier than usual and had rushed back to the ranch house. More than once he'd been tempted to go upstairs and wake her but he knew if he did they might end up staying in bed the rest of the day. He then thought about the phone call he'd received an hour ago from Charm. It seemed Charm couldn't wait to meet her look-alike and asked that he fly Bailey to Fairbanks this weekend. He hadn't made any promises, but he'd told her he would talk to Bailey about it.

Moments later, he heard her upstairs and felt his sex stir in anticipation. Only Bailey could put him in such a state, arousing him so easily and completely. And he would admit that her mere presence in his home brought him a kind of joy he hadn't thought he would ever feel again.

But then he also knew it was the kind of joy he couldn't allow himself to get attached to. Just as sure as he knew that when he got up every morning the strait would be filled with water, he knew that when Bailey's days were up, she would be leaving.

Already he'd detected a longing in her and figured she'd become homesick. It was during those times that he was reminded of the first day they'd met. She'd told him about her rules and her love for Westmoreland Country. She'd said she never intended to leave it. And since he never intended to leave Kodiak, that meant any wishful thinking about them spending their lives together was a waste of his time.

Walker's grip on the cup tightened. And hadn't she told him about men getting possessive, becoming territorial and acting crazy sometimes? Sadly, he could now see himself doing all three where she was concerned.

It was nobody's fault but his own that he was now in this state. He'd known her rules and had allowed her to get under his skin anyway. But he could handle it. He had no choice. He would store up memories of the good times, and those memories would get him through the lonely nights after she left.

He heard her moving around upstairs again and sat his coffee cup down. Temptation was ruling his senses now.

Desire unlike anything he'd ever felt before took control of him, had him sliding back from the table and standing.

Walker left the kitchen and moved quickly toward the stairs, seeking the object of his craving.

Thirteen

"What am I going to do, Josette? Of all the stupid, idiotic, crazy things I could have done, why did I fall in love with Walker Rafferty?" Bailey asked. She held her mobile phone to her ear and paced Walker's bedroom. Talk about doing something dumb.

She had woken up that morning and glanced out the window on her way to the bathroom. She'd seen Walker and his men in the distance, knee deep in snow, loading some type of farm equipment onto a truck. She had stared at him, admiring how good he looked even dressed in a heavy coat and boots with a hat on his head. All she could think about was the night before, how he had made love to her, how he'd made her scream a number of times. And how this morning before leaving the bed he had brushed a good-morning kiss across her lips.

Suddenly, while standing at the window and ogling him, it had hit her—hard—that all those emotions she'd been feeling lately weren't lust. They were love.

She had fallen head over heels in love with Walker.

"Damn it, Josette. I should have known better."

"Calm down, Bailey. There's nothing stupid, idiotic or crazy about falling in love."

"It is if the man you love has no intention of ever loving you back. Walker told me all he could ever offer is a meaningless affair. I knew that and fell in love with him anyway."

"What makes you think he hasn't changed his mind? Now that the two of you have spent time together at his ranch, he might have."

"I have no reason to think he won't be ready for me to leave when my two weeks are up. Especially after that stunt I pulled the other day. Inviting his men for breakfast without his permission. Although he didn't say anything, I could tell he didn't like it."

"Are you going to tell him how you feel?"

"Of course not! Do you want me to feel even more stupid?"

"So what are you going to do?"

Bailey paused, not knowing how she intended to answer that. And also knowing there was really only one way to answer it. "Nothing. Just enjoy the time I have with him now and leave with no regrets. I believe the reason he refuses to love anyone else is because he's still carrying a torch for his late wife. There's nothing I can do about that and I don't intend to try."

Moments later, after ending her phone call with Josette, Bailey walked back over to the window. Today the weather appeared clearer than it had been the past couple of days. She missed home, but not as much as she'd figured she would. Skype had helped. She communicated regularly with her nieces and nephews and little cousins and, according to Ramsey, although several wives were expecting new babies in the family, none had been born.

Everyone was expecting her home for Thanksgiving and was looking forward to her return.

She had worked out a system with Lucia where she could work remotely from Alaska. Doing so helped fill the long days when Walker was gone. In the evenings she looked forward to his return. Although they had established an amicable routine, she knew it was just temporary. Like she'd told Josette, there was no doubt in her mind Walker would expect her to leave next week. Granted, she knew he enjoyed her as his bedmate, but she also knew that, for men, sex was nothing more than sex. She had found that out while watching her then-single Westmoreland brothers and cousins. For her and Walker, there could never be anything between them other than the physical.

Even so, she could sense there was something bothering Walker. More than once she'd awakened in the night to find him standing at the window or poking the fire. And then there had been the night he'd woken up screaming the words, "No, Kalyn! Don't! Connor! Connor!"

She had snuggled closer and wrapped her arms around him, and pretty soon he had calmed down, holding her as tightly as she held him. The next day over breakfast she had expected him to bring up the incident, but he hadn't. She could only assume he didn't remember it or didn't want to talk about it. But she had been curious enough to check online and she'd found out Kalyn had been his wife and Connor his son.

Bailey turned when she heard the bedroom door opening, and there Walker stood, looking more handsome than any man had a right to look. As she stood there staring, too mesmerized by the heat in his eyes to even speak, he closed the door and removed his jacket, then tossed it across the chair.

She'd seen that look in his eyes before, usually in the evenings after he'd spent the entire day on the range. It wasn't quite nine in the morning. She swallowed. Now he was unbuttoning his shirt. "Good morning, Walker."

"Good morning, Bailey." He pulled the belt from his jeans before sitting in the chair to remove his boots and socks. His eyes never left hers.

"You've finished your chores for the day already?"

"No."

"No?"

"Yes, no. The guys took my tractor over to the Mayeses' place for Conley to look at it. He's the area mechanic. Nothing much to do until they get back, which won't be for hours."

She nodded. "I see."

"I came in for coffee and had a cup before hearing you move around up here, letting me know you were awake." Now he was unzipping his pants.

"And?" she asked, as if she really didn't know.

He slid his pants down muscular thighs. "And—" he crooked his finger "—come here a minute."

He stood there stark naked. She couldn't help licking her lips as her gaze moved from his eyes downward, past his chest to the thatch of dark hair covering his erection. "Before or after I take off my clothes?" she asked.

"Before. I want to undress you."

At that moment she didn't care that she'd just finished putting on her clothes. From the look in his eyes, he was interested in more than just taking off her clothes.

Drawing in a deep breath and trying to ignore the throb between her legs, she crossed the room on wobbly knees. Was she imagining things or was his erection expanding with each step she took? When she stopped in front of him, he placed both hands on her shoulders. She felt the heat of his touch through her blouse.

"You look good in this outfit," he said, holding fast to her shoulders as his gaze raked over her.

"Thanks." It was just a skirt and blouse. Nothing spectacular.

"You're welcome." Then he captured her lips with his.

Her last coherent thought was *But this kiss is spectacular.*

Walker was convinced, and had been for some time, that Bailey was what fantasies were made of. What he'd told her was the truth. She looked good in that outfit. Truth be told, she looked good in any outfit...especially in his shirts. Those were the times he felt most possessive, territorial, crazy with lust...and love. All the things that she'd once stated were total turnoffs for her.

He continued kissing her, moving his mouth over her lips with a hunger he felt all the way to his toes. He had wanted this kiss to arouse her, get her ready for what was to come. He figured she knew his motives because of the way she was responding. Their tongues tangled madly, greedily, as hot and intense as it could get.

His hands left her shoulders and cupped her backside, pressing her body against his. There was no way she didn't feel his erection pressing against the juncture of her thighs.

He'd watched her crossing the room and noticed her gaze shifting from his face to his groin, checking him out. He really didn't know why. Nothing about that part of his body had changed. She had cupped it, taken it into her mouth and fondled it. So what had she found so fascinating about it today?

As if she'd guessed his thoughts, she glanced up to meet his eyes just seconds before reaching him. The tint that darkened her cheeks had been priceless, and instead of stripping her clothes off like he'd intended, he kissed her. He'd overplayed his hand with Bailey. This young woman had done what no other could have done. She was on the verge of making him whole. Making him want to believe in love all over again. Restoring his soul to what it had been before Kalyn had destroyed it.

He slowly broke off the kiss. His hands returned to her shoulders only long enough to remove her blouse and un-hook her bra. And then he tugged her skirt and panties down past her hips and legs to pool at her feet. He looked his fill. Now he understood her earlier fascination with him because he was experiencing the same fascination now.

Yes, he'd seen it all before. Had tasted and touched every single inch. But still, looking at her naked body al-most took his breath away. She was beautiful. His body ached for her in a way it had never ached for another woman...including Kalyn.

That realization had him lifting her into his arms, car-rying her to the bed. He placed her on it and joined her there. He had intended to go slow, to savor each moment as long as he could. But she had other ideas.

When they stretched out together on the huge bed, her mouth went for his and kissed him hungrily. The same way he'd kissed her moments ago. The only difference was that her hands were everywhere, touching, exploring and strok-ing. He joined in with his own hands, frenzied with the need to touch her and let his mouth follow. She squirmed against him, biting his shoulders a few times and licking his chest, trying to work her mouth downward. But he beat her to the punch. She released a gasp when he tightened his hold on her hips and lowered his head between her legs.

He'd only intended to lick her a few times, but her taste made that impossible. He wanted more, needed more, and he was determined to get everything he wanted.

He heard her moans, felt her nails dig deep into his shoulders. He knew the moment her pleasure came, when she was consumed in an orgasm that had her writhing be-neath his mouth.

Lust ripped through him, triggered by her moans. He

had to be inside her now. Easing his body over hers, their gazes held as he slowly entered her. It took all his strength not to explode right when she arched her back and lifted her hips to receive every last inch of him. She entwined her arms around his neck and then, in a surprise move, she leaned up slightly and traced his lips with the tip of her tongue.

Something snapped inside him and he began thrusting in and out of her, going deeper with every downward plunge. Over and over, he fine-tuned the rhythm, whipping up sensation after exquisite sensation.

"Walker!"

When she screamed his name, the same earthshaking orgasm that overtook her did the same to him. A fierce growl escaped his lips when he felt her inner muscles clench him, trying to hold him inside.

This was how it was supposed to be. Giving instead of taking. Sharing instead of just being a recipient.

When their bodies had gone limp, he found the strength to ease off her and pull her into his arms, needing to hold her close to his heart. A part of him wished they could remain like that forever, but he knew they couldn't. Time was not on their side.

He knew her rules, especially the one about staying in Westmoreland Country. And he knew the promise he'd made to his father, about never taking Hemlock Row for granted again. That meant that even if Bailey agreed to a long-term affair, there would be no compromise on either of their parts.

Even so, he was determined to stock up on all the memories he could.

"Charm called."

Bailey's body felt weak as water but somehow she managed to open her eyes and meet Walker's gaze. She was convinced the man had more stamina than a bull. And wasn't she seven years younger? He should be flat on his back barely able to move…like her.

She found the strength to draw in a slow breath. Evidently he was telling her this for a reason and there was only one way to find out what it was. "And?"

"And she asked me to bring you to Fairbanks this weekend. Let me rephrase that. She kind of ordered me to."

Bailey couldn't help but chuckle. "Ordered. I didn't think anyone had the nerve to order you to do anything."

"Charm thinks she can. She considers me one of her brothers and she thinks she can wrap all of us around her finger. Like you do with your brothers and cousins."

That got another chuckle from her. "I don't know about that anymore." When he eased down beside her, she snuggled against him. "So are you going to do it? Are you going to take me to Fairbanks?"

He looked over at her. "I thought you didn't want to have anything to do with the Outlaws."

"I never said that. I just didn't like how they handled their business by sending you to Denver instead of coming themselves." Reaching up, she entwined her arms around his neck. "But I'm over that now. If they hadn't sent you, then we would not have met."

She grimaced at the thought of that, and for the first time since meeting Walker she decided the Outlaws had definitely done her a favor. Even if he didn't love her, she now knew how it felt to fall in love with someone. To give that person your whole heart and soul. To be willing to do things you never thought you would do.

Now she understood her sisters. She'd always thought Megan and Gemma were plumb loco to consider living anywhere other than Westmoreland Country. Megan not so much, since she stayed in Westmoreland Country six months out of the year and spent the other six months in

Rico's hometown of Philly. But Gemma had made Australia her permanent home and only returned to Denver to visit on occasion. Megan and Gemma had chosen love over everything else. They knew home was where the heart was. Now Bailey did, too.

"You've gotten quiet on me."

She glanced over at Walker and smiled. "Only because you haven't answered my question. So are you going to take me to Fairbanks?" She knew that was a big request to make, because he'd mentioned once that he rarely left his ranch.

She could tell he was considering it and then he said, "Only if you go somewhere with me tomorrow."

She lifted a brow. "Where?"

He pulled her closer. "You'll know when we get there."

She stared at him silently, mulling over his request. She was curious, but she knew she would follow him to the ends of the earth if he asked her to. "Yes, I will go with you tomorrow."

Fourteen

The next morning Walker woke up with a heavy heart, pretty much like he'd done for the past ten years. It was Connor's birthday. In the past he'd spent the day alone. Even Garth knew not to bother him on that anniversary. Yet Bailey was here, and of all things he had asked her to go to Connor's grave with him, although she had no idea where they were headed.

"You're still not going to give me a hint?" Bailey asked when he placed his Stetson on his head and then led her outside. Bundled up in her coat, boots, scarf and a Denver Broncos knitted cap, she smiled over at him. Snow covered the ground but wasn't as deep as yesterday.

He shook his head. "Don't waste your smile. You'll know when we get there." She had tried to get him to tell her last night and again this morning, but he wouldn't share. He had thoroughly enjoyed her seductive efforts, though.

"I didn't know you were so mean, Walker."

"And I've always known you were persistent, Bailey. Come on," he said, taking her gloved hand to lead her toward one of his detached garages. When he raised the door she got a peek of what was inside and almost knocked him down rushing past him.

"Wow! These babies are beauties," she said, checking out the two sleek, black-and-silver snowmobiles parked beside one of his tractors. "Are they yours?"

He nodded, leaning against the tractor. "Yes, mine and Garth's. He likes to keep his here to use whenever he comes to visit. But today, this will be our transportation to get where we're going."

"Really?" she gasped excitedly, nearly jumping up and down.

Walker couldn't ignore the contentment he felt knowing he was the one responsible for her enthusiasm. "Yes. You get to use Garth's. I asked his permission for you to do so. He figures any woman who can shoot a grizzly from one hundred feet away should certainly know how to operate one of these."

Bailey laughed. "It wasn't exactly a hundred feet away and yes, I can operate one of these. Riley has one. He loves going skiing and takes it with him when he does. None of us can understand it, but he loves cold weather. The colder the better."

Walker opened a wooden box and pulled out two visored helmets and handed her one. "Where we're going isn't far from here."

She looked up at him as she placed her helmet on her head. "And you still won't give me a hint?"

"No, not even a little one."

Of all the places Bailey figured they might end up, a cemetery wasn't even on her list. When they had brought the snowmobiles to a stop by a wooden gate she had to blink to make sure she wasn't imagining things.

Instead of asking Walker why they were there, she followed his lead and got off the machine. She watched as he opened a box connected to his snowmobile and pulled out a small broom. He then took her gloved hand in his. "This way."

Walking through snow, he led her through the opening of the small cemetery containing several headstones. They stopped in front of the first pair. "My grandparents," he said softly, releasing her hand to lean down and brush away the snow that covered the names. *Walker and Lora Rafferty.*

She glanced up at him. "You were named after your grandfather?"

He nodded. "Yes. And my father."

"So you're the third?"

He nodded again. "Yes, I'm the third. My grandfather was in the military, stationed in Fairbanks, and was sent here to the island one summer with other troops to work on a government project for a year. He fell in love with the island. He also fell in love with a young island girl he met here."

"The woman who could trace her family back to Alaska when it was owned by Russia?" Bailey asked, letting him know she remembered what he'd told her about his grandparents that first day they'd met.

A smile touched one corner of his mouth. "Yes, she's the one. They married and he bought over a thousand acres through the government land grant. He and Lora settled here and named their property Hemlock Row, after the rows of trees that are abundant on the island. They only had one child. My father."

They then moved to the second pair of headstones and she guessed this was where his parents were buried. *Walker and Darlene Rafferty.* And the one thing she noticed was that they had died within six months of each other.

She didn't want to ask but had to. "How did they die?"

At first she wasn't sure he would answer, but then his voice caught in the icy wind when he said, "Mom got sick. By the time the doctors found out it was cancer there was nothing that could be done. She loved Hemlock Row and wanted to take her last breath here. So we checked her out of the hospital and brought her home. She died less than a week later."

Bailey studied the date on the headstone. "You were here when she died?"

"Yes."

She did quick calculations in her head. Walker had lost his wife and son three months before he'd lost his mother and subsequently his father. He had fled Hollywood to come here to find peace from his grief only to face even more heartache when he'd arrived home. No wonder he'd shut himself off from the world and become a loner. He had lost the four people he'd loved the most within a year's time.

She noticed his hold on her hand tightened when he said, "Dad basically died of a broken heart. He missed Mom that much. Six months. I'm surprised he lasted without her that long. She was his heart, and I guess he figured that without her he didn't need one."

Bailey swallowed. She remembered Ramsey telling her that at least their parents had died together. He couldn't imagine one living without the other. Like Walker's, her parents had had a very close marriage.

"My father was a good one," Walker said, breaking into her thoughts. "The best. He loved Hemlock Row, and when I was a teenager he made me promise to always take care of it and keep it in the family and never sell it. I made him a promise to honor his wishes."

She nodded and recalled hearing her father and uncle had made their father and grandfathers the same such promises. That was why her family considered West-moreland Country their home. It had been land passed to them from generation to generation. Land their great-grandfather Raphel had worked hard to own and even harder to maintain.

Walker shifted and they moved toward the next head-stone. She knew before he brushed the snow off the marker who it belonged to. His son. *Connor Andrew Rafferty.*

From the dates on the headstone, he'd died four days after his first birthday, which would have been…today. She quickly glanced over at the man standing beside her, still holding her hand as he stood staring at the headstone with a solemn look on his face. Today was his son's birthday. Connor would have been eleven today.

There were no words Bailey could say because at that moment she could actually feel Walker's pain. His grief was still raw and she could tell it hadn't yet healed. So she did the only thing she could do. She leaned into him. In-stead of rejecting her gesture, he placed his arms around her waist and gently drew her against his side.

They stood there together, silently gazing at the head-stone. She was certain his mind was filled with memories of the son he'd lost. Long minutes passed before Walker finally spoke. "He was a good kid. Learned to walk at ten months. And he loved playing hide-and-seek."

Bailey forced a smile through the tears she tried to hold back. She bet he was a good daddy who played hide-and-seek often with his son. "Was he ever hard to find?"

Walker chuckled. "All the time. But his little giggle would always give him away."

Walker got quiet again, and then he turned her in his arms to face him. He touched her chin with his thumb. "Thanks for coming here with me today."

"Thanks for bringing me. I know today has to be painful for you."

He dropped his hand and broke eye contact to look up at the snow-covered mountains behind her. "Yes, it is every year. There are some things you just can't get over."

Bailey nodded. She then glanced around, expecting to see another headstone, and when she didn't, she gazed at Walker and asked, "Your wife?"

He looked back down at her and took her hand. "What about her?"

"Is she not buried here?"

He hesitated a moment and then said, "No." And then he tightened his hold on her hand. "Come on. Let's head back."

Later that night as Walker lay in bed holding Bailey in his arms while she slept, he thought about their time together at the cemetery. Today had been the first time he'd allowed anyone in on his emotions, his pain, the first time he'd shared his grief. And in turn, he had shared some of his family's history with her. It was history he hadn't shared with any other woman but Kalyn. The difference in how the two women had received the information had been as different as day and night.

Kalyn hadn't wanted to hear about it. Said he should forget the past and move on. She was adamant about never leaving Hollywood to return here to live. She never even visited during the three years they'd been married. How she had hated a place she'd never seen went beyond him. And she had told him that if his parents died and he inherited the place, he should sell it. She'd listed all the things they could buy with the money.

On the other hand, Bailey had listened to his family's history today and seemed to understand and appreciate everything he'd told her. She had even thanked him for sharing it with her.

He hadn't been able to verbalize his own appreciation so he'd expressed it another way. As soon as they returned to his ranch, he had whisked her into his arms, carried her up the stairs and made love to her in a way he'd never made love to any other woman.

Walker released his hold on Bailey now to ease out of bed and cross the room. He stared into the fire as if the heat actually flickered in his soul. Today, while making love to Bailey, he kept telling himself that it was only lust that made him want her so much. That it was appreciation that drove him. He refused to consider anything else. Anything more. And yet now he was fighting to maintain his resolve where she was concerned.

He didn't want or need anyone else in his life. And although he enjoyed her company now, he preferred solitude. Once she was gone, everything in his life would get back to normal. And she *would* leave, he didn't doubt that. She loved Westmoreland Country as much as he loved Hemlock Row.

He inhaled deeply, wanting to take in the smell of wood and smoke. Instead, he was filled with Bailey's scent. "Damn it, I don't want this," he uttered softly with a growl. "And I don't need her. I don't need anyone."

He released a deep breath, wondering whom he was trying to convince.

He knew the answer to that. He had to convince himself or else he'd end up making the mistake of the century, and one mistake with a woman was enough.

When Bailey had noticed Kalyn wasn't buried there, for a second he'd been tempted to confide in her. To tell her the whole sordid story about his wife and her betrayal. But he couldn't. The only living person who knew the whole story was Garth, and that was the way Walker would keep it. He could never open himself up to someone else—definitely not another woman.

He heard Bailey stirring in bed and his body responded, as usual. He wondered how long this erotic craving for her would last. He had a feeling he would have an addiction long after she was gone. But while she was here he would enjoy her and store up the memories.

"Walker?"

He turned and looked toward the bed. "I'm over here."

"I want you here."

His thoughts were pensive. He wanted to be where she was, as well. He crossed the room and eased back into bed, drawing her into his arms. They only had a few more days together and then she would be gone. She would return to Westmoreland Country without looking back. In the meantime, he would make sure the days they had together were days he could cherish forever.

Fifteen

"I don't believe it," Charm Outlaw said, caught up in a moment of awe as she stared at Bailey. "We do favor. I didn't believe Garth and Walker, but now I do." She gave Bailey a hug. "Welcome to Fairbanks, cousin."

Bailey couldn't help but smile, deciding she liked Charm right away. Everyone had been right—they did look alike. Charm's five brothers also favored their Westmoreland cousins. "Thanks for the invite. I hadn't expected all of this."

"All of this" was the dinner party Charm had planned. Walker had flown them to Fairbanks and Garth had sent a limo to pick them up from the airport. The limo had taken a route through the city's downtown. Even though a thick blanket of snow covered the grounds, Bailey thought downtown Fairbanks was almost as captivating as downtown Denver.

Walker had given her a bit of Fairbanks's history, telling her that it was a diverse city thanks to the army base there. A lot of ex-military personnel decided they liked the area and remained after their tour of duty ended. He also told her Alaska had the highest ratio of men to women than anywhere else in the United States. Online dating was popular here and a lot of the men actually solicited mail-order brides.

After resting up at the hotel for a couple of hours, another limo had arrived to deliver them to the Outlaw Estates. Bailey couldn't help but chuckle when she remembered the marker at the entrance of the huge gated residence. It said, "Unless you're an outlaw, stay out. Josey Wales welcomed." Walker had told her the sign had been Maverick Westmoreland's idea. He was a huge fan of Clint Eastwood. The Outlaw mansion sat on over fifty acres of land.

Already Bailey had met Charm and Garth's brothers—Jess, Sloan, Cash and Maverick. In addition to their resemblance to the Westmorelands, they carried themselves like Westmorelands, as well. All five were single and, according to Charm, the thought of getting married made her brothers break out in hives. Jess, an attorney, seemed like the least rowdy of the four, and she wasn't surprised that he had announced his candidacy for senator of Alaska. He indicated he knew of Senator Reggie Westmoreland and although they hadn't met yet, Jess had been surprised to discover they were related. He looked forward to meeting Reggie personally. He'd been following Reggie's political career for a number of years and admired how he carried himself in Washington. He also knew of Chloe's father, Senator Jamison Burton, and hoped as many others did that he would consider running for president one day.

"Every Outlaw is here and accounted for except Dad. He's not dealing with all this very well and decided to make himself scarce tonight."

Garth cleared his throat, making it apparent that he felt

Charm had said too much. Bailey hadn't been bothered by Charm's words since on the flight over Walker had prepared her for the fact that Bart Outlaw still hadn't come around. For the life of her she couldn't understand what the big deal was. Why did Bart Outlaw refuse to acknowledge or accept that his father had been adopted?

Walker had also shared that Garth, his brothers and Charm all had different mothers but the brothers had been adopted by Bart before their second birthdays. Charm hadn't joined the group until she was in her teens. Her mother had sent her to Bart after Charm became too unruly. It sounded as if Bailey and Charm had a lot in common, although Dillon never entertained the thought of sending her anywhere.

One thing Bailey noted was that Walker never left her side. Not that it bothered her, but his solicitous manner made it obvious the two of them were more than friends. Every so often he would ask if she was okay. He'd told her before they'd arrived that if the Outlaws got too overbearing at any time, she and Walker would return to the hotel.

She saw a different Walker around the Outlaws. She knew he and Garth were best friends but it was obvious he had a close relationship with the others, as well. This Walker was more outgoing and not as reserved. But then he'd acted the same way around her brothers and cousins once he'd gotten to know them.

"How long are you staying in Fairbanks, Bailey?" Charm asked her. "I'm hoping you'll be here for a few days so we can get some shopping in."

Before she could answer, Walker spoke up. "Sorry to disappoint you, Charm, but Bailey's returning to Denver on Monday."

"Oh," Charm said, clearly disappointed.

Bailey didn't say anything, merely took a sip of her wine. It sounded as if Walker was counting the days.

"Well, I guess I'll have to make sure I'm included in that trip to Denver with my brothers later this month."

"Then, you'll be in luck because the women who married into the family, as well as me and my sister Megan, all love to shop," Bailey said, trying to put Walker's words to the back of her mind.

Charm's face broke into an elated grin.

Garth shook his head. "Shopping should be Charm's middle name." He checked his watch. "I hate to break up this conversation, but I think dinner is ready to be served."

Charm hooked Bailey's arm in hers as they headed toward the dining room and whispered, "So tell me, Bailey. Are there any real cute single guys in Denver?"

Walker sat with a tight jaw while he listened to Garth give his father hell. Deservedly so. Although Bart had finally shown up for dinner, he'd practically ignored Bailey. It had been obvious from his expression when he'd walked into the dining room and saw Bailey sitting beside Charm that he'd done a double take. He'd definitely noticed the resemblance between the two women. Yet that seemed to spike his resentment. So, like Garth and his brothers, Walker couldn't help wondering why Bart was so dead set against claiming the Westmorelands as kin. It seemed Garth was determined to find out.

After dinner, even before dessert could be served, Garth had encouraged Charm to show Bailey around while he and his brothers had quickly ushered their father upstairs. Garth had invited Walker to sit in on the proceedings.

"You were outright rude to Bailey, Dad."

Bart frowned. "I didn't invite her here."

"No, we did. And with good reason. She's our cousin."

"No, she's not. We are Outlaws, not Westmorelands."

"You're not blind, Dad. You saw the resemblance between Charm and Bailey with your own eyes. Bailey even remarked on how much you favor her father and uncle."

"That means nothing to me," Bart said stubbornly.

Garth drew in a deep breath, and Walker knew his best friend well enough to know he was getting fed up with his father's refusal to accept the obvious. "Why? Why are you so hostile to the idea that your father was adopted? That does not mean he wasn't an Outlaw. All it means is that he had other family—his biological family—that we can get to know. Why do you want to deprive us of that?"

A brooding Bart was silent as he glanced around the room at his sons and at Walker. It was Walker who received the most intense glare. "You were to take care of this, Walker. Things should not have gotten this far. You were to find a way to discredit them."

"That's enough, Dad! How could you even ask something like that of Walker?" Garth asked angrily.

Instead of answering, Bart jerked to his feet and stormed out of the room.

His sons watched his departure with a mixture of anger and confusion on their faces.

"What the hell is wrong with him?" Jess asked the others.

Garth shook his head sadly. "I honestly don't know. You weren't there that day Hugh first told us about the Westmorelands. Dad was adamant that we not claim them as relatives no matter what. When he found out I sent Walker anyway, he was furious."

Sloan shook his head. "There has to be a reason he is handling things this way."

"I agree," Maverick said, standing. "Something isn't right here."

"I agree with Maverick," Walker said. There was something about Bart's refusal to accept that his father was adopted that didn't make sense. "There has to be a reason

Bart is in denial. He might have his ways, but I've never figured him to be an irrational man."

"I agree," Cash said, shaking his head. "And he actually told you to find a way to discredit the Westmorelands?"

Walker nodded slowly. "You heard him for yourself."

"Damn," Sloan said, refilling his glass with his favorite after dinner drink. "I agree with Maverick and Walker. Something isn't right. Since Dad won't level with us and tell us what's going on, I suggest we hire someone to find out."

Cash glanced over at his brother, frowning. "Find out what?"

"Hell, I don't know" was Sloan's frustrated reply.

The room got quiet until Walker said, "Have any of you considered the possibility that there's something that went on years ago within the Outlaw family that you don't know about? Something that makes Bart feel he has to maintain that his father was the blood son of an Outlaw?"

Garth sat down with his drink. "I have to admit that thought has occurred to me."

"In that case," Jess said, "we need to find out what."

"You worried it might cause a scandal that will affect your campaign?" Sloan asked his brother.

"I have no idea," Jess said soberly. "But if there's something I need to worry about, then I want to find out before the media does."

Garth nodded. "Then, we're all in agreement. We look into things further."

Everyone in the room nodded.

"I'm sorry about my father's behavior at dinner, Bailey. I honestly don't know what has gotten into him," Charm said apologetically as she led Bailey back to the center of the house.

"No apology needed," Bailey said. "I was anticipating

such an attitude. Walker prepared me on the flight here from Kodiak. He said Bart might not be friendly to me."

"Um," Charm said, smiling. "Speaking of Walker. The two of you look good together. I'm glad he's finally gotten over his wife."

Bailey drew in a deep breath, not sure that was the case. It was quite obvious to her that he was still grieving the loss of his wife and son. And because of the magnitude of that grief, he refused to open up his heart to anyone else. "Looks can be deceiving, Charm."

She raised a brow. "Does that mean you're actually leaving to return to Denver on Monday?"

"No reason for me to stay. Like I said, looks can be deceiving."

Charm lifted her chin. "In this case, I think not. I've noticed the way Walker looks at you. He looks at you—"

Probably like a horny man, Bailey thought silently. There was no need to explain to Charm that the only thing between her and Walker was their enjoyment of sex with each other.

At that moment, Bailey's cell phone went off. At any other time she would have ignored it, wishing she'd remembered to turn off the ringer, but not this time. This particular ringtone indicated the call was from her cousin Bane.

"Forgive my rudeness," Bailey said to Charm as she quickly got the phone out of her purse, clicked it on and said to the caller, "Hold on a minute."

She then looked at Charm. "Sorry, but I need to take this call. It's my cousin Bane. He's a navy SEAL somewhere on assignment, and there's no telling when he'll have a chance to call me again."

"I understand. And if you need to talk privately you can use any of the rooms off the hall here. I'll be waiting for you downstairs in the main room."

Bailey gave Charm an appreciative smile. "Thanks." She quickly stepped inside one of the rooms and turned on the lights. "Bane? What's going on? Where are you?"

"Can't say. And I can't talk long. But I'm going to need your help."

"My help? For what?"

"I need to find Crystal."

Bailey frowned thoughtfully. "Bane, you know what Dillon asked you to do."

"Yes, Bay. Dil asked that I grow up and accept responsibility for my actions, to make something of myself before thinking about reclaiming Crystal. I promised him that I would and I have. Enough time has passed and I don't intend to wait any longer. In a couple of weeks I'll be on an extended military leave."

"An extended leave? Bane, are you okay?"

"I'll be better after I find Crystal, and I need your help, Bay."

Everyone had left the family room to return to the dining room for dessert except for Garth and Walker. Garth refilled Walker's glass with Scotch before proceeding to fill his own.

"So," Garth said, after taking a sip. "Do you think there's something Dad's not telling us?"

Walker, with his legs stretched out in front of him, sat back on the sofa and looked at Garth before taking a sip of his own drink. "Don't you?"

"Yes, and I'm going to hire a private detective. I don't want Hugh involved. He and Dad go way back, and there might be some loyalty there that I don't want to deal with."

"I agree. What about Regan? Isn't some member of her family a PI?"

Garth nodded, studying the drink in his glass. "Yes, her sister's husband. I met him once. He's an okay guy.

I understand he's good at what he does. I might call him tomorrow."

"I think that's a good idea."

They were silent for a spell and then Garth asked, "So what's going on with you and Bailey?"

Walker took another sip of his drink. "What makes you think something is going on?"

Garth rolled his eyes. "I can see, Walker."

Walker met his best friend's stare. "All you see is me interested in a woman who's hot. That's nice to have on those cold nights, especially for a man who's been without a female in his bed for a while. You heard her. She's leaving on Monday. Good riddance."

Bailey paused outside the closed door, not wanting to believe what Walker had just said. She'd been making her way back downstairs when she'd heard voices from one of the rooms. The voices belonged to Garth and Walker and when she'd heard her name she'd stopped.

Backing away from the door now, tears filled her eyes. She quickly turned and bumped right into Charm.

"Bailey, I was downstairs wondering if you'd gotten lost or something and—"

Charm stopped talking when she saw the tears in Bailey's eyes. "Bailey? What's wrong? Are you all right?"

Bailey swiped at her tears. "Yes, I'm fine."

Charm frowned. "No, you're not." She then glanced beyond Bailey to the closed door and the voices she heard. "What's going on? What did you hear? Did someone say something to upset you? Is Dad in that room with Garth and Walker? Did you overhear something Dad said?"

When Bailey didn't say anything, an angry Charm moved past her toward the door, ready to confront whoever was in the room about upsetting Bailey.

Bailey grabbed her hand. "No, please. Don't. It's okay."

She swiped again at her eyes. "Thanks for your family's hospitality, Charm, but I need to leave." Bailey wanted to put as much distance between her and Walker as she could. "Will you call me a cab? I need a ride to the airport."

Charm frowned. "The airport? What about Walker? What am I supposed to tell him?"

To go to hell, Bailey thought. But instead she said, "You can tell him I got a call…from a family member…and I need to get back to Denver immediately."

Charm's frown deepened. "Do you really want me to tell him that?"

"Yes."

Charm didn't say anything for a minute, then nodded. "Okay, but I won't call you a cab. I'll take you to the airport myself."

Garth stared hard at Walker. "What you just said is nothing more than bull and you know it."

Walker took another sip of his drink before quirking a brow. "Is it?"

"Yes. You've fallen in love with Bailey, Walker. Admit it."

Walker didn't say anything for a long minute. Garth knew him well. "Doesn't matter if you think it's bull or not."

"It does matter. When are you going to let go of the past, Walker? When are you going to consider that perhaps Bailey is your future?"

Walker shook his head. "No, she's not my future. She has these rules, you see. And one of them is that she will never leave Westmoreland Country. And I, on the other hand, made a deathbed promise to my father never to leave Hemlock Row again."

"But you will admit that you love her?" Garth asked.

Walker closed his eyes as if in pain. "Yes, I love her.

I love her so damn much. God knows I tried to fight it, but I couldn't. These past three weeks have been the best I've ever had. I thought I could live my life as a bitter and lonely man, but she's made me want more, Garth. She's made my house a real home. And she likes Hemlock Row."

"Then, what's the problem?"

He met Garth's inquisitive stare. "The problem is that I can't compete with her family. She needs them more than she could ever need me."

"Are you sure of that?"

"Yes. She's been homesick. I honestly didn't expect her to stay in Alaska this long. Already she's broken one of her rules."

"Maybe she had a reason to do so, Walker. Maybe you're that reason."

"I doubt it."

Garth was about to say something else when there was a knock on the door. "Come in."

Sloan entered. "Charm just left with Bailey."

Walker raised a brow. "Left? Where did they go? Don't tell me Charm talked Bailey into hitting some shopping mall tonight."

Sloan shook his head. "No. It seems Bailey got a call from some family member and had to leave. I don't know all the details but Charm is taking her to the airport. Bailey is booking a flight back to Denver. Tonight."

Sixteen

"Ma'am, please buckle your seat belt. The plane will be taking off in a minute."

Bailey nodded and did what the flight attendant instructed. She'd arrived at the Fairbanks airport with no luggage, just the clothes on her back. Charm had promised to go to the hotel and pack up her things and ship them to her. She would do the same for the clothes Bailey had left behind at Hemlock Row.

Luckily Bailey could change her ticket for a fee. And she didn't care that she had two connecting flights before she reached Denver, one in Seattle and the other in Salt Lake City. All she cared about was that in twelve hours she would be back in Westmoreland Country. She hadn't even called her family to let them know her change in plans. She would get a rental car at the airport and go straight to Gemma's house. She needed to be alone for a while before dealing with her family and their questions.

She drew in a deep breath, not wanting to think about

Walker. But all she could remember were the words he'd told Garth. So he would be glad when she was gone, would he? Well, he was getting his wish. She had been a fool to think he was worthy of her love. All he'd thought was that she was a hot body to sleep with.

But then, hadn't he told her up front all he wanted from her was a meaningless affair? Well, tonight he'd proved that what they'd shared had been as meaningless as it could get. Knowing it would take at least two hours before the plane landed in Seattle, she closed her eyes to soothe her tattered mind. At that moment she hoped she never saw Walker again.

"Damn her," Walker growled, taking his clothes out of the drawers and slinging them into the luggage that was opened on his bed. He intended to fly back to Kodiak Island tonight. There was no need to hang around. Bailey was why he'd left Hemlock Row to come here in the first place. And then what did she do? She hauled ass the first time she got a call from home.

However, now he knew that even that was a lie. Thinking she'd had a real family emergency, he'd placed a call to Dillon, who didn't know what he was talking about. As far as Dillon knew, nobody had called Bailey.

So now, on top of everything else, she had lied to him. She couldn't wait until Monday to leave? She had to leave tonight? Hell, she hadn't even taken the time to pack her clothes. What the hell was he supposed to do with them?

But what hurt more than anything was that she hadn't even had the decency to tell him goodbye. He felt like throwing something. Why did falling in love always end in heartache for him?

He continued to throw everything in his luggage when he heard a knock on the door. He hoped it wasn't Garth, trying to talk him out of leaving. There was no way he could stay. He wanted to go home to Hemlock Row, where loneliness was expected. Where he could drown his sorrows in a good stiff drink.

When the knocking continued, he moved to the door and snatched it open. Both Garth and Charm stood there. "I'm leaving tonight, Garth, and there's nothing you can say to stop me."

Garth and Charm walked past him to enter the hotel room. "I agree you should leave tonight, but not for Hemlock Row."

Walker looked at Garth. What he'd said didn't make any sense. "Then, where the hell am I supposed to go?"

"To head off Bailey. Stop her from making it to Denver."

That statement came from Charm. He glared at her. "And why on earth would I do that?"

Charm placed her hand on her hip and glared back at him. "Because you and Garth are the reason she left. I don't know what the two of you said about her while huddled in that room together tonight, but whatever you said, she overheard it and it had her in tears. I thought Dad was in there with you and figured he'd said something rude and gave him hell about it. But he said what Bailey overheard must have been a conversation between the two of you," she said, shifting her furious gaze between him and Garth.

Walker frowned. "For your information, I didn't say a damn thing that would have…"

He stopped speaking, swallowed hard and then glanced over at Garth. "Surely you don't think she heard—"

"All that crap you said?" Garth interrupted to ask, shaking his head. "I hope not. But what if she did?"

Walker rubbed a hand down his face. *Yes, what if she did?* "Damn it, I didn't mean it. In fact, later on in the conversation I admitted to falling in love with her."

"You love her?" Charm asked, smiling.

"Yes."

"Well, I doubt she heard that part. In fact, I'm one hundred percent certain she didn't. She was crying as if her heart was broken."

Walker checked his watch. "I've got to go after her."

"Yes, you do," Garth agreed. He then looked at Charm. "Do you have her flight information? I'm sure she has a connecting flight somewhere."

"She has two," Charm answered. "The first is in Seattle and then another in Salt Lake City."

Garth checked his watch. "I'll contact Regan and have her get the jet ready. If we act fast, you can get to Seattle the same time Bailey does. Maybe a few minutes before. And in case you've forgotten, Ollie is director of Seattle's Transportation Security Administration. Knowing the top dog of the TSA might prove to be helpful."

Walker nodded. He, Garth and Oliver Linton had served in the marines together and the three had remained good friends. "You're right." Walker was already moving, grabbing his coat and hat. Like Bailey, he was about to fly with just the clothes on his back.

Bailey took a sip of her coffee. She hated layovers, especially lengthy ones. She had another hour before she could board her connecting flight to Salt Lake City. And then she would have to wait two more hours before finally boarding the plane that would take her home to Denver.

Home.

Why didn't she have that excited flutter in her stomach that she usually had whenever she went on a trip and was on her way back to Denver? Why did she feel only hurt and pain? "That's easy enough to answer," she muttered to herself. "The man you love doesn't love you back. Get over it."

She drew in a deep breath, wondering if she ever would get over it. If it had been Monday and she'd been leaving

because her time in Kodiak was over, it probably would
have been different. But hearing the words Walker had
spoken to Garth had cut deep. Not just into her heart but
also into her soul. Evidently, her time at Hemlock Row had
meant more to her than it had to him. All she'd been to him
was a piece of ass during the cold nights. He'd practically
said as much to Garth.

After finishing off her coffee, she tightened her coat
around herself. For some reason she was still feeling the
harsh Alaskan temperatures. She hated admitting it, but she
missed Hemlock Row already, although she refused to miss
Walker. She wished she could think of his ranch without
thinking of him. She would miss Willie, Marcus and the
guys, as well as Ms. Albright. She would miss standing at
Walker's bedroom window every morning to stare out at
Shelikof Strait. And she would definitely miss cooking in
his kitchen. When she finally got around to designing her
own home on Bailey's Bay, she might steal a few of his
kitchen ideas. It would serve him right if she did.

"Excuse me, miss."

She glanced up into the face of an older gentleman
wearing a TSA uniform. "Yes?"

"Are you Bailey Westmoreland?"

"Yes, I'm Bailey Westmoreland." She hoped nothing
was wrong with her connecting flight. She didn't want
the man to tell her it was canceled or delayed. She was
ready to put as much distance between herself and Alaska
as she could.

He nodded. "Ms. Westmoreland, could you please come
with me?"

She stood. "Yes, but why? Is something wrong? What's
going on?" She didn't have any luggage so there was no
way they could have found anything in it. And her ticket
was legit. She had made the proper changes in Fairbanks.
As far as she was concerned she was all set.

"I'm unable to answer that. I was advised by my director to bring you to his office."

"Your director?" She swallowed. This sounded serious. She hoped she and some terrorist didn't have the same name or something. *Oh, crap.* "Look, sir," she said, following the man. "There must be some mistake."

She was about to say she'd never had done a bad thing in her life and then snapped her mouth shut. What about all those horrific things she, Bane and the twins had done while growing up? But that had been years ago. The sheriff of Denver, who was a good friend of Dillon's, had assured him that since the four of them had been juveniles their records would be wiped clean, as long as they didn't get into any trouble as adults. She couldn't speak for the twins, and Lord knew she couldn't vouch for Bane, but she could certainly speak for herself.

So she did. "Like I said, there must be a mistake. I am a law-abiding citizen. I work for a well-known magazine. I do own a gun. Several. But I don't have any of them with me."

The man stopped walking and looked over at her with a keen eye. She swallowed, wishing she hadn't said that. "I hunt," she quickly added, not wanting him to get the wrong idea. "I have all the proper permits and licenses."

He merely nodded. He then opened a door. "You can wait in here. It won't be long."

She frowned, about to tell him she didn't want to wait in there, that she was an American with rights. But she was too tired to argue. Too hurt and broken. She would wait for the director and see why she was being detained. If she needed an attorney there were a number of them in the Westmoreland family.

"Fine. I'll wait," she said, entering the room and glancing around. It was definitely warmer in here than it had been at the terminal gate. It was obvious this was some kind of meeting room, she thought, shrugging out of her coat and tossing it across the back of a chair. There were no windows, just a desk, several chairs and a garbage can. A map of Washington State was on one wall and a map of the United States on the other. There was a coffeepot on the table in the corner, and although she'd had enough coffee tonight to last her a lifetime, she crossed to the pot, hoping it was fresh.

That was when she heard the door behind her open. Good, the director had arrived and they could get down to business. The last thing she needed was to miss her connecting flight. She turned to ask the man or woman why she was here and her mouth dropped open.

The man who walked into the room was not the TSA director. It was the last person she figured she would see tonight or ever again.

"Walker!"

Seventeen

Walker entered the room and closed the door behind him. And then he locked it. Across the room stood the woman he loved more than life itself. She'd overheard things straight from his lips that had all been lies, and now he had to convince her he hadn't meant any of what he'd said.

"Hello, Bailey."

She backed up, shock written all over her face. "Walker, what are you doing here? How did you get here? *Why* are you here?"

He shoved his hands into his pockets. He heard the anger in her voice. He also heard the hurt and regretted more than ever what he'd said. "I thought we had a conversation once about you asking a lot of questions. But since I owe you answers to each and every one of them, here goes. I came here to talk to you. I got here with Garth's company jet. And I'm here because I owe you an apology."

She stiffened her spine. "You should not have bothered.

I don't think there's anything you can do or say to make me accept your apology."

He recalled when he'd said something similar to her the day she'd shown up at Hemlock Row. "But I did bother, because I know you heard what I said to Garth."

She crossed her arms over her chest. "Yes, I heard you. Pretty loud and clear. And I understood just what I was to you while I was at Hemlock Row and how you couldn't wait for me to leave."

"I didn't mean what I said."

"Sure you did. If nothing else, I've discovered you're a man who says exactly what he means."

He leaned against the wall, tilted his hat back and inhaled deeply, wishing her scent didn't get to him. And he wished she didn't look so desirable. She was still wearing the outfit she'd worn at the Outlaws'—black slacks and a bronze-colored pullover knit sweater with matching jewelry. She looked good then and she looked good now, four hours and over two thousand miles later.

But he liked Bailey best when she wasn't wearing anything at all. When she lay in his bed naked, with her breasts full and perky, the nipples wet from his tongue, and her feminine mound, hot, moist and ready for—

He sucked in a sharp breath and abruptly put an end to those thoughts. "Can we sit and talk?"

She frowned. "I honestly don't want to hear anything you have to say."

"Please. Both times when you apologized to me, I accepted your apologies."

"Good for you, but I have no intention of accepting yours."

She was being difficult, he knew that. He also knew there was only one way to handle Bailey. And that was by not letting her think she had the upper hand. "We are going to talk whether you want to listen to what I say or not. I locked that door," he said, removing his hat to place on a rack and then crossing the room to sit in one of the chairs. "And I don't intend for it to be opened until I say so. I forgot to mention that the director of the TSA here is an old marine friend of mine."

She glared at him. "You can't hold me here like some kind of hostage. I will sue you both."

"Go ahead and do that, if you desire. In the meantime you and I are staying in here until you agree to listen to what I have to say."

"I won't listen."

"I have the time to wait for you to change your mind," he said, leaning back in the chair so the front legs lifted off the floor. He closed his eyes. He heard her cross the room to the door and try it. It was locked. He didn't reopen his eyes when he heard her banging on it, nor when he heard her kick it a few times.

He knew the exact moment when a frustrated and angry Bailey crossed the room to stand in front of him. "Wake up, you bastard. Wake up and let me out of here."

He ignored her, but it wasn't easy. Especially when she began using profanity the likes of which he'd never heard before. He'd heard from one of her cousins that she used to curse like a sailor—worse than a sailor—as a teen, and Walker had even heard her utter a few choice words that day in his bedroom when he'd pissed her off. But now, tonight, she was definitely on a roll.

He would let her have her say—no matter how vulgar it was—and then he would have his. He would tell her everything. Including the fact that he loved her. He didn't expect her to love him back. It was too late for that, although he doubted it would have happened anyway. Bailey loved Westmoreland Country. She was married to it.

It seemed her filthy mouth wouldn't run out of steam anytime soon, so he decided to put an end to it. He'd gotten the picture, heard loud and clear what she thought of him. He slowly opened his eyes and stared at her. "If you recall, Bailey, I once told you that you had too delicious a mouth to fill it with nasty words. Do I need to test it to make sure it's still as delicious as the last time I tasted it?"

She threw her hair over her shoulder, fiery mad. "I'd like to see you try."

"Okay." He grabbed her around the waist and tumbled her into his lap. And then he kissed her.

She tried pushing him away, but just for a minute. Then, as if she had no control of her own tongue, it began tangling with his, sucking as hard as he was. And then suddenly, as if she realized what she was doing, she snatched her mouth away, but she didn't try getting off his lap.

"I hate you, Walker."

He nodded. "And I love you, Bailey."

She'd opened her mouth, probably to spew more filthy words, but what he'd said had her mouth snapping closed. She stared at him, not saying anything, and then she frowned. "I heard what you told Garth."

"Yes, but if you had hung around, you would have heard him say that I was talking bull because he knew how I felt about you. He's been my friend long enough to know. And then I admitted to having fallen in love with you."

She stared at him, studying his face. How long would it be before she said something? Finally she did. "You can't love me."

He shifted her in his lap, both to keep her there but also to bring some relief to the erection pressing painfully against his zipper. "And why can't I love you?"

"Because you're still in love with your wife. You've been grieving for her for ten years and you want me to believe I came along and changed that in less than a month?"

He knew he had to tell her the truth. All of it. He had to tell her what only he and Garth knew. Doing so would bring back memories. Painful memories. But he loved her. And he owed her the truth.

"Yes, I guess that would be hard to believe if I had been grieving for Kalyn for ten years. But I stopped loving my wife months before she died. I stopped loving her when I found out she was having an affair with another man."

Bailey swallowed. Of all the things she'd expected him to say, that wasn't it. "Your wife was unfaithful?" she asked, making sure she'd heard him correctly.

"Yes, among a number of other things."

She lifted a brow. "What other things?"

Walker drew in a deep breath before lifting her from his lap to place her in the chair beside him. He paced the room a few times before finally leaning against the wall.

"I need to start at the beginning," he said in a low, husky tone. But she'd been around Walker enough to detect the deep pain in his voice. "I was in the marines, stationed at Camp Pendleton. A few of the guys and I took a holiday to LA, preferring to tour the countryside. We came across a film crew making a movie. Intrigued, we stopped and, believe it or not, they asked us to be extras."

He paused before continuing, "One of the women who had a small role caught my eye and I caught hers."

"Kalyn?"

He looked over at Bailey. "Yes. That night she and I met at a restaurant and she told me her dream was to become an actress, that she was born in Los Angeles and loved the area. We slept together that night and a few times after that. I was smitten, but I thought that would be the end of it. It was only a few months before my time in the marines ended and I was looking forward to heading home. Both Garth and I were."

He paused. "Dad had written and I knew the ranch was

becoming a handful. He couldn't wait for me to come home to help. I told him I would. Practically promised."

He moved away from the wall to sit in the chair beside her. "I basically broke that promise. A few days before I was supposed to leave I got a call. Someone had viewed a clip of me as an extra and liked what they saw. They didn't know whether I could act or not but thought I had what they termed 'Hollywood looks.' They called me to try out for a part in some movie. I didn't get the part but they asked me to hang around for a week or two, certain they could find me work."

He leaned back in the chair as he continued. "Kalyn said she was happy for me. She also told me she thought she was pregnant. I never questioned her about it, although Garth suggested I should. I didn't listen to him. Nor did I listen when he tried to get me to leave California and return home, reminding me that my dad needed me. All I could think about was that Kalyn might be pregnant and I should do the honorable thing and marry her. So I did."

"Was she pregnant?" Bailey asked curiously.

"No. She said it was a false alarm, but I was determined to make my marriage work regardless. I loved her. I suggested we leave LA and move to Kodiak Island, but she wouldn't hear of it. She would cry every time I brought up the subject. She told me she hated a place she'd never seen and she never wanted to go there."

Bailey couldn't imagine anyone not liking Hemlock Row, especially before they'd seen it.

"I talked to my dad and he told me to stay with my wife and make my marriage work and that he would hire a couple more men to help out around the ranch," Walker continued. "Although he didn't say it, I knew he was disappointed that I wasn't coming home with my wife.

"A few months later I got the chance at a big role and my career took off from there. Kalyn was happy. She loved being in the spotlight as my wife. But I missed home and when I told her I'd made up my mind to leave and return to Alaska, she told me she was pregnant."

Bailey lifted a brow. "Was she really pregnant this time?" she asked in a skeptical voice. It sounded to her as though Kalyn's claim that first time had been a trick just to get Walker to marry her.

"Yes, she was this time. I went with her to the doctor to confirm it. Things got better between us. I fell in love with Connor the moment I heard his heartbeat. And months later, when I felt him move in Kalyn's stomach, I think my son and I connected in an unbreakable bond. I couldn't wait for him to be born. When he finally arrived I thought he was perfect. I couldn't wait to take him home for my parents to meet their grandson."

"You took him home to Hemlock Row?"

"Yes, but not until he was almost a year old. Kalyn refused to let me take him any sooner than that. Connor loved it there with his grandparents. I took him everywhere and showed him everything. Kalyn didn't go with us and told me I could only be gone with Connor for a week. I was upset about it but was grateful that my parents got to meet Connor and he got to meet them. A few months after I returned to LA I learned my mom was sick and the doctors couldn't figure out why. I went home a few times and each time I did, Kalyn gave me hell."

Bailey frowned. "She didn't want you to go home to check on your sick mother?" she asked, appalled.

"No, she didn't. Things got pretty bad between us, although we worked hard to pretend otherwise. In public we were the perfect, happily married Hollywood couple, but behind closed doors it was a different story."

He stood again to pace and when he came to a stop in front of where she sat, her heart almost stopped. The look on his face was full of hurt and anguish. "Then one day

I came home and she dropped a bombshell. She told me that for the past year and a half she'd been having an affair with a married man and he'd finally decided to leave his wife for her."

He drew in a deep breath and closed his eyes. When he reopened them, he said, "And she also wanted me to know that Connor was not my son."

"No!"

The pain of his words hit Bailey like a ton of bricks, so she could imagine how Kalyn's words must have hit him. The son he'd fallen in love with was not his biological son. She couldn't imagine the pain that must have caused him.

"I told her I didn't care if Connor was my biological son or not. He was the son of my heart and that's all that mattered. I loved him. She only laughed and called me a fool for loving a child that wasn't mine."

There were a lot of words Bailey could think of to describe Walker's deceased wife, and none of them were nice. "What happened after that? Did she move out?"

"No. Her lover must have changed his mind about leaving his wife. When I came home one evening after picking up Connor from day care, she ignored both of us and stayed in her room. I knew something was wrong, I just didn't know what.

"A few days later, on the set, I got a call letting me know there'd been an accident. It seemed Kalyn lost control of the car in the rain. She was killed immediately but Connor fought for his life. I rushed to the hospital in time to give my son blood. He'd lost a lot of it."

"So he *was* your biological son!"

"Yes, Connor was my biological son. She had intentionally lied to me, or she might have been sleeping with both me and her lover and honestly didn't know which one of us was Connor's father. Connor lasted another day and then I lost him. I lost my son."

A tear slipped from Bailey's eye, and when more tears began to fall, she swiped at them. He hadn't deserved what his wife put him through. No man would have deserved that.

"But that wasn't the worst of it," she heard him say as she continued swiping at her tears.

"It wasn't?" She couldn't imagine anything worse than that.

"No. After the funeral, I came home and found a letter Kalyn had written to me. She left it in a place where she figured I would find it."

Bailey's brows bunched. "A letter."

He nodded. "Yes. She wanted me to know the car wreck wasn't an accident. It was intentional."

Bailey's heart stopped. "Are you saying that…" She couldn't finish the question.

"Yes," he said softly with even deeper pain in his voice. "Kalyn committed suicide. Being rejected by her lover was too much for her and she couldn't live another day. She wanted to take her lover's son with her."

She saw the tears misting his eyes. No wonder his son was buried in his family's cemetery but his son's mother was not. The awful things she'd done, and the fact that she'd hated Hemlock Row sight unseen.

"Nobody knows about that letter but Garth. He was with me when I found it. We decided turning it over to the authorities would serve no purpose. It would be better to let everyone continue to believe what happened had been an accident."

Bailey nodded. "Did you ever find out the identity of Kalyn's lover?"

"No, although I had my suspicions. I never knew for certain." He paused. "I told myself that I would never love or trust another woman. And I hadn't. Until you. I didn't want to fall in love with you, Bailey. God knows I fought it tooth and nail. But I couldn't stop what was meant to be. Yes, I said what I said to Garth, but I was in denial, refusing to accept what I knew in my heart was true. I'm sorry for the words I said. But the truth is that I do love you. I love you more than I've ever loved any other woman."

She eased out of the chair and went to him, pulled him to her and held him. He had been through so much. He had lost so much. He had experienced the worst betrayal a man could suffer. Not only had Kalyn intentionally taken her life, she had taken the life of an innocent child.

Walker pulled back and looked at her. "I know there can never be anything between us. You don't love me and I understand that. You're in love with your land, and I accept that, too, because I'm in love with mine. I made Dad another promise, this one I intend to keep. I'll never leave Hemlock Row again."

She stared deep into the dark eyes that had always mesmerized her. "You just said you loved me, yet you're willing to let me go back to Westmoreland Country?"

"Yes, because that's your real love. I know your rules, Bailey."

A smile touched her lips. "And I'm breaking the one I thought I would never break."

He looked at her questionably. "What are you saying?"

She wrapped her arms around his neck. "I'm saying that I love you, too. I realized I loved you weeks ago. I think that's why I came to Kodiak to personally apologize. I missed you, although I would never have admitted that to myself or to you. I do love you, Walker, and more than anything I want to make a home with you at Hemlock Row."

"B-but what about Westmoreland Country?"

She chuckled. "I love my home, but Gemma and Megan were right. Home is where the heart is, and my heart is with you."

He studied her features intently. "Are you sure?"

She chuckled again. "I am positive. I'm officially breaking Bailey's Rules."

And then she slanted her mouth over his, knowing their lives together were just beginning.

A few days later, Walker eased out of the bed. Bailey grabbed his thigh. "And where do you think you're going?"

He smiled. "To stoke the fire. I'll be back."

"Holding you to it, Alaskan."

Walker chuckled. He couldn't believe how great his life was going. Everyone was happy that he'd gotten everything straightened out with Bailey and she had decided to stay. Next week was Thanksgiving and they would leave Kodiak Island to spend the holiday with her family in Westmoreland Country.

After stoking the fire and before he returned to bed, he went to the drawer and retrieved the package he'd put there earlier that day. Grabbing the box, he went back to the bed.

"Bailey?" She opened her eyes to look at him. "Yes?"

"Will you marry me?"

When she saw the box he held she almost knocked him over struggling to sit up. "You're proposing to me?"

He smiled. "Yes."

"B-but I'm in bed, naked and—"

"Just made love to me. I can't think of any other way to complete things. I want you to know it's never been just sex with us…although I think the sex is off the charts."

She grinned. "So do I."

He opened the box and she gasped at the ring shining back at her in the firelight. "It's beautiful, Walker."

"As beautiful as my future wife," he said, sliding the ring on her finger. Halfway there, he stopped and eyed her expectantly. "You didn't say yes."

"Yes!"

He slid the ring the rest of the way and then pulled her

into his arms. "My parents would have loved you," he whispered against her ear.

"And I would have loved them, too. And I would have loved Connor."

He pulled back. "He would have loved you." Walker held her hand up and looked at it. "I thought the timing was right since I'll be taking you home next week. I don't want your family to think I'm taking advantage of you. When they see that ring they will know. I love you and intend to make you my wife. Just set the date. But don't make me wait too long."

"I won't."

He brushed his thumb across her cheek. "Thanks for believing I was worthy of breaking your rules, Bailey."

"And thanks for believing I am worthy of your love and trust, Walker."

Their mouths touched, and she knew tonight was the beginning of how things would be for the rest of their lives.

Epilogue

Thanksgiving Day

Bailey looked around the huge table. This was the first time that every one of her brothers, sisters and cousins—the Denver Westmorelands—had managed to come home for Thanksgiving. Even Bane was here. The family had definitely multiplied with the addition of wives, husbands and children. She and Walker would tie the knot here in Westmoreland Country on Valentine's Day.

Everyone was glad to see Bane. It had been years since he'd been home for Thanksgiving. In fact, they hadn't seen him since that time he'd shown up unannounced at Blue Ridge Land Management, surprising Stern and Adrian.

Bailey wondered if she was the only one who noticed he seemed pensive and preoccupied. And not for the first time she wondered if something had happened on his last covert operation that he wasn't sharing with them.

"You okay, baby?" Walker leaned over to ask her.

She smiled at him. "Yes, I'm fine. You love me and I love you, so I couldn't be better."

The announcement that she was marrying and leaving Westmoreland Country had everyone shocked. But all they had to do was look at her and Walker to see how happy they were together.

Thanks to Lucia and Chloe, Bailey would still work for *Simply Irresistible*, working remotely from Kodiak Island. She'd been doing it for a while now and so far things were working out fine.

The Outlaws, all six of them, had come to visit, and just like Bailey had known, everyone had gotten along beautifully. They were invited to the Denver Westmorelands' annual foundation banquet and said they would return in December to attend. That way they would get to meet their Westmoreland cousins from Atlanta, Montana, North Carolina and Texas. Word was that Bart still hadn't come around. According to Walker, Garth intended to find out why his father was being so difficult.

Since Gemma, Callum and their kids were in town, Bailey and Walker were staying at the bed-and-breakfast inn Jason's wife, Bella, owned. It was perfect, and she and Walker had the entire place to themselves.

Bailey figured she would eventually get around to building her own place so she and Walker could have somewhere private whenever they came to visit, but she wasn't in any hurry.

After clinking on his glass to get everyone's attention, Dillon stood. "It's been years since we've had everyone together on Thanksgiving, and I'm thankful that this year Gemma and Bane were able to come home to join us. And I'm grateful for all the additions to our family, especially one in particular," he said, looking over at Walker and smiling.

"I think Mom, Dad, Uncle Thomas and Aunt Susan

would be proud of what we've become and that we're still a family."

Bailey wiped a tear from her eye. Yes, they were still a family and always would be. She reached under the table for Walker's hand. She had everything she could possibly want and more.

"You wanted to see me, Dil?" Bane asked, walking into Dillon's home office. Out the window was a beautiful view of Gemma Lake.

Dillon glanced up as his brother entered. Bane appeared taller, looked harder, more mature than he'd seemed the last time he'd been home. "Yes, come on in, Bane."

Dinner had ended a few hours ago and after a game of snow volleyball the ladies had gathered in the sitting room to watch a holiday movie with the kids, and the men had gathered upstairs for a card game. "I want to know how you're doing," Dillon said, studying his baby brother.

"Fine, although my last assignment took a toll on me. I lost a good friend."

Dillon shook his head sadly. "I'm sorry to hear that."

"Me, too. Laramie Tucker was a good guy. The best. We went through the academy together."

Dillon knew not to ask what happened. Bane had explained a while back that all his assignments were confidential. "Is that why you're taking a military leave?"

Bane eased down in the chair across from Dillon's desk. "No. It's time I find Crystal. If nothing else, Tuck's death taught me how fragile life is. You can be here today and gone tomorrow."

Dillon came around and sat on the edge of his desk to face his brother. "Not sure if you knew it, but Carl Newsome passed away a few years ago."

Bane shook his head. "No, I didn't know."

"So you haven't seen Crystal since the Newsomes sent her away?"

"No. You were right. I didn't have anything to offer her at the time. I was a hothead and Trouble was my middle name. She deserved better, and I was willing to make something of myself to give her better."

Dillon nodded. "It's been years, Bane. The last time I talked to Emily Newsome was when I heard Carl had died. I called to offer my condolences. I asked about Crystal and Emily said Crystal was doing fine. She was working on her master's degree at Harvard with plans to get a doctorate."

Bane didn't say anything as he listened to what Dillon was saying. "That doesn't surprise me. Crystal was always smart in school."

Dillon stared at his brother, wondering how Bane had figured that out when most of the time he and Crystal were playing hooky. "I don't want to upset you, Bane. But you don't know what Crystal's feelings are for you. The two of you were teens back then. First love doesn't always mean last love. Although you might still love her, for all you know, she might have moved on. Have you ever considered the possibility that she might be involved with someone else?"

Bane leaned back in his chair. "I don't believe that. Crystal and I had an understanding. We have an unbreakable bond."

"But that was years ago. You just said you haven't seen her since that day Carl sent her away. For all you know, she could be married by now."

Bane shook his head. "Crystal wouldn't marry anyone else."

Dillon lifted a brow. "And how can you be so sure of that?"

Bane held his brother's stare. "Because she's already married, Dil. Crystal is married to me, and I think it's time to go claim my wife."

* * * * *

Don't miss the final Westmoreland hero!
BANE
Available December 2015,
only from New York Times *bestselling author*
Brenda Jackson

If you loved Bailey's story,
pick up the very first Westmoreland novels,
now available in a convenient box set!

Volume One
Brenda Jackson's THE WESTMORELANDS
Books One to Five

DELANEY'S DESERT SHEIKH
A LITTLE DARE
THORN'S CHALLENGE
STONE COLD SURRENDER
RIDING THE STORM

"God, woman, you do turn me inside out. You always have."

"I'm sorry. I didn't mean to send mixed signals—" Alaina stammered.

He traced her lips. "You turning me inside out has always been a good thing. We may have argued about a lot of issues, but we always connected on a physical level. I meant it when I said I wouldn't pressure you to take this faster than you're ready."

"That's good to know. The attraction between us is…problematic."

"We were married for years. Even if your brain doesn't remember, I believe that on some level your body does. We'll just take things slow until your mind catches up."

He offered her another piece of dark chocolate. Her fingertips gingerly brushed his as she took it. Another confusing jolt of desire burst through her.

"What if my mind doesn't ever catch up?"

A devilish smile spread across his lips. "Then we'll start over."

* * *

A Christmas Baby Surprise
is part of Mills & Boons Desire's No 1 bestselling series Billionaires and Babies: Powerful men… wrapped around their babies' little fingers

A CHRISTMAS BABY SURPRISE

BY
CATHERINE MANN

Published in Great Britain 2015
by Mills & Boon, an imprint of Harlequin (UK) Limited,
Eton House, 18-24 Paradise Road, Richmond, Surrey, TW9 1SR

© 2015 by Catherine Mann

ISBN: 978-0-263-25284-2

51-1115

Harlequin (UK) Limited's policy is to use papers that are natural, renewable and recyclable products and made from wood grown in sustainable forests. The logging and manufacturing processes conform to the legal environmental regulations of the country of origin.

Printed and bound in Spain
by CPI, Barcelona

USA TODAY bestselling author **Catherine Mann** lives on a sunny Florida beach with her flyboy husband and their four children. With more than forty books in print in over twenty countries, she has also celebrated wins for both a RITA® Award and a Booksellers' Best Award. Catherine enjoys chatting with readers online—thanks to the wonders of the internet, which allows her to network with her laptop by the water! Contact Catherine through her website, www.catherinemann.com, find her on Facebook and Twitter (@CatherineMann1) or reach her by snail mail at PO Box 6065, Navarre, FL 32566 USA.

To my awesome editor Stacy Boyd!

One

Alaina Rutger was living her childhood dream—a family of her own. Her charismatic husband was driving her home from the hospital with their infant son strapped into a car seat. She had the perfect life.

If only she could remember the man who'd put the four-carat diamond wedding ring on her finger.

A man who called himself Porter Rutger. Husband. Father of her child. And a man who'd been wiped from her memory along with the past five years of her life.

She tore her eyes away from his broad shoulders and coal-dark hair as she sat in back with their baby. Her baby. Alaina tucked the monogrammed red blanket over the infant as he slept, one foot in a booty, the other in a cast that had begun the repair on his clubfoot.

Another person she didn't remember. Another heart-break in her upside-down world. A week ago, she'd woken in the hospital with no memory of the man sitting by her bedside or of the blue bundle in the bassinet.

Waking up from a coma had felt a lot like coming to after the worst hangover ever, her head throbbing so badly she could barely move. But a quick look around showed her a hospital room rather than a bedroom.

And a hot man sleeping in the chair, his dark hair rumpled. His black pants and white button-down wrinkled.

Her own Doctor McDreamy?

"Hello," she'd croaked out, her throat raw for a sip of water.

McDreamy bolted awake quickly. "Alaina?" He blinked, scrubbed his hand across his eyes in disbelief, then shot to his feet. "Oh, God, you're awake. I need to get the nurse."

"Water," she rasped out. "Please, a drink."

He thumbed the nurses' call button. "I don't know what the doctors will want. Maybe ice chips. Your IV has been feeding you. Soon, though, I promise, whatever you want, soon."

The nurses? Doctors? He wasn't Doc McDreamy? Then ... "Who are you?"

He looked up from the control panel of buttons slowly, his eyes wide with disbelief. "Who am I?"

She pressed her fingertips to her monster headache. "I'm sorry, but I feel like hell. What happened?"

"Alaina..." He sank slowly into the chair, his voice measured, guarded. "We were in a car accident."

"We?" She knew him?

"Yes," he said, leaning closer to cover her hand carefully. "Alaina, my name's Porter and I'm your husband."

The shock of that revelation still echoed through her.

Once the nurse and doctor had checked her over Porter had further explained they'd been in a car wreck a month prior, after picking up little Thomas from the adoption agency. Her husband… Porter. Porter Rutger. God, she still struggled to remember his name. Porter told her the baby had a birth defect and had spent the past month going through surgeries while she'd been in a coma from the accident.

Too soon, before she felt ready to handle this life she'd landed in, it was time to leave the hospital. She'd been told many first moms felt that way.

But not all new mothers had amnesia.

Her throat burned with bile and fears that hadn't abated since she'd woken from the coma a week ago thinking it was November, only to find it was December.

Five years later.

Five years of memories simply gone, pushed out of her head in the course of a month. Most devastating, she'd lost the four and a half years Porter had been in her life.

How was it that four weeks asleep could steal so much of her life? That coma had left her mind missing a substantial chunk of memories and yet her body felt 100 percent normal. She'd even been attracted to her stranger husband, so attracted that the aches and lethargy left over from her coma hadn't dulled the shiver of awareness she'd felt at the brush of his hands against her as he helped her from the hospital bed and into the car.

She swallowed hard and turned to look out the window at the rolling waves as the Mercedes traveled the Florida coastal road toward what Porter had told her was their beach mansion. They also owned a home in Talla-hassee but they'd been closer to the beach home when picking up the baby, then having the wreck. Traveling with their infant son so fresh from surgery and her so recently out of a coma hadn't seemed wise. The doctors had advised they stay close for the short term at least.

Porter had quickly suggested they stay at their nearby vacation home. Apparently her tall, dark and studly hus-band was wealthier than Midas, thanks to his construc-tion empire that won major contracts to build corporate structures around the country. They had no financial worries as she recovered, he'd told her. Another reason to be grateful.

But instead of gratitude, she could only feel fear at the imbalance of power between her and this man who was her husband. She was adrift with only the facts he told her about her past. No family since her par-ents were dead. No friends, other than people she ap-parently hadn't seen in five years, since her breakup from an abusive boyfriend. She'd cut herself off from everyone then.

Still, she was missing the months following that breakup, the months leading up to her meeting Porter. Falling in love with him. Marrying him. He said after they married, they'd moved to southeastern Florida, away from her hometown in North Carolina. She be-lieved what he said, but wondered what parts he might not have mentioned. Men could be so brief in their ex-planations, leaving out details or emotional components a woman would find crucial.

Porter glanced in the rearview mirror, his brown eyes as dark as undiluted coffee full of caffeinated energy.

Jolt.

"Alaina, is everything all right?" he said, his Southern drawl muted by some experience in another region.

Something else she didn't know about him unless he told her.

What kind of answer did he expect from her? More of the same dodgy responses they'd given each other over the past week since she woke up? Guarded words spoken in front of doctors or said out of fear her fragile world might shatter into a somnolent fog again?

Each mile closer to a vacation home she couldn't recall stretched the tension inside her tighter until she snapped softly, "Did the doctor give you any more insight as to why can't I remember the past five years? Nearly a quarter of my life is just gone."

"The doctor spoke with you. He has an obligation to be honest with you. You're his patient." The man in the front seat who called himself her husband was unfailingly polite but lacked the kind of warmth that Alaina would have envisioned in a man she'd married.

Her husband.

What had made her choose this coolly controlled male for a mate? Another question she couldn't begin to answer. In spite of the spark that seemed to arc between them amidst the questions.

"I haven't forgotten that conversation. It was more of a rhetorical question because there are so many other things I don't understand." She glanced down at her sleeping son in his impossibly cute elf pajamas. "Such as, how could anyone forget a child this precious?"

Her heart swelled to look at Thomas, his tiny nose and Cupid's-bow mouth calling to her every maternal instinct. She'd always wanted children, dreamed of having a big family after growing up an only child. If she and Porter had been married for almost four years, what had made them wait to start their family?

"You'd only known him for a couple of hours before the accident." Porter turned onto a secluded drive where mammoth houses were hidden by manicured privacy hedges on one side, although she knew the other side opened to the water.

"The length of time shouldn't matter. He's a child, my child—" she paused, brushing her fingers across the top of an impossibly small and soft hand "—our child. That's life changing. A minute. An hour. A couple of hours. That should be burned in here." She tapped the front of her head.

"Even if your marriage wasn't?" he asked wryly.

Contrition nipped. This had to be tough for him, too. "I'm sorry. This can't be easy for you, either."

"You're alive and awake, more than I ever expected to have again." He said the emotional words with a harsh rasp as he guided the car along the palm tree–lined road. "I can deal with the rest."

"You make me feel as if I shouldn't be frustrated."

"Give yourself time." He kept both hands on the wheel, the late-day sunshine glinting off his Patek Philippe wristwatch. "You've been through a lot."

How did she know the brand of his watch but not know if the band on his ring finger had an inscription? But then, she remembered studying art history when she'd got her bachelor's degree. Recalled a love of finely made things and beautiful objects. Maybe that was why the watch resonated and the ring…nothing.

"What about you? What have you been through this past month? It must have been horrible, with a child in surgery and a wife in a coma."

"That doesn't matter," he said, his voice clipped. "I'm fine now."

Her mouth twitched with amusement as the car braked at a stop sign wrapped in garland. "Are you one of those men who's too tough to be vulnerable?"

His eyes met hers solemnly in the mirror. "I'm a man who thought he'd lost everything."

And just that fast, she felt her terrified heart melt a little for this stranger husband of hers. "You still have, in a way," she said sympathetically, "because of me and how I've lost any sense of us and our memories."

At the deserted intersection, he twisted to look over the seat at her, his elbow resting along the back and tugging his button-down shirt across his muscular chest. "You and our son are alive. That truly is what's most important to me."

There had been tension between them since she'd woken up in the hospital. He still held all the answers she couldn't access. But now, with the sincerity shining in his eyes, she wanted to hug him, ached to wrap her arms around him and have him do the same to her. Most of all, to have that feel familiar. She stretched a hand out to touch his elbow lightly—

A car honked behind them and she jerked her hand back. What was she thinking? Except for the few things he'd told her, she knew nothing about him or her or what kind of life they'd built together. Or what kind of future they might have because these events had changed them. Undoubtedly.

However for Thomas, she and Porter had to try for a level of peace between them. Could the Christmas spirit work a miracle for her family?

Shifting nervously in her seat, Alaina toyed with

the reindeer baby rattle, gathering up her rapidly fraying nerve. "May I ask you questions about the past?"

"Why didn't you question more before?" He kept his eyes on the road this time.

In some ways maybe that made this conversation easier.

"Because...I was scared you wouldn't answer."

"What's changed?"

"We're not in the hospital. There are no doctors who make me do all the work thinking, insisting I should only remember what I'm ready to know. They kept asking me not to push to remember, but that's causing me even more stress, wondering." She needed to know. How could she be a real wife to Porter and a mother to Thomas if she didn't even know who she was or how they'd become a family?

"You trust me to answer truthfully?" He glanced back at her, his eyes darkening.

"What do you have to gain by lying?"

Now wasn't that a loaded question? One that called for total trust in a man she barely knew. But she had no other choice, not if she wanted to reconnect as a family. "How did we meet?"

"My firm was handling building an addition to a museum where you worked. You saw me flex my muscles and here we are."

He sure did have muscles, and if they'd enticed her half as much then as they did now she could see how he would have caught her attention. His humor made him even more appealing. "You're funny, after all, Porter."

"You think I don't have a sense of humor? You've wounded my ego."

"There hasn't been a lot of room for levity this week."

She'd been so damn scared in the hospital. Walking the halls at night when she couldn't sleep. Obsessively checking on the baby and praying she would remember something, anything from the past five years.

Most of all, wondering about the mysterious, handsome man who'd spent hours with her each day.

"True enough. Hopefully we can fix that. We have the whole holiday season to relax, settle our child and get to know each other again." Through the rearview mirror, he held her eyes with a determined intensity. "Because, make no mistake, I intend to remind you of all the reasons we fell in love in the first place."

His words made something go hot inside her, a mixture of desire and confusion and, yes, nerves. She swallowed hard. It didn't help. But even if she didn't remember it, this was her life. There was no choice but to push on. To regain her memories and her life.

And figure out just what this man—her husband—meant to her. Not just in the past. But now.

Porter Rutger had been through hell.

But for the first time in a long time he saw a way to climb back out.

His hands clenched the steering wheel as he drove his wife and son home from the hospital. The past month—worrying about how Thomas would recover from his first surgery for his clubfoot, wondering about possible hidden effects of the accident on the baby...

And all the while his wife had been in a coma.

Porter's jaw flexed as he studied the familiar beach road leading to the vacation home they'd chosen after their third in vitro failed. Before they'd adopted

Thomas, their marriage had showed signs of fraying from years of struggling with the stresses of infertility.

He and Alaina had been in hell for a long time, even before the accident. He'd thought they'd hit rock bottom when they'd contacted a divorce attorney. They'd been so close to signing the divorce papers when the call came about a baby to adopt. A special-needs baby, difficult to place, an infant who required surgeries and years of physical therapy. While foster care would have provided the basics, the search for a home would have to start all over again if they backed out, leaving the baby adrift in the system.

They hadn't made the decision to adopt on a whim. They'd started the adoption process two years ago when the reality of infertility had become clear. Then they'd faced more heartache waiting. Their already strained marriage hadn't fared well under the added stress.

To this day, he couldn't remember which of them had asked for a divorce. The words had been thrown out during an argument and then taken root, growing fast, lawyers involved. It had damn near torn him apart, but their constant arguments had made it impossible to envision a future together bringing up the family they both wanted so much. Even marriage counseling hadn't helped.

They'd reached the end—and then the call had come about Thomas.

He and Alaina had put their differences aside to adopt the baby and stay together temporarily. Her soft, open heart had welcomed the baby from the second the call had come. Thomas needed them. That had cinched the deal for Alaina.

Then the accident happened and the possibility of losing her completely had made him want to shred the documents. Maybe he could have that family he wanted after all.

And he'd had no idea how quickly that little bundle in the back would steal his heart. He would do anything for his son. Anything.

While he would also do anything to have Alaina healthy, he couldn't ignore the fact that he had a second chance to win her over—for himself and for their son. This could be a fresh start, a way to work through all the pain they'd caused each other in the past.

Yes, he'd made mistakes in their marriage, but this was a new opportunity to build the family he'd always wanted. Growing up with a single-mom lawyer who worked all the time and husband-hunted during her hours off, he'd craved stability, love.

If he could only gain Alaina's forgiveness, or convince her that he was in it for the long haul this time, that he'd changed. Hell, if he could just make Alaina realize he wasn't the man he'd been a few weeks ago, then he could have the family he'd always dreamed of. The one they'd both wanted.

He'd never been one to procrastinate or waste time. He was a man of action.

And the stakes had never been more important than now.

Porter glanced in the rearview mirror at his blonde wife, the woman he'd fallen head over heels in love with four and a half years ago. Her intelligence, confidence and artistic flair had mesmerized him. He'd seen her discussing gallery art with a visiting class of elementary school students and he'd known. She was the one. She was his every perfect fantasy—soft, openhearted. He could envision her cradling their babies. Making sand castles with toddlers. Painting with children.

And it hadn't been just the maternal images that drew him. She had a passionate nature that set him on fire. Even now, the memories turned him inside out.

But the more they'd argued, the more he'd realized how shaky their foundation had been.

"What did you want to know?"

"We didn't talk much at all in the hospital." Her blue eyes held his for an electric instant before she looked away.

"The doctor's orders. And things were hectic, with Thomas's physical therapists and your tests." He'd been pulled in two different directions even though he'd taken time off from work, passing over control of his construction firm to his second in command until he had his family in order. Seeing her so helpless in the hospital had sucker punched him. Their love for each other might have died, but they still shared a history, an attraction, and now a child. His need for the picture-perfect family had destroyed their marriage and their love for each other.

But he owed it to her to take care of her while she healed and while they figured out how to parent Thomas.

"I'm not blaming anyone," she said quickly. "I'm just trying to fill in the blanks so I can function. I felt so... limited in the hospital."

He wouldn't sabotage her recovery. The doctors had said she shouldn't push to remember, and he planned to honor that directive. He wasn't that ruthless, no matter what his competitors said. But he sure as hell wasn't going to squander this chance to convince her to stay.

He would do whatever it took to keep her in this family. He wasn't interested in being a part-time father, and had never been, even when he'd agreed to sign those damn divorce papers. He'd regretted that decision the moment he'd made it. How could he have the family he needed if he let his wife walk away? Even then, regardless of their problems, he'd wanted things to go back to the way they'd been in the beginning.

He didn't know what had gone wrong, what more she expected of him. And now that she couldn't remember their life together, he might not ever find out. "The doctor wanted to see how much you recalled on your own. We didn't want you to confuse memories with things you'd been told."

"Maybe hearing about us might help jog those memories."

He noticed she didn't mention the whole trust issue again. Did that mean she'd put it on the back burner? Or she was willing to take him at his word?

She sure as hell hadn't trusted him at the end of their marriage, before the accident. Would that distrust eek through even her thick fog of amnesia? He steered off the highway onto the access road to their security gate.

"Porter, I don't have a choice but to ask you these questions. There's no one else from my past I still have a relationship with. If I want to find out anything about these past five years, it's you or Google."

He chuckled darkly. "A ringing endorsement if ever I heard one."

A smile played with her full lips. It was almost comfortable and it caused his chest to tighten. He remembered a time when he'd been able to make her smile every day, back before their relationship had deteriorated into loud fights and long silences.

"Porter, I'm not going to apologize for speaking the truth." The smile faded. "Why didn't anyone come see me in the hospital?"

"When the accident happened, we were far from home, picking up the baby. Our friends weren't nearby." And no doubt they would have felt awkward coming to visit the couple given the impending divorce. "I saved the cards from the flowers and balloons that came at the start. I'll show you when we get home."

She chewed that full lip. "What about phone calls to quiz people? Who can I call to help me?"

He wouldn't isolate her, but he didn't want to make it easy for her to take off again, either. He just wanted a little time for them to cement their relationship again, to rediscover what they'd once had—and to parent the baby they'd always wanted. They needed this time to become the family he'd always imagined they could be.

"The doctor warned you to be careful and take it slow. You'll have to ask your physicians near the beach house. Whatever they say is good by me." It surprised him that she hadn't asked many questions publicly at the hospital, but whatever had held her back, now that they were alone, she was more relentless about getting answers. There was an urgency and an edge to her now that she hadn't possessed before the accident.

Or had she kept it hidden the way she'd hidden so many of her motives in the last months of their marriage?

"So you have no trouble giving me those phone numbers? If the doctor says it's okay." She leaned forward, resting her arms on the back of the seat as they waited at an intersection.

"No problem at all." People would be eager to hear

from her after the accident, but they'd also be busy with the holidays. And the doctor had given them no reason to think her memory would return so soon. He needed the next two weeks' Christmas holiday with her and their son to tell her his side of the story. To see if they could make this work. Maybe, just maybe they could build that family after all. For Thomas. "Whatever you want from me, just ask. We're married."

Her quick gasp brushed across his neck, and her gaze met his, her eyes wide. "Whatever I want?"

The air went hot between them. Could she see the memories in his eyes? Could she sense just how damn good they had been together? How good they could still be?

There was desire and apprehension in her eyes. Her gaze broadcast loud and clear that she might not share the same memories, but she felt their connection—and it made her nervous.

He needed to proceed carefully. He hadn't told her about their decision to divorce. He wanted the chance to convince her to stay first. He also didn't want her asking questions that would box him into lying—or telling a hard truth. Like the fact they hadn't slept together for a month before the accident. "I can promise you, I'm not about to demand husbandly rights or anything else from you until you're ready."

"That's for the best," she said a little too fast. "I'm not ready for—"

"You don't need to say anything more." He punched in the security code to open the scrolled gates that were designed like a pewter clamshell gaping wide. Christmas lights glistened on the palm trees lining the path to the yellow stucco mansion, the glimmer growing brighter with the setting sun.

"You've been very understanding the past week, Porter. I know this has been difficult for you, too, and I appreciate that you've worked to make things as easy for me as possible."

There was a time not so long ago she'd made it clear she felt just the opposite. She'd insisted he only wanted her as a place holder in the mother role. That any woman would have done, that he didn't really love her and that she was damn well tired of him hiding at the office to avoid facing their problems.

He kept his silence.

"What? Did I say something wrong?"

"You've been through a lot the past month." They both had. He steered toward the three-story mansion perched on an ocean bluff, holiday decor in full glory of wreaths, bows and draped garland as he'd ordered. "Of course you deserve understanding. I just want you to be clear that while I'm giving you time and space to remember your past, that doesn't mean I won't be trying to fill your head with happy new memories."

Her eyes went wide again. God, she was beautiful but too frail after all she'd been through. Protective urges fired to the fore. They might not be the couple they'd been before, but he needed her to make his family complete. He would do whatever it took to woo her over these next couple of weeks. And he wouldn't let anyone stand in his way.

He put the car in Park in front of the sweeping double staircase just as the groundskeeper stepped into another car to valet park…and…

Damn. Porter felt the sucker punch clear through to his spine.

He recognized that Maserati sports car well. Heaven help them all.

His mother had come to visit.

Two

Home sweet home?

Sorta.

Her eyes flitted to the sprawling house before them. Poinsettias lined the double staircase, adding Christmas spirit to the green and vibrant Florida winter. A giant wreath trimmed in gold and silver hung on the door, warm and inviting.

The warmth made her heart sink a bit. Had she picked out all of these decorations? Were they supposed to carry some sentimental value? She had been with Porter for almost five years. They owned years' worth of memories and items they had collected—and all of it was a mystery to her. Taking a deep breath, she turned her attention to Thomas and his monogrammed blanket.

As she unbuckled the baby from his car seat, Alaina couldn't miss the tension radiating from Porter. Of course he'd been under a tremendous stress, too, during this whole situation. He had just been so stalwart until now; she was surprised he let his emotions show.

Even if he'd opened up only briefly before he became the ultimate in-control guy again. Was that an act just for her? Was that how she'd preferred him to be? She'd liked seeing the emotion on his face, in his eyes. The controlled expression he wore now seemed to shut her out.

She cradled the sleeping infant in her arms, taking comfort from the scent of baby shampoo and innocence. She didn't remember becoming a wife or a mother. She didn't *feel* like a wife or a mother.

But she knew without question she would do whatever was needed to make sure this innocent life in her care felt loved and secure.

Porter opened the back door of the car, the setting sun casting a nimbus around his big body, which blocked out the rest of the world. God, he was a gorgeous hulk of man. She could see him in a painting of Atlas holding the world on those broad shoulders. He made her feel safe, protected. She could lean on him.

He propped a hand on the roof. "Are you feeling steady enough to carry the baby?"

"I'm fine, but thank you for asking." She stepped out, her hold careful on Thomas.

Porter cupped her elbow in a steadying grasp, his touch warm and gentle, sending tingles through her. She glanced at him quickly. Did he feel it, too? What was he thinking? He had to want his wife back. She wanted that for him, but even so, she couldn't shake the feeling that something was off between them. She couldn't miss how he only answered what was needed, never offering one snippet more. And his shoulders seemed so braced, tense. Where was the joy in this homecoming?

She straightened and adjusted her hold on the baby. "Thank you. I really am okay to walk on my own."

It was strange how she'd been in a coma for a month and yet her body acted as if she'd simply taken a long nap. She'd spent a week doing physical therapy and eating high-nutrient meals to regain strength in her muscles. Other than tiring quickly, she felt no ill effects from her ordeal. At least not physically. How surreal.

"I'll get the car seat and diaper bag, then." He reached to lift them out, the navy blue Burberry bag looking tiny and incongruous in his large hands. "Before we step inside, I should warn you."

Foreboding gelled in her belly. Here it came. Whatever awful thing she'd feared her amnesia had been hiding from her. "Warn me about what?"

"My mother's here," he said with a heavy sigh.

She almost laughed in hysterical relief. She walked beside him toward the towering doors, inhaling a bracing breath of salty ocean breeze. "Your mom?" If he had a mother, why hadn't she come to the hospital? That seemed strange. She hadn't thought to question him about his family in the hospital since her memories stopped just before her relationship with Porter began. "You have a mother?"

"I wasn't born under a rock," he said with a sense of humor that still surprised her.

Another intriguing element to this man.

Chewing her bottom lip, Alaina eyed the door with trepidation. The gold and silver of the wreath caught in the amber sunset. "I wish you would have mentioned her arrival before now."

"I didn't know she was coming until I saw her car as we pulled up. It's very distinctive."

"Is your father here, too?"

"If so, that would be an even bigger surprise since I've never met the man."

"Oh, um, I'm sorry." Another thing about her husband she should have known.

"Thank you, but I'm long past looking for father figures around every corner. I'm looking forward to *being* a father." He reached to lift out the infant seat. "Let's go find out what coerced my mother to drive up from Miami."

Something about the way he said that made her sad, reminding her again of all the ways this should have been a happy day for him. His family was returning home from the hospital in good health. But she again felt that their life together—whatever it was now—couldn't be summed up that easily.

She wanted to trust him.

But something deep inside her, something beyond memory and born of instinct, held her back.

Luckily for him, his mother had been settling into her suite when he and Alaina brought Thomas into the house. His wife was in the nursery with their son now, which would give him a chance to talk to his mother alone first in his study. She needed to understand that he would toss her out on Christmas Day itself if she did one thing to upset this chance he had to win back his wife and keep his family intact.

He paced restlessly, his eyes drawn to the brass clock on his desk. What the hell was taking his mother so long? This wasn't the best of times for unexpected company, damn it.

Wooing Alaina back into his life and into his bed was going to be tough enough without having his mother throw verbal land mines into the mix with no warning. Courtney Rutger was a shark in the courtroom and in life. Their relationship had been strained since he'd walked out at eighteen and put himself through college working construction rather than take her money.

There were too many strings attached to his mother's gifts. The extravagant presents had clearly made Alaina uncomfortable given her less affluent upbringing and he couldn't blame her. Still, he'd never been quite sure how to navigate the tense waters between his mother and wife.

Finally, she glided into his study in a swirl of expensive perfume and one of her favored fitted Chanel suits. She leaned toward him for an air kiss on the cheek. "Porter."

He complied, as expected, wondering if she'd ever carried him around the way Alaina cradled Thomas. Making real contact, rather than an air kiss or half hug.

"Mom," he answered, angling away and leaning against his desk. "Why are you here?"

"To celebrate Christmas, and to help you with your new baby and your *wife*."

Help now? He wasn't buying it. His mother had visited only on holidays during his marriage, and she hadn't done more than come to the hospital the day after the accident. She'd seen her grandson, brought some gifts and flowers and left. She sure as hell hadn't cooed over her grandchild, much less snapped photos on her cell phone to share with her pals. "You've never been interested in babies before."

"I've never been a grandmother before."

"Mother..." He raised an eyebrow impatiently.

"Son," she answered with overplayed innocence.

"Is that what you're about? I'm your son. I know you. And you're not going to cause mother-in-law troubles."

"I don't know what you're talking about."

"Oh, Mother, please. You've made it clear for years that you don't like Alaina." The friction between his wife and mother, which had grown over time, had added pressure to an already strained marriage. "She's working to regain her memory and the last thing she needs is you tossing in digs or telling her things she's not ready to hear. She needs to be kept calm and happy while she recovers. She should remember the happy times first."

His gaze gravitated to the framed reproduction of a map of the Florida East Coast Railway from the Flagler Museum, an anniversary gift from Alaina two years ago. She'd respected his work, complimented him on being an artist in his own right through his construction company. She'd bought the gift in commemoration of another Florida builder/entrepreneur from the past.

Some people went on cruises for vacation. He and Alaina had spent their time off touring historic sites and discussing the architectural history of the buildings.

There had been good times between them... God, he missed what they'd once had.

And now he had a second chance. He wouldn't let anything or anyone stand in his way of repairing his relationship with Alaina. Of building a family together. It was too important.

"Your wife is ill now. I understand that and will

be nice. If you're not ready for her to hear about the 'bad memories,' then okay. I'm here for all three of you." Courtney clicked her manicured nails. "I do have a heart."

She placed her hand dramatically on her chest, and gave a picture-perfect smile. It was with just such finesse that Courtney Rutger won over jury after jury—if not her son.

His mouth twitched with a smile. "That's questionable."

"And you're just like me." She winked. "Makes a mother proud."

He shook his head. "You're something else."

"That's one way to put it." She clapped her hands together. "Now where's my grandson?"

"He's getting his diaper changed."

Frowning, she smoothed back her French twist, her dark hair showing only a few threads of gray. "Then I'll wait a couple of minutes until he's through with that." She hesitated, shrugging. "What? I like to watch babies nap."

"Since when?"

"Since always. They're easier then." She grinned unrepentantly. "Now smile. It's the Christmas season. Your family is under one roof. And I certainly wouldn't have wagered a chance in hell on that happening this year."

Neither would he.

A creak of the door snapped his attention across the room. Alaina stood in the doorway frowning. Damn it. How much had she heard? Had his mother's strategic verbal land mines already blown his second chance all to hell? Courtney might have said she intended to respect his wishes, but he wasn't 100 percent certain she wouldn't try to find some way to finagle her way past on a technicality.

"Alaina?" he asked, waving her inside.

She stepped deeper into the room. "Please introduce me to your mother." She tugged a Christmas plaid burp cloth off the shoulder of her blue cotton dress that skimmed her curves. "I'm sorry I don't remember you, ma'am, but you're right. We're all lucky to be here together since I very well could have still been in that hospital bed. Or not here at all."

He exhaled hard, grateful she'd misunderstood his mother's comment. But he couldn't count on continued luck. He needed to make progress with his wife and get his family back. The sooner the better.

Two hours later, Alaina opened the closet in her bedroom. Hers and Porter's.

The space was larger than her first college studio apartment.

One side was lined with rows of Porter's clothes, suits and casual wear, each piece hung and arranged with precision, even down to sleeve length. She walked along the row, her fingers trailing the different textures. She could almost imagine the cloth still carried the heat of the man who wore them.

A half wall sectioned the male and female side of the "closet." Shoes fit into nooks, purses, too. And somehow she knew to push the button on the end—jewelry trays slid out in staggered lengths and heights. The stones that winked at her varied from semiprecious to mind-bogglingly expensive.

Who was she now? In this life? This house with an apartment-sized closet?

Even that thought gave her pause, reminding her that she hadn't grown up with finer things like the ones in this house. How comfortable had she been living here? Had she grown jaded and used to these luxuries?

Glancing back at the elegant driftwood four-poster bed, she began to seriously consider their arrangements as they became reacquainted. He'd said he wouldn't pressure her and she hoped he meant that. He couldn't possibly think they would be sharing a bed. Not yet. In spite of the attraction that still simmered between them, she wasn't ready for intimacy just now.

But someday?

She could barely envision getting through the night, much less through the next few weeks. She turned to the closet again and studied the racks of clothes and rows of shoes and purses and her clothes as if they could give her some hint about the woman she'd been in those missing five years. Certainly one who enjoyed shopping and bright patterns. Grasping at the clothes, she enjoyed the cool feel of the silks and satins. This closet was luxurious—the kind women might fantasize about. Alaina half hoped one of these garments would stir a memory, and the past five years of her life would come rushing back to her.

No such luck.

She released a floor-length gown with a jeweled bodice and glanced down at the simple cotton dress she wore, so different from the rest of her clothes. Had Porter packed this for a reason or had he simply grabbed the first item his hands fell on?

The cotton dress didn't feel like the artsy sense of

herself she remembered from five years ago. In fact, the house didn't much reflect her, either. Where was her love of Renaissance art? There were no paintings or statues she would have chosen. Everything was generic, decorator style, matching sets. Had she really spent time here? Been happy?

Where had the traces of herself gone?

The sense of being watched pulled her back into the room, where she found her husband standing by the four-poster bed with a tray of food. He wore a T-shirt and jeans now, the pants low slung on his hips as if he'd lost weight recently. Perhaps he'd been worried sick about her and Thomas. She tried to imagine what the past month had been like for him, but came up empty. It was hard enough for her to grasp her own situation, let alone empathize with his when she didn't know him beyond what the past week had shown her. But all of those interactions had been in the hospital with its sterile environment and lack of privacy. The four and a half years they'd supposedly known each other were wiped clean from her mind. Not so much as a whisper of a memory.

"I thought you might be hungry. There wasn't much of a chance to eat with the trip home, settling Thomas and my mother's surprise arrival." He set the tray on a coffee table in front of the sofa at the foot of their bed. His thick muscled arms flexed, straining against the sleeves of the cotton tee. She tried not to notice, but then felt slightly absurd. He was her husband and yet a stranger all at once.

"That's thoughtful, thank you." She watched him pour the tea, the scent of warm apples and cinnamon wafting upward. "Between a night nanny for the baby and a full-time cook-maid, I'm not sure what I'm going to do to keep myself occupied."

"You've been through a lot. You need your sleep so you can fully recover. I'm here, too. He's my child."

"Our child."

"Right." Porter's eyes held hers as he passed over the china cup of tea with a cookie tucked on the saucer. "He needs you to be well. We both do."

The warmth of the cup and his words seeped into her and she asked softly, "Where are you planning to sleep?"

He studied her for a slow, sexy blink before responding, "We discussed that in the car."

"Did we?" She wasn't certain about anything right now.

"We did." He sat on the camelback sofa, the four-poster bed big and empty behind him as he cradled a cup of tea for himself in one hand. "But just to be clear, nothing will happen until you're ready. You're recovering on more than one level. I understand that and I respect that. I respect you."

His sensitivity touched her. She should be relieved. She *was* relieved.

And yet she was also irritated. She couldn't help but notice he still hadn't said he loved her, that he wanted her. He wasn't pushing the physical connection that obviously still hummed between them. Was he giving her space? Was he holding back because she couldn't possibly love a man she didn't know? She kept hoping for some kind of wave of love at first sight. But they were fast approaching more than a few hundred sights and still that wave hadn't hit.

Attraction? Yes. Intrigue? Definitely. But she was

also very overwhelmed and still afraid of what those memories might hold. She wasn't able to shake the sense that she couldn't fully trust him. If only he would say the right words to reassure her and calm the nerves in the pit of her belly.

She looked around the room, everything so pristine and new looking, a beach decor of sea-foam greens, tans and white. More of the matched set style that, while tasteful, didn't reflect her preferences in the least. "How often did we come here?"

"I have a work office in the house. So whenever we needed to."

She set aside the tea untouched. "You're so good at avoiding answering my questions with solid information."

A flicker of something—frustration?—flexed his jaw. "We spent holidays here and you spent most of your summers here."

"Then how do I not have any friends in this area?" Where were the casseroles? The welcome home cookies? Or did the überwealthy with maids and night nannies not do that for each other?

"Many people around here are vacationers. Sometimes we invited friends or business acquaintances to stay with us, but they're back home in Tallahassee or at their own holiday vacation houses. We also traveled quite a bit, depending on my work projects."

"So I just followed you around from construction job to job?"

"You make that sound passive. You're anything but that. You worked on your master's degree in art history for two years. One of your professors had connections in the consulting world and our travels enabled you to freelance, assisting museums and private individuals in artwork purchases. You did most from a distance and we flew in for the event proper when artwork arrived."

That was the most he'd said to her at once since she'd woken from her coma. And also very revealing words. "We sound attached at the hip."

He rested his elbows on his knees, staring into his empty teacup. "We were trying to make a baby."

His quiet explanation took the wind right out of her sails. She'd guessed as much since they were adopting and had no other children, but hearing him say it, hearing that hint of pain in his words, made her wonder how much disappointment and grief they'd shared over the years while waiting for their son. Then to have that joy taken from them both because she couldn't remember even the huge landmarks in their relationship that should be ingrained in her mind—when she'd met him, their first kiss, the first time they'd made love…

"And starting our family didn't work the way we planned."

He looked up at her again. "In case you're wondering, the doctors pinpointed it to a number of reasons, part me, part you, neither issue insurmountable on its own, but combined…" He shrugged. "No treatment worked for us, so we decided to adopt."

Thomas. Their child. Her mind filled with the sweet image of his chubby cheeks and dusting of blond hair. "I'm glad we did."

"Me, too," he said with unmistakable love.

The emotion in his voice drew her in as nothing else could have. She sat beside Porter, their shoulders brushing. It was almost comfortable. Or did she want it to be that way? So many emotions tapped at her, dancing in her veins. "He's so beautiful. I hate that I don't remember the first instant I laid eyes on him, the moment I became his mother."

"You cried when the social worker at the hospital placed him in your arms. I'm not ashamed to say I did, too."

Oh, God, this man who'd not once mentioned love could make a serious dent in her heart with only a few words. It was enough to make her want to try harder to fit into this life she didn't remember. To be more patient and let the answers come.

She touched his elbow lightly, wanting the feel of him to be familiar, wanting more than chemistry to connect them. "This isn't the way Christmas was supposed to be for us."

"There was no way to foresee the accident." He placed his hand over hers, the calluses rasping against her skin, another dichotomy in this man who could pay others to do anything for him yet still chose to roll up his sleeves.

"I never did ask how it happened. There have been so many questions I keep realizing I've forgotten to ask the obvious ones."

"We picked up Thomas at the hospital. Since it was so close to our beach house, we considered staying here for the night, but instead opted to drive back home to Tallahassee. A half an hour later, a drunk driver hit us head-on."

"We wanted our son in our own house, in his nursery."

"Something like that."

"What does his nursery look like at our house in Tallahassee?"

"The same as here, countryside with farm animals. You said you wanted Thomas to feel at home wherever he went. Even his travel crib is the same pattern. You even painted the same mural on the wall here."

She remembered admiring the artwork when she'd laid the baby in his crib, enjoying the quiet farm scene with grazing cows and a full blue moon.

"I painted it?" Finally, something of herself in this house of theirs. Her eyes filled with tears. Such a simple thing. A mural for their son in their two homes—or did they have more?—and yet she couldn't remember painting the pastoral scene. She couldn't remember the shared joy over planning for their first child, or the shared tears.

And right now she was seconds away from shedding more tears all over the comfort of Porter's broad chest.

When would she feel she belonged in this life?

Three

Porter woke from a restless sleep. He would have blamed it on staying in the guest room, but he'd bunked here more than once as his marriage frayed. He knew that wasn't the reason he couldn't sleep. Sitting up with the sheets tangled around his waist, he listened closer and heard it again. Someone was awake.

The baby?

He swept the bedding away and tugged on a pair of sweatpants. Even having a night nanny, he couldn't turn off the parenting switch. Over the past few weeks, the accident and time in the hospital had kept him on high alert, fearing the worst 24/7.

A few steps later, he'd padded to the nursery, determined to relieve the night nanny and watch Thomas himself. He'd worked with minimum sleep before. Actually, this past month had made him quite good at operating on only a few hours of rest. He was still so glad his son was okay that being with him was reassuring, even in the middle of the night. Those quiet hours also offered the uninterrupted chance to connect with his child.

Stepping into the doorway, he stopped short. Instead of the matronly granny figure he'd hired to help out, he found his wife feeding their son a bottle in a rocker by the crib.

"Hey, little man," she said softly, propping the bottle on her arm, "I'm your mommy. Forever. And I do want to be your mother. Who wouldn't love that precious face of yours? I wish we could have had the past month together, but that wasn't my choice."

Alaina took his breath away.

Though her pale pink T-shirt was crumpled from sleep, it still hinted at the shape of her curves and the matching pale, striped shorts exposed her beautiful legs.

But Porter couldn't see her face. Like any new mother, she was focused, homed in on her child. Her head was tilted down toward Thomas, blond hair spilling over her right cheek and shoulder.

She was beautiful and the warmth of her love for Thomas pulled at him. For the first time since she had woken up from the coma, she looked at ease. She looked almost happy. If he were being honest with himself, it was the first time she had looked truly happy in months.

A pang of guilt welled in his chest. Porter wanted to do anything—give anything—for her to stay like that. For her to be happy with him again. And she deserved it. Relationships hadn't always been kind to her.

When they'd first started dating four and a half years ago, she had recently left an emotionally abusive boyfriend. He had controlled all aspects of her life, telling her who she could and couldn't see. He'd shown up to check in on her. Slowly isolating her so she would have no one to turn to for help.

That was one of the reasons she didn't have friends around to help now. She'd told him it had been hard to make friends after that experience. Possibly that was why she was struggling so much to trust him now.

He couldn't blame her for feeling that way.

Five years ago, she'd tried to take charge of her life when she'd left the boyfriend. But the abuse hadn't stopped. He'd stalked her. Only the restraining order had given Alaina her life back.

And even after all she'd been through, Porter admired the hell out of that. Her capacity to still love, to still believe in people. It was one of the things that had drawn him to her.

And tonight, he saw that spirit, that beautiful resilient spirit fill the room. A pang of guilt flooded him for not telling her about their marital struggles, but damn it, he couldn't shake the sense he would lose her altogether if he did that. He would do whatever it took to get his family back. He would make sure she had no wants or desires not satisfied.

How had it taken such a terrible accident for him to appreciate how important his family was to him? Shouldn't he have realized all of this on his own, without the fear of almost losing this chance to have a family he of his own?

She must have felt his eyes on her, because she abruptly looked up and met his stare, and the relaxed expression on her face faded. "Porter?"

He quirked an eyebrow. "What good is a night nanny if you don't let her work?"

"I've already missed out on a month of his life. I want him to bond with me."

"You shouldn't push yourself."

"I'm an adult. I know my limits," she said with a tight, bristly tone. Thomas squirmed and whined. She brought him to her shoulder like a natural, patting his back and tapping the rocking chair into motion. "Do you?"

He chuckled drily. "Now that sounds like the wife *I* remember. Yes, I'm a workaholic." He gave her a sideways smile. "But you taught me to slow down and admire art."

"That's a nice thing to say." She patted Thomas's back faster, and still he fussed and squirmed, kicking his casted foot.

"Here, pass him to me." Porter walked deeper into the room, his arms outstretched.

Hurt and irritation flashed in her blue eyes, but she handed over the baby, anyway. "Sure. I want him to be comfortable."

"Alaina," he said, taking the baby and cradling him like a football, while massaging his little leg above the cast, "you aren't expected to know everything any more than I am. We're a team here and together we'll get it all covered."

She nodded once, shoving up from the rocker. "I know. It's just difficult feeling like I bring so little to the table right now."

"You told me once that marriage isn't always fifty-fifty. The pendulum swings back and forth." His mind drifted back to when she'd spoken those words.

She'd been so angry. He'd come home with a cast on his wrist, fresh out of the emergency room because he'd fallen off a scaffold while inspecting a work site. He'd broken his wrist, but he hadn't wanted to worry her. She'd made it clear she should have been called and included, allowed to help him and drive him home. She'd wanted to tend him and he'd wanted to get to change clothes to go back to work…

He damn well wouldn't let his job interfere with repairing his family now.

Porter felt Thomas drift off to sleep again, his body relaxing. Later he would tell Alaina the baby hadn't been hungry. His leg had been aching from the weight of the cast and the surgery. Alaina felt insecure enough right now. "Let's pass over the nursery monitor to the woman paid to stay awake."

"Sure, but I'm not tired. Maybe it has something to do with that month-long nap I took."

He stifled a laugh to keep from waking the baby, glad that she could joke about their ordeal. He set Thomas in his crib again, stroking the baby's head for a few seconds before turning the monitor back on. Porter nodded to the door and walked into the hall. The night nanny, Mrs. Marks, poked her head out of her bedroom, waved with her puzzle book and ducked into the nursery.

Porter held out a hand to his wife. "Want to see the beach view from the balcony? It was too foggy at supper time to enjoy much. The Christmas lights along the yachts will be more visible now."

"Yachts?"

He winced. From the beginning, she hadn't been comfortable with some parts of their wealthy lifestyle. She'd grown up with hardworking parents who ran a beach food cart in North Carolina's Outer Banks. Their business had paid the bills, but hadn't provided much in the way of extras. What would she say when he told her one of those yachts anchored off the shore was theirs?

"Forget it. You should rest even if you can't sleep."

"I can make decisions for myself," she said with blue fire in her eyes. "Show me the lights."

"Right this way," he said, once again extending his hand to her. Gingerly, she took it, but her grip was loose, as if she was ready to tear away from him at any moment.

Porter led them down the stairs, guided by the muted twinkle of Christmas lights that were twined with garland and wrapped around the banister.

There was an audible silence that followed them, but Porter tried to focus on the fact that she had chosen to come with him instead of retreating to the privacy of her room. It was a good sign.

They reached the stairway landing where the sleek black baby grand piano stood beneath one of Porter's favorite portraits: Alaina in her wedding gown. Her hair had been curled in loose waves that framed her face and the lace wedding gown accentuated her slender figure. She had looked like a princess that day. And it was Porter's renewed intention to make sure he treated her like royalty so she would want to stay once her memory came back. So the good now would overshadow the bad then. That she could forgive and move forward with him and Thomas, building a future.

And if her memory didn't return? He still needed to convince her to stay and build that life with him and their son. Family was everything and he refused to lose his.

Alaina squeezed his hand as they passed in front of the portrait. He watched her gaze lock on the photograph. She didn't say anything for several minutes, and he didn't push her as they strode out onto the patio that overlooked the Atlantic.

Rebuilding his family was a game of growing trust. And she deserved to raise questions without him dumping information on her. He wanted to give her the space she needed to realize she belonged here.

"Tell me about our wedding." The words came out almost like a prayer. Soft. Earnest.

"There's a photo album around the house somewhere. And plenty of extra pictures on the computer."

"But here's the bridal portrait, and it doesn't tell me anything. Not really. I feel a disconnect with the person in the pictures you've already shown me. Maybe if you tell me, then I will recognize the emotions of the moment."

"Maybe?" His heart hammered.

"Men don't get all emotional about weddings."

He considered her for a moment. She dropped his hand and moved to the piano bench. She sat with her back against the keys, eyes fixed across the room and on the ocean. The Christmas lights from the yachts illuminated the edges of her face, framing her in an otherworldly glow. Damn. She was gorgeous, even when she was stormy. He wanted her in his bed now as much as he ever had. But he wanted to put his family back together even more, and he had to remain focused on the end goal.

Quietly he offered, "I was happy the day we married."

It was true. He had been so entranced by her sense of the world, by the family they could make together, that he hadn't been able to marry her quickly enough. They'd started trying for children right away. His mother had told him that he and Alaina should take time to cement their relationship. He hadn't given much thought to that—until now.

"How long had we known each other?" Her eyes searched his. He could feel her trying to grasp hold of the past. Of who *they* were.

"We met a year prior. We were engaged for four months of that."

She slid over on the bench and motioned for him to sit next to her. He sat sideways so he could look at her directly.

"Why the rush?"

"We loved each other, knew it was right. Why wait?"

"I wasn't pregnant?"

"No, you weren't. We were never able to conceive."

It had been no one's fault. And they had Thomas now. They had taken in a child who desperately needed a home and stability. And somehow, that seemed to soften the animosity they had felt. They'd agreed to a temporary truce and now he planned to make them a permanent family.

"I hate being dependent on you for all my memories." Her eyes were shining with frustration. But, Porter realized, the frustration wasn't entirely directed at him.

He gently lifted a wisp of hair out of her face and tucked it behind her ear. "Then tell me what your dream wedding day would be like and that will be our wedding memory."

Her eyes went whimsical, a smile pushing dimples into her cheeks. "I would want to get married at a museum, or some historic site on the grounds, but with a preacher there."

Porter nodded to encourage her. "What else?"

"I think I would want a vintage gown and you in an old-school tuxedo, tails perhaps. And if I could dream big—sky's the limit—I would want flowers, so many flowers, all different colors. Southern flowers, magnolias and azaleas, too."

A long sigh escaped her lips, and she turned in her seat to face him.

"And the reception?"

"A band, so people could enjoy themselves. A buffet meal so people could eat or dance or talk, whatever they wish. I would want there to be children there, activities and a tent where they could play, sitters on hand. How does all of that sound?"

"Very close to the wedding we planned." He took her hand in his and ran his thumb over her silk-smooth palm.

"Planned?"

He shrugged. "My mother put in her two cents, your friends put in theirs. Weddings get complicated and we both let them have their way to get things moving so we could start our life together. To be truthful, I just remember you and how beautiful you looked and how damn lucky I was to have convinced you to marry me."

More memories hit him, about how later she'd come to resent not having stood her ground to have the wedding of her dreams. Her insistence that her style and wishes got pushed aside by his mother and wedding planners.

She inched toward him on the bench, resting a hand on his knee. Her touch made his blood surge hot beneath his skin. Damn. He wanted to take her in his arms. Wanted to taste her kiss. To taste *her*—over and over until they both stopped thinking and remembering.

"That's lovely, what you just said and the way you described the feelings. I wish I recalled even a part of that." The murmur leaped from her lips as her eyes searched his face. There was intrigue there, sure. Attraction, definitely.

"You will. Someday."

Another deep sigh. "And if I don't?"

"Then we'll keep taking things a day at a time and looking to the future. Marriage isn't perfect, Alaina. You've forgotten the arguments and disagreements, too. So perhaps it's a trade-off, getting to start over with a clean slate."

Alaina shook her head, but didn't pull away. Her fingers continued to trace light circles on his knee. "Amnesia is a horrible illness, not some trade-off. I would gratefully welcome one bad memory now from those years, just to open the door. To see our life together."

"What if that one memory made you stop loving me because you couldn't recall the rest?"

He wanted this fresh start for their family so badly. He needed it down to his core. And he was afraid that if she recalled any of the past year, she'd pack up and be out of his life the way she'd intended to do before the accident.

"I don't mean to be harsh, but I can't remember falling in love with you. So how is that a point?"

He threw her a playful wink. "I guess I'll just have to help you fall in love with me again."

She didn't smile back, her gaze narrowing with intensity. "So do you still love me?"

"Of course I do," he said automatically because that's what she needed to hear.

But from the look in her eyes, he could tell that on some level, behind the amnesia, she sensed the truth.

This wasn't about loving or not loving each other. After all, they hadn't spoken those words to each other in over a year. This second chance was about finally building the family he'd always wanted and doing whatever it took to make that happen.

Alaina leaned against the door frame of Porter's home office, making the most of the moment to study him unobserved. Much like as he'd watched her last night in the nursery. She'd been more moved by the way he'd looked at her, almost as if he was thinking the words he never spoke. Words about loving her.

Why was it so important to hear that from him when she didn't know how she felt about him? When she couldn't remember meeting him, marrying him— falling for him? And some men weren't overly demonstrative.

What about him?

She searched for clues as she watched him work at his computer, seated behind an oversize desk. He wore casual clothes, jeans and a polo shirt, his watch the only cue to his wealth. She liked that about him, how if she'd met him on the street she wouldn't have guessed he had all these houses—and a closet as big as some apartments.

She also liked the artwork on the wall behind him. Nice choice. It fit him more than a lot of things in this elaborate vacation place. She wondered if she'd picked it out for him.

He wore thick black-framed glasses as he typed, something she hadn't noticed before. There was so much about him she didn't know. So much to learn and on the one hand, some would say she had all the time in the world. But she felt an urgency to settle her life, for Thomas's sake.

And she couldn't ignore how much it touched her heart to see her son snoozing in a bassinet beside Porter's leather office chair. That he'd made arrangements to watch the baby while working spoke volumes. She could see that Porter wanted to be a good father, that he wanted to be active in his son's upbringing. She wanted to trust her impressions of him and accept that she had an amazing life. She wanted to quit worrying about the past she couldn't remember.

And yet she couldn't dismiss the sense that she should be wary of assuming everything was as it seemed.

Porter glanced up, as if sensing her gaze. He tucked his reading glasses on top of his head, his eyes were full of awareness from their almost kiss earlier.

Even if she couldn't remember what they'd had, she could swear she felt all those shared kisses in their past on some level. Did he have regrets about them as a couple? Was that the unsettled feeling she sensed in him?

Had he appreciated what they had?

"Alaina," he said softly, rocking back in his chair. "I've got this. Easy. He's sleeping. Go relax. Take a walk on the beach. Read a book."

Or stay with Porter and be tempted even more? How long would she be able to resist?

Not long.

She backed out of the door. "Sure, thanks. I'll have my cell phone with me. Don't hesitate to call if you need me to come back for him. I want to be with him whenever he's awake."

She'd missed so much already. Oh, God, she was going to start crying if she kept thinking about it.

Her emotions were swinging from desire for her stranger of a husband to grief over all she'd lost. She needed to get herself under control or she would be a nervous wreck. Thomas didn't need to have all those negative feelings around him. Maybe Porter was right about her taking time to decompress for a while.

With determined strides she moved toward the kitchen, scarfed down some toast and tea, and contemplated the events of her past twenty-four hours.

A whirlwind didn't even begin to cover it.

Glancing around the open space, she couldn't help but feel the decor looked as if it had been directly lifted from a catalog. Everything was gorgeous—stainless steel appliances with rustic wooden accent bowls—but it all felt too…put together.

Was this the kind of woman she had become over the past five years?

Unable to suppress her need for more answers, Alaina began to explore the house. Their house, she reminded herself. This was supposedly all hers, too, even if it felt alien in comparison to her more Spartan upbringing. She needed to learn to be comfortable here again.

Porter had made it clear that he wanted her to relax. To take time for herself. And while that was sweet, she wasn't entirely sure she enjoyed being forced into downtime. She had lost so much of her life that downtime intimidated her.

But she had to admit she admired Porter's dedication

to Thomas. It was endearing. He had found a way to integrate work and family. And that trait was sexy as hell.

She searched for more signs of encouragement regarding their life, but the rest of the house mirrored the kitchen. It was also well put together. So manicured and manufactured. She couldn't seem to find a trace of her artistic side at all.

Alaina thought back to the last apartment she could remember, the one she'd had five years ago. It had been modest, but hanging above her bed, she had placed a Renaissance-style painting. The myths drew her in. She loved that each painting captured a Greek tragedy or legend.

There wasn't one painting like that in this whole place.

Did Porter hate that sort of thing? Had she given up her taste in favor of his? And should she just start changing things now?

The bramble of her thoughts was interrupted as she came to the staircase and practically walked into her mother-in-law.

Courtney's hair was swept into a tight but elegant topknot. Polished. Her green dress swished as she moved toward Alaina. Jimmy Choo heels clicked with each step.

The poised, older woman waved with long, manicured nails. "Come with me. I need coffee. Or a mimosa. Unless you would rather some time by yourself?"

"Of course not." Alaina had too much time to spend with a jumble of questions about her missing thoughts. "I would love the chance to visit with you."

Her mother-in-law cast her a sidelong glance. "Dear,

it's all right. You don't have to tiptoe around my feelings."

"I welcome the chance to get to know you. You're Porter's mom." She extended her arm for Courtney to take. It was time to start to get to know her family. Her old life.

Had they got along before?

Courtney linked her arm with Alaina's. "I'm also your mother-in-law. Thomas's grandmother. I'm here to help however I can. Not that you really need it. You're very good with Thomas."

Was she? God, she hoped so. "I don't know anything about babies."

"Maybe not before you got married, but since I've known you? You've learned a lot about infants. You volunteered in the NICU three times a week, holding the newborns or just talking to the ones too tiny and fragile to be held." Her mother-in-law guided her back toward the kitchen.

Back toward Porter.

"I did that?" Another thing to add to the list of things she was learning about her life during these missing years. Fancy art exhibits. A postgraduate degree. NICU babies. She had certainly filled her time while married to Porter.

"It was hard for you, wanting to be a mother so desperately." Courtney patted her hand. Sympathy radiated from her touch.

There was a certain calm that settled between them. An understanding Alaina seemed to be close to grasping, but couldn't quite settle. Not yet. Although it wouldn't hurt to ask a few questions.

"What about Porter? Does he want to be a father?"

"Of course he does. You've seen how he is with Thomas."

Alaina thought back to the way he had massaged Thomas's hurt leg last night. About how he had insisted on watching him as he worked. He was taking his fatherly duties seriously. And it made her heart melt.

"Whose idea was it to adopt?"

Her mother-in-law hesitated midstep before walking again, heels clicking on travertine tiles. "You would have to ask him that question."

Did Courtney not know or was there something deeper here? An argument within the family? "I'm so tired of asking him about every single detail of our lives together. I was hoping you could help fill in some details."

"I'm sorry about the amnesia, dear." She squeezed Alaina's hand, her touch lotiony soft. "That has to be so frustrating, but maybe you can focus on the good things, like your child, your marriage, your home. Not everyone has all of that."

The woman was such a mix of coolness and warmth. One minute Alaina was certain her mother-in-law disapproved of her, and the next Courtney was offering genuine comfort. Navigating life lately was like walking through a maze with a blindfold on.

"I hear what you're saying and I appreciate your trying to help. Really." They were practically at Porter's office now. Alaina glanced at the wall that housed photographs in handsome frames. Not one photograph had Alaina side by side with Courtney.

Glancing at her mother-in-law, Alaina chewed on her lip. What had their relationship been like? Judging by the photo albums she'd pored over, there wasn't much of a relationship between them. She forced herself to ask the question that had weighed on her mind since Porter announced that Courtney was at their vacation house. "Did you and I like each other?"

Arched eyebrows lifted. "Honestly? Not very much. We don't have a lot in common."

Finally, what felt like an honest answer from someone. "I think I like you now."

"That's probably because you don't feel married to my son."

True as it was, the declaration stung. Alaina spun her wedding ring around on her finger. "And could it also be that you don't see me as Porter's wife anymore?"

"Maybe…" Courtney paused, worrying one fingernail with another. "I made my mistakes—you made yours. But lucky for us, we get a fresh start."

There was a lot of fresh-starting going around. A lot of work going into creating a second chance at her life. If only she knew how long it would be until her memories came back. If they ever would. Was the effort to start over wasted—or vitally necessary?

Either way, right now, Alaina had no choice but to press on. "Courtney, will I dislike you again if I remember? Was it that bad?"

And if she remembered, what would she think of her marriage? That was a question she couldn't bring herself to ask.

"Somehow, I think we've found a middle ground that will stick regardless of what you remember."

"Good. I need a friend I can trust." And she meant it. Whatever had been in the past between them—well, it didn't matter right now. Alaina wasn't that person anymore. While it hadn't been long ago since she'd woken up in that hospital, the accident and the amnesia had changed her irrevocably. "So? Can we be friends?"

"Friends. I like that. No mother-daughter mess. I'm not your mother. Hell, I'm having enough trouble getting used to being a grandmother. And just so we're clear, I don't change diapers. But I excel at watching while a baby naps and I'm superb at holiday shopping." Courtney winked a perfect smoky eye.

"I'm not going to be ready for that anytime soon." The idea of going out in public was absolutely overwhelming. And venturing out in public at Christmastime? That sounded dreadful.

Claustrophobic.

"That's why we're going to shop online. Later, of course, once you've had time to settle in and recover." Courtney stopped outside her son's office door and tapped lightly until Porter glanced up. "Since the baby is napping, that's my call to be a grandmother. Son, take your wife out and romance the socks off her."

Four

His mom walked away from the office door, heels click-clacking in time with her singsong voice as she spoke to Thomas. He hadn't expected his mom to embrace the grandmother gig so wholeheartedly, but then his life was anything but predictable these days.

Porter searched Alaina's expression. The tension in her jaw. The way her brow furrowed as she subconsciously drew one arm across her midsection to grasp the opposite upper arm.

She gave him a good-natured grin, but it was clear she was still unsure of how to act around him. He couldn't blame her for that.

But she also looked ready to bolt and that's the last thing he wanted, so he took the time to take her in. Alive. Vibrant. Here, with him and Thomas. Thank God.

On top of her head, she'd piled her hair in a loose,

messy bun. Wavy blond strands fell out of the bun, framing her slender face.

Her white dress hugged her breasts, drawing his eyes. Tempting him. Reminding him of the heat they'd always found in bed. The passion that still simmered between them, that they could find again if he could make the most of this time. His hands ached to stroke the fabric along her skin, to caress her along the length of the dress that fell in rolling pleats from her waist, to trace the red flower embroidery snaking around at midthigh.

To press his mouth behind her knee and tunnel his way up her skirt.

She looked like a vision right out of *The Nutcracker*. Clara, as she ran away with the Nutcracker Prince. The only question was, could he be that prince again? Could he charm her, show her how damn great they were together? Somewhere along the years the fantasy had given way to a reality that neither of them had anticipated.

And he hated that.

And he hated that the reality had broken their family, nearly ending the life he'd dreamed of as a boy.

Though she lacked memories, every item she'd added to the house screamed its sentimentality. It was like alarms blaring. The dress she wore was no different.

It was the same dress she had worn two years ago, on their vacation to St. Augustine. They were only supposed to be in town for the night. He had surprised her after a major art opening by booking a charming bed-and-breakfast room for the weekend. They'd spent the whole time laughing, drinking local wine. Back when things were simpler. When they still sparkled and sizzled together.

It could be that way again.

It would be that way again. He refused to accept any other outcome.

"Don't let my mother get to you or put pressure on you when it comes to our marriage."

It was the best he had to offer. Wooing her back into this family was a delicate task requiring finesse.

"There's not much you could do to romance a new mom who's recovering from amnesia." She tapped her forehead in jest.

"That sounds like a challenge." He thrived on a challenge.

"Okay—" she spread her arms wide "—give it your best shot."

"Really? You want me to sweep you off your feet?" He cocked his head to the side, a thrill zipping through him.

"Sure, what woman wouldn't want to be swept off her feet?" Inclining her head, she dramatically twirled. The fabric of her skirt tightened and loosed as she turned. She was so damn sexy.

And he wanted her for his own.

"Challenge accepted." Progress. He could practically taste it.

She stopped midspin. "Wait, never mind. This shouldn't be a game."

"Believe me—I understand that all too well." Closing the gap between them, he rested his hands on her shoulders. "So relax. I've got this under control. Let me pamper you, and you focus on recuperating."

"You're right. The best thing I can do for my family is to regain my memory so we can move forward with our future rather than staying here in limbo with you working from home at a vacation house." She twisted her hands nervously, glancing out the window. "Honestly, I believe it's too soon for us to go on some extravagant outing."

So large gestures were out of the question. It was time for a game plan. He knew he had to be quick. They couldn't hole up in this house forever. Her memory would slowly come back into focus. It was time for action. Now.

Still, he said, "Of course. I agree and I have a few ideas, but I'll need a half hour to pull things together. There's a hammock past the pool, by the shore. I'll meet you there."

Her smile was hopeful. Beautiful. "Sounds perfect."

Alaina inhaled deep breaths of ocean air, one after the other, a foot draped over the side of the hammock, toe tapping to keep the steady swaying motion. The hammock was attached to two fat palm trees, branches and fronds rustling overhead.

Could Porter really find a way to put her fears to rest? Could regaining her memory be as simple as relaxing and enjoying time with the man she'd married?

She wanted to believe that. It had only been a week since she'd woken up after all. Yet, every hour that passed with no breakthroughs knotted the anxiety tighter within her.

Answers. That was what she needed. She was desperate for them. She kept hoping the scenery would jog her memory. Bestow the memories that were locked away somewhere in her mind.

Glancing at the harbor, she tried to imagine what sort of person she had grown into. A twenty-eight-year-old woman with a husband rich enough to bump elbows with the incredibly wealthy. And, judging by the sheer size of the yachts before her, incredibly wealthy didn't even begin to cover it.

Yachts spotted the water with the same frequency as white caps in a storm. A few of them looked like personal cruise ships.

Had she been out on any of these? Did she move comfortably in a world like this? Knowing what her life had been like before, she couldn't imagine it.

Her thoughts were cut short as a sun-bronzed woman approached. Alaina guessed the woman was probably a decade older than her. Maybe more. But older, Alaina realized, was a matter of perspective. She still felt as if she was looking through the eyes of a twenty-three-year-old.

The woman bustled toward Alaina, brunette hair flapping beneath an oversize white floppy hat. Cat-eyed sunglasses shielded the majority of her face, concealing her eyes from view. The gust of wind tugged at her bright pink-and-peach shift dress.

Alaina stood with mixed feelings. On the one hand, she was glad to have someone else to talk to, but on the other, she was nervous. It was too soon. What if the woman asked something Alaina couldn't answer?

But then hadn't she just thought how she needed to push ahead? She had to be strong, brave, for Thomas.

And Porter.

The woman jogged the last few steps and hugged Alaina hard before stepping back, her hands clasped to her chest. "Oh my God, Alaina, I thought that was you." The woman scrunched her nose, crinkling zinc oxide into the creases. "I forgot for a minute you can't remember all of us. I'm Sage Harding. Your neighbor. I like to think I'm your friend, even if we only see each other a couple of times a year for holidays."

A couple of times a year? But Porter had said they came here often. Perhaps Sage didn't come as often and so their paths only crossed a couple of times a year. Alaina wanted to believe that. Porter had no reason to lie.

She didn't understand her need to believe the worst in him, to be so suspicious of his every word.

They were married. There was ample proof. And they'd adopted a child together. They had a beautiful life—if she could just bring herself to accept it.

"Thank you for coming over to speak to me, Sage. That makes me feel less like an amnesia freak or a patient."

"Honey, you can't help what happened to you." Sage sat on a teal Adirondack chair next to the hammock. "You were in a car accident."

"I understand the facts in my mind, but it's difficult to trust my mind these days." She rolled her eyes at her own lame joke. "But enough about my medical woes. Tell me about yourself. Where are you from? Are you here with your family? How did we become friends?"

"Wow, that's a lot of questions." Sage held up her fingers, holiday-green glitter polish on short nails. "I'm from the D.C. area. My husband's in the House of Representatives, so we keep this house to stay Florida residents. Our two kids go to boarding school. And you and I became friends at an art gallery fund-raiser for the homeless."

That all rang true and fit with everything Porter had been telling her. "What type of art do you enjoy?"

"Oh, I don't know jack about art." Sage waved a self-deprecating hand. "I was there for the canapés, champagne and movie-star company. And helping the homeless. I like being a part of charity work. It's a rewarding way to spend my time."

"That's nice." Alaina wasn't sure what else to say to this refreshingly honest woman.

Sage leaned closer, her elbows on her knees. "Are you okay, really okay? I've been so worried. I came by the hospital when I heard and left flowers. But you weren't allowed to have visitors. I would have a baby shower for you, but that might be awkward just now. Maybe we'll wait until you get your memory back."

"I think that's best. And I'm still…resting."

"Oh, right. Silly me. I didn't mean to intrude. I was just so glad to see you and wanted to make sure you and Porter are doing okay."

Now that was a loaded statement. Alaina opted for an answer that wouldn't land her in hot water. "We're enjoying being parents."

"How is your little guy's foot?"

"Healing."

"I'm so relieved." Sage studied her matching Christmas-green toenails for three crashes of the waves. "I wasn't sure you would be back this year after, well, your male visitor last Christmas."

Alaina forced herself to stay still. There was no answer to that revelation and she sure as hell wasn't going to quiz a virtual stranger. "Thank you for stopping by."

"I shouldn't have said anything. I thought maybe he'd contacted you and I wanted to be sure you knew. I mean well." She pushed to her feet and dusted sand off her legs. "Please accept my apology."

"Accepted. It's tough to know the right thing to say. Amnesia isn't an everyday occurrence and it's difficult to know how to handle it." Alaina stood and saw Porter walking down the bluff carrying a picnic basket and an insulated bag. "There's my husband."

Sage crinkled her nose again. "That's my cue to leave."

"Merry Christmas to you and your family."

"To you and yours, too, honey." Sage squeezed Alaina's hand quickly. "Enjoy your baby's first visit from Santa Claus."

Santa Claus?

Of course. She should be focusing on Thomas's first Christmas. On doing normal family things like picking out toys for him to enjoy over the next year. Or making Christmas cookies, as her mother had always done as far back as Alaina could remember. Starting her own family traditions with Porter.

Or had they had traditions? Tough to tell in this generic-looking house without her own personal stamp.

She wanted that homey holiday life so desperately. Wanted to be normal again. To be herself again. Whatever that meant and whoever that was.

If things were normal, she and Porter might be standing in line somewhere, debating how to spoil their beautiful new son.

Anxiety ebbed back into her chest. Not that it was ever far away.

The thought of melting away into a crowd sounded a lot more appealing now than it had earlier.

A quick glance back down the sandy path toward the vacation home revealed that Porter had already started to make his way toward her. He was only about ten feet away and just the sight of him took her breath away all over again.

She allowed herself to examine him fully as he approached, basket in hand. His broad shoulders and chest, the clear suggestion of muscles beneath his casual light blue button-down. The way his jawline appeared to be chiseled out of marble. Strong. Defined. Like some of the statues she used to have in her old apartment.

But it was the lightness in his demeanor, the force of his smile that made her heart hammer. While he was made up of hard angles, his smile made him seem approachable. Understanding. Maybe even affectionate.

Was that what she'd seen in him from the first?

She wanted to kiss him. To know what they were like together. In bed. Or in the shower. Or in the dozens of other places her imagination wandered with fantasies.

Or were those memories? She couldn't be sure. There had been an undeniable physical connection between them from the moment she'd seen him in the hospital. It had laced each of their conversations so far. Amnesia or not, that much of a connection had persisted.

How could she have looked at another man as Sage had not too subtly insinuated?

Alaina had wondered more than once if Porter had been hiding something from her. She just hadn't considered that whatever he might be hiding was her fault.

Sunglasses shielding his eyes from the late-morning sun, Porter jogged down the last step cut into the bluff, his deck shoes hitting sand. He'd expected to find his wife napping in the hammock. Not chatting with their gossipy neighbor. Hell, he'd even checked with the staff to make sure the Hardings wouldn't be here for Christmas.

Apparently, staff intel was wrong.

Sage Harding fanned a wave at him as she slid her own sunglasses back on her face and sashayed through the sea oats and around a bluff back to her white mansion on stilts.

Between his mother and Sage, he couldn't catch a break. Although a voice in the back of his mind persisted that he didn't deserve one. He was deliberately keeping parts of their past from his wife. He tamped down that voice, not just for his own reasons but for her sake, as well. The doctor had said not to push her, but rather to let her recover the missing years on her own.

All the CT scans and MRI scans hadn't shown any brain damage, and yet her coma had persisted. The doc had said her mind was most likely protecting herself from something she wasn't ready to deal with. Again that voice piped up that maybe she didn't want to recall how close they'd been to signing the divorce papers their lawyers had drawn up. That she wanted this second chance at creating a family every bit as much as he did.

His pace quickened as he approached. He could see that there was something sparking beneath the surface of her eyes. It was in the way she cocked her head to the side and studied him up and down. A question in her expression. A curiosity. One he wanted to answer.

Time was limited now as their son napped—and the holidays were a brief interlude, too. Soon, they would have to return home. She would find out all that he'd been keeping from her and all hell could break loose. He intended to use this time with her, away from all that, wisely.

Porter placed the picnic basket and insulated bag

on the Adirondack chair so there would be nowhere to sit except beside his wife. "You'll want to stay clear of Sage Harding."

"Sage?" Alaina shifted, the roped hammock swaying beneath her. "Why on earth should I avoid her?"

"Because she's not as genuine as she tries to appear. She's cultivating wealthy friends to fund her husband's run for the US Senate. Plain and simple, she uses people."

Alaina slowly nodded as if she was unsure how to respond. As if she didn't trust his word. Ouch.

"Okay. That's sad to hear, that someone's using others."

"You're not sure if you believe me about Sage's motivations for coming over?"

She shook her head. "It's not that. But people can have different impressions of someone."

A diplomatic answer. But one that reminded him he still had to earn her trust. Well, re-earn. "Fair enough. It's your judgment call to make. Just promise me you'll be careful around her."

"I will." She chewed her bottom lip. "Maybe I was too eager to believe what she said about being friends because I feel so isolated. There's no one I know outside of our family."

"You asked for phone numbers. I looked up ones for your old friends." He held out a sheet of paper with scribbled names and numbers. It was a small gesture, but he hoped it would matter to her. Show her that he was committed to making their family work.

"*Old* friends? We're not friends anymore?"

"You moved away from North Carolina years ago. They got married, too, and many of them relocated, as well." He shrugged. "People lose touch with each other. It happens."

She pressed her forehead. "Not that it really matters anyway, I guess. They would only know what I already recall. They won't have much of anything to offer about the past five years other than maybe one of those 'the world is rosy' Christmas letters I must have sent out." The hurt and frustration in her voice filled each syllable.

"Maybe there's something they can offer. I want you to be happy. I'm trying to help you, Alaina."

"And I'm not trying?" she snapped. "This is so very hard, not remembering even meeting you, yet trying to be a wife and a mother in a completely alien world."

This wasn't going the way he'd planned. He didn't want her to feel more isolated, more alone. "I'm sorry. I know this is a million times tougher on you, and I want to help you." He smoothed back her hair, his hand resting lightly on her shoulder. "I didn't mean to upset you. Can we start over? I've ordered brunch. You barely touched breakfast. Okay?"

"Sure, Porter, that's probably a good idea. I'm sorry for lashing out at you like that. I know this has to be difficult for you, too. And I can see you're truly trying to make things easier for me." She pressed her fingers to her temple again as if her head was throbbing. "Did we used to argue like that a lot?"

Arguments?

He needed to tread warily as hell on this topic.

It was such a loaded question she'd asked. And a difficult one to answer.

Porter reached into the basket to give himself time to think, and hefted out an impressive spread. Brie. Herbed crackers. Fresh fruit, cut and quartered. Dark chocolate–covered nuts. All of her absolute favorites. Years ago, when things were easier between them, they had made brunches on the beach a ritual. It was also how they had spent their first date. A picnic on the beach.

"We exchanged words, and yes, we argued." He glanced back at her, looking over the top of his sun-glasses. "Our reconciliations were incredible." He handed her a piece of chocolate.

She eyed him pensively for a few seconds before her shoulders relaxed and she took the truffle with a play-ful smile, blue eyes twinkling like the ocean reflect-ing the sun. "It's not sexy to hit on a woman who just came out of a coma."

"Why?" He pivoted on one knee, cupping the side of her face in one hand. "You're beautiful."

She didn't pull away. "I'm pasty and exhausted."

"That's why this is the perfect place to rest." He pulled a slice of cheese from the cutting board and popped it into her mouth before she could respond. "Now eat. You need to put back on the weight you lost."

Her throat moved in a swallow before she said, "Was that an insult?"

"I just told you. You've always been beautiful to me." He traced her bottom lip with his thumb. "I'm more than willing to practice our reconciliation skills whenever you're ready."

She nipped the pad of his thumb and sent a jolt of arousal clean through him.

"Porter, I would be lying if I said I wasn't tempted. So much." She pressed a kiss into his work-roughened palm before moving his hand away. "But you're right about me lacking energy and needing to refuel. And you were right about me needing to decompress. My emo-tions seem to swing from high to low without warning."

"Damned by my own words," he said, but glad for the reminder to put her needs first.

"And we should go back soon. The baby…"

"Is sleeping. With my mother watching and a nanny as backup." He frowned, shaking his head. "Because I would never trust my mother as the sole caregiver of a child. Our child."

"That's sad."

"I meant it as a joke." Sorta.

"Really? Because I don't think it's funny. Is that why you have the nanny? Because you don't trust me?"

He could hear her winding up again.

"I trust you with our child, unequivocally. Truly, I only want you to rest." They needed the extra help right now until things returned to a normal routine. Because it had to return to normal. He refused to accept the possibility he could lose the family they had created for their son.

"You're maxed out, as well."

He rubbed the back of his neck and didn't answer.

Didn't quite look at her.

She ran her hand slowly along his shoulders. Her fingers lightly tracing circles down his back, reigniting his desire. She inched closer, so her head was inches from his. Her voice lowered, filling with concern. With understanding.

"And having your mother here stresses you more."

He reached out, closing the distance between them. Hand to her cheek, he stroked her skin with his thumb. She sighed into his hand, her breath warm against him. Sexy and moist. He wanted her so damn much.

"Damn it, Alaina, you always did read me well, right from the start."

Unable to resist a taste, just this one moment to connect with his wife again, Porter leaned in to kiss her.

Five

The warmth of his lips sent an electric pulse through her, and she hungered for more. His hand wound into her hair. Alaina's own body melted into his as she pressed herself against his hard, muscled chest.

The kiss deepened, mouths opening, hands stroking. Alaina's desire became more urgent as she tasted a hint of raspberries on his tongue. He angled her closer, tongue exploring. Testing. Her fingers curled into the fine texture of his shirt. Everything about him drew her, from the way he looked at her to the way he made her smile. From the way he touched her to the care he gave their child.

Right now, she could easily envision how she'd fallen in love with this man and married him. She ached to remember the passionate experiences they'd shared, words they'd exchanged. Anything. And she hated that he had it all and she had nothing.

But she reveled in how hard he was working to win her over. That thrilled her and excited her—

From somewhere outside of this wonderful moment, she heard the distinctive hum of a speedboat skidding across the water. It snapped her to her senses. Reminded her of the fact she was kissing a man she didn't really know, a man she didn't fully trust, which complicated her feelings even more.

She pushed against his chest. Broke the kiss and connection before looking shyly at him.

She laughed self-consciously. "I shouldn't have done that. You have an amnesiac wife and a new baby and here I am making a move on you."

He burst out laughing, the sound rolling out on the ocean breeze. He laughed again, his head falling and broad shoulders shaking. Pinching the bridge of his nose, he said, "God, woman, you turn me inside out. You always have."

The words sent a shiver through her every bit as arousing as his kiss had been. There was emotion behind the words.

Had there been emotion in his touch, as well? She didn't trust her judgment yet.

The wind blew her hair across her face and she swept it away again. "I'm sorry. I, um, didn't mean to send mixed signals and mislead you—"

He traced her lips. "You turning me inside out has always been a good thing. We may have argued about a lot of issues, but we always connected on a physical level." He tapped her lips a final time. "But I meant it when I said I wouldn't pressure you to take this faster than you want to take it."

"That's good to know." She shot to her feet restlessly,

gathering up their lunch and putting it back in the basket. "The attraction between us is…problematic."

An urgency to move filled her. They needed to get back to the baby, anyway. She gathered more remnants of the picnic, sliding the lids onto the various containers. But not before she snagged another piece of brie and popped it into her mouth. She reveled in the creamy texture, using the food-induced silence to steady herself.

"We were married for years," he said into the silence. "Even if your brain doesn't remember, I believe that on some level your body does. We'll take things slowly until your mind catches up." He offered her another piece of dark chocolate. Her fingertips gingerly brushed his as she took it. Another confusing jolt of desire burst through her.

"What if my mind doesn't ever catch up?"

A devilish smile spread across his lips. "Then we'll start over."

"And what if I'm not the same woman I was?" In her chest, her heart pounded. Tension rose again, unmistakable.

"You are the woman I met five years ago."

She left the hammock, placing the basket on the chair and stacking the containers inside. "But I'm not. I recall what I was like then. It feels like it just happened. But the past week, waking up and finding out that I'm married and a mother and I have this whole chunk of life I lived? That was a surprise. That's changed me. Immeasurably."

"Sure, of course it did."

"You say that. But I don't think you're hearing me. Not really. You seem to want to pick up where we left off."

On a certain level, she could understand that desire. On the logical level. But the emotional one—that was an entirely different scenario. How could she make him understand how overwhelming all of this was?

His jaw flexed and he left the hammock, helping her pack their meal, kneeling beside her. "I'm trying to help you remember, like you asked."

"I don't believe that. You want me to be the woman you married. To have our lives back the way they were."

He snorted on a dark laugh. "You couldn't be further from the truth."

She went still, sagging back to sit on her butt in the sand. A chill settled in her stomach. "So things weren't great between us."

"I didn't say that."

"When I asked you if we argued a lot, you answered that we exchanged words and had great make-up sex."

"We did."

"But we argued. A lot." She packed up the last few items into the basket. And shut it hard.

"Married couples do that."

"We did."

"Yes, Alaina, we did." He clasped her shoulders. "We weren't perfect. We still aren't. But we have a chance here to build our family. We've been wanting this for a long time. Can you believe that much at least?"

He searched her face, scrutinized her expression. Cheeks ablaze, she tried to work out the harrowing emotions that knocked against each other inside of her like kids in bumper cars. He was asking for her trust. And she *should* trust him. They were married after all—but she had been close to having an affair, if Sage Harding was to be believed. What did all of that add up to?

Porter was practically a stranger to her. And his desire to have her put her faith in him frayed her nerves more. It didn't make sense. The Porter she was meeting now had never given her a reason not to trust him. But deep down, something stopped her from giving herself over to him completely.

"Sure," she said, knowing her answer was a brush-off and not able to come up with more than, "I believe you want to build a family."

Dizziness hit. Her chest tightened. She felt a moment of panic over being confined even though he was just holding her. She knew the fear was unreasonable, but still, given what had happened in that past abusive relationship. she couldn't help but feel nervous over how isolated she'd allowed herself to become. And how some might say Porter had taken away her resources by bringing her here where she wasn't close to anyone, just as her old boyfriend had done before.

What did she really know about this man beyond that he was gentle with Thomas?

Her arms began to tingle. Alaina felt so boxed in by the weight of the past she remembered and the past she didn't. Space. That's what she needed. She shot up from their beach picnic, turned on her heel...

And ran.

The pounding of her feet hitting the ground reverberated in her mind. She hadn't even noticed she had balled her hands into fists until she made it to the kitchen. The sticky sweet remains of a raspberry fell into the sink as she unclenched her fingers.

One deep breath. And then another.

There was no one to call. It was times like these that she desperately wished she could talk to her mother or

father. They had always known what to say, how to help
her parse out a situation. But they had died during her
junior year of college. The memory of that moment,
of that horrible phone call, was still fresh in her mind.

She'd give anything for her family to be intact.

Didn't Thomas deserve the same? An intact, func-
tional family? Parents who adored him? She already
loved her son so much. And if she were being honest
with herself, she wanted a family just as much as Porter seemed to. She wanted them to be a complete and
intact unit.

More than her own happiness was at stake now.

And for the first time, she was more afraid of what
might happen to her marriage if she remembered, than
if she left those five years buried.

Relieved Thomas's checkup had gone so well, Porter shut the door of the car behind his wife in the parking lot of the pediatrician's office. This had been their
first joint trip off the property since the family had left
the hospital together last week. He glanced in the backseat, where Thomas smiled at him in his "Santa's Little
Helper" onesie.

The doctor had confirmed that Thomas was healing well. It would just take time. That seemed to be the
theme of his life recently. Wait. Be patient.

It was damn hard to do sometimes. Porter strode
around the car and positioned himself in the driver's
seat. On the one hand, he was grateful they were all
still together. On the other hand, he felt as if things had
stalled since their beach picnic. She had built a wall
around herself and he didn't understand why. Since that
kiss, she'd been antsy, jumpy over being touched. Only

when they were with Thomas were they both at ease. He didn't doubt for an instant—she loved their son every bit as much as he did. That baby boy had them wrapped around his finger.

Porter had built multimillion-dollar homes around the country. He'd built a billion-dollar corporation on his own, with no help from his wealthy mother. And yet those accomplishments didn't mean as much to him as coaxing a big belch from Thomas or laughing with Alaina as they struggled to work a tiny flying fist into a sleeper.

He wanted a family no matter what. People accused him of being determined at work, but that was nothing compared to how hard he would devote himself to making this come together. He wouldn't give up what he was building in his life. It was a helluva lot more important than any structure put up by his corporation.

Porter started the car and adjusted the radio. "Would you like to pick up carryout on our way home or stop by a deli? The weather's perfect to eat on the deck."

Would she be interested in unwinding later in the hot tub? He didn't know what to expect from her after she'd welcomed his kiss on the beach, and then proceeded to push him away.

"Porter, do you mind if we do something away from the beach house? I don't want to be cooped up all day. It's too nice of an afternoon to spend inside." Alaina stared out the window as they drove past a team of reindeer made of bent willow branches in the courtyard of the doctor's office.

A smile pulled at his lips. Perhaps this patience thing was paying off. Alaina hadn't wanted to do anything outside of the house since they'd arrived there. This was a good sign. Maybe she was beginning to trust him.

"Of course. I have to swing by a job site for a final walk-through. Then the rest of the day is ours." He reached for her hand and gave it a gentle squeeze.

"I don't mind that at all. Besides, I'd like to see you in action."

She flashed him a quick smile as she turned the radio to a Christmas station. Her head bopped along to a jazzy rendition of an old classic as they drove through town, where lighted white snowflakes hung from palm trees lining the village's main thoroughfare.

It didn't take long to reach the job site. This was an up-and-coming section of town. The beach stretched and wound lazily in front of them, beyond the Spanish-influenced mansion Porter needed to inspect.

"Porter, this place is beautiful. It's so exotic looking." Her eyes darted to the lattice that was pressed against the side of the house between the garage and door. Scores of plants were strategically placed around the yard.

He slowed the car to a stop. "It is. It's been my favorite recent project. Do you want to stay in the car or come with me?" He searched her eyes for a clue as to what she was thinking. She glanced behind him, over his shoulder to the two men who were talking to each other by the large arched doorway.

"I want to come. But first, can you tell me who they are?" She gestured toward the men.

"The taller man with the buzz cut is my second-in-command. His name is Oliver Flournoy. He's a smooth-talking guy, but he's still single. The man he is talking to is Micah Segal, our CFO. Sometimes we go out with him and his wife, Brianna. They have a toddler, Danny. He adores you. Like all kids do."

"Okay. Oliver and Micah. Got it in here." She tapped her temple and let out a shaky laugh. She unclipped her seat belt and pushed herself out of the car so she could unbuckle Thomas.

Alaina really was something else. This was a huge step for her and seeing her step back into the world so fearlessly even in the face of her amnesia impressed him in a major way. She was an amazing woman, more than just beautiful. She had an inner strength that shone— and drew him. How had he lost sight of this side of her?

What a helluva time to want to tuck her away from prying eyes and kiss her until she sighed, and more.

He cleared his throat and his thoughts, narrowing his focus back on the moment at hand. By the time Thomas was out of his seat, Micah and Oliver were over at the car. Palpable silence descended on the group. Alaina rocked Thomas back and forth, eyes flicking from Oliver to Micah and back to Porter.

Oliver, a slim man with deep brown hair, cleared his throat to break the silence.

"How are you feeling, Alaina?" he asked, clearly feeling awkward as hell with her amnesia.

"Well. All things considered… And how are you, Oliver?"

"Doing well, doing well," he answered, repeating her polite words, bobbing his head. "Just gearing up for Christmas at my sister's."

"That's…good." She rocked Thomas, turning her attention to the shorter man with auburn hair. "And how are things with you, Micah?"

"No reason to complain, ma'am." He blinked fast

as if forcing himself to make eye contact. "All's quiet and well at home."

More awkward silence descended. Damn. This was not going the way he'd thought it might.

"We are glad you are feeling better," Micah added. Blink, blink. Blink, blink.

"We are, too," Porter said, wishing he could say something to smooth things over. "Alaina, why don't you let me hold Thomas and you can go explore the grounds. The view from the back deck is stunning. Oliver, would you unlock the door for her?"

Alaina nodded, visibly relieved at the opportunity to escape. Brushing his hands along her arms, Porter took Thomas from her.

"Of course." Oliver unlocked the door and strode inside, flipping on lights. Alaina walked through the door frame, her movements quick and brisk. She was taking everything in. Seemed to love the driftwood-colored hardwood floors, the crisp white trim. She flashed Porter a quick smile over her shoulder before walking across the rooms to the patio door.

His eyes stayed on her a moment longer. He was struck by her bravery in facing this amnesia head-on, even when it wasn't easy. In the old days, he might have asked her about artwork for the place. Her expertise was always coveted by home buyers. He missed seeing the way her artist's mind worked. It had been one part of their marriage where they shared an easy accord.

"How are you handling the new kid? This father-hood gig is something else." Micah made small talk with Porter as they moved through the house.

"It's everything I wanted and nothing I imagined." He would do anything for his son. Anything. He'd never expected to feel this much for another living being—the love, the protectiveness, the pride. "He's fun."

"And cute as hell." Micah tugged Thomas's healthy foot lightly. "How's his clubfoot healing? Gotta confess, I don't know a lot about this type of issue."

"He'll need two more surgeries and physical therapy, but the doctor expects a full recovery. I just hate that he has to hurt."

Micah nodded sympathetically. "He smiles when he sees you. That rocks."

"Truth." At least he had that going for him. The bond he was already creating with his son made his heart swell. It made the dream of a family of his own more real—and more important.

"And Alaina?"

"She's a natural mother. No amnesia could steal that from her."

"I'm sorry, man. I wish I could say it's for the best, since y'all— Hell, that sounds insensitive."

Micah's features tensed. But Porter knew he didn't mean anything by the comment. Things had been so difficult before the accident. So rocky. It wasn't something they could keep hidden.

"Don't worry. I know you mean well." Their voices bounced around the skeleton of the house.

"Come have dinner with us. Let's hang out like old married couples." Micah's face showed genuine concern and interest. He was a good guy. The type Porter could always count on.

"I'll talk to Alaina. We'll see if she's up to it. She wants to talk to people from our past, and I want to give her whatever she needs. We just have to tread carefully and follow the doctor's instructions." Porter explained a little of the situation to Micah, but his gaze moved to the side. Toward Alaina.

She was walking around the property, taking in the features of this house. She seemed to belong in the place. The softer, more classical lines and arches fit her better than the angles and modernism of their beach home.

Why hadn't he perceived this before? His mind filled with all the times she'd catered to his tastes and desires. He couldn't escape the realization that he needed to appreciate her for who she was, not just how she fit into his vision of the perfect family.

"Of course. Let's talk more and pick a time. Dinner at our place. Or a restaurant." Micah clapped him on the shoulder. "Or even go to the ballet."

"Seriously? The ballet?" Head cocking to the side, Porter snapped his attention back to the conversation.

"Just checking to be sure you're still listening. You were so busy staring at your wife."

It was hard not to stare at her. Alaina captivated his attention, his thoughts.

Seeing her in this house he wondered if surprising her with the beach house after finding out they would need fertility treatments a few years ago had been the right call. Should he have had her pick out a house with him instead? He'd cut her out of the decisions sometimes, telling himself he was surprising her. Yet then she was stuck pretending to be pleased.

He needed to set his mind on ways to fix that in the future, when he was considering major changes like remodeling or even relocation. Big changes he couldn't tackle right this second. But he could—and wanted—

to do something special for her now, something she would like.

After they were back in the car, Porter started to drive toward a place they hadn't been to in ages. Fishin' Franks—her favorite restaurant. He wanted today to be special.

Lunch was absolutely delicious. Cajun fish tacos. Fresh avocados. Live music.

All things considered, Alaina was having a decent time being out of the beach house today. Porter was as charming as ever, completely sensitive to her every whim and desire. And to Thomas. Seeing them together made her heart surge. Porter was dedicated to the boy. Completely devoted to becoming a family.

For a moment, she considered what it would be like if her memories never came back.

Maybe this was all they needed. A completely fresh start. A new house for a new family. A house like the one at the job site. One that fed into her eclectic sensibilities and symbolized their new life together.

She could practically picture Thomas taking his first steps on the driftwood-colored hardwood floors. And art hanging all over the living room.

As they walked into the Baby Supplies Galore store, she scanned the faces of the other shoppers. In true Florida Christmas fashion, babies were dressed in shorts and tanks that sported flamingos in Santa hats.

The aisles were packed with late-December holiday shoppers. Christmas music mingled with the rush of families debating gifts.

Porter kept stride next to her as she pushed the cart down the least crowded aisle. His hand went almost instinctively to the small of her back. The warmth of his touch begged her to recall their past again. It clouded her sense of the present. Even knowing that they could be a family with a fresh start, she yearned to remember what they'd shared.

"What was the best present you ever received from me for Christmas?" she asked, looking at the blanket sets.

Glancing at the prices, Alaina quickly realized this was a high-end baby store. Just one item probably cost as much as five of her childhood Christmases altogether. This was a completely different level of shopping.

"Hmm. There was one year that you did a painting based on the blueprint of the building project that launched my career. I loved that. It's hanging above my desk in my office."

"I'd like to look at that more closely. Get an idea of the direction of my art. And what was my favorite Christmas present from you?"

"I think the best gift I ever gave you may have been the surprise trip to Paris. We spent a week in art galleries eating brie and bread."

"Ah, bread and cheese. Such a solid combination." She laughed to cover her regret that she couldn't remember what sounded like a beautiful trip. "What about your Christmases as a child?"

She slowed down beside a tower of holiday-themed baby rattles—penguins with red-and-green scarves, polar bears with fuzzy hats and deer with jingle bells.

"My mom went all out. Good God, she went all out. Mom's a lawyer. Did I tell you that?" He plucked a snowy owl out of a bin and waggled it in front of the baby, who rewarded him with a gummy grin.

"I don't believe anyone thought to tell me that detail, actually." She'd taken in so much information in such a short time it was hard to keep the facts straight. "I assumed she was independently wealthy. She took time off to be here? That's really sweet."

He waggled his hand. "Taking time off work is a way to put it, I guess. My mother sneaks off to work just like I do. Neither of us has ever been big on sleep."

"That's funny, given the impression she relays, snoozing in, preferring the baby be asleep."

"That's my mom. Contrary."

Alaina hugged a stuffed bear against the ache in her chest. "I wish my mother could be here to meet Thomas. She would love him."

His forehead furrowed with deep creases of concern. "I wish she could be here for you."

She set the bear back on the shelf, arranging him precisely. "Your mother's been surprisingly easy to get along with. This fresh start has been helpful perhaps. We don't feel threatened."

"You have no reason to feel threatened by my mother."

"She's certainly got it all together."

And what about her own life? Nothing about it felt together. A whole degree and career she couldn't remember participating in. What kind of exhibits had she been a part of?

There was no sense dwelling on it, though. Instead, she would put all of her energy into the present moment. Focusing on the past wasn't doing anyone any good.

For now, she would worry about making Thomas's first Christmas something special.

Porter picked a reindeer and snowman ornament that read Baby's first Christmas. He flipped it over in his hand before handing it to Alaina. "What do you think of this one?"

She traced the ceramic ornament. "It's perfect. And speaking of firsts, since I haven't remembered anything, let's choose some new traditions to start today."

The fresh start she'd been daydreaming about could begin now.

"Such as?" he asked.

So many traditions to pick from. She opted for the simplest, one that connected so many families at the holidays. "Let's start with meals. What do we usually eat for Christmas?"

"Traditional turkey and a duck with all the trimmings. You like oyster stuffing so we have that. I like cranberry pie."

"While that sounds delicious, let's do away with it or eat it all on another day. For Christmas let's serve something totally different this year. A standing rib roast…" She snapped her fingers. "Or I know—how about we have a shrimp boil?"

"A shrimp boil? For Christmas?"

"Yes," she said, warming to the idea, feeling in control of the holiday and her new life for the first time. "In the Carolinas we call it frogmore stew, but down here it would be a shrimp boil. Shrimp, corn, new potatoes, maybe crawfish or crab or sausage in it, as well. We could have corn-bread stuffing, or crab and corn bread stuffing. What do you think?"

He held up a Santa hat and plopped it on her head.

"I think you're so excited I'll eat anything if it makes you smile like that." His hand slid down to cup her face. "I've missed your smile."

Again, she thought about how he must feel in this situation. He'd lost his wife, for all intents and purposes. First to the coma and now to her inability to remember what they'd been to each other. And this certainly couldn't have been how he'd envisioned their first Christmas with their child. "I'm sorry for all the pain this is causing you."

"I'm not in pain right now. I'm happy. Really happy."

His eyes shone with sincerity that sent tingles into her stomach.

"Let's shop. This is one time I won't complain about all that money you have. Let's be Santa."

She pushed the cart forward to the next line of plush toys.

"I like the way you think. And I'm a sucker for stuffed animals." He tossed a giant polar bear at her. She caught it easily.

She waved it in front of Thomas, and even gave the bear a voice. Porter pulled down a small duck and started to play along with her.

It felt so natural. As if they were a normal family. As if they all belonged together. The baby giggled at the impromptu theater provided by his parents.

An elderly lady walked up to them. "If all parents were like you two, the world would be a wonderful place. You're giving that child the gift of imagination. It's lovely. What a beautiful family." The elderly lady grabbed a small teddy from the shelf.

"Thank you, ma'am." Porter rubbed his hand over Alaina's shoulder.

His hand sent her senses tingling. It had felt so natural. So perfect. Maybe there was a shot for them all after all.

"Merry Christmas. Y'all enjoy him while he's that small and adorable. Before you know it, he'll be a teenager asking for a car." She smiled at them and continued farther into the store.

"A car?" Porter chuckled, plucking up a rattle shaped like a race car. "Easy enough for now. And clearly the polar bear and duck have to come home. They have Thomas's stamp of approval."

"I think you are right. I really like this elephant, too, though." She scooped the blue elephant off the shelf and her hand tightened.

The inky tendrils of a memory pushed into her mind. It felt as if she was underwater without goggles. It was unfocused at first. She and Porter at a friend's baby shower around the holidays. Laughing at the party. Overwhelmed with joy for their friends, for the baby that was about to come into their lives.

But knowing all the while that a baby wasn't about to enter her and Porter's life. How hard it was for them to go back home to their house on Christmas knowing they couldn't conceive. How much pain welled in her chest even now at the thought of that Christmas.

"What is it? What's wrong?" Porter asked, concern flooding his voice as he took the elephant from her.

The memory evaporated and she sank down, sitting on the edge of a display platform. "I just remembered something. From before. From a Christmas a few years ago, I'm not sure exactly when."

"Tell me," he insisted, kneeling beside her while keeping his hand securely on Thomas.

She struggled to remember every detail as if that might pry out more. "We went to a baby shower after finding out we couldn't conceive… I just…" Her voice trailed off. The words faded and closed in her throat.

"Shhh. It's okay." He wrapped an arm around her. Drew her close as ragged breaths escaped her throat. His embrace was somehow more familiar than the kiss, more real.

He stroked her back, murmured into her hair. This moment felt like the first thing she'd really shared with Porter since waking from the coma. And she sank into that feeling.

Would she be able to hang on to that once they returned home? Or would it evaporate like that ethereal memory?

Six

Porter had a knack for presentation and plans. It was a skill he'd picked up as he grew his construction empire. And it was something easily transferred to romance. He was a big-picture kind of guy.

And if any of his visions needed to pan out, it was this one.

The day after their shopping outing, he led Alaina through the house, hands covering her eyes.

"You swear you can't see?" His body pressed against hers as they shuffled forward. The light scent of her coconut shampoo wafted in the inches between them, making him remember the countless nights they'd spent together. How he wanted that now. Wanted her now.

But he had to put recovering their family first. Taking her to bed would jeopardize his plans since she didn't trust him yet.

"I swear. But what is all this about?"

"It's a surprise. You'll just have to trust me."

Damn. If that wasn't the statement of the moment. Trust him that the surprise was worth it. And that he was, too.

He spun her around the room, turning in circles until there was no doubt in his mind that she was completely disoriented.

Two turns later, and they were in the family room. Dropping his hands, he waited while she surveyed the room and the additions he'd purchased just for her.

A ten-foot-tall live Christmas tree stood centered in the three bay windows. It was already lit, the white lights bathing the room in a warm glow.

Two boxes of decorations—special ordered and newly delivered—were stacked on the white-and-tan-striped couch, pushed up against the blue pillows of embroidered crabs and starfish. The shelving unit behind the couch had been emptied of the normal knick-knacks of lighthouses, shells and boats.

A blank canvas. Perfect for making new memories. And maybe uncovering other old ones that would bring them closer together. Of course there was also the risk that she would remember the wrong ones. That she would realize how close they'd come to divorcing and wonder why he hadn't told her.

This was how they would build a family together. She had been right earlier. It was time to start creating family traditions. Ones Thomas would grow into.

Traditions grounded a person, gave them a firm foundation to build a life upon, and clearly Alaina had a gift for that he hadn't recognized before. Maybe because he'd been too busy trying to wedge her into his preconceived notions of a family portrait rather than letting them make it together.

He wanted to create the family he'd never had as a kid. It was always just him, his mom and whatever guy she was pursuing at the time. There had been no long-standing traditions on Christmas or any other time. He loved his mother, of course, but they were distant. And he wanted better for his son.

He'd always wanted this. It was why he'd grabbed this second chance. But he was starting to see he'd sacrificed some of Alaina's preferences to reach his goal.

"How did you get this here so quickly?" Gesturing to the boxes and the tree. Blue eyes dancing in the muted light.

"The idea came to me while we were shopping and I had it all delivered."

"But you already had the decorations in place for when we arrived."

"Those were the ones here before, the ones outside and in the living room. It struck me today we didn't have anything less formal, for us as a family here, to open gifts with Thomas."

She hugged him hard. "Thank you, it's perfect." Then she froze, stepping back and turning away fast to dig around in the box closest to them. She lifted the decorations out and stacked them on the coffee table in front of the couch.

"Did I choose those others in the main living room? They don't seem like me." She shot him a look. "They're so…matchy…modern art deco rather than the smoother Renaissance palettes I gravitate toward."

"You're right." And he was seeing how he'd missed the mark and wished that he'd paid more attention.

"Most of the decorations came with the house. I bought the place as a gift to you."

"You didn't build this?" Surprise cut into her voice as she lifted the palm tree crèche out of the box. Leaning against the space between the boxes on the couch, she placed the crèche on the center shelf.

"Oh, I did. But for another family. They had everything in place, ready to move in and then they split up. I picked up the place for a song…um…not that I wouldn't have spent a fortune for you." A sheepish grin pulled on his cheeks. He placed a running silver reindeer on the lowest shelf behind the couch.

"I know that. Clearly."

Was that a dig? Was she complaining about their lifestyle? He shook off the defensiveness and thought about her, her wants and preferences, and recalled how uncomfortable she'd always been with his wealth. "We always planned to redecorate and never got around to it. I should have insisted."

"Or I should have insisted. I'm an adult. I take responsibility for decisions I made, even if I can't remember them." She rolled her eyes.

"Would you like to redo the whole place? Or our primary residence?"

"Primary residence? Hmmm. That still feels so… surreal. Like everything else in my life." She toyed with a red satin bow. "I haven't even seen our regular house in Tallahassee yet. Is it like this?"

"No, you had carte blanche there."

"How long have we lived in that house?" She sat on the tile floor between the couch and the coffee table with the box of new tree ornaments in front of her. Each one unique and made by a local artisan. Reaching into the box she began to remove all kinds of ornaments. It was a mismatched set. She set them down, one by one, on the coffee table, eyes sharp with obvious approval.

He thought back to those early days when they'd had so much hope for their future, planning a big family, children, grandchildren, growing old together. "We had it built when we got married."

"So we made those decisions together."

"We did." Kneeling, he helped her take the remaining ornaments out of the box. He lifted the first ornament they'd ever got together as newlyweds: two penguins on a snowbank holding hands. Gently, he set it next to the ornament that sported a snowman made of sand.

"I wish we'd gone to our house first." Her fingers roved gently over top of all the decorations. It was as if she was trying to gain memories by osmosis. She stopped over a Santa Claus ornament. He was posed in a Hawaiian shirt and board shorts, and he had a pink flamingo beneath his hands. A small laugh escaped her lips and she brought the Santa to the tree and hung it on a bough.

"We still can." He brought a snowflake ornament with him and hung it slightly below hers.

"But we're settled for now and have the follow-up appointments with Thomas's doctor. After Christmas we can settle into a new routine."

"It's a lot to take in at once, both places."

"That's perceptive of you."

They kept bringing ornaments to the tree, filling the boughs until they grew heavy with their collective past. He enjoyed the way that she laughed over the ornaments. The way each one was an act of discovery for her.

The evening was too good to be true.

Just as they were getting ready to put the angel on top of the tree, his mother's laughter floated into the room a second before she entered, hanging on the arm of a man with salt-and-pepper hair.

She waved her son over. "Come here, darling. You too, Alaina."

What the hell? Porter pushed to his feet and silently fumed. Who was this man? Didn't his mother realize they needed a calm and quiet family holiday? Her surprise visit had already added enough additional chaos to the equation.

"Mom, what's going on?"

"I want you to meet my new friend Barry. He's a tax attorney."

Now that seemed right. He was as polished as she was.

Barry thrust out his hand. "Nice to meet you both. Your mom has been telling me a lot about you." His grip was tight as he shook Porter's hand. "Oh, you're putting up another tree? Best part of the whole Christmas season if you ask me."

The guy was nice enough. Smooth. But so were most attorneys. They knew how to read people and work a room. This guy was no exception.

"I feel the same way, Barry." Alaina's voice cut his thoughts in half.

Courtney hugged Barry's arm closer. "I'm so glad he's joining us for dinner tonight. It'll be a little party."

"Mother, I need to talk to you. Mind if I show you something?" And with that he hooked Courtney's arm in his. Smiling tightly, he led her out of the family room and into the hallway.

He glanced back into the room to see his mother's newest suit-of-a-boyfriend helping Alaina put the angel on the tree. Something he had wanted to do with her. Damn it. Who pushed in on someone else's Christmas decorating?

"Mom," he hissed softly, "did you have to bring your boyfriend over now? Alaina's condition is delicate and we have a new baby."

"First—" she held up a slim finger "—Alaina is stronger than you give her credit for. Second, your child is asleep. And third, he's not my boyfriend. We just met at a local fund-raiser I was attending at the invitation of your neighbor Sage."

How freaking perfect. Sage was up to her usual tricks. She'd probably invited his mother to glean some information about what was going on with Alaina. She'd use their struggle as gossip at the next society function.

"There's a helluva lot going on here without adding strangers to the mix. You should have spoken to me."

"Let me get this straight." His mother folded her arms. "I showed up uninvited and brought my uninvited pickup. That makes you uncomfortable."

Always the lawyer. Even out of the courtroom.

"You're leading the witness, Mother."

"Fair enough." She held up both hands. "Barry and I will go out."

He gave an exasperated sigh as he put his hand to the back of his neck. "No, stay. It'll only be more awkward if you haul him back out after announcing he's staying for dinner."

She clacked away from him, back into the great room, heading to the last box of Christmas decorations.

So much for creating stable traditions and experiences like a normal family. Tonight was supposed to have been calm. Relaxing. A night for him and Alaina to grow closer. To move toward becoming a family. Turns out that was just as difficult for him as it was for her.

Alaina cut through her petite filet with ease. Shoveling a forkful into her mouth, she watched the verbal volleyball tournament between her mother-in-law and Porter. The tension in the room rolled in waves.

"I'm just saying, sweetie, that if you move the Christmas tree closer to the fireplace in the family room, there will be enough room for us to sit comfortably and display all of Thomas's gifts." Courtney used her fork to slice up the asparagus before continuing. "Think of how visually appealing that will be. Think of the pictures of Thomas's first Christmas. You only get one first Christmas, you know."

Porter set down his crystal water goblet. "Yes, Mother, that is true, but—"

"But what? You're not worried about the pictures. Believe me, you'll regret that in a few years."

Porter let out a deep sigh, and speared a piece of his medium rare steak with his silver fork. His face remained calm, but Alaina noticed the way his jaw flexed. It was a small movement but it was there and had nothing to do with eating his meal.

"So, Barry—" Alaina broke into the conversation in an attempt to let the heat fade "—have you always lived in Florida?"

"No, no. Though I have been here for forty years, so it seems funny to claim another state when I've acquired the Florida tan we all get from simply walking around. I'm actually from Colorado originally. Just outside of

Denver. Have you ever been there?" Barry sipped his wine, eyes as keen as the cut crystal.

Such a simple question. Yet panic filled her. Had she been to Colorado? That was the tricky part about conversations with strangers.

"Oh, Barry, you can't put Alaina on the spot like that right now." Courtney chimed in, touching his arm. "She was a victim of a terrible car accident. She's got a mild case of amnesia."

Porter pinned Courtney with a glare. She merely blinked in response. Alaina's eyes slid from Courtney to Porter. While it was true, she didn't like the ill effects of her accident being casually brought into conversation. So she decided to take charge of this conversation.

"By mild amnesia, my mother-in-law means I've forgotten the past five years." Alaina tapped her fingernail on her water glass. "Other than that, I'm fine and prefer people not treat me with kid gloves."

"All right, then," Barry agreed. "I can understand that—"

Courtney stopped him with another touch to the arm. "It's just easier if people know what they are dealing with up front. They get a fact pattern and suddenly, they understand how to handle a situation."

"Spoken like a true lawyer. Give me the facts." Barry wheezed out a laugh.

Porter's jaw flexed again. His disapproval of the way his mother had introduced the life-changing accident was more than apparent. Alaina could tell that any second now, he might explode, and that was the last thing she wanted or needed. Not to mention their reactions confused her. What was with all this tension? What was she missing—well, other than five years. So much of her life was confusing.

But right now wasn't about her. It was about her husband, who was clearly upset. She reached under the table to touch his knee, squeezing lightly until he looked at her. She pleaded with her eyes and somehow he seemed to understand.

Was this what it was like to be married? Was this an almost memory, the way they could communicate without words? It felt good.

"Amnesia, huh," Barry said between bites of his dinner. "That's rotten luck, Alaina. I wish you a speedy recovery."

"Thanks. I'm lucky to have such a great support system here." It was the most diplomatic answer she could manage. She gave Porter's knee another quick squeeze of thanks. And then returned her attention to her filet.

From the other end of the room, Thomas erupted in a gut-wrenching cry.

Alaina and Porter both sprang to their feet and rushed to the jungle-themed baby swing. She eased Thomas out and up, cradling him in her arms, rocking him back and forth. He still fussed.

"He's hungry," she said, glancing down at her watch. It was definitely dinnertime.

"I've got it." Porter's murmur was low, almost too soft to hear. Porter left the dining room and jogged into the kitchen. Moments later, he reemerged with a burp cloth and bottle, already a seasoned pro at this dad thing.

How long had they wanted this?

A whispery memory rippled through her mind of her looking at Porter as he held an infant swaddled in blue. But the baby boy wasn't Thomas—somehow she knew it was the son of Porter's CFO, the boy who was now a toddler.

Her heart ached to see the longing in his face, and then the memory faded, the rest gone. She swallowed down the lump in her throat and looked at her husband, the man still so new to her now but who had felt so familiar in the memory.

Courtney set her Waterford wineglass down on the table, half rising from her chair to get a better look at them. "Don't you have a live-in nurse to take care of him, Porter?"

"I just want to make sure I'm there for my son and that he knows who I am." He tested the milk on his wrist, then handed it to Alaina.

"And you are, Porter." Courtney dabbed at the corners of her mouth. "But you hired help. So let them help. You don't need to hover. I certainly never hovered over you and I was a single parent. I wouldn't steer you wrong. Not when it comes to my grandson."

"I appreciate that, Mother." Porter's tone was level as if he knew to keep it calm for his son, although the set of his broad shoulders made it clear his patience with his mother was nearing an end. "But I think a mix of help and hands-on work is best. Besides, we won't use the help forever. That's just until we've settled back into a routine."

So he had been serious when he'd said the night nurse was a component of her recovery. He was sincere about being a fully involved parent. She admired that. Wanted to be part of that unit. Thomas deserved that dedication from both of them.

His mom's counter came within seconds. "That's

where I think you might be wrong. I think the full-time help is wonderful. It really expands what you can do at the company. You know he's in good hands. And you can work more, grow the empire and make sure he has whatever he wants in his life."

Alaina assumed her mother-in-law's advice was coming from a good place. But it seemed more than a tad controlling. She admired Porter's restraint in not calling out his mom on that and wondered if he was holding back to keep things peaceful, not just for Thomas, but for Alaina, too.

Maybe this had been why she and her mother-in-law hadn't gotten along before the amnesia. She didn't need her memories to clue her in on *that*.

She just resented the way Porter's and his mother's issues were intruding on what had been the best day Alaina could remember having with her husband, when there were precious few to remember.

In spite of knowing there was so much of her life left to uncover, she found herself wanting more of those new memories.

He closed the door behind his mother. Finally. And not soon enough.

He'd known this was a bad idea, having his mom here for Christmas. She hadn't ever been the home and hearth for the holidays sort, and she certainly hadn't got along with Alaina. This wasn't the joyous, peaceful atmosphere he'd been attempting to create with his wife. This evening was a prime example. His day with Alaina had been derailed by that damn awkward dinner.

At least Courtney was out for the evening with Barry the tax attorney. Just like that, she'd become the mother of his youth. The one who was interested in men more than family. The one who put boyfriends first.

Alaina's misfortune was that she couldn't remember a thing. His great curse was that he couldn't forget a single damn moment. What a pair they made.

Cricking his neck to the side, he strode to his office computer and uploaded some videos of their Tallahassee house onto a disc for Alaina so she could see where they'd lived. Maybe that would jostle a memory. And maybe she would see her own stamp on their life in a way she hadn't here.

He was struck by the irony. Even with streaming music, some people still made music mixes on CDs as a gift, full of "their songs." Not him. But then he wasn't sure she would even like the same music anymore. His whole life felt upside down lately.

He thought all he'd wanted was the family he'd dreamed of having, but in getting to know Alaina again, seeing her in a new way after the accident, his feelings were mixed up.

Even his mother's behavior tonight had rocked him. It's not that he minded that she had a new beau. She was a grown-up, after all. But it brought the weight of his past crashing down on him.

Needing to calm himself, Porter made his way to Thomas's nursery. Seeing his son was a way to remind himself that this was not the past. That he was going to be an active part of his son's life. That he was making the family he'd always wanted.

Porter had never lacked material objects as a child. His mother was a brilliant attorney and made a decent salary.

But he had been profoundly lonely. And he never

wanted Thomas to experience that. Never wanted him to feel as if he wasn't welcome, as if he wasn't wanted.

Courtney had chased love for Porter's whole life. Moving from man to man. Men who seldom bothered to learn Porter's name, always settling on the generic "sport" or "son." Nameless. Invisible.

He'd attended an elite boarding school from middle school through high school. He was home for three weeks over Christmas and two months over the summer.

It was common for his mother to promise to spend time with him only to bail in favor of a date and time at the bar. She'd always promised to take him to movie releases, or ice-skating or bowling. But more often than not, Porter did all those things with a nanny instead of with his mother. He was frequently sent to his room so his mother and her current boyfriend could have the run of the house, child-free.

But there had been one Christmas break when he was in seventh grade that completely changed their relationship forever. It was part of the reason he still felt so distant from his mother. The experience left him feeling like a part-time son in a part-time family.

Alaina might not have ever gone to Colorado, but he sure as hell had.

He had come home from break, excited for the plans he had made with his mother over the school year. They were supposed to go skiing in Colorado. It was going to be a winter wonderland filled with snow, hot chocolate and sports.

They had gone to Colorado. But Courtney had brought a nanny along for the ride. As well as her boyfriend. She'd enrolled Porter in a snow camp for the day and the nanny entertained him at night while Courtney wined and dined. He'd even discovered she planned the whole trip around her meet-up with the guy. Porter had felt completely let down. He'd wanted to spend time with his mother. Even as a teen, he'd been seeking that connection. But it was on that trip that he'd realized it would never happen. If he wanted a family of his own, he would have to create it himself.

Shoving the memory aside, Porter stood over the crib. Thomas snoozed, breathing light little breaths. He was so peaceful.

It would be different for Thomas. Porter and Alaina would figure out how to be around each other. They would move past the temporary truce they'd erected before the accident and live as a family. Alaina seemed to feel their connection as much as he did. Even if she regained her memories, surely she would forgive the past and stay this time. And they both already felt so bonded to their son.

A muted knock sounded from behind him. Porter wheeled around to see Alaina standing in the doorway. She'd already changed for bed. She was in a racerback tank top that showed off her ample curves. The black shorts hugged her legs, inching up her strong thighs. His gaze lingered on her smiling face.

"Hey. You know, today was pretty amazing. Maybe you're not so terrible at that romance thing." Her voice was low, but playful. Almost like the Alaina he had first fallen in love with. He ached to grab her, to draw her into his arms.

"Well, I only know how to go big or go home."

"Today was great. All the things we found for Thomas. You bringing the decorations out for us tonight. Trying to get our own holiday traditions started. It was sweet and it meant a lot to me." She stepped close to him. Just barely out of reach.

Close enough that the coconut scent of her shampoo teased his senses. Close enough that he ached to pull her to him and take her to bed. Patience be damned. But there was too much at stake. Keeping them together. Keeping her happy. Keeping her.

He forced himself to measure his words.

"I want us to be a family." He stuffed his hands into his pockets to keep from grabbing her and saying to hell with talking. "And I think your idea of a shrimp boil is a great follow-up to what we did tonight. We are a team. Input from both of us matters."

"I think so, too. The time we're spending here is helping." She paused, her beautiful blue eyes glazing over with her attempt at looking inward. "I also vaguely recall making the painting I gave you. I can see it in my mind. It's a bit fuzzy, but I can remember the colors I used, the brushes…"

Memories. He should be rejoicing. And he *was* glad for her, but he couldn't stop the impending sense of doom. What would happen when she remembered all the mistakes he'd made? When she realized those were the questions he had avoided answering?

"It's great that you're starting to remember. I love your paintings. Your colors. I can't wait for you to re-see our house in Tallahassee."

He just prayed they could mend their marriage—their family—before the rest came rolling in. The bad parts. The possible divorce.

And God—that sucker punched him. The stakes

were higher than ever. They had a child now and Porter felt he was getting to know Alaina all over again.

"What other kinds of things did you give me over the years? You know, aside from a beautiful beach house?" Leaning over the crib, she rearranged the baby blanket.

"The humanities, art specifically, is clearly important to you. In Tallahassee, you're extremely active in the Art Association. And you wanted elementary school kids to be exposed to art. So I started a scholarship program in your name that brings artists into the classroom."

"Porter, that's so generous of you. I don't know what to say."

Her face flushed with such gratitude he felt guilty for keeping other facts from her. Facts about their marriage. But he was focused on the bigger picture, a long-term answer for them. Their future as a family. She would see that, if she suddenly remembered everything. She had to.

"You don't have to thank me, Alaina. You deserve it. And the program has been a success. The kids really benefit from it."

She looked at him them. Really and truly looked at him. He held her gaze, reading the warmth in her sky-blue eyes. The eyes of his wife and the eyes of a stranger at the same time.

Thomas began to stir, making little clucking noises. Poor guy. They were disturbing his much-needed sleep.

"I think we might be too loud."

"I guess that's our cue. We've got to let sleeping babies sleep." He took the monitor so he could give it to the matronly night nurse. "Besides, there is one more surprise for you. But it's back downstairs."

* * *

Alaina followed him back down the stairs and into the family room. They didn't bother with the actual light, but chose to sit beneath the glow of the Christmas tree.

"Close your eyes." His whisper tickled her ear. She let her eyes flit shut. A box was placed gently in her lap.

"All right. You can open them. And the present." Porter sat across from her, on the ground. Eyeing the box, she tore into the perfectly wrapped package. She lifted the flap.

And gasped in delight and breathed in the scent. Her soul sang.

Canvas paper. Acrylic paint. Oil paint. Chalk. Paintbrushes and sketching pencils. Everything she needed for a quick art set.

"Oh, Porter. You didn't have to… I mean…you could have waited for Christmas…" Her voice hitched in her throat. Emotions pulsed. Her breathing sped up in anticipation. She couldn't wait to pour out her emotions on the page.

He cupped her shoulders. "I'm a pretty simple guy. I want my family to have what they want. What they need. And I thought it would be a good outlet for you. I think this is the longest you've ever gone without some creative project."

In the deepest part of her being, she was truly touched. He had been trying so hard to connect with her. To do things to make her feel more comfortable. Even if their life before the accident hadn't been perfect, the man before her now was putting in a real effort.

"Porter, it's perfect. Thank you." She grabbed his

hand, beginning to feel as if she knew the texture and feel of him. He tucked her hair behind her ear.

"Of course."

"Can I ask another question?"

"Always."

"How did we decide on the name Thomas?" It had been her father's name. She hoped that had been the reason, but she didn't trust much about her instincts these days. A pang of sorrow shot through her. Her father would never know her son. She took a shaky breath. His loss felt so recent.

Porter inched toward her. They were side by side. His shoulder brushed hers and she leaned into him. Breathed in the dark clove scent of his cologne.

"We chose the name for your father. It wasn't much of a discussion. I never had a father and your father sounded wonderful even if I never had the honor of meeting the guy. It seemed right. Fitting." He wrapped his arm around her, and she buried her face in his chest. The tightness of his arm on hers ramped up her heartbeat. He was beginning to feel like someone she could talk to. Trust was still an iffy idea, but she was moved by his actions today.

She couldn't deny it. She was ready to take this to the next step. She craved intimacy with him. Her body ached for him, recognizing him on an instinctive level that went beyond memories.

"I know there must have been difficulties between us. Probably a strain because of the infertility," she began to say. She had to finish before she lost her nerve. "And probably a bunch of other things that I don't need to know right now…but I'm glad that we are trying to become a family now. And I was wondering if you could stay the night with me. Just sleeping. Nothing else. What do you think?"

His eyebrows shot upward. "I think I would be an idiot to say no."

Seven

Alaina couldn't believe she'd asked to share a bed with her husband. Not sex. Just sleeping.

She stood in her bathroom, changing into the pajamas she'd chosen. Choosing them had been tough. What to wear to sleep with a man she was attracted to, but wasn't ready to have sex with? If she wore a nightgown or a T-shirt, that would invite his hand to tunnel upward.

If she wore something silky, then that would feel like skin, sexy. But she didn't want to be frumpy. She couldn't help but feel vain in wanting to look attractive for her husband. So she'd opted for colors that flattered her. A pale pink tank top, cotton but thin. And a striped pair of shorts, so yes, their legs could brush.

Because she wanted this. Needed this, to be close to another human being. To her husband. Some part of her body knew they'd been together. Often. For a long time. There was a synchronicity in the way they moved through life that spoke of having done things together as a team, everyday things, sexual things.

When she'd first woken up from her coma, she'd felt as if the past five years hadn't existed. That it had only been a few months since she'd broken off her relationship with Douglas and taken out a restraining order.

But during the week in the hospital and then the week at the beach house, she had gained a sense of distance from the past. These weeks had helped ease the initial tension that had made her feel stuck in another time.

Had she moved beyond all those awful feelings left over from Douglas? She must have, since she'd got married. Even with her memories of the past five years gone, her sense of Douglas felt further away than when she'd first woken up in the hospital. It was as if her body was moving forward to absorb the lost time even if her brain didn't fill in the missing pieces.

Her past with Porter hadn't returned, but her feelings for him were definitely growing. Strong. Real.

Powerful.

She looked down at her engagement ring and the wedding band. For the first time, she felt as if maybe, just maybe, they fit.

When Porter had given her those art supplies, she'd felt connected to him. She'd been given a link to her past with those supplies in hand. It made her want to find more links to the past, make more connections. It made her want this night with her husband.

She tugged on her pj's, the soft cotton brushing against her breasts and sending a shiver of awareness through her.

This wasn't going to be as easy as she'd thought.

Deep breath in. One foot in front of the other. She could do this.

The bedroom was washed in warm yellow light from the oversize candle emblazoned with an anchor on the mahogany dresser. It cast flickers on the ship steering wheel that leaned from dresser to wall.

Matchy-matchy. Maybe she would try her hand at redecorating this place. Make it feel less like a page out of a catalog and more like a home for a family always on the go. But she'd only make those decisions with Porter. Joint decisions. Like the decisions they had made earlier today with Thomas's gifts.

Porter slouched against the door frame, half looking at her. His black sweatpants hung low on his hips. A white T-shirt for a local Tallahassee baseball team enhanced his athletic frame. Damn, he was sexy.

And he was hers.

Alaina toyed with the band on her shorts. "This is a little awkward."

"I'm sorry you feel that way."

"Me, too, but I said it, and then I couldn't take it back."

"You don't have to."

She took a deep breath. "I think I do." She yanked back the covers, then paused, inhaling hard. "I don't even know what side of the bed I sleep on."

"You're fine," he said.

"Are you saying that to be accommodating? Or is that the truth?"

"The truth. Your instincts are right. That's your side of the bed."

Something eased inside her. Maybe she needed to follow her instincts more with him.

Alaina climbed into bed and patted the space beside her. "Okay. Join me."

He lay on top of the spread. "Done, as requested."

"And I didn't die."

"Wow, now that's a turn-on."

Laughing, she shoved him gently with both hands and felt the resistance in his muscles as her skin met his. He let out a low chuckle, clearly amused.

She sagged back into the fluffy feather pillow. He reclined on his side, propping his head on his hand.

Alaina picked at the down comforter. "What's next? Our situation is so unconventional I don't know what the rules are."

"No rules as far as I'm concerned. We're making this up as we go."

Still, she wanted details, a sense of who'd they'd been. "How did we used to sleep? Did I sleep on your chest? Did we spoon? Me against you? You against me? Opposite sides of bed?"

"Why don't we just see where we end up?" He held out an arm.

After only an instant's hesitation, she rested her head on his shoulder and his arm wrapped around her. A sigh filled her. This. This was right. The feel of her body fitting against her husband's.

Sleep pulled at her eyelids. It had been an exhausting day. Being here with Porter felt so damn right. Familiar. As if by muscle memory, her body curled around him, and she took comfort in the steady rise and fall of his broad chest.

Her eyelids fluttered shut. How was it possible to be entirely at ease and so on edge all at once?

Sleep was the furthest thing from Porter's mind.

Then again, that was nothing new. Not since the accident. Since the endless blur of days and nights at the hospital. He'd taken to doing work in the odd hours of the evening. Using work as a way to keep his mind off the dire situation of his family.

But tonight, he was working for different reasons. He needed to keep himself occupied, to keep his hands off his wife. Tonight, concentration was difficult. Near impossible, with Alaina pressed against him.

It had been so damn long since he'd held her like this. Since the warmth of her body melted with his. He absently ran a hand through her hair. She drew in closer.

How had it been so long since they'd done this? Been in bed together, nestled against each other.

Too long.

Yes, he wanted to touch her, to make love to her, but he had to keep his goals in mind. For the first time in months, he felt as if they were working together. That they were in this for real. Not just him, but her, too. They were becoming a family. At least, he thought they were. His own experiences with family were shaky at best. And her family was gone. But *this* family—this family had a shot.

He returned his attention back to his tablet. Looked over some reports. Started to feel the pull of sleep.

But something was wrong. Alaina started to shake. She twisted away from him.

"Stop it." Her voice was a murmur. But there was desperation in it.

"Let go. Just…just. No. Stop." Her lovely face contorted with fear. She continued to thrash against an invisible assailant.

She was having a nightmare.

Gently, he shook her shoulder. "Alaina. You're okay. You're okay."

She gasped in air. Her blue eyes suddenly alert. Scanning the room. Focusing on him. Breathing rapidly, her body twitchy. "I'm sorry. I didn't mean to wake you. Oh, God, this plan isn't working out like I meant it… I should just go."

He clasped her arm. "Stay. Do you remember what you dreamed? Did you recall something from the past?"

"No, not really." She sagged back against him. "I was just having a nightmare about Douglas, about that time with him. Things get muddled in dreams, feeling out of control and scared. Did I tell you about Douglas?"

"Your ex-boyfriend before you met me? Yes, you did."

"What did I tell you?"

"Are you trying to pull information out of me? Have you forgotten parts of that time in your life, too?"

"I remember. He was verbally abusive. I didn't see that for a long time. Then he hit me…" She shook her head. "And then I was done. I walked out."

"That's what you told me." Once he'd learned about the jerk, Porter had made a point to keep tabs on the guy, make sure he honored that restraining order. "I'm sorry tonight is bringing back bad memories for you. This was supposed to be a positive experience."

"It would have been worse if I'd been alone. Let's try again."

"I'd like that, too." She maneuvered into the crook of

his arm. Laid a hand on his chest. He pulled her tightly against him, his mind churning with ways to help her feel at ease, to know he wouldn't let anything happen to her. Her breathing slowed, falling into the rhythmic pattern of a deep sleep.

And even with the determination to keep her safe from threats like Douglas, and to keep his hands to himself until she was ready for more, Porter couldn't deny he had no way to keep her safe from thoughts of the past.

The yellow-orange rays of dawn's first light filtered in between the tulle-like curtains, nudging Alaina awake. She glanced over at her husband, whose eyes were still closed, heavy with sleep.

Quietly, she slid from bed and crept down the hall to check on the baby.

Thomas greeted her with a chubby-cheeked smile.

"Are you hungry, my love?" she cooed, picking him up out of bed. She sat with him in the rocker while he drank from the bottle. This was her favorite time of the day, just the two of them alone. She fed him and rocked him even though he was awake. She talked to him and sang to him. Time passed in a vacuum, a couple of hours sliding by in a beautiful haze.

This was everything she'd always hoped motherhood would be. A calmness descended on her as she sat with Thomas. And a desire to crawl back into bed with Porter. To memorize all of his features. To hold these moments close so they couldn't slip away like the others.

Maybe it was time to start drawing again. A family portrait. She'd start with Porter. Capture the angles of his face, the strength in his chest. And the smile lines in his face. And somehow, maybe their years together would come rushing back as she revisited him.

After finishing with Thomas, she set him down for a nap. Kissed his forehead. Filled with love for the making of her little family. She'd sketch him next.

On tiptoe, she made her way downstairs, grabbed her new sketchbook and pencils and crawled back into bed. Sunlight streamed over Porter's face.

She began to outline him. Rough strokes on paper. She worked first on his face. She started to lose herself in the drawing, the world ebbing away from her.

Until a knock sounded from behind her. Alaina practically leaped out of her skin.

"Sleeping Beauty's still asleep, I see." Her mother-in-law called from the door, a diamond-and-silver snowflake broach pinned to the collar of her shirt. Porter let out a loud snore and turned on his side.

"Have breakfast with me? I could use some toast. And girl time." She motioned for Alaina to follow her down the hall.

"Sounds great. I am a bit hungry myself." Alaina stacked her sketchbook and pencils on the bedside table. If she stayed here much longer, she might not be able to resist temptation. She needed some space to gather her thoughts—and her mother-in-law might well have insights that could help her decide how to move forward in the marriage.

She hurried after Courtney into the hallway toward the back stairway leading to the kitchen.

When she'd caught up to her mother-in-law, Courtney glanced over her shoulder on her way down the steps. "I've never seen you draw before. You know, you get the same look on your face as Porter does when he is working on a building design."

"I do?"

She nodded, clasping the polished steel railing. "Porter's always been a hands-on guy. Started back in middle school. He was always building things. Once, he built a table for me for Christmas. He was sixteen then. Said he'd loved the sweat equity of the project. The ability to create something from nothing. I guess that's a bit like art, isn't it?"

"I suppose it's actually a similar process. Built not bought. I think that's why this house feels foreign to me. It's cookie cutter decor in a lot of ways other than some of the artwork. I'll take some imperfections in my decorations if it's coming from scratch."

"You sound like him. When he built that table, I think that's when he decided he didn't need me anymore." Courtney gave a slight laugh. But the sound was tinged with sadness.

They turned the corner into the kitchen and sat on the bar stools facing a view of the water, where a holiday boat parade was organizing. Festively decorated boats of all sizes congregated. A blow-up Santa in a bathing suit sat on the deck of one, but most of the vessels were outfitted more simply with green garland boughs.

"I'm sure he still needed you then. You helped shape him into the person he is today." A person she was still trying to understand. To relearn.

Her mother-in-law's eyebrows arched as she popped two slices of bread in the toaster. "Sometimes I wonder. He's built every house he's lived in as an adult. Sometimes I'm surprised he didn't build the yacht, too."

Alaina said, "Whoa, wait. We own one of those yachts?"

"You do. Usually my son has me stay out there rather than in the house, which, quite frankly, is an amazing spin on a mother-in-law suite. But still. We've always had troubles, my son and I."

Her mother-in-law straightened the rings on her fingers before she continued. "You know, I was madly in love with Porter's father. I was young—and the whole world seemed open to me when we were together. But he had other dreams. Other desires. He left shortly after Porter was born."

"I'm sure that was difficult. Raising Porter alone and working so much."

"Would you like the truth, Alaina? I was—and still am—brilliant in the courtroom. I can dissect a case like nobody's business. But motherhood? That never came to me. Not like it does to you."

Alaina nodded sympathetically, but didn't say anything. She knew Courtney had her quirks, but she never doubted that the woman loved her son. Family was just complicated. Alaina felt as if she knew that better than anyone. Funny what a few weeks in a coma had done for her perspective.

Porter was a man whom she was only just beginning to understand. But the tension between her husband and mother-in-law was starting to make sense to her. Courtney was all about buying premade items. It's why she'd insisted on the night nurse tending to Thomas.

But Porter—Porter was a man intent on creation. On actively building. He'd built a construction empire the same way he'd built that table. To prove he could take scraps and turn them into something usable. He'd built his life from the ground up, even though he could have easily used his mother's fortune. He hadn't backed down from the work it required.

And what about her? Alaina had spent the past two weeks in the haze of amnesia. Afraid of what she'd find if she pressed too hard. But Porter was aware of their history. Aware of their struggles. And he was still dedicated to their family. Maybe she needed to become aware, too.

And that meant digging around in the dirt a bit. And possibly talking to Sage.

As Alaina poured two cups of coffee in holiday mugs painted with angels, she made up her mind. Today was a day for exploring. And she would start with all the pieces of her past—even the uncomfortable ones. The time had come to reconstruct her life.

Starting with finding out more about how and why they'd purchased that yacht when she could have sworn such flashy purchases weren't her style.

Eight

Porter was still stunned over Alaina suggesting they go out to the yacht. He couldn't recall her ever suggesting that. In fact, the eighty-foot *Sunseeker* had been a contentious issue between them since he'd bought it two years ago. But he wasn't turning his back on the chance to get closer to her.

In the past, she'd always hated the vessel. Said it was too showy. Too flashy. It screamed their wealth, and that bothered her down to the core.

But Porter had never felt that way about the purchase. To him, it represented freedom. A chance to leave the world behind. To be completely untethered from the responsibilities of work and reliant on himself. And yes, he'd hoped it would offer them more time to relax together, bring them closer as their marriage began to fray.

The Florida winter sun warmed him. The captain had

dropped anchor and gone into town about a half hour ago. The luxury craft happily rocked with the waves and the current, other boats far enough away to give him and Alaina a sense of privacy he welcomed. Water lapped against the sides and a healthy breeze coated the deck. They'd intended to take Thomas with them, but his mother had offered to watch him. She had even insisted. Though they did hire a backup sitter for all the tasks Courtney was not enthusiastic about performing.

He'd come out of the cabin with two bottles of water. One for him and one for Alaina.

Every day he was feeling closer to her, closer than he could remember feeling before. They were building something, a new connection. And since last night he felt a change between them. Something that had been missing for a long time before the accident.

He took a moment to appreciate her. Just the way she was in this moment. She'd dressed in layered tank tops and leggings, flip-flops half on, half off. She was sprawled on the white cushioned deck chair. Hunched over a pad, sketching furiously. The wind teased her blond hair. She was beautiful.

"May I see your drawings?"

She sketched with charcoal, not looking up. "Are you sure you want to look? There are ones of you in here."

"Did you draw me as a gargoyle? Or a cyclops?" he asked, lounging back in a deck chair and propping his foot on the bolted down table between the seating.

She glanced up. "Why would I do that?"

"Since we talked about our past arguments."

Fish plopped in the brief silence before she answered, "You've been nothing but understanding and patient with me, with this whole situation. No matter what else happens, I won't forget that."

"Whatever else happens?" Trepidation kinked the muscles in his neck.

"If you get tired of having an amnesiac wife."

"I could never get tired of you."

Her cheeks flushed pink as she glanced at him through her eyelashes. His mind swirled, thinking of last night. Of her body pressed against his and the scent of her coconut shampoo. And how he'd wanted so much more than to just sleep next to her.

How he still wanted that.

She seemed to read his thoughts, her blush fading. Awareness flitted across her face. An expression that almost looked like longing.

The sound of another fish jumping out of the water brought them back to reality. He shook his head.

She passed over the pad of drawings. "Here. Feel free to look."

She tucked her hair behind her ear and chewed her nail as he flipped through the book.

There were pages upon pages of sketches. Some scenes of the beach house. Some of boats in the harbor. Thomas in a Santa hat.

All so damn good, the details grabbing his heart. "You've been busy."

"I feel like there are thoughts needing to pour out. I don't have to think or talk, just… Oh, I don't know how to describe it other than to say it's like meditation."

He flipped to the next page. Half-finished drawings of him sleeping. She seemed to fixate on his face. Mostly his eyes. As if she was trying to figure out something about him. Her sketches were beautiful. Hyperrealistic. He'd forgotten how talented she was with charcoal and pencils.

The last sketch in the book sucked the air from his chest. It was a montage of images. Items of their joint past. Did she remember?

It was a scene of a room. On the desk, there was a globe with a cracked stand. A Moroccan rug on the ground. All souvenirs—all representing moments in their life together. If she didn't know what these were, what did the drawings mean? Why had she stumbled onto these particular items? He couldn't decide whether to tell her or not. What would be helpful?

Truth. As much as he could give her.

"There are items here that you received over those missing years, gifts I gave you."

She gasped. "Like what?"

"The rug right here." He pointed to the sketch, careful not to smudge the material, "It was the first gift I ever gave you. When you were living in that tiny apartment with the tile in your bedroom. You said you hated how cold your feet were in the mornings. Even then, I knew you liked those rich colors. Items with a bit of history. I picked it up on a business trip."

She considered his words, staring hard at the sketch. "I woke up with this scene in my head. I thought it was from a dream…but maybe my memories are trying to come back after all."

"It's quite possible."

"What else is from our past?"

"The globe with the cracked stand."

"That's a strange gift. Where's it from?" She crinkled her nose and adjusted her sunglasses again.

"Well it didn't start out cracked. It cracked in our

move. But I got it for our one-year anniversary. It was a blank globe. Ceramic. You painted it. It's got quotes over where the countries ought to be. Quotes about art and life. I've always thought you should replicate it and sell them."

She smiled at him. "Do you think the art supplies gift made me think of that?"

"Could be."

"What about being on the yacht? What will that help me remember?"

"Honestly? Arguing. You were angry with me for buying this. You thought the money could have been better spent. But then we fought about pretty much everything then."

"I appreciate you being honest."

"I want you to trust me. You believe that, right?"

"I do. I'm just not sure you want me to remember everything. You seem very into this fresh start. All the control is on your side since you have the pieces of the past and I only get what other people tell me."

He couldn't deny the truth in that. He owed her more, better. Hell, he owed her the unvarnished truth, but couldn't bring himself to go quite that far when they were so close to having everything they'd wanted. Time on the yacht offered them a window of time away from the world and he needed to embrace that fully.

"Alaina, I have an idea. Let's use this time to pretend we're two different people. Strangers who've met and are stuck on this ostentatious yacht together. Strangers attracted to each other and ready to get to know each other." He loosened the cap on the water bottle and handed it to her.

His gaze met hers, and he could swear the air crackled with the static of a lightning strike even though there wasn't a cloud in the sky.

She grabbed it and flashed him a grin. "I'm game."

Vibrant pinks of the sunset blurred into deeper purples. The heat of the day was behind them, the cool ocean breeze nudging Alaina's skin toward goose bumps. She ran a hand over her exposed leg, hoping to generate some warmth.

Embers of sunlight caused the yacht to glow. While she was conscious of how expensive this outing was, she had to admit there was some charm to it all. The lulling rock of the yacht in the water. The heavy smell of salt in the air. Relaxing. Intimate. It was easy to feel as if they were the only two people in the whole world with the captain and crew dismissed for a few hours and other boats so far away.

And in some ways, that'd been a good thing.

But she still couldn't help feeling slightly uneasy. He hadn't denied wanting this fresh start, or taking the power it gave him. Even when she agreed to get to know him anew, she wondered what he really thought of her. Of all of this.

"You look chilled." Porter pushed his deck chair closer to hers. He had a thick blanket in his hand. It was covered in a sprawling cursive print. She squinted in the dying light to see what it said. Looked like lines from a novel. Was that a purchase she'd made?

"I've definitely been warmer. That's for sure." Although there was heat building inside her just from looking at him, having him near. Their night sleeping together had brought a new level of intimacy to their relationship. One that made her yearn to take that to the next level.

"Luckily for you, I come prepared." He draped the blanket across her shoulders, his hands brushing her shoulders and sending another shiver through her.

Definitely the electric sort of shiver born of heat not cold.

She pulled the blanket tight, closing it around her body against the ache for contact with him. Did he want this as much as she did? What would happen afterward?

"So generous," she teased him, but she was grateful for his attentiveness. Even her nose was cold.

"I don't know about that. There is a catch, you see." The sunset glinted in his eyes. His beard-stubbled face was serious.

"Oh?"

"It's going to cost you a date, lady. And you're going to have to share that blanket." A mischievous twinkle danced in his dark eyes, reaching his lips.

Butterflies filled her stomach, and her breasts tingled with increasing need. His relaxed smile sparked a fierce need for him; the new ease of being with him stirred her. Deeply.

He was asking for more than a shared night in a bed and she could sense they both knew that.

Clenching the blanket tighter in her fists, she returned his gaze steadily. "I don't know about that. That's a pretty tall demand."

Feeling bold and ready to take a risk that she prayed would pay off, she held out a side of the blanket for him to sit next to her. He filled the gaping space in an instant with his big, warm presence.

"How 'bout a game?" he asked, gathering her closer, his hard thigh against her legs.

"I like games." She liked *him*. A lot.

"Thought you might. I'll ask a question. And you have to answer it. And then you can do the same to me." He pivoted his body to face her.

She nodded, her hair snagging on his five o'clock shadow. "I like it. But I'm going first. Worst drink you've ever had?"

"Worst drink? Hmm. In college, a friend dared me to drink a bar mat—which is basically a mix of all the alcohol that spills during the night as a shot. I never made that mistake again." He shuddered at the memory.

"That is absolutely disgusting." She laughed, unable to imagine him losing control in any way. "What in the world made you go along with that?"

"Now, now, Alaina." He nudged her shoulder gently. "You only get one question at a time. It's my turn. If you had to be stuck in one television show for the rest of your life, which one would it be?"

Now that was a hard one. "Well. And you keep in mind I'm working with outdated information. But I'd have to say I'd like to be stuck in *Scooby-Doo*. The original series. I could totally drive around in the Mystery Machine. I half wanted to be a detective when I was younger because of that show. Definitely my favorite growing up."

"*Scooby-Doo?* I would never have guessed that one. You'd have the brains of Velma and the beauty of Daphne. You would've been the powerhouse." He put his arm around her back, drawing her closer to him as he leaned them down to look at the first evening stars.

She turned to half lie on his chest, her ear pressed

against the steady thud of his heart. "Ha-ha. Absolute favorite meal? Like the kind you could eat again and again and never get sick of?"

He exhaled deeply. "You do know how to ask the tough questions. I would eat Dunkaroos for every meal. I love the frosting."

"Porter…really? Out of all the food in the world… Dunkaroos?" She lifted her head off his chest to stare at his face. Smile lines pushed at his cheeks as he attempted to look completely serious.

"Oh, yeah. Completely." She arched her brow at him. But the smile stuck to her face, anyway.

"My turn again. Let's see—who was your first kiss?"

"Oh, lord. I haven't thought about Bobby Dagana in ages. I was fourteen. He walked me home and kissed me on my doorstep. But my mom saw the whole thing happen and teased me for the rest of the day."

"If I had known you when we were younger, I would have kissed you before Bobby Dagana had ever thought about it." He massaged the back of her head. Fingers tracing circles in her scalp.

"Mmm. That feels nice. Could you keep doing that while I think of another question?" She held on to his side, hooked her fingers in his belt loop. She could have sworn the vessel rocked under her feet even as she knew that would be virtually undetectable on the large luxury yacht.

"Nope. Sorry. That's your question… I'm kidding." He captured a lock of her hair and wrapped it around his finger.

"What are you thinking about right now?" Her heart was in her throat as she waited for the answer. The seconds felt like mini eternities.

"Honestly? You. How beautiful you are. How lucky I am." He said it without a trace of sarcasm or humor. He squeezed her arm. Silence fell between them.

She swallowed hard. "Really lucky to have your life turned upside down because I can't remember even meeting you?"

Her eyes stung with tears.

"Ah, Alaina," he sighed, stroking her face. "I don't deserve you."

"Why do you say that?"

"Because you came out here with me today, even though you seemed to have sensed the yacht wasn't neutral territory for us. Why *did* you come out on the yacht with me?"

Where the hell had that come from?

Porter wanted to kick himself. He'd been five seconds away from romancing his wife back into his bed again. Then he'd sabotaged it by asking a question to stop their progress in its tracks.

"The yacht seems to have been a bone of contention between us and I wanted to try to heal that."

"Did you remember something about it?" He felt as if his marriage was one big ticking time bomb, set to explode the second she regained her full memory. He had to make the most of their time together before that happened.

"It's more like a sensation, feelings." She tapped her temple, her forehead furrowed. "Intuition, I guess. But no, I don't remember."

A reprieve. For now.

He searched for the right words to strike a balance between honesty and gaining her trust without spilling all. "We did argue, pretty heatedly. You thought it was a waste of money, that we didn't need it, wouldn't be using it often enough to warrant the expense."

"It is a nice boat." She drew a lazy circle on his chest with her finger.

He struggled to focus.

"Boat? That's something you ski behind or paddle."

"Ah, so the big boat is important to you." She patted his chest. "That's rather Freudian."

He didn't take the bait and argue with her as he would have in the past. Instead, he worked to explain his feelings rather than offer up a knee-jerk reaction. Over the past few weeks, he'd pushed aside her feelings for his own, and he knew if he wanted his family to stay intact, he needed to try a different strategy.

"The escape is important to me. There's no office here. It's the anticonstruction site, no land."

"Oh." She blinked fast, her hands falling to her lap. "Did you tell me that before?"

"I didn't," he admitted. "I should have."

She stayed silent so long he wondered if she would change the subject altogether.

Then she looked up at him, her blue eyes searching his face. "Would I have heard you?"

He hadn't expected that from her. Maybe they were both changing, making something good happen from the hell of the car accident that had stolen her memory.

"Maybe. Maybe not. I honestly can't answer that, Alaina. And you've mentioned before that it's not fair I'm the filter for all your memories and questions." He reached forward and slid a disc holder off the table. "We're tied to this house for now. But I compiled all the videos and photos of our Tallahassee home. When we get back, if you're ready and want to, I will try my best to help you connect with people who knew both of us."

"Thank you. Truly. This means more to me than… well, more than any expensive gift." She took the disc from him and held it to her chest. "This is what I'm talking about. You're really trying to hear what I need, to help us trust each other. I can feel that."

Trust. Now that was a sticky word. But the doctor had warned against pushing her too fast. Maybe that was a convenient excuse now for not being more open, but damn, she felt good in his arms. He didn't want to say anything to make her pull away.

She set the disc aside and rested her palms on his chest, the invitation clear in her gaze. "And I want to be closer to you, even if it's just on a physical level."

They'd been married a long time. He recognized the authenticity of the desire in her eyes, the passion in her husky voice. Some things between them didn't need words or memories. Their bodies recognized each other.

Still, he had to ask, to keep what fragile trust they'd built.

"Alaina," he said, taking her face in his hands, "are you sure this is what you want?"

"Absolutely certain," she whispered against his mouth an instant before she kissed him.

In a flash of insight, as he wrapped his arms around her, he realized why he'd asked about the boat. To deflect her from pressing for more on why he felt he wasn't a good husband. He was changing, learning from his mistakes, but he still wasn't ready to admit he hadn't been up-front about how close they'd been to divorce before the accident. He wanted to make his family whole before they dealt with that truth.

He was a jerk.

And the worst part? He still couldn't bring himself to back away from this chance to have Alaina again.

Every step of the way to their cabin below, she kissed him. Deeply. Urgently.

Hungrily.

Alaina savored the taste of Porter on her tongue. The sensations pulsing through her were new and familiar all at once. Surreal. Sensual.

The touch of his hand, the rasp of his beard-stubbled face, the scent of him—all of it turned her inside out. Nothing in her life made sense. Her past was a jumble. Her present a strange haze.

But she was certain of this. Of needing Porter. Of their undeniable chemistry. Of the evening that had sparked her back to life in a way she was somehow certain she'd never felt before.

Her feet tangled with his as they moved through the corridor, sconces lighting the way toward the main cabin. He met her kiss for kiss, snaking his hands into the mess of her wavy hair. His steps slowing, he pressed her against the wall to deepen the contact. Pressed her closer to him. Her back against the polished cypress wainscoting.

And then he broke the kiss to stare at her. His coal-dark eyes searched her face, looking for an answer to his unasked question. And she knew. He was wrestling with this step and the fact that she didn't recall their marriage.

But she recalled their now. She felt the connection. She didn't believe in love at first sight, but there was a sense of their history still binding them, curling through some part of her mind.

So she leaned in for another kiss and reassured him.

"I want this." She breathed against his mouth. Then nipped his lower lip. She let her hand travel to the tender flesh between his shirt and pant line.

His head fell back with a growl of desire. Need fueled the air between them. He lifted her legs to wrap around his waist. She hooked her heels behind him, her core pressed to his, her arms looped around his neck. Her body was on fire for him.

Porter.

Her husband.

He carried her the rest of the way down the hall, past framed photos of Florida island scenery and fishing expeditions. And she had to admit, this yacht had a romantic appeal. She appreciated the sense of escape, being away from the world, just the two of them floating alone in the world.

Porter shouldered open the door to their master bedroom, and then shouldered the door closed after him. The lighting was dimmer here, but she didn't care much about the surroundings anymore. Only the man touching her.

And that big bed waiting for them.

Gently, he eased her back onto the soft comforter carefully, stretching out on top of her. He propped himself on his forearms, but there was no missing the rigid length of him pressing against her belly.

A smile spread across her lips as she met his gaze. In his face, she saw his desire matched hers. Frenzy. Fire. Longing.

"Alaina. I've missed you. So damned much." He

punctuated each word with a kiss before angling back up onto an elbow, putting enough space between them to pluck at their clothes.

One, then the other, he peeled off her layered shirts and bared her lacy bra to the moonlight and low flickering sconces. Reverently, he ran gentle fingers across the peaks of her breasts. Her nipples tightened in response. Anticipation lit beneath her skin and she reached for him, needed to feel his bare flesh against hers. She skimmed off his shirt and unzipped his jeans with impatience, her hands brushing his as he peeled away her leggings.

Finally, finally, they were both naked. The heat of his skin seared her and she wondered how she could have ever forgotten this man.

Porter lowered himself on top of her. Skimmed her collarbone with kisses. Traveled with soft lips back to her mouth. He held one of her hands above her head as he skimmed off her underwear.

She arched her body toward him. Slick with need for him. His fingers teasing her, taking her desire to another level.

His breath was against her skin again. Kissing her hip, hands sketching along her breasts, then his mouth there as well, licking and drawing her in until she bit back a cry of ecstasy.

She pushed herself up, meeting Porter's eyes as she reached for the hard length of him. His jaw flexed, eyes fluttering as she stroked him. His lips found hers again. Needing the contact.

Hooking her legs around his waist again, she pulled him closer. Pulled him into her, the thick press of him filling her. They were anchored together. Joined by something more than the physical.

There was a deliberate rhythm to their coupling. The frenzy shifting into something even more intimate. Something that didn't rely on the past, that only existed between the people they were now. A throaty moan rolled through her. Made her dizzy as he stroked her. She writhed, hands twisting in the blanket.

Each deep thrust sent her closer to a wave of ecstasy about to crest. They pushed farther up the deck chair until she was pressed up against the edge. Their bodies moved as one in a familiar rhythm.

He kissed her deeply on her mouth. Her neck. She practically melted into him as he brought her to the cusp of release, slowed, held back, then thrust deeper to drive her the rest of the way into completion.

She wrapped her legs tighter around him, her heels digging into his ass. She kissed him, fiercely, deeply, taking his hoarse shout of completion into her mouth, aftershocks rippling through her again and again.

Their first time together.

Or rather her first time with him.

That thought threatened to steal the bliss still shimmering through her.

As she held him, their bodies slick with sweat, she knew. They'd done this before. She knew him, not in a concrete memory, but in an elusive feeling she wanted to grasp and hold on to but couldn't quite reach.

However she knew, this man was her husband.

Nine

Peace settled inside him like a whisper, like the breeze coming in off the ocean. Alaina had pulled on his polo shirt to keep out the night chill. It looked right on her. She pressed herself against him, head resting on his shoulder. Her soft arms draped over his bare chest. The downy blanket closed them in together, cocooning them in that peace.

Except with that peace came the reminder that he still hadn't told her everything about the state of their marriage before the accident. They'd moved to another level here and he couldn't keep hiding the facts from her for much longer under the excuse of protecting her or rebuilding their family.

She had always been a strong, independent woman. That hadn't changed. He could feel the restlessness in her to regain her life. He owed it to her to do everything he could to help. And he would. He resolved to give her—them—the foundation, the memory, of a beautiful Christmas together, and then just before New Year's he could tell her everything he could about their past. Hopefully she, too, would see that the New Year offered a new beginning, symbolically and literally.

At first, keeping Alaina had been about re-establishing their family at all costs, but as he learned new things about her and realized the mistakes he'd made that had contributed to their discord, he knew he didn't just want the family. He wanted her. He wanted them. Together. In love.

He'd do anything to keep her with him like this. He hadn't realized how broken they'd been before. But tonight—tonight they'd connected as they had when they were just falling in love.

A new conviction overtook him. Porter wanted to help ease her memories back. He was not afraid of her leaving. Of her wanting a life without him. They fit. They were a team.

A family.

"What was our first time together like?" Alaina's voice carried on the wind.

Porter took a deep breath. "Are you sure you wouldn't rather remember that on your own and not have my words tangled up in those memories?"

She looked up her chest at him, her blue eyes still hazy with passion. "I want to hear how you remember us."

"Okay, then." His hand settled on the soft curve of her hip. "I'll do my best to set the stage for you. I came to your apartment for dinner. You swore you could make the best steak and stuffed mushrooms. I brought a bottle of wine. You were in a bright green dress. Red lipstick. Your hair was curled. We ate. And you were right." Paused to kiss her. He never wanted to stop kissing her.

He whispered in her ear, "Best steak and stuffed mushrooms ever. And then." He nipped down her neck again, tasting the mix of sea salt and sweat. "The rest is history."

A breathy sigh escaped her lips a second before she angled to press her mouth to his. "Let's make history again."

He growled his approval.

Her hands slid around his waist and shifted on his lap. He spanned her waist and brought her closer. She wriggled against his erection, sending a fresh jolt of desire through him. The scent of her shampoo, the salty air and their lovemaking combined into a heady aphrodisiac.

The blanket, in addition to the dark, gave them an air of privacy. And even though all the boats were too far away for anyone to see them, there was also a sexiness to being out in the open this way with her, under the stars. Sex between them had always been good, even with the stress of the fertility treatments, but there was a freedom between them now.

A new connection tonight.

Her hands skimmed across his bare chest, her head falling back to expose the curve of her neck, encouraging him wordlessly. He didn't need more of an invitation to make the most of this chance to be with her again.

He slipped his hands under the shirt—his shirt on her, the cotton warm from her body. Her silky smooth skin called to him, enticed him to explore further. He skimmed up to cup her breasts, circling his thumbs over her nipples as he kissed the curve of her neck. Her low moan of excitement encouraged him to continue. He stroked down her side, tucking his fingers into her panties, the string along her hip a fragile barrier that gave way with a twist and snap.

Humming her approval, she made fast work of unzipping his jeans. He swept away her underwear, the scrap of satin almost as soft as her skin. The moist heat of her pressed against him. He'd never wanted her—or anyone—more than at this moment. She was everything, his every fantasy come to life. She was… Alaina.

Resting her hands on his shoulders, she raised up, then lowered herself onto him, taking him inside her. Exactly where he wanted to be for as long as possible. A challenge with her hips rolling against him in an arousing wriggle.

He cupped her bottom and brought her closer still, thrusting up as she threaded her fingers through his hair, tugging slightly. Her husky sighs drove him crazy with wanting her, drove all thoughts of their past away until only the present mattered.

And hell yeah, he knew he was making excuses to be with her even with secrets between them. But right then, he didn't care.

The wind blew her hair forward and around his face, as if binding them more closely. The silky strands teased his senses. Everything about her was sensual. Her hair, yes, even her hair turned him on, drove him closer to the edge until he bit back the urge to come, waiting for her. Touching her and stroking her until her breath hitched in that way he knew meant she was close, so close. And then her orgasm massaged him over the edge to his own release. Their groans tangled up, tossed around in the wind like her hair.

Each ripple of his release rolled through him like waves along the water, one after the other. Elemental. So damn perfect, all the more so because she sighed her bliss against his neck.

Cradling her to him, he reclined back onto the deck, holding her, the blanket still secured around them. He drew in ragged breaths of ocean air, his heart hammering in his chest.

Alaina sagged back until they lay side by side with a deep exhale. "Porter, it's not fair that you know exactly what I want and I know so little about what turns you on."

"So little?" He laughed. "Trust me—your instincts are spot-on."

"Hmmm... Maybe I'm remembering things on a subconscious level."

Her words chilled him into silence for an instant before he said, "Like what?"

"Nothing specific really." She linked hands with him. "Just impressions. A sense of knowing you."

He squeezed her hand. "I like the sound of that. We're still married underneath everything that's happened."

She just made that *hmmm* noise again and let the silence settle.

He rolled onto his side, propping his head on his hand. "Should we turn in?"

She traced his bottom lip. "I want to sleep here with you on the boat, but I can't leave Thomas overnight. Even knowing he's just there on shore—"

Porter kissed her fingertips. Drew her close. "I understand and I agree. Let's go see our son."

He wanted their focus to be on their family, their future, and Thomas was an important part of what would bind them together even after she regained her memories. If Porter could give Alaina the perfect family Christmas, she would understand why he wanted their family to remain intact, why he'd waited to tell her the truth about their tumultuous past. She'd understand, and she'd forgive him so they could create a happy, stable family environment for their son.

Or at least he thought she would forgive him. The trouble with Alaina's amnesia, however, was that she wasn't the same woman he'd once known.

The moon glow washed the beach in a pale silver light, softening the edges of their mansion like a watercolor image. Alaina took it in, seeing a beauty in the place she'd missed before. This might not be her personal pick of a home, but there was a blessing in having access to this kind of magnificent landscape and a peaceful escape where she could recover.

She curled in a tight ball, hugging her knees, wrapped in a blanket on the hammock. The light breeze rocked her back and forth, keeping time with the crash of the waves.

She'd come out here after they'd checked on Thomas while Porter went to scavenge for food. She'd brought a laptop with her to watch the disc he'd made, filled with images of their home. Such a thoughtful gesture.

And the more she glanced at the photographs of her life, the more she was excited for the return trip to Tallahassee. For life with Porter and Thomas. For her shot at having a family.

She looked up from the laptop, glancing at the house next door, Sage's home. Could the woman's comment about another man visiting be trusted? Was there a hidden agenda in her statement?

Or could there have been another man? Alaina didn't feel as if she ever could have been the sort to cheat on her husband but what did she really know about their marriage?

A burn started along her skin as she thought of her stalker ex-boyfriend from long ago. Could he have been lurking around again after so many years? Porter hadn't mentioned him, but perhaps she should bring up the subject of Douglas and simply ask that they look into his whereabouts.

An outline of an approaching figure took shape out of the misty night. Her eyes adjusted from the glare of the laptop to the darkness of the moonlit beach and she recognized her husband. Sagging with relief, she closed her laptop and set it aside to focus on this renewed connection with Porter. He strode down the bluff, sure-footed, a pizza in one hand, baby monitor in the other.

His smile widened as he placed the box on the Adirondack chair and sat next to her on the hammock.

"You're the only woman I ever met who would rather be romanced with deep-dish pizza than the offer of lobster." Porter passed her a slice.

Steam oozed off the cheese—the scent of tomatoes, garlic and oregano dancing around her. She blew cool air on her slice, eager to dive in. "The videos you put together of the Tallahassee house were very thoughtful.

I haven't gotten to watch them all, but I took a quick peek and I like the house."

"I'm glad. We'll be celebrating New Year's there with our son."

"And your mom?"

"She won't be with us. I'm still not sure why she's here." Even in the muted light, she could see his eyes darken at the mention of his mother. His mouth went tight.

In the deepest part of her core, Alaina wanted to set her family right. Her whole family, which included Courtney, too.

"She loves you. She wants to see your child." She set the plate of pizza down and ran a comforting hand down his back.

"Our child. You're a good mother, Alaina." He kissed her forehead.

"Thank you. These definitely aren't the easiest of circumstances to become a first-time parent." She looked down at her slice of pizza. "Your mother said I used to volunteer in the NICU, back when we were trying to conceive."

"You did. You were so generous and brave to do that. Like I said, you're a born mother."

She'd tried to envision herself in the hospital holding babies. Had volunteering helped ease the ache inside her over not being able to become pregnant? Or had it deepened her sense of loss?

"Your mother and I may be different, but that doesn't mean she loves you any less than I love Thomas."

"Like I said, you're generous. She wasn't very nice to you when we got married."

"Why was that?" She'd gathered that much. Pieced

it together from her conversations with her mother-in-law. But Alaina wondered if that even mattered now. The introduction of their child reminded Alaina that there was more at stake in this family than petty fights.

"I was never really sure and you didn't bad-mouth her so I never found out."

Alaina nodded, wondering if the animosity had just been a misunderstanding. And realizing that her mother-in-law had never intentionally sabotaged them. She'd kept her reservations about Alaina to herself. And there was something to be said for that. "She must not have bad-mouthed me, either, or you would know what the problem was."

"I hadn't thought about that."

"I just think it is something to consider. And besides, your mom and I are fine now. We have a fresh start. And she wants to be a part of the family—a part of our lives. Part of Thomas's life. I can feel it." A gust of wind pushed the ends of her hair into her eyes. She removed a ponytail holder from her wrist and piled her hair on top of her head in a messy bun.

"Oh, yeah. She wants to be part of the family. But only when it suits her." Bitterness dripped from his words. He ran a hand through his hair, exhaling deeply.

She picked up his hand in hers and twined their fingers together. "So...what should we get your mom for Christmas? And should we think of a neutral gift for her tax-attorney boyfriend? You know, just in case he is here. I'd hate for him to have nothing to open up if he spends Christmas with us."

Porter's jaw tightened and he dropped her hand. "I'm cold, aren't you?"

"Not terribly. Not with you and this blanket." She

tried to catch his eye. To get him to stay and talk to her. To calm down and let her in. They could work through this together if he would only open up.

Was this something that used to happen in the past? Were these the kinds of arguments they'd had before?

"I think it's time to go inside. We have a big day tomorrow. Lots of wrapping to do. We don't want to get sick." He started to gather the remains of the pizza and dishes. He kissed her forehead again, then he started for the beach house, retreating into the dark space between the beach and the mansion.

Leaving her with a cold feeling in her stomach no blanket could insulate.

Of all the times for his temper to explode, this was probably the worst one imaginable.

Porter had sought sanctuary in his office. Tried to lose himself in work. To cool down. To figure out why he had got so angry with Alaina.

He knew he'd been unreasonable. And he was afraid he'd blown his second chance with her. Maybe she'd see he wasn't worthy of her love and time. Maybe this would be the trigger that brought all of her memories rushing back. But not the good memories. The dark ones. All of their fights.

Without even realizing it, he'd bumped over from his spreadsheet and projections charts to the internet. He'd begun to scour his normal stockpile of online shopping websites. Looking for a gift for his mother. Alaina was right. He needed to figure something out.

And not just a gift for his mom. Also how to fix the space he'd placed between him and his wife. Again. Had he been too selfish keeping their past a secret? Put

Alaina at too much of a disadvantage by not sharing the darker parts of their marriage?

A knock pulled his attention to the door, and damn, how ironic, there his mother stood.

"Good evening, Porter. I was just thinking about what I should get Thomas for Christmas. Now, I know you and Alaina just finished your big shopping trip, but I thought we'd compare lists."

Now his mother was ready to play Santa? After all these years of virtually ignoring the holidays? Not that he begrudged his son the presents by any means, but he also didn't want Thomas to expect something from Courtney only to have her go back to her old ways later. Porter pursed his lips. Felt them turn white with tension.

"Clothes would be fine." It came out like a bark. "Or set away money for his college education. Whatever you want."

Courtney nodded, straightening her green silk scarf as she stepped deeper into the room. "This place reminds me so much of that Christmas we spent in the Keys when you were younger. Do you remember?"

"I do. But I think the beach house is closer to the house you rented the Christmas we went to Virginia Beach."

"Sometimes the places run together for me. I never liked to repeat holiday locations. Too depressing." A sad sort of smile set on her mouth.

Old habits died hard. When was the last time he and Alaina had spent a holiday in Tallahassee? He could have brought them home. To start their lives together in the space they'd cocreated. But instead, he'd fled and brought them here. Maybe there were some similarities between him and his mother after all.

"So are you serious about this guy?" Porter asked, shutting down his computer for the night.

Courtney shook her head. "No. I'm done with the search for my forever love. After your father left me... well, I'm not sure I've ever been the same. I loved him. I really did. But then he left and I was pregnant..." Her voice trailed off. She stared at her son with shining eyes.

"Mom...I'm sorry." A pang ricocheted through his heart. He'd had no idea she'd ever felt that way about anyone.

"Oh, honey. Don't look at me like that. I know things haven't been perfect for us. But I'm so glad that this was the path of my life. It gave you to me, and I've never once regretted it," she said, wrapping him in a hug.

It wasn't a particularly tight hug, but it wasn't one of those air hugs that she normally gave. From his mom, this was a lot.

He'd been so focused on his experience of childhood, on what she'd lacked as a mother, that he'd failed to see she was every bit as damaged as he was by the guy who'd bailed on them.

Never before had he considered what his father had done to his mother. Never had he thought about how betrayed and lonely his mother must have felt.

He was a selfish bastard for missing that.

"Thanks, Mom. I'm glad you're in Thomas's life." He hugged her back before stepping away.

Just as Alaina's scream echoed from above.

Ten

Alaina shot upright on the bed where she'd fallen asleep on top of the covers. The nightmare filled her brain like toxic fumes. Except it wasn't a dream. It was a memory, but from five years ago. One she hadn't forgotten but had instead pushed back because it was too painful to remember on a daily basis.

Why was she dreaming of an ex-boyfriend now? Of that hellish last time she'd seen Douglas? Of what he'd done to her?

Porter charged through the door, looked around the room as if searching for an intruder, then rushed to their bedroom, his face filled with concern—and fear. "Alaina, what's wrong? Are you okay?"

Thomas started shrieking in the next room, his plaintive cries cutting through the fog in her mind. She slid her feet off the bed. "I need to go to him—"

Courtney called from the open doorway, apparently having followed her son upstairs, "I'll take care of the baby. You two...talk. I promise not to drop him," she said in a halfhearted joke that fell a little flat. Then she left, heels clicking double time down the hall.

Heart still racing, Alaina waited until her son's cries quieted at Courtney's cooing and only then did she sag back against the headboard. Porter crossed to close the door, then returned to her, sitting on the edge of the bed while she tried to catch her breath. Returning to the present was tough. The night terror's claws were still buried deep in her.

Porter stroked her tangled hair back from her face. "What's going on?"

"I had another nightmare about Douglas." It seemed a pale word for what she'd experienced. Especially since the event had really happened to her five years ago.

She shivered at the thought. Intellectually, she knew it was long ago, but it felt so much closer to the present because of the amnesia. The chill settled deep in her gut and she tugged the down comforter tighter around her even though it made no sense that she would be so cold.

"How was this dream different from the other one about him?"

"This time, he didn't just stalk me, or slap me. Douglas hurt me...more. So much more."

He went still. Very still. "More?"

"You know what I mean." She made a vague gesture with her hands, as if they could speak what she hated to verbalize.

"I'm not sure I do."

"You must know." She looked up at him sharply. "We were married for almost four years. You have to know what he did to me." A desperate, fearful note entered her voice as she searched his face. Hoping the answers were there.

It was bad enough she had to relive it in her dreams. She didn't want to. So many times she'd resented that Porter needed to fill in the blanks in her memory. But she didn't want to recall one second more of this than she already did.

His eyes narrowed. "You told me how he verbally abused you. Your fights escalated and he hit you. You left him because of that, then he stalked you. Completely unacceptable, and you told him it had to stop." He grabbed for her hand gently.

A simple touch, but it gave her the courage she'd been lacking.

A courage that was all the more necessary as she realized she might have omitted a very big facet of her past from him. Why would she have done that?

"I honestly never explained to you what happened after I left him?" she pressed. "Why I got the restraining order?"

"I assumed you spoke with the police right away." He frowned. For an odd moment their roles were reversed as she had answers that he didn't know about.

She couldn't say she liked the feeling on this side of the fence, either. "I did speak to the police, then and later. And you really don't know this? You never did a background check on me?"

"I'm insulted you would think that of me."

"You seem like the kind of guy who would learn as much as you could about an important person in your life."

"I seem like a control freak, you mean?" A laugh escaped his lips, an effort to put her at ease she realized.

"No, um, you just seem assertive." She searched for the right words but her nerves were so damn frayed. "Detail oriented."

"Well, that's diplomatic."

She dropped her gaze, cheeks burning at the memory. The reality catching in her throat. "You're not like Douglas at all." She understood that absolutely. "But I think maybe since I woke up from the coma I've been fearing that you're like him. That the amnesia upsets the balance of control between us, and on some level that's been frightening to me."

"I'm not sure I'm following what you're trying to tell me." He pinched the bridge of his nose. "What happened that gave you nightmares? Did you remember the time he showed up here?"

She looked up sharply. "He came *here*?"

"Once, yes, he did. You freaked out. I arrived home just in time, and…" He clenched his hands in fists. "I hit him and the police were called. He did a little time in jail for violating the restraining order and that was that. We never saw him again. Last I heard he got arrested for assault and is back in prison."

That must have been what Sage saw. There wasn't some other man she'd been seeing during her marital troubles. There hadn't been cheating in the marriage because no way in hell would she have ever, ever slept with Douglas again. And thank God, he was out of her life, unable to reach her.

Relief melted through her, dulling the edges of her fear enough that she could say the words out loud to Porter.

Her husband, a man who'd been there for her, who supported her as an equal. She might not have shared the full truth before, but she needed to share it now.

"Douglas did more than hit me once before we split up. When he started stalking me, I thought he would lose interest in time but it got worse." Even thinking about it, just remembering those months brought back the old terror, and then the pain.

Porter rubbed a hand along her back in soothing circles, staying silent but present, waiting.

"One night, after work, he was lurking around my apartment. I don't know how many times he'd done it before. He said he'd been watching me, studying my habits. And the time had come for us to be together again."

A breath hissed between Porter's teeth.

"Usually I had someone walk me to my car, but not that night. So yes, he'd probably been waiting every night and stayed away those other times because he was such a coward. He would have never dared come after me if I had a protector."

"Please don't say you're blaming yourself for whatever happened. You have to know you didn't deserve the hell and the betrayal that bastard brought into your life."

"No, I don't blame myself. I understand he would have found me alone sometime. It's impossible to stay on guard 24/7. He preyed on me because my family was dead and I had very few connections to check up on me." She said the words by rote, knowing them to be true, but still wondering what else she could have done. Maybe she should have moved across the country. "It's not unreasonable to expect to live my life."

His throat moved in a hard swallow. "Do you want to tell me what happened?"

She covered his hand quickly, realizing she should have told him right away. "He didn't rape me, if that's what you're thinking."

"I'm not thinking anything. I'm waiting for you to tell me."

She exhaled hard. "He beat the hell out of me in the parking lot. Completely. He hit me and kicked me, damn near killed me before he walked away as if we'd just had a disagreement over what cereal to have for breakfast. I crawled into the car and tried to drive myself to the hospital."

"Why wasn't he locked away for good, then?"

Alaina picked at an imaginary piece of lint. The memory swelled before her again, rising up in the depths of her stomach. She took a steadying breath. She needed more air in her lungs. "Family connections and a good lawyer were able to convince a jury my injuries resulted from driving into a ditch as I tried to take myself to the hospital."

"The auto accident that made it difficult for you to conceive." A flicker of understanding passed over his face.

"Yes. Except it wasn't an accident. And the jury didn't believe it, in spite of the restraining order. His lawyers said I was unbalanced and trying to set him up. They convinced the jury."

"That's such bull," he blurted out.

"I agree."

She'd felt so helpless and alone without even someone to sit by her side in court. She'd isolated herself from everyone but her work friends by then, not wanting Douglas to lash out at someone close to her. It was the double cruelty of domestic abuse—an abuser isolated a woman and then, scared and mortified, a woman isolated herself more.

"What happened?" he asked.

"In the end they settled on a restraining order against both of us." She stared at her hands. "And you truly didn't know this? I never told you?"

"You didn't." He shook his head, and then, looking at her, his shoulders tensed. "I hope you believe me."

"I do believe you, actually. But that makes me wonder why I didn't share this before now, though." Had she clung to some kind of old sense of shame? Or simply hoped for a new start? "It's strange, especially since that played a part in our inability to have kids—you said it was both of us, though."

"It was. The scar tissue around your fallopian tubes and my low sperm count worked against each other." He took her hands in his. "But that's all a moot point. I am so sorry for what you went through."

"You're not angry with me for not telling you?"

"I'm…frustrated. I wish I'd known. I wish you'd trusted me enough to tell me."

She wanted to ask him what was wrong between them that she wouldn't share something so important, but maybe he was puzzling through that even now. What was wrong with her? Why hadn't she trusted him? That question scared her most of all because in spite of her concerns since coming home from the hospital, she'd grown closer to him over the past couple of weeks. She could see them building a life together with their child.

But that nightmare was a threat to her future. She could feel it. A simmering unease filled her, rooted in the fact that she hadn't trusted him with such fundamental knowledge about her as a person. She hadn't confided her deepest fears to him and she didn't like what that revealed about their relationship. Or at least, their old relationship.

Was it foolish of her to hope they had started to build something stronger than what they'd had? Something that could really last? More than anything, she wanted to keep the connection they'd found. Especially when she felt so completely adrift in the world.

She needed Porter. Needed to reclaim that connection to him on an elemental level.

The last thing Porter expected right now was for Alaina to push him back onto the bed and straddle his lap. No doubting her intent, though. She planned for them to have sex. Now.

She unbuttoned his shirt with impatient fingers, crawling up his chest as she leaned down to kiss him. Thoroughly. With open mouth and open passion.

Sweeping his shirt away, she kissed her way down his chest, pausing to circle his flat nipples with her tongue. His body reacted even as his mind shouted to know what the hell was going on with her.

She kissed lower and lower still, unzipping his fly and freeing him. Stroking. Inching closer until her mouth closed over him and his head dug back into the pillow. Her tongue circled him, her hand working up and down the length of his shaft. His fingers twisted in the sheets as he held back the urge to pulsate to completion.

His heartbeat throbbed in his ears. Sweat beaded on his brow from the restraint of holding back.

She looked up at him through her lashes with a sultry expression. He wanted her to have whatever she needed, whatever would bring them closer, even on an elemental level.

His hands roamed along her shoulders and he lifted her upward before he lost control altogether. Even though it damn near killed him to stop.

He owed her the honesty he'd planned for the New Year. Except he couldn't seem to dismiss the knowledge that she hadn't been honest with him for their entire marriage, and about such an important part of her past.

A huge, daunting piece of her. Obviously, the fact that she'd battled through that nightmare of a relationship didn't change how he felt about her. But he worried what it suggested she felt about him that she'd withheld the truth.

"Alaina—"

She tapped his lips before sweeping off her nightgown. "Don't even try to talk me out of this. I know what I want. I know what I need. You. Now."

The sight of her naked other than her panties stunned him silent and made him burn to have her. Only her words stopped him short.

Did she sense that they were headed for trouble once she remembered? Did she know on some subconscious level that memories of their marriage were not all good? Is that why she wanted this moment before their future was taken away?

And then he realized he couldn't do this. Not this way, with so many secrets between them. He couldn't make love to her again until they had more level ground between them. She deserved better from him.

She'd been hurt enough. He couldn't undo his past

deceptions. But he could start fresh now and be the man she deserved.

He scooped up her nightgown, the silky fabric still warm from her body. He resisted the urge to press the nightie to his face and take in the scent of her.

Porter cleared his throat and tossed the gown onto the bed. "Alaina, this may be the right time for you, but it's not the right time for me."

She angled up and stared down at him, horror on her face. "Did what I told you about Douglas turn you off?"

Guilt kicked him. How could she think that? He hated that she'd entertained that thought for even an instant.

Sexy as hell, she was all defiance and challenge, inventing obstacles when they needed to talk. Really talk.

"No, I don't think that. Not at all." He sat up and wrapped a sheet around her. "I want you so much my teeth hurt. But, now that you're having these nightmares and flashes of memories, I wonder if we should be careful." His mind was racing with—hell, he didn't know what exactly. He just felt unsettled. "What if all of this is too much for you, stirring up too many emotions too fast, upsetting you. Maybe we should talk to the doctor again about working on helping you recover your memory."

She bowed her head, eyes averted. "Do you see me as flawed?"

The defiance slid away, leaving behind a vulnerability that rocked him.

He touched her chin, tipping her face so she could see the truth in his eyes. "Don't put words in my mouth. I care about you. I want what's best for you."

"Care? You *care* about me," she hissed, stepping

backward. "Be honest with me, Porter. Did we love each other?"

They did. So much. And yet still, he'd lost her. They'd decided to divorce, only reconciling temporarily for the baby.

"Then what's stopping you now? I don't understand."

Of course she didn't because he was holding back so damn much from her. He kept their past a secret out of fear of destroying this new peace between them, this chance to rediscover what they'd had.

The thought of losing her again shredded what was left of his restraint. "Nothing's stopping me." Not tonight. "Absolutely nothing."

He angled forward to kiss her and her purr of approval vibrated up her throat. Things were so right here between them. If only the outside world and concerns—and memories—didn't lurk just outside that door.

For now, he would have her, take and give all he could, hope that she would feel and understand how much she meant to him. He rolled her to her back on the bed, the mattress giving beneath them. With sure but swift hands, he swept off the rest of his clothes and her panties, his urgency sending them fluttering to the floor.

Her milky white skin glowed in the moonlight beaming through the window. She took his breath away.

"Alaina, I could never see you as anything but beautiful, magnificent. Mesmerizing. You take my breath away now every bit as much as you did then. I want you, Alaina, every single day, every minute since I met you, I have wanted you."

When they'd first been married, he'd taken his time learning every curve of her, every freckle and dimple.

They'd both talked of being made for each other. How had he lost sight of that?

Almost lost her?

He stretched out over his wife. Flesh to flesh. Truly becoming one as he slid inside her. Moved within her. The warm clamp of her body around him made his heart hammer harder in his chest,

Framing her face in his hands, he kissed her, openmouthed, tongues mating, as well. He couldn't be close enough to her. Wanted more. He wanted forever. The reality of that exploded inside him, filling every corner. It wasn't just about making a family or being parents together. This was about being her husband, her lover, her love.

His feelings for her were more intense than before, steeled by the challenges they faced. He wouldn't take her or what they had for granted.

He loved her.

Three simple words that unleashed everything inside him, sending him over the edge into throbbing release as her cries of completion breathed over his ear. Her fingernails dug into his back as if she ached to stay anchored in this moment every bit as much as he did.

Forever.

His forehead fell to rest on her shoulder and he inhaled the sweet sultry scent of her mixed with an air of their perspiration mingling. The perfume of them together.

Wrapping his arms around her, he tucked her to him and slid onto his side. Her cheek pressed against his chest and she trailed her fingers along his stomach. The ceiling fan spun lazy circles overhead, cooling the air around them.

Reminding him the outside world and concerns couldn't be kept at bay forever. At any moment, she could remember. His time was running out. And even if it wasn't, he owed her the best he had to offer in all aspects of their life together.

"Porter, you never answered my question."

He searched his passion-fogged brain for exactly what she meant. "Which question?"

She raised up on one elbow to look into his eyes. "Did we love each other before I lost my memory?"

He weighed his answer carefully, because yes, he had loved her, so very much. But their past hadn't been as simple as that, and he owed her a more honest future. And he would give it to her.

Still, he needed to be careful not to put too much stress on her, especially so early in her recovery. The nightmares made it clear how her feelings were in turmoil. She was a strong woman, but she'd been through so much. So he would tread warily, step back, figure out and plan the best way and time to tell her.

For now, he had a question to answer. Did they love each other before she'd lost her memory?

He couldn't be sure how she felt at the end, but he'd loved her. Did he still?

God help him, could he love a woman who didn't even remember the first time they met? A woman who didn't know him well enough to love him and might never love him again?

Alaina's frustration level was through the roof. Porter had become distant, and was spending more and more time in his study.

Where was the tender lover? The attentive father?

Between the nightmares and being rejected by Porter, her brain was spinning.

Her life had been frustrating every day since she'd woken from the coma with five years of her life missing, but Porter had counseled her to be patient, all the while romancing her to restore their marriage.

And when she needed romance he shut her out.

Now it was only two days away from Christmas and she couldn't recall ever feeling less in the holiday spirit. How unfair to Thomas. This was his first Christmas. He deserved a house full of love and happiness.

Knotting the belt on her bathrobe, she walked down the quiet hall toward the nursery, the scent of pine from the tree filling the whole giant house. She needed to be near her son and soak up his sweet innocence. To find the peace of rocking him in her arms. And maybe she needed to cry.

Silently nudging the door open, she tiptoed into the room. Her son still slept, his chest rising and falling evenly as he sucked on his tiny fist. Needing the comfort of being close to him, she turned to settle into the rocker.

And stopped short.

Courtney slept on the daybed, a baby bottle of water and powdered formula on the end table. Her arm draped over the side. Why hadn't she noticed before now how much Porter looked like his mother?

Perhaps Alaina made a noise because her mother-in-law startled awake, yawning. "Oh, wow, I must have fallen asleep. I vow that night nanny has the best job ever."

Alaina laughed softly, chocking back the tears in her throat. "We all love Thomas, and I have to confess I appreciate the help." She mixed the bottle and shook the contents. Thomas would be awake at any moment and he would be hungry. "This has been an, um, unusual foray into motherhood."

"You would have done fine on your own. But I'm glad to be here. I thought, well, I wasn't sure how things would be between you and Porter. So I'm here." She stretched, her silk shirt untucked from her skirt. She reached down to retrieve her Jimmy Choo heels. "And I'm seriously in need of a bathroom and a cup of coffee. Do you need anything from the kitchen?"

"Coffee and a biscotti would be nice. No need to hurry, though," she answered, mulling over what Courtney had just said about being unsure of their marriage.

Or, wait, had she put it a different way... Alaina tried to recall the shifting words in her mind. She was having trouble sorting what was real or remembered, or just an impression.

Kind of like those drawings in her sketchbook— she didn't know which images came from real life and which ones were simple dreams until Porter told her.

Her brain was so rattled. She was such a freaking mess. She just wanted to feel certain about something. Anything. When Thomas made a soft cry, Alaina was only too glad for the reprieve from her thoughts.

She turned off the monitor and lifted him from the crib; his casted leg hung heavily. Her little boy needed her so much.

A quick diaper change later, she settled into the rocking chair and popped the bottle in his mouth, savoring the simple joy of snuggling him close and feeling his warm weight in her arms. She bent to brush a kiss through his baby-fine hair while his little fingers flexed and curled haphazardly around the bottle.

So precious.

More than anything she wanted to remember the day she and Porter had first met Thomas, the day they'd picked him up from the hospital. She ached to recall that moment when they'd first become parents to this beautiful boy. She wanted to be grateful for all she had, but she still couldn't shake the feelings of frustration for all that she'd been denied.

What would happen if she never remembered anything more? Just that thought sent a bolt of panic through her.

Three deep breaths later, she saw her mother-in-law in the doorway with two cups of coffee. Courtney set one mug down beside Alaina with a small plate of biscotti before sitting elegantly on the edge of the day-bed.

"Hmmm." Courtney sighed, holding her mug under her nose and inhaling. "Manna for an exhausted mama."

The java scent wafted from the cup, teasing the air. Alaina's mouth watered but she didn't want to hold the hot drink near her son. "Thank you again for your help caring for him since we brought him home from the hospital."

"Of course I want to help. I'm not the most maternal figure in the world, but we *are* all family." Courtney blew into her mug, then sipped. "I'm just so glad you and Porter have worked things out between you."

Worked things out?

Alaina schooled her face not to show her surprise. Her mother-in-law had let something very telling slip. This was Alaina's chance, the one she'd been waiting for, to unwittingly pry a piece of important information about the past from someone. But getting those words from Courtney wouldn't be easy. The woman was a savvy lawyer.

Alaina opted to encourage Courtney to finish her thought. "Porter and I have come to an understanding thanks to Thomas."

"Good. I'm so glad the two of you are staying together." She shook her head sadly. "Divorce is tough on children. Although, of course, Porter's father and I were never married, but I think you get my point. It was difficult on my son not having his dad in his life."

Divorce.

There it was. The word she'd feared. The secret Porter had been keeping from her.

They'd been on the brink of splitting up.

Eleven

The family room was still littered with wrapping paper and baby toys. Porter's eyes roved over the chaos, and he couldn't help but smile. It was exactly the way a child's Christmas should be. Presents spread all over the place and a room filled with family. His family.

So far, Thomas's first Christmas had been a success. Porter and Alaina had unwrapped all of Thomas's gifts and taken so many pictures. Even Barry had brought Thomas a gift—a giant puppy stuffed animal that took up a whole couch cushion on its own.

Everything was as it should be. Except for Alaina's demeanor. That had shifted over the past few days. He could sense her growing frustration. She was angry with him for the time he spent locked away in his office, but it had been all he could do to keep his hands off her while he figured out the best way to tell her he had been holding back important parts of their past. Yes, he'd done so in hopes of rebuilding their family and along the way rediscovered his love for her.

A love that was now in danger again.

If only the doctors could give him concrete answers on her recovery and the odds that painful news could set her back? He knew she was strong. He wanted to trust in what they had.

Except how did a man tell his wife during the holidays that oh, by the way, they'd been talking to lawyers about a divorce shortly before that car accident?

That stark truth didn't fit well into a Christmas bag.

But he wasn't so good at pretending all was well anymore. So when he stepped out of his office, conversation between them had been stiff. Formal.

His mother and her boyfriend had already retired for the evening, leaving Alaina and Porter alone. They'd put Thomas down for the night.

Alaina had begun to stuff a trash bag with the discarded and ripped wrapping paper. She moved with an efficiency and fluidity that radiated anger.

He moved the framed drawing of Thomas she'd given him for Christmas onto the shelf behind the couch. This would be the start of the redecorating process. The process of making this house a home, one that reflected their joint, eclectic tastes.

Assuming he could figure out how best to ease into telling her about their past without destroying their future—while still making sure he didn't somehow harm her recovery.

The radio played through a medley of Christmas songs, filling the space between them. This was his chance. He picked up a neatly wrapped box. He'd given her a ring earlier with Thomas's birthstone, circled with diamonds. But he still had another present for her, something more personal rather than just focused on them as parents, and he'd hoped that in this stolen moment, he would be able to show her how much he cared.

Cared?

He needed to stop using that lukewarm word. He knew he loved her. Deeply. There was no denying that.

The only question? Did his wife still love him?

He tightened the bow on the box and hoped like hell he could get this right with her.

He loved her, more than he could have thought possible.

Her voice halted him. "Were we on the edge of divorce when we adopted Thomas?"

Porter stared at her, unblinking. Heart hammering. "Why would you say that? Do you remember something?"

"Just answer my question." She set aside the bag of discarded wrappings, her posture tense. "Was our marriage over? Were we on the brink of splitting up when I had my accident? Answer me, damn it."

He could feel her anger and her worries even though her voice remained low, her body rigid.

"Our marriage was in jeopardy. Yes. How did you find out?" Were her memories warning her about how close they'd been to throwing it all away? He set aside the package he'd been about to give her.

"Your mother told me." Her tone was flat. Sharp. Accusatory.

He bit back a curse. Why would she do that? Clearly he hadn't told his wife yet and it was his place to share. The betrayal cut deeply. He was disappointed in his mother—and in himself for not handling this better. "I had hoped to wait until after Christmas to tell you, but I see that's only made things worse."

"You're right about that. This can't wait. Not any longer."

"I'm sorry, Alaina, so damn sorry for bungling this. This amnesia... Well, no more excuses. I'm sorry." He thrust a hand through his hair. "The truth is, yes, we planned to get a divorce."

"A divorce," she echoed hollowly. "We were truly on our way to divorce."

"We discussed it with an attorney. But even though we talked about it, we hadn't started official proceedings."

"Why not?" Her eyes flashed with a hint of hope, as if she wanted him to say they'd reconciled.

But he wouldn't lie to her. Not again.

"We'd decided to stay together temporarily, because of Thomas."

"I meant why didn't you tell me sooner, before Christmas week?"

"What good would that have done when you didn't remember? I wasn't supposed to push you—"

"Stop. Just stop the excuses. You misled me. Deliberately." Alaina's eyes narrowed.

"Excuse me for wanting to hold my family together. Yes, I saw it as a chance to repair things so you, Thomas and I could have a future together. Then along the way it became about more. I wanted to romance you. I wanted to win my wife back."

"Win? *Win?*" Her voice rose along with her obvious anger—and hurt. "Win me like I'm some kind of prize?"

Damn, that sounded cold. The truth really did sound better. "Win back your love."

"Marginally better," she conceded, "but still done in a way where you kept me in the dark. You could have said something, done something, to let me know things were more strained than just arguments." Her voice cracked and she paused to take a deep breath. "You know how hard this has been for me, to struggle with not having any memories of you."

Her accusation stung.

"You kept secrets of your own. You never told me what Douglas did to you. We were married, for God's sake. And you never told me." That truth had hurt. But he'd swallowed down the pain in an effort to solidify their future.

"Sounds to me like our marriage was a sham." She clenched her hands into fists. "I love that child in there, but I don't understand why we chose to adopt if we were about to divorce."

"We weren't about to divorce, damn it."

"Don't quibble. That's the same as lying to me. That stops now." The pain in her voice was audible. "Tell me exactly what happened before I lost my memory. What was the state of our relationship?"

The frustration and agony of those days were indelibly etched in his mind. He paced restlessly, but there was no escaping the past—or the present. "We'd been waiting for a child for a long while. Then right when we'd given up hope on each other, we got the call about Thomas. It was the wrong time, but he needed us. The surgery. We were afraid he would go into the foster system. So we agreed to stay together until the adoption became final."

"And you didn't think this was important for me to know?" Her arms crossed over her chest. Closing him out. Shutting him out.

"You were in no shape—"

"So you decided to climb into my bed again?"

"I wanted to put my family back together. I wanted to win you back and I saw the chance." He stopped his restless pacing and rested his hands on her shoulders. How could he make her see how far he'd come? How much he'd changed? That he wanted this second chance to work between them, not just for their family, but because he loved her.

"The chance to get your way." She shrugged off his hands. "Forget it. Forget everything. This hurts, Porter. This betrayal hurts too much for me to forgive."

Alaina rocked her baby. The nursery provided her with a calming reassurance. She belonged here with him and her heart swelled in pain at the idea of not having this part of her life. Despite the mess of the past few weeks, she knew that a family was all she'd really ever wanted. The time in the nursery with her son was healing to her soul.

Such a precious child. Hers.

And Porter's.

Thomas yawned in her arms, blinking up at her, eyes heavy with sleep.

"Thomas, you know I'll always love you. Always." Her murmur mixed into the gentle lullaby music playing from the mobile over the crib.

She shook her head, still trying to piece together the latest revelation.

Surveying the mural on the wall—the one she'd

painted—fuzzy images wafted in and out of her mind. Visits to doctor's offices and specialists. Vacations and hotel rooms. Snippets of a past half remembered, feeling a bit like a dream upon waking.

For a moment, she held her breath, almost afraid breathing would chase the memories away. But instead, the thoughts became clearer, more vivid. Pieces of her past five years began to materialize and to make sense.

And then something else entered her mind that left her stomach in knots.

With a clarity that frightened her, she remembered the car ride home after picking up Thomas. Things had been so strained in the last few months leading up to the adoption. And their inability to conceive had dredged up old memories. Memories of Douglas and the attack and what might have been if he'd never beat her senseless. All of that had come crashing back at her when they'd picked up Thomas and she'd had an all-consuming headache. The pain had only grown worse when she'd realized their son had reminded her of her past. The past she'd been running and hiding from.

A past she'd hidden from Porter. A man she had married and had loved.

A man she loved still.

Porter was on the hunt, storming through the house looking for his mother. He needed to talk to her. To figure out why she'd jeopardized his second chance with Alaina.

He found her in the kitchen, scooping out heaps of mint-chocolate-chip ice cream into a silver bowl embellished with mistletoe.

"Mother, what the hell were you doing?"

"What are you talking about?" She piled more ice cream into the bowl, staring coolly at him.

"You told Alaina that we were getting a divorce."

Courtney's face was impassive. She shrugged nonchalantly. "I told her the truth. Somebody needed to."

"That was my place." Leaning against the counter, he crossed his arms over his chest. He felt betrayed. It wasn't his mother's place to tell Alaina anything about their marriage. Porter inhaled deeply.

"So one would think. Too bad you didn't bother to give her that courtesy before you climbed back into bed with her." She fixed him with an unflinching gaze. The one she was famous for in the courtroom.

"That's really none of your business. I'm acting on the advice of her doctors, trying to ease her memory back."

As she shook her head dismissively, a tight grin spread across her face, not reaching her eyes. "You're using that as a cop-out so you can pursue her."

"I want my wife back. What's the problem with that?"

"The problem is the way you're going about it. I love you, son, but I also love Alaina. And no woman deserves to be tricked by a man who is supposed to love her."

She turned and walked away.

Tricked?

He wanted to call her back. To demand that she listen. He wasn't trying to fool anyone; he'd simply been trying to buy some time to get his family in order. He was simply trying to make Alaina fall in love with him again so she would love him as much as he loved her.

Love?

Yes, he loved her. Just because he hadn't said the words didn't make them any less true.

So why hadn't he thought to tell her?

Now that her initial shock had eased, Alaina wanted to do something to fix the rift between her and Porter. She didn't know exactly how much could be repaired, but she couldn't leave things this way. The only question was where to start. She took a deep breath of the salt air, watching the lights on the yachts twinkle in the twilight, remembering her time on *their* yacht.

She tugged her gaze back to her drawing pad, needing the comfort of her art now more than ever. Sketching a whimsical family portrait—a dream really—she whipped the charcoal across the pad. Pushing with her left foot, she rocked the hammock back and forth. An idea would come to her if she sat here long enough, she was sure of it.

Her brow furrowed as she ran through potential ways to start her conversation with Porter. To make him understand what she'd learned about herself since the accident. About her feelings for him.

If only she could voice her feelings with words as easily as they flowed from her fingertips onto paper— the three of them on their yacht in a tropical locale with a baby palm tree for a Christmas tree and toddler Thomas playing with a new toy boat. She had faith in them as a family. Faith that they could build a future with or without all her memories.

She had her faith in what she wanted from the future.

The sound of shoes shuffling on the ground drew her attention back to the present. Eyes focusing, she saw

Porter approaching, a box with glittering gold wrapping paper in hand.

Cocking her head to the side, she peered sideways at him. "What do you have there? You already gave me a gift." She held up her hand with the ring featuring Thomas's birthstone circled by diamonds." The setting was a delicate band of filigree that looked handcrafted.

"I have something else for you. Do you mind if I sit with you?"

She swung her feet off the side of the hammock. "Please."

He lowered himself to sit beside her, his strong shoulder brushing hers and reminding her of the physical chemistry they'd always shared, the heightened awareness she'd always felt around him.

She knew that because she remembered it now.

Wordlessly, he passed her the large gold box. She opened it to find—a binder full of house designs.

"I thought you would want to choose a new house yourself rather than having me assume I know what you want. I would like for us to live in that house together, but that's up to you."

Words failed her. His gift touched her, deep in her soul. She tore her eyes away from the drawings and sketches to meet his gaze, still stunned silent.

"Alaina, I apologize for not being up-front with you from the start."

"I'm the one who owes you an apology." She sighed deeply.

"I'm not sure what you mean."

Bracing for the talk they needed to have, she told herself that honesty and communication were their only hope at this point. That was how they'd patch things together. And it started now.

"I think I lost my memory before the accident," she admitted, although she wanted to see a specialist to discuss it. "I think it had something to do with being afraid to be a parent, being afraid of what happened to me with Douglas."

"I'll never let him near you again." Porter made it sound so simple, but her fears were far more jumbled than that. She didn't fear Douglas coming after her. She feared the wreck of a woman the attack had left behind.

"I realize he's back in jail. I should have told you years ago about what happened and I didn't. I'm in no position to judge you for holding things back. I think I spent so long telling myself that I would be okay, I forgot to show you the weakness behind the mask." Maybe she had hoped that if she forgot about it, that if she never brought it into their relationship, that would be almost the same as if it had never happened.

After her struggle with amnesia, she knew the brain had its own complicated coping mechanisms.

"Seems to me we both have issues with trust." He brushed a hand along her hair, a light caress she wanted to lean into. "What about now that you remember?" Even in the dying light, she could read the worry and fear sparking in his eyes. She was starting to realize just how afraid he was of losing her, of them drifting away from each other.

"I don't remember, not everything. Just snippets about the day of the accident."

"I assumed you remembered…" He rested his head against hers. "My mother said you deserve better from me, better than me. And God, Alaina, she's right. I should have handled everything differently from the moment you woke up in the hospital, from before then, actually."

The bits of Porter she remembered from before the accident would have never said something so tender or allowed himself to be so vulnerable. She recalled how locked in he'd been on the goal of building the family and life he'd thought they should have. She glanced at his gifts—the choices for house plans, the understated but heartfelt ring. These were the gifts of the man she had sensed he might become.

A man she could build her life with.

"I trust you. If you say you love me, then you do."

"But I haven't said it."

"Yet. You will." A smile spread across her lips as she reached for him, fingers twining with his.

"Confident, are you?"

"I'm learning to trust my feelings rather than rely on some black-and-white memory of the past. Feelings, emotions…love…well, that comes in layers and textures that defy simple images."

"Love, you say?" He moved closer. "You love me?"

"I'm still waiting for you to say the words first."

He squeezed her hand tight. Brought his lips to her fingertips and kissed her gently. Butterflies stirred in her stomach.

His mouth brushed hers again. "Then by all means, I'm more than ready. Alaina Rutger, you are the one and only woman for me, the love of my life, the mother of my child. My partner. My lover. My life."

She took his face in her hands. "Porter, my love, my partner, father of my child. You are my soul mate for all time even if our minds and memories fade." And she meant it. Every syllable.

Porter dropped to one knee. "Will you marry me?"

"But we're already married." Her eyes widened in a mixture of disbelief and excitement.

"You'll get your memory back someday. I'm confident of that. But even if you don't, I would like for us both to remember the day, the vows." The starlight and Christmas lights caught in his eyes, making them dance with the promise of family and love.

"I adore that plan. I adore you. Yes. Let's get married all over again."

"Renew our vows on New Year's at our Tallahassee house?"

"Perfection." She kissed him deeply. So sure of him. Of them. Of what they could accomplish together as a team.

He pulled away to whisper in her ear. "Yes, you are perfect, Alaina. Absolutely perfect."

Epilogue

One Year Later

"Merry Christmas, my love," Porter said, kissing his wife, the sun warm on his shoulders as they lounged on the upper deck of their yacht.

"Merry Christmas to you, too." She slid from her lounge chair to his, curling up beside him with a happy sigh. "This has been the most amazing family Christmas ever."

Their son napped in his cabin with his grandmother and her new husband keeping watch. Who would have thought Barry would be a keeper? But his mom was happy.

And so was Porter.

He stroked down his wife's arm, linking fingers with her. "I'm glad you found a way to enjoy the yacht."

"Trips together have been a fun escape—" she squeezed his hand back "—and a chance to grow closer as a family."

Waves slapped the side of the craft, chimes singing on their Christmas palm tree. He never would have believed this possible before her accident. But then, he hadn't bought the yacht with the intent of traveling. He'd missed the whole point of a vacation home and the boat, a symbol for his bigger problem.

Life was meant to be enjoyed.

And this past year he'd enjoyed his life more than he could ever remember doing, thanks to his fresh start with Alaina and Thomas.

He stroked a loose strand of blond hair behind her ear. "So you never told me. Why did you choose the Florida Keys for Christmas?"

She tapped her temple. "A week with minimal contact from the outside world?" She grinned. "What's not to love? I have my husband and son, my family, for the holidays."

Thomas was out of a cast for now, due for another surgery later, but free to crawl around in the sand. He would be a late walker because of his clubfoot, but the doctors expected a full recovery. He was a gloriously healthy child.

They had everything in their life that mattered.

It hadn't always been easy. But they worked at it, finding new paths to make their marriage thrive.

They played this game of surprise often. Her memory had never returned fully, so Porter had suggested she make choices and surprise him. Some small things like dinner dates or larger plans like vacations.

He soaked up the feeling of her skin against his, her

bikini leaving a delicious amount of flesh for him to explore with his eyes and hands. "I enjoy your choices for vacations."

"And I appreciate the way you've worked to help me feel more in control of my world. I wish I could have regained all of those missing years, but I'm beginning to accept that may never happen."

He searched her eyes for signs of the pain she'd experienced last year as she began to accept that her memory might not ever come back. She'd remembered good moments and some arguments they'd had, as well. He'd asked to hear every one of them, and as he'd listened, it had helped him hear her side of things. Helped them cement the bond they'd found after the accident.

They had made peace with that past and grown individually, as a couple, too.

He kissed her on her pink nose. "You still haven't fully answered my question. Why the Keys? There are plenty of places for isolation."

She sat up and pulled a box from under her lounge chair. "Why don't you pull the wrapping from your gift and see. That's why I asked you to come up here."

She passed him a two-foot square box with a huge red bow.

They'd already exchanged presents earlier and one of his had a note inside promising his "special" gift would be given later on the top deck. He'd assumed she meant sex.

This was another surprise.

He tore the large red ribbon from the gift box, lifted the lid. A framed sketch rested inside a satin lining. The charcoal image showed a family of three on their yacht in a tropical locale with a baby palm tree for a

Christmas tree and toddler Thomas playing with a new toy boat.

She rested her hand on his elbow. "I was drawing that a year ago when you found me in the hammock and told me you love me. This," she said, tapping the edge of the gift, "was my dream for our family. My hope. And now it's our reality."

"It is, isn't it?"

"The very best Christmas gift ever and I get to enjoy it year-round." Her smile was brighter than the noonday sun. "Thank you."

He traced her mouth and winked. "I guess that means I should cancel our flight out of Miami to Paris."

Laughing, she kissed him, her palms flat against his chest. "Don't you dare. I can't wait to go to the Louvre."

She'd seen the photos of their first trip, one she'd forgotten. Seeing the frustration on her face over that lost moment, he'd known right away what to get her for Christmas.

He set aside the incredible sketch, a treasure for his office, and gathered his wife into his arms to make love. They would experience Paris all over again for New Year's. Some couples didn't get second chances at forever.

He was grateful for every minute of this second chance with Alaina. Each day a beautiful surprise with the love of his life.

* * * * *

If you liked this tale of family drama and romance,
pick up these other stories from
USA TODAY *bestselling author Catherine Mann*

HONORABLE INTENTIONS
BILLIONAIRE'S JET SET BABIES
YULETIDE BABY SURPRISE
FOR THE SAKE OF THEIR SON

And don't miss the next
Billionaires and Babies story
TRIPLETS UNDER THE TREE
from Kat Cantrell
Available December 2015!

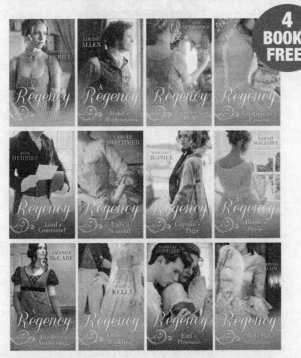
_ST19

MILLS & BOON®

Desire™

PASSIONATE AND DRAMATIC LOVE STORIES

A sneak peek at next month's titles...

In stores from 20th November 2015:

- **Bane** – Brenda Jackson *and*
  Triplets Under the Tree – Kat Cantrell

- **Lone Star Holiday Proposal** – Yvonne Lindsay *and*
  A White Wedding Christmas – Andrea Laurence

- **The Rancher's Secret Son** – Sara Orwig *and*
  Taking the Boss to Bed – Joss Wood